FAR FROM BOTANY BAY

FAR FROM BOTANY BAY

a novel

Rosa Jordan

OOLICHAN BOOKS

LANTZVILLE, BRITISH COLUMBIA, CANADA

2008

Library and Archives Canada Cataloguing in Publication

Jordan, Rosa
Far from Botany Bay / Rosa Jordan.

ISBN 978-0-88982-249-8

1. Bryant, Mary, b. 1765—Fiction. 2. Women prisoners—Australia—Fiction.
3. Penal colonies—Australia—Fiction. 4. Escapes—Australia—Fiction. I. Title.

PS8619.O74F37 2008   C813'.6   C2008-903044-3

We gratefully acknowledge the financial support of the Canada Council for the Arts, the British Columbia Arts Council through the BC Ministry of Tourism, Small Business and Culture, and the Government of Canada through the Book Publishing Industry Development Program, for our publishing activities.

Published by
Oolichan Books
P.O. Box 10, Lantzville
British Columbia, Canada
V0R 2H0
Printed in Canada

To my oldest and dearest friends

Esther and Lester Cole
and
Grace and Phil Hampton

who always helped me get to where I wanted to go
even when they and I didn't know where that was.

1

Upon the Sea, Beyond the Seas

Was it Mary Broad's upbringing that caused her to do what she'd done—for which she was sentenced to hang, and more? Those who knew her as a child said, with some reservations, that her parents did their duty. More likely it was an inherited flaw, for wasn't the propensity to break the law handed down, generation to generation, like the colour of one's eyes? "Blood will out and blood will tell," people told each other, as if they had known all along that the girl was in league with the devil. "Like father, like daughter."

Few recalled that Silas Broad had lived some fifty years without committing a crime, and was not descended from anyone known to have been convicted of an unlawful act. What was remembered was the wild light that blazed in his eyes when a stranger walked into the pub and how, before that stranger spoke a word, Silas had broken a full bottle of rum over his head and fled. Naturally the sheriff had to go after him, for it had been an unprovoked attack plain and simple—not to mention his running off without paying for the rum.

Until that year, Silas Broad had been a seafaring man, that occupation dating to before his marriage to Grace. Silas was only a bosun, but the captain, who had been his friend from boyhood, allowed him to bring his bride aboard rather than lose his most trusted crew member. Grace didn't care for the sea but adored her husband, and so came with him on many voyages.

It was on the first day of May, 1765, that Grace gave birth to Mary. The baby was born in Cornwall, not at sea, but sailed with her parents soon thereafter. Whether Mary loved the ship because she was the only child aboard and the centre of everyone's affection or just because she was her father's daughter, who could say? All her parents were certain of was that even as a toddler she was never seasick and had no fear of the water.

Had Mary been set to work at a tender age, as children of her class usually were, it's likely she would have been an unattractive child with mouse-brown hair and sallow skin. But her early years were spent scampering about the ship, and in that way, she grew to be a sturdy child. The sun turned her skin to gold, her hair to honey blonde, such hair as her mother brushed until it gleamed, and wove into a braid that hung down to her waist.

Mary's intelligence was, like her looks, merely average. Yet with both parents and every hand on board having time to spare, she got an exceptional education in those early years. She learned to tie all kinds of knots, play simple tunes on the flute, and read the sky like a sailor. Old salts told her Greek myths, Norse legends, and hair-raising yarns of their own adventures. Her mother taught her to read a bit from the Bible, not knowing that Mary took its tales to be like all the others, which Grace had explained were a mixture of fact and fantasy and wishful hoping.

Silas himself was barely literate, but he did read navigational charts. When the captain caught him teaching Mary to trace their route across the map, he laughed and said it was like teaching a dog to dance, for what use could a girl ever have for such knowledge? Yet the captain sometimes amused himself by inviting the child to his cabin for tea and biscuits, and taught her elements of navigation that even Silas had never mastered.

It was when Mary turned ten that Grace set foot upon land and said they would not go to sea again. "It's bad enough our Mary's not had the company of other children," Grace told Silas. "But to grow into a young woman in the company of women-hungry men isn't safe or decent."

Silas agreed, and so for the next ten years Mary remained with her mother in a thatch-roofed cottage there on the Cornwall coast. Grace's way of mothering was strange, although Mary, having seen little of ordinary family life, didn't know that when she was young. Most of England's poor—men, women, and children alike—worked unendingly from daybreak on and fell asleep at night like exhausted animals. When the men had had too much, they went down to the pub and drank. The women, who had a harder time unloading their burdens, added to everyone else's troubles with their whining and carping.

Not so Grace. Mary's memories, during that decade when she and her mother lived alone and saw Silas only between sailings, were of being wakened at daybreak by a mother full of surprises. "Come," Grace might cry, "sunrise is bright as a rose. Let's take our porridge and have breakfast down on the beach!"

Another day Grace might sniff the air and announce, "I smell berries ripe for picking. Let's take pails and see what we can find. If there's plenty, we'll stop by Farmer Smith's and trade him some for a cup of cream. What a treat we'll have!"

Or on a cold winter morning Mary, who was never sent to school, might wake to find Grace sitting by the fire with the Bible, which was their only book. "Come sit here on the hearth," she'd say, placing a mug of hot milk in Mary's hands, "and listen to this story of what Delilah did to poor old Samson. Bless me, but that man was a fool!"

What made Grace truly different was that she played with her daughter not after her work was finished, but during the first hours of the day when she was at her liveliest. Later, when the chores must begin and, it seemed, were never altogether done, they worked side by side, each trying to take the heaviest part, to lighten the other's load. It was how her parents treated each other, and Mary knew no other way.

In time Mary came to understand that because Grace was different from other mothers, her life was different from that of other poor children, who were little more than small bodies in bondage to the family's struggle for survival. Once, skipping gaily ahead of her mother en route to the forest to search for a treasure of mushrooms, a neighbour's wife, hoeing in the field, had given them a sidelong glance and said to her daughters in a tone that carried condemnation, "Out larking about as usual."

Grace smiled and waved as if she hadn't heard. When Mary asked her about it later, Grace said, "Poor Mrs. Mullen. If I had thirteen children as she does, I'm sure my life would be as full of work and as empty of joy as hers."

"Why did she choose to have so many?" Mary asked.

"God and men have their way with women's bodies," Grace replied shortly.

Mary, whose only experience with birth had been watching baby chicks emerge from the shell, found Grace's answer more confusing than clarifying.

"Do babies come from God, or from men?" she asked. "Who decides how many?"

"They come from both, my love, and it seems to me that neither give it much thought. Men plant their seed in women as they please, and that seed grows or not as God sees fit. Some, like Mrs. Mullen, seem to give birth every year, while others like me have only one, no matter how often the planting or how ready the soil."

Mary knew the tool her father used for planting, for their one-room cottage offered not a shred of privacy. Although it was not as big as a spade, it was, she thought, much larger than the hole in her body where, her mother explained, the seed must be put to make a baby.

"What if I don't want any babies?" Mary asked.

Grace laughed and said, "Then get thee to a nunnery, my dear."

"Doesn't God give babies to nuns?"

"I'm sure He would, if men were allowed behind the cloister walls. Only because nuns live without men can they live without giving birth. If this is a choice you'd make, you'll need be making it before you're bedded by a man."

"I'll not be locked up for any cause," Mary pouted. It piqued her that women, who carried the burden of children, were given so little choice in the matter of their making.

Though there were days during her teens when Mary felt as restless as the waves, her imagination and that of her mother kept her from being bored. Most of what she lacked she'd never known. What she missed most keenly was her father. It was ever a topic between her and Grace: what they would do when he returned, how good it would be to have him home again. It wasn't just the gifts he brought and money to tide them through another winter, but the tales he spun night after night, which took Grace and Mary with him wherever he'd been. Long after they had gone to bed, Mary would hear her parents' cooing whispers. Thus were all his homecomings, until the last, the terrible one.

Silas hadn't been away many months, only up to Norway and back along the English coast. But the man who crashed through the door that night wasn't the husband and father they knew. It was a wild-eyed beast caked in filth, half-starved, dragging one leg. Silas was barely able to speak, and gave them only scraps of the story.

Scavengers, he said, had lain in wait and, with misplaced lanterns, had lured the ship upon the rocks. Silas had made it to shore, clinging to a splintered mast, and over a period of weeks had dragged his broken body along the coast to home.

How had he got the awful gash on his thigh that left him too crippled to ever walk right again? Why did he come the whole distance, from the point on the coast where the ship went down to the cottage where his wife and daughter waited, without seeking food or medical care? Why had he not asked for help from good folk along the way? The only answer they got was a frightened look in his eyes. Even Mary could see that what he had not told them was worse than what he had.

It was from Silas's nightmares that the truth emerged, in bits and pieces at first. Later, when they had heard it all, he would tell it all, again and again. It never really went away. Any number of nights his screams would wake them, not piercing but strangled, as if something had him by the throat. He would jerk erect and fling his feet to the floor to flee. Grace would wrap her arms around him and hold him fast, speaking in a soft voice, repetitious as a lullaby, until he was fully awake. Mary would cross the room from her cot on the opposite side of the hearth, shivering, for the fire would have long since gone out. She would crouch on the earthen floor, embrace his shins, and lay her head against his wounded thigh. He would stroke her hair in the absent way one pets a cat, drawing calm from its silky warmth.

If they were lucky, he would relax before he was fully awake, and would lie back down and fall asleep. But often he could not sleep again till daybreak, and he would tell them what happened when the ship went down and he'd swum for his life and finally managed to catch a spar which was tossed by the waves up onto a rock-strewn beach. Mary often fell asleep with her head on his knee, for by now she had heard the story so often it had lost its horror, like a rough path made easier by repeated passage.

"'Twas her again," he'd mutter. "Hanging over me with the axe. Still drippin' blood it was, from havin' chopped into the cabin boy what washed up along side me."

The scavengers killed four of his shipmates, all who had made it to shore except for himself. The thing that saved Silas was the moon, which came from behind a cloud for the briefest moment. He saw the woman silhouetted against the light as she swung the axe, and he rolled not away but against her, so that the blade meant for his belly had hit his thigh instead. He had brought her down on top of him and, with her face staring into his, choked the life out of her.

That was not the end of it. There had been days and nights of terror as he dragged himself from one hiding place to another while her companions sought him, wanting to avenge her death and not wanting to leave alive a witness to their deeds. More than once they had come so close to where he lay hidden among weeds or rocks that he fancied he could smell their rummy breaths. Sometimes he dreamed of them, too, of being surrounded, and there being no escape. But mostly he dreamed of the woman.

Then came that night in the pub. Although Silas had no chance to tell them what happened, once Grace and Mary heard the story from the bartender, Mr. Strobe, they knew the why of it.

"He wasn't drunk, I swear ye that, for he'd just come in and ordered a bottle of rum. I'd barely slid the bottle across the bar. He picked it up in one hand and a glass in the other and turned around, and there was this stranger coming our way. A rough-looking bloke he was, but nothing out of the ordinary." Strobe stared hard at the floor as if a picture of the stranger was painted there. "I took him to be a traveller with some-thing of a thirst, 'cause he come fast through the door and straight for the bar. Just then Silas turned around and, droppin' his glass on the floor, he took the bottle by the neck and laid it against the feller's head with a force ye can't imagine."

The bartender shook his head and gave up trying to see more than he had seen that night. "Bless me if I know what brought it on, for I've known Silas Broad since he was a boy, and drunk or sober, I've never known him to brawl."

Grace and Mary knew that the stranger was, or had seemed in Silas's mind to be, one of the scavengers. In his tortured brain he believed himself still hunted, and yet on the run.

Silas fled home that night with the posse behind. He burst into the cottage and by the things he snatched, Mary knew he intended to take the boat. In the distance they heard horses' hooves ringing on the rocky roadway. "The sheriff," he muttered, "but he'll not find me here!"

"No, Silas, my love!" Grace cried, clinging to his sleeve. "It's only your body they'll take! Your soul will still be free!"

"Don't preach rubbish, woman! Me soul lives in me body. They take one, they got the other." He kissed her hard, pushed her away, and banged the door on his way out.

Mary ran down the slope after him and saw, through the blinding rain, that the waves that windblown night could have washed over their cottage had it been on the shore instead of on the hill above.

"Father, don't go!" she screamed. "You'll die."

"Then I'll die a free man," he bellowed, and pointed the bow of his little boat into a watery mountain.

Then the lawmen's horses were around her, snorting and circling until she thought she would be trampled.

A shot exploded above her head, causing the horses to rear. Had the bullet found its mark? She stared hard beyond the turbulent surf in the direction her father had gone.

There was nothing but darkness to see.

Then lightning split the sky and she glimpsed the small boat, high on a monster wave. Silas, illuminated in blue-white brightness, half-turned and raised one arm to the sheriff's men in a defiant salute.

Thunder rolled, and the world went dark. Mary would never see her father again.

⊕

Well before Silas disappeared, Mary and her mother had grown accustomed to a harsher kind of poverty. In Silas's last year at home, crippled as he was, they no longer had his seaman's wages to tide them over. They ate what came from Grace's garden, which in winter was barely more than dried beans and shrivelled potatoes. Occasionally, when it seemed sure that they would starve, a boat-building neighbour would give Silas a bit of work. On those days he went without breakfast and ate only when Mary came at noontime with a pot of soup, thick or thin as their larder allowed.

On one such trip she had seen, from the hill above the boat yard, a lean young man bending over a boat turned up for repair. Her father saw her coming and limped quickly up the path to take the kettle from her.

"Get ye home," he said.

It was an unusual way for Silas to behave, for normally he looked forward not merely to the food but to an hour of Mary's cheerful company. Mary suspected that the command had to do with the young man and, not being fearful of her father, asked with a tease in her voice, "Who is he you don't wish me to meet?"

"A smuggler," Silas told her, unsmiling. "Such men live for money, and have no loyalty to country, mates, nor kin. Men like that," Silas wagged his finger in her face, "bring naught but grief to the women they bed."

"Do you imagine that I can't tell a good man from a bad one?" Mary retorted. "As a child I knew that much."

It was true. Those years she'd spent on shipboard had taught her that there were some crew members who had a look in their eye of wanting something—what she didn't know—but something they had no right to ask and she was sure she did not want to give. Even before they tried for a whiskery kiss on her mouth, she learned to keep her distance from them, no matter what treats they offered.

"I know ye've not been courted," said Silas, "and when ye are, by the seat of me britches, it'll not be by the likes of that one yonder."

Mary said no more, but handed over the soup and started back along the path. At the rim of the hill she stopped and looked back at the likes of that one yonder. She couldn't see his face, only the top of his hat. He was standing with one foot up, his long legs wide apart.

She considered how peculiar it was that men, whose private parts hang out, so often sit or stand like that, their crotch exposed to the world but for a covering bit of cloth, while women, with everything tucked neatly inside, conceal what little there is to see with layers upon flared-out layers. She stopped on the other side of the ridge and put one foot up on a rock, cocking her leg the way men do, to get the feel of what it was like to have the most tender part of her body so exposed. It was a cool, free feeling, yet a troubling one. It took, she deemed, greater confidence than most women have to sit or stand in such a vulnerable way. Perhaps it was a matter of size. If she had six feet of hardened muscles like that man down at the boat, maybe she could stand with her legs apart without fearing molestation.

Mary took her foot off the rock and walked on down the path, for it wasn't a fantasy worth cultivating. Her imagination ran to daydreams which, although improbable, were at least in the realm of possibility. She would fantasize doing some favour for a wealthy person who, in gratitude, would give her enough money to make life easy for her parents in their old age. Or she would dream of meeting and marrying a local lad who would love her company as much as her parents loved each other's. Or she would catch the eye of a ship's captain who would take her, in marriage or not, on all his distant voyages.

Mary's fantasies about men had little basis, for during her teens she met very few. The nearest she had come to being courted was an exchange of bashful glances with the vicar's son in church, when the rest of the congregation's heads were bowed in prayer. All of her twenty years had been spent under the watchful eyes of one or both of her parents. That, of course, would change after her father sailed his boat into the storm and was never seen again.

She and Grace could not survive on garden vegetables alone, although her mother's thinness, Mary suspected, came as much from grief as from being half-starved. Mary sought work and found it, cleaning up a doctor's operating room. Poorly paid and disgusting work it was, but at least the hours were good. The doctor only did surgery in the mornings, so she was home each day well before dark. She would return bone tired from scrubbing, but what a pleasure it was to see the thatch of the cottage, golden in afternoon light, and to find her mother crouched among the greenery of her garden. Mary would drop onto a wooden bench by the door, and tell Grace of the day's events.

"'Twas a body we had to move today," Mary said. "Mrs. Crumb. Her heart stopped when he took the knife to her tumour. Seemed like no one, not the doctor nor her kin, really cared."

Mary was silent a moment, then continued. "They say God takes care for every one of us, but I'd swear He took no notice of Mrs. Crumb. I wonder if the Greeks and Romans might have been right about Them Up There being so busy with their own affairs that they scarce notice humans unless one gets in the way?"

Grace said nothing, but sat there in the garden, stroking the sun-warmed earth as if it was a living thing.

"Aye, Mother, get your hands out of the dirt!" Mary exclaimed.

"Why?" asked Grace, wiggling a hand into the soil until it was covered up to the wrist. "'Tis the body of God."

Mary's lips parted in surprise, for her mother read the Bible daily. Mary could not recall her ever saying an unconventional thing about religion.

"Earth? The body of God?"

"Why not?" Grace asked, looking off into the distance. "Don't they say we will all be taken to His bosom, and become one with Him? And aren't we put into the earth, and don't we become part of it?"

"Taken to His bosom, yes—" Mary began, but her mother interrupted.

"Sure and it can't be a bosom like yours or mine, not if it's to hold all the good folks that ever lived." Grace chuckled, for between her and Mary, the smallness of their breasts was a teasing matter.

A kind of fear, rising, perhaps, out of having seen death earlier that day, kept Mary from laughing at the joke. "Call the earth God if you like," she retorted. "But to see you put your hand in the dirt and talk of becoming part of it gives me no comfort."

Grace's reply was stern. "Only children who die young have the comfort of parents to the end of their life. I'd not wish that on either of us."

"The least you could do is comfort me while you live," Mary pouted, tears unexpectedly forming in her eyes.

Grace's voice softened a little. "That's what I'm trying to do, Daughter. I'm speaking to you now of when I'll not be here, because it won't be long, and you must get used to the notion."

Mary, not a whiner by nature, but because she was so tired, began to bawl like a baby.

Grace lay back between the rows and gazed up at the sky. "I shan't mind. The earth is bountiful and the earth is God, and I shall be alive there, one way or another."

"What about Father?" Mary choked. "He went down at sea."

Grace, her face framed by potato plants, shrugged her thin shoulders, still flat upon the ground. "It comes to the same thing. Have you never noticed how sand and sea rush into each other's embrace and churn up together into something that's neither one or the other? As did your father and I, he smelling of sea and I of earth." Grace lay there a moment longer, watching clouds move across the sky. Then she lifted a dirt-soiled hand, and said, "Come, child. Stop your sniffling. Help me up, and let's go put together a bite to eat."

Mary grasped her mother's hand and pulled her to her feet. There was something frighteningly insubstantial in Grace's lightness, as if her bones were hollow, like the bones of a bird. Grace stood there, wavering unsteadily, until Mary put an arm around her waist and walked her to the house.

That conversation occurred on the last sunny day of

fall. Before winter was full on them, Mary knew what Grace knew: that her mother was dying. What surprised them both was how long it took.

Mary could not stay home to nurse her mother for, without her pittance of a salary, they surely would have starved. She would stoke the fire before she left, and would hurry home after work, only to find it gone out and the cottage icy because Grace was too weak to keep it going. The woman who had never complained now always complained of the cold.

One morning Mary found it particularly difficult to leave, for her mother continued to shiver even with the fire ablaze. At the door, Mary hesitated. "Shall I stay home today?"

"No. I'm tired. I rest better when I'm alone."

"I'm just afraid—" Mary began, but dared not put into words what she feared.

"I'm trying," Grace said, as if reading her mind, "to hold on till spring when the ground gets warm. Just now it's so cold. And I've no cloak for you to wrap me in."

Mary came back and stood over the bed. Grace looked up at her, questioningly. "You shall have a cloak," the girl said fiercely. "The warmest cloak in Cornwall!"

Then she went out and up the hill to the road. It was a grey morning, the thatch of their cottage grey, the smoke rising from the chimney, the frozen grey field fringed with black rocks that divided it from the sea, itself countless shades of grey. It was like a painting done in charcoal; soft-edged, with no colour brighter than that of smoke and steely dark water.

Mary had a sudden sense that, inside the cottage, her mother was already dead and turning grey. She felt an urge to rush back. But she was a sensible girl not given to impulsive behaviour—not yet. She set her foot hard on the road and walked in the direction of town. For that decision, right or wrong, Mary would never know whether her mother had died that moment or much later, waiting for a daughter who would not return.

Mary walked quickly, head filled with thoughts of how she would get a cloak this very day. She would go to the store, buy the fabric on credit, and by the evening fire she would cut and stitch it, working all night if need be. If the merchant refused her, she would go to a seamstress, and promise to pay whatever she asked, week by week as her salary allowed.

But Mary would do neither. Unbeknownst to her, something was about to break. It was as if since birth she had been attached to one end of a rope by which her mother pulled her, hand over hand, through infancy and youth to the crest of womanhood. In that high place Mary had expected to find a broad, smooth path to follow. But just as she was about to set her foot there, the rope, which perhaps never had been more than a thread, would snap. Mary Broad would fall, not back into childhood but into a chasm deeper than the ocean. She could swim, climb, save herself. But not for a very long time. Not until the falling stopped.

It was a busy morning in the surgery and then, in

the afternoon, when she would normally have started the cleaning, the doctor undertook an amputation which left the room splattered with blood. It took two hours to clean up afterwards, with hands which were soon half-frozen, for the water she carried from the well was bitter cold.

She was fetching water when a coach pulled up, discharging a lady whose face she did not see. Mary only glimpsed the coachman, very grand, as he climbed down to open the door of the coach. Mary entered the surgery by the back way as the lady entered the waiting room by the front door. She heard the doctor say, "Just let me take that, Mrs. Trump. If you'll step this way, into my office?"

The lady fluttered words of thanks and must have handed him her wrap for, through the doorway that joined the rooms, Mary saw the doctor's hand as it hung the cloak on the waiting room rack. Their voices moved away from her and were silenced when the door into the doctor's private office clicked shut.

Mary finished the floor, which was always the last of the scrubbing. She would have to hurry to see the merchant and, at that, would be late getting home. A vision of her mother's uncontrollable shivering gripped her and she, with her aching cold hands, began to shiver too.

She stepped to the door of the waiting room. "I'll be going now, Sir," she said into the empty room. It was merely habit, this announcing her daily departure, for the doctor, still sequestered with the lady, could no more hear Mary's voice than she could hear his.

Her foot nudged something soft. She looked down and saw that the lady's mauve cloak had fallen to the floor. She bent to pick it up, intending to hang it back on the peg. But as her hands sank into its softness, something in her went wild, perhaps in the same way some wild thing had taken hold of her father that night in the pub, to do a thing not in his nature and never done before.

Mary did not notice the pink silk bonnet attached, nor concern herself with what weighted the pocket. All she felt, all she knew, all she wanted, was the warmth of the cloak. Swiftly she bundled it under her shawl. Holding the wrap tight against her belly as a woman might hold an unborn child, she fled out the side door of the surgery.

She cut across the lot to a narrow alley behind a row of shops already beginning to close. Because she was running, and because her head was down, she did not see the coachman until his crop came down with a slash and barred her way.

The thread had broken; the fall had begun.

Mary cared not what dank floor she lay upon, so great were the pains in her face and private parts. Nor could she imagine, when she opened her eyes, what hell this was. What she saw in the gloom above her were the faces of women she had never seen before.

"They've had their way with 'er, all right," said a voice as deep as a man's.

"Musta been a virgin. Ain't she bleedin' like a stuck hog!" said a frail girl who could not have been more than fourteen.

The deep-voiced woman jabbed a finger into the ribs of the girl. "Lend a hand, you simperin' tart. Pull up her skirt so's it don't get soaked."

Mary felt her hips being lifted and her skirt tugged above her buttocks. She opened her mouth to speak, but it hurt so much she merely moaned.

"Must've given them some backtalk, to've been beat about the face so," said a third woman, with frizzy red-orange curls matted around her face.

"Country girl," said the deep voice. "Wouldn't know any better."

The red-haired woman lifted Mary's head into her lap. "I'm called Colleen," she announced in a lilting Irish brogue. "What're you in for, lass?"

"Thieving," Mary whispered, through swollen lips.

"Me, I got caught with my Johnny and our bunch, freedom fighters, you know."

Colleen motioned to the teenaged waif. "Florie there tried her hand at whoring." She jerked her chin at the deep-voiced woman. "Cass claims all that and murder to boot."

"Murder?" Mary's body spasmed with fright.

"Murder and more," Cass bragged. "If there's a crime I've not committed, I ain't heard of it yet. Me family's been highwaymen and the like for ten generations. Lie still, girl, so's I can wipe you up."

As she spoke, the older woman's hands moved

between Mary's legs like a nurse's, wiping away the blood. "Gad, but you are a mess!"

"I don't know what happened," Mary said. "I had the cloak in my arms, and then the men . . . ." She stopped. Although she knew there had been men, many men, and many questions, she could not clearly recall anything beyond the face of the coachman. "I don't remember."

"Lucky you," growled Cass.

Mary turned her head and saw a fourth woman, slender, almost pretty, leaning against the bars. Florie saw the direction of her gaze and said, "That's Grace. She stole some ribbon from the millinery where she worked."

"My mother's name was Grace," said Mary. She was unaware of having used the past tense, yet she used it naturally, either because she had sensed her mother's passing that grey morning, or because she wanted it to be true; wanted her to have died before someone came next day to explain why her daughter had not returned.

Although she had never been in a court of law before and many words were unfamiliar, Mary understood well enough what was said. The things she had stolen were described in detail and held up for display. "Valued at eleven pounds, eleven and sixpence," the prosecutor said. He portrayed Mary as a vain and greedy girl, a menace to society in general and to England's gentlewomen in particular.

Mary listened curiously, as if they spoke of a stranger.

She herself had never given a fig for fashion. She believed, like her mother, that it was the durability of a garment that counted, with some consideration for softness against the skin when one had the luxury, as they had rarely ever had, of choosing. All that mattered by way of style was that its design didn't hamper the job at hand.

Once, as a child during their days at sea, Mary had begged her mother to make her trousers so she could learn to climb the mast. Silas thought it would do no harm but Grace had refused. "No harm to Mary perhaps, but to see my child high on a swaying mast would make me faint away!" Grace claimed. "What can't be done in a simple dress I'll not have my little girl doing." And so it was. The only exception was allowing the child to strip down to her underwear to learn to swim; that being permitted because her mother feared her falling overboard and wanted to be sure she could stay afloat until someone came to the rescue.

As Mary sat thinking of the kind of clothing she had never had and never wanted, she heard, in another part of her mind, the judge's words, " . . . on this 20th day of March, 1786, Mary Broad be sentenced to hang." He asked if there was anything she would like to say, anyone's pardon she would like to ask, before being taken to the gallows.

Mary stood, looked up at the judge, and said in a low, clear voice, "I never noticed the bonnet, nor what was in the pockets. 'Twas the cloak I wanted, not for myself but for my mother, who was always cold."

Someone whispered something to the judge. He looked sternly down at Mary and said, "Your mother is dead. It was your wicked deed, perhaps, that sent her to the grave."

Mary's eyes locked his, measuring the truth of his words. They were, she decided, only half-true, for if her mother had not died that morning after Mary had left, in that moment when she had felt the world turn grey, then Grace would surely have died in the freezing night when no one returned to light the fire. In either case, she would have died alone, and cold. Mary bowed her head and said, "Truly, I deserve to hang."

The judge had sat too long in judgement of others to be taken in by remorse which in reality was merely evil-doers' tears for their own lives, which they were about to lose. But he noted that the condemned girl was six weeks short of her twenty-first birthday. He fancied himself a Christian, and had a Christian's belief in the possibility of redemption for those who genuinely repented their misdeeds. Rarely had the judge felt himself in the presence of such soul-deep remorse. He ordered Mary Broad returned to her cell.

The judge was no fool, but neither was he clairvoyant. He had no way of knowing that Mary's remorse was not for having stolen the cloak, but for having failed to bring its soft warmth to her mother before she died.

Some days later Mary was taken into court again and there told that her sentence to hang had been commuted to "transportation upon the seas, beyond the seas" for a period of seven years. Then she was crammed into a wagon and taken to the port, along with the women in her cell and many others. Exactly where beyond the sea they would be sent was a mystery, for it was well known that since the Americans declared independence a decade earlier, the break-away colonies no longer permitted the Empire to dump its unwanted citizens there.

The crowded wagon rumbled its way along the muddy track until they were in sight of the waterfront. As far as the eye could see, the harbour was lined with rotting ships, each one overflowing with stinking humanity. Slops, they observed, were poured straight down the sides of the ships into the scummy water below.

"Some's been confined in these hulks for ages," Cass said stoically. "Reckon it can't be much worse than other places I've been."

But when their longboat reached the *Dunkirk*, its excrement-encrusted side rising above them like a cliff, even Cass blanched.

"This old hulk?" Mary exclaimed. "I've seen driftwood more seaworthy than this!"

"You think they'd care if the lot of us went to the bottom of the sea? Girl, that's what they're hoping," Cass sneered. "That, or we all be carried off by gaol fever."

Ships allowed little enough space for crew, and in these rotting hulks-turned-prisons, six were crowded into places designed for one. Mary's bed was a single plank, and she rarely moved from it except when compelled to some task, ordered by a guard. The girl, Grace, lay next to her, mostly silent, for which Mary was grateful, as she had no desire to speak. It was as if a great fog had rolled in, dulling her mind and all her senses.

From time to time Cass intruded on Mary's isolation, pulling her roughly from the plank and pushing her into line for gruel.

"I know you're aiming to starve yerself," Cass growled. "But not whilst I'm about. This hell-hole is foul enough without the stink of your corpse adding to it."

When the night visits began, they only drove Mary deeper into herself. Spence, a big man with muscles wrapped in middle-aged fat, was less brutal than other guards, but by far the most lecherous. Some of the women tried to entice him, hoping for favours in return. But Spence's taste ran to the youngest women and the most withdrawn. He called them "little virgins", though there would not be one among them who, if she'd had her maidenhead when taken prisoner, hadn't already lost it to the police or a prison guard. Florie was the youngest in their corner of the ship, but her pathetic mewing was too much like that of a motherless kitten. It caused Spence to want to kick instead of caress her. It was Mary, silent on her plank, who made his loins burn. He had seen her kind before. Lying so still, moving only when bade to do so, never weeping, asking for nothing, she was like a living doll. A man could do as he liked with her, and imagine her to be anything that pleased him.

It was some weeks before he took her; saving the best for last, he told himself, as he dallied with others newly arrived. But finally his lust peaked, and he gave himself permission, under cover of darkness, to writhe against Mary's slight but definite curves.

The doll-like quality was as Spence had imagined. Her limbs lay loose, moving only as he moved them. At first he was thrilled by the sense of power this gave him, the thought that he could manipulate every part of her body to pleasure his own. But there was more to her stillness than he had bargained for. She did not turn, twist, gasp, or moan. Even her breathing, so light he scarcely felt it, did not change. Frustrated by her stillness, he slapped her. Her face rolled to the side under his blow, and lay there, eyes open, staring emptily, like a dead person.

As well she might have been, for from the first moment the guard lowered his bulk on top of her, Mary had withdrawn deep into herself. She imagined herself to be dead, and his weight to be the press of moist stinking earth such as one shovels from a barnyard.

Spence had known unresponsive women before, but a few blows and the reward of a kind word or two was usually enough to wake them up. With Mary, though, the coldness remained, and seeped up from her body into his. Each of the three nights he lay with her, he had a horrible notion that his engorged penis was in the frigid vaginal grasp of a dead person.

Then he felt a hand, warm upon his thigh, and thought for an instant that Mary had finally been roused. But when his own hand followed the arm, he found it attached to the raven-haired girl Grace, who shared Mary's plank. He rolled over onto Grace, and molested Mary no more.

Grace was bony as a skeleton but definitely alive. Her silence soon gave way to whispered pleadings, but she didn't ask for much and, when he gratified her whim for a comb, her body amply repaid him. It was on the night he gave her the comb that their thrashings pushed Mary onto the floor. There she remained, preferring its sticky filth to the nauseating odour of their unwashed private parts.

One morning Grace woke with fever. She begged Spence to take her to the infirmary but he refused, and came that night as usual, to root about in her burning body. Only on the third night, when he found Grace unconscious, did he order her taken out.

"You can have your bed back now," Florie whispered to Mary.

Mary looked toward the plank, but others were already fighting for it. She shook her head and stayed where she was.

"Grace is gone for good," Florie whispered. "Died on the way to the infirmary."

Mary wound a long strand of unwashed hair around and around her finger and said in a distant voice, "Now all the Graces I've known are dead."

Within the week, the guard, Spence, disappeared, and his death, also of fever, may have been what saved the others. Word got out that typhus was spreading from the prison ships to the mainland. Citizens began to clamour that criminals confined on the hulks must be taken out of the harbour and away.

Thus, five months after Mary set foot on the *Dunkirk*, she and many other prisoners were loaded into long-boats and taken to the *Charlotte*. The *Charlotte*, along with ten other sailing vessels, was anchored on the Motherbank outside Portsmouth. This "First Fleet", as it was called, consisted of two warships, three supply ships, and six convict transports. Its assignment was to convey seven hundred and fifty-six prisoners to a distant land. Of the prisoners, one hundred and nine-ty-two were women and five hundred and sixty-four were men. They, along with the mariners who trans-ported them, were to found a prison colony in a place called, by Captain Cook in his log, Botany Bay.

"A wild and woolly place it is," said a young sailor who rowed them from the *Dunkirk* out to the *Charlotte*. "A fit place for you lot."

"Botany Bay," Mary mused. She recalled her father's praise for Captain Cook's navigational adventures down on the bottom of the world. Her mother had looked bewildered and remarked that the Good Book spoke of the four corners of the earth, so how could anyone sail across the bottom side? Her father had only smiled. "You've been to sea with me, my love, and seen ships and shores come up over the curve of the earth. Two hundred years and more it's been known that if one sails forever east or west, them that survive the journey end up back where they started out, same as a bug that walks around an apple."

"How far is this Botany Bay?" Mary asked the sailor at the oars.

"Some twelve thousand miles and across two seas."

The boy looked grim and it occurred to her that he was more frightened than she. "They say the voyage will take the best part of a year."

"Doesn't matter to me how far it is," Colleen said, looking radiant. "My Johnny's being transported, too."

"Twit!" snorted Cass. "You and the boy charged with treason, and you think they passed on hangin' to give you a honeymoon? It's some greasy sailor you'll be layin' under, and lucky if it's only one."

Colleen bit her lip and turned away.

"Try to catch the eye of an officer," Cass muttered to Mary. "Or a kitchen hand."

"What will they do to us?" Florie asked fearfully.

"Same as always," Cass said heavily. "Whatever they like."

As Mary stepped onto the deck of the *Charlotte*, the ocean breeze dissipated her mental fog. For the first time in many months she took note of her surroundings.

⊕

The *Charlotte* did not have the jerry-built lean-tos, platforms, and deckhouses that had given the *Dunkirk* hulk the feel of a tenement slum. There was confusion on the deck with so many new arrivals, but signs of order, too.

"Name?" asked a man with a ledger in his hand. By the soft look of the hand that held the pen, Mary took him to be an officer.

Before she could answer, the quartermaster shouted, "Hey, Brown!"

Brown turned to answer and she saw that his shirt was split up the back. So he was a prisoner, same as her. The man handed the quartermaster a list from the ledger, then turned back and looked Mary in the face. Like his name, his hair and eyes were brown.

"Mary Broad." She watched as he wrote it on the page, marvelling at the cleanliness of his hands and the beauty of the letters formed by those long, tapered fingers.

Then he looked past her to Florie, who was next in line, and asked again, "Name?"

The quartermaster stood with the captain, a small, dry-looking man whose name, she would learn, was Arthur Phillip. They were comparing a list with a pile of barrels. The lid of one had been pried off. Captain Phillip did not like what he saw inside.

"How the devil can I keep fifteen hundred people alive for nine months feeding them dung such as this?" the captain stormed. "Don't stow it; I'll have a word with Lord Sydney."

Florie sidled up to Mary and whispered, "Wouldn't I like to catch the eye of that one!"

"Which one?" asked Mary, who had been gazing about the ship. The old transport was about a hundred feet long, and no more than thirty feet wide. Although she had not been aboard a ship since she was ten years old, she saw that the *Charlotte* was in a better state of repair than the *Dunkirk*. Everywhere men were at work, scraping, caulking, and mending. Something like excitement welled in her breast. This ship was being readied for a voyage on the high seas!

Florie jerked her chin at the man called Brown. "You didn't see his eyes? Imagine lashes like that brushing your cheek!"

In fact, Mary had noticed his eyes, but only much later did she realise what it was about his brown eyes that she found so different from those of other men she had encountered during her imprisonment. They were kind.

For the next two months, the *Charlotte* lay at anchor. It was far enough from shore that the roll of sea and ship was constant, yet close enough that desperate convicts might attempt to escape. Thus, only prisoners with some task to perform were allowed on deck. The majority were confined below in windowless, unlighted quarters. The rocking motion of the old wooden ship rarely bothered Mary, but most of her companions were terribly seasick. The reek of vomit and the stench of diarrhea were ever in the air.

At last, on May 13, 1787, the First Fleet set sail for what was to be the longest voyage ever made with so great a number of people. Once each ship cleared the harbour, its prisoner passengers were allowed on deck. Mary climbed the ladder up into fresh air with the relief of one being released from the hole of a stinking privy.

Few of the convicts had ever been more than a dozen leagues beyond where they were born. Had they been bound for America they would have felt less hopeless, for it was a known place, and some who had gone there had returned. Botany Bay was infinitely further away. For all they knew, it lay within the boundaries of Hell itself.

They lined the railing and strained their eyes for a last glimpse of England, which most of them would never see again. Women wept without restraint and many men sobbed with them. One could almost imagine, as the *Charlotte*'s sails billowed out, that it was not the wind that filled them but the convicts' keening cries of anguish.

Of the convict women, only three were dry-eyed: Cass, who prized her toughness too much to let anyone see her carry on; Colleen, who believed her Johnny was aboard although she had not yet glimpsed him; and Mary, who, along with a handful of crew members, stood at the opposite railing, staring not back at England but out to sea. It was but two weeks past her twenty-second birthday. Next to freedom itself, she could not have asked for a better gift.

From what Mary had overheard of the captain's curses the day she came aboard, she knew that the contractor had short-changed them on rations. If the sailors knew hunger on this voyage, the convicts would know more. But hunger was not something Mary feared. She filled her lungs and thought that if she could draw the clean salt air into her belly, she could live on it alone. Then she remembered that her belly already held a load, which was daily growing. Although hunger didn't concern her for herself, a child had been planted in her womb. It had only her body for nourishment, and it must be fed.

It took about two weeks to reach the Canary Islands. Mary had been there on one of her father's voyages, but it was when she was very young and she remembered little of their time on shore. Even so, as she watched the crewmen jauntily coming and going, she felt pangs of envy, and a deep loneliness for her parents. She thought of trying to escape, but something held her back. It was not the baby, for, in truth, that unseen, unborn thing meant little to her yet. She stayed aboard because the journey itself called to her. This might be a prison ship, but for Mary, as for her father, any voyage had always been a kind of freedom.

Also, she reasoned, the Canaries were islands; thus even if she escaped the ship she would still be trapped. A lone Englishwoman in this land of dark-skinned people would certainly draw attention. Her judgement proved correct for, when a convict named John Power stole a dinghy and slipped away to a small outlying island, he was captured by a search party the very next morning.

The weather had been fine for the two-week run down to the Canaries, but when the fleet picked up the Brazil Current and started across the Atlantic toward Río de Janeiro, they encountered intolerable heat. Rats, cockroaches, fleas, and lice proliferated, driving them to distraction. Then came tropical downpours and that was worse. Most stayed below, gagging on vile fumes from the bilge. Mary had never felt so ill. She made her way up onto deck to vomit over the railing.

A hand in the small of her back made her jump. "A wee bit seasick are we?" asked a teasing voice with a Cornish accent.

Mary glanced around to see a convict whose name she knew to be Will Bryant. He had a cheerful disposition, and was often called upon by the crew for one task or another. He stood leaning on a mop. The rain had soaked his hair, making it appear even blacker than it was.

"Speak for yourself," Mary snapped. "I've been to sea with my old dad and it takes rougher than this to turn my stomach."

"Funny," he said, looking down at her with amused eyes as blue as her own. "I could swear you're a bit green about the gills. But maybe not. Might be you just need a taste of rum and a little fun tonight?"

She turned on him, furious. "Can't you see, boy? I'm pregnant!"

Will looked down at her waist, which in truth was not much thickened. "Well then," he grinned, "we can be all the merrier and no harm done."

Mary landed him a slap on the face that would have cracked the neck of a smaller man. Will flinched and his grin went a little crooked. He gave a can't-blame-me-for-trying-shrug, picked up the mop bucket, and sauntered off.

Tensed to vomit again, Mary turned back to the

railing. But the rain, a warm drizzle, fell soft on her face and arms, and the nausea passed.

Florie sidled up to Mary and nudged her in the ribs. "Making eyes at you, is he? Good-looking bloke is Will Bryant, them blue eyes under that mop o' curly black hair."

Mary glanced in the direction Will had gone. He was standing at the far end of the ship with one long leg up on an overturned lifeboat, his head bent to study the water below. A thought—no, not a thought, a feeling—jolted her. Hadn't she seen him before, long ago?

"What's he in for?" she asked Florie.

"Smuggling. They catched him off the coast of Cornwall."

"Smuggling," Mary mused. Then it came to her— that man whose boat her father had repaired, whom she had looked down on from a hill above. She had not seen the stranger's face, but he had stood so, with one foot up on an overturned boat, his long legs wide apart, as if proud of his manly parts. Yet many men, especially long-legged ones, struck such a pose. No reason to imagine that the man sharing this voyage to Botany Bay was the same one she had seen that sunny day in Cornwall.

Even so, her father's words came back to her. "A smuggler," he had said of the man in the boat yard. "Such men live for money, and have no loyalty to country, mates, nor kin. Men like that bring naught but grief to the women they bed."

Will looked up and Mary turned away so that he

should not take her stare for interest. "Not for me," she said to Florie. "If I had the stomach for any on this ship, it would be Mr. Brown. At least he's got something on his mind besides—" She stopped, for already she had said more than she had intended.

Florie looked surprised, and a little awed. "'Tis him you crave? Why, convict and all, Mr. Brown is as good as an officer!"

"I crave none," Mary snapped.

That was not entirely true. Mary had taken the measure of every man aboard, and had already made her choice. "Try to catch the eye of an officer," Cass had said the day they were rowed out in the longboat. "Or a kitchen hand."

It was good advice. Mary saw, more clearly now than before, that it might well be the only way to keep from fetching up half-starved in Botany Bay. But she might be needing more than food. There were no midwives on this ship. Back in Cornwall, women in the agony of childbirth had sometimes been brought to the doctor. That was always a last resort, but on occasions it had been the salvation of mother or child or both. There was a good chance that the ship's surgeon had had some experience in birthing babies under difficult circumstances. Thus Mary made up her mind to find favour with him.

It would not be easy. Dr. White was a harsh man, not even slightly gentle with the women who came to him in distress. Mary had first thought that he might be one of those who hated women and had gone to sea to escape them. But as she watched him—and she did watch him when she could—she saw that he was just as rough with the men. She judged him to be an unhappy person; an officer, yes, but like most on this ship, not wanting to be here.

Mary often stood sideways to the railing as if she were looking ahead in the direction the ship was going, but where she stood was across from the surgery. When Dr. White appeared in the doorway, she stole quick glances to decipher his moods and his needs. The question was how to approach him, this man supposedly here for healing, who used his tongue like a lash and handled his patients, convicts and crew alike, with no more sympathy than a farmer might have for cattle being hauled to slaughter.

The doctor's mood varied little, remaining as sour on sunny days as in stormy weather. Fairly soon, Mary noticed that his feet gave him pain. When there was no one in the surgery he often sat down, unlaced his boots and rubbed his feet. Indeed, he frequently went about with laces dangling, so as to remove the boots more quickly when he had a moment to rest. It was the only weakness she saw in him.

It was when they lay in the doldrums, on the passage between the Canaries and Brazil, that Mary made her move. She entered the surgery toward the end of a busy day, when there was but one patient remaining. It was the boy, Pip, who had been fettered so cruelly back on the *Dunkirk*. When the convicts were brought on board the *Charlotte*, Captain Phillip had ordered all fetters removed. But that year on the *Dunkirk*, dragging the iron ball and chain, had given Pip an unnatural walk. With each step he took, now that the fetter was gone, one bone-thin leg jerked high of its own accord. But Mary saw, when she entered the surgery, that something else had brought him here. His skinny forearm oozed blood from a horrible gash.

Dr. White stared at the wound with a look of pure disgust. "Metal or wood?" he asked.

"Metal," the lad replied in a voice that belied his agony.

The doctor began to clean the wound, not seeming to care that his roughness left Pip gasping with fresh pain. "No room for clumsiness on a ship."

"'Twern't clumsiness, Sir," the boy shot back. "'Twas that lout Scrapper what swung a grappling hook at me when I wouldn't give him me victuals."

The doctor bound the gash shut, pushed Pip out of the room, and gave Mary a cursory glance. "You look fit enough."

"I am fit, Sir. It's not for doctoring I've come."

White dropped into a chair and pulled his boot from first one aching foot then the other. "Out," he growled. "I've no time for the likes of you."

"You misunderstand, Doctor. I—"

Mary took a deep breath, went down on her knees, and lifted his foot into her lap. His eyes flew open but already her fingers were moving over the foot, gently at first, then firmly, as she felt where the pain must be. Her father's foot had required massaging after the injury to his leg, but that was a task her mother had performed. Later, when her mother lay in sickbed, Mary had often rubbed her feet when she came home and found them aching with cold. This was the first time Mary had touched a man's foot, but a foot, she figured, was a foot. What took the pain from one would likely take it from another.

Mary quickly massaged the first foot then moved to the other one, not knowing how long the doctor would remain still. As it turned out, not long. He may have allowed her three minutes, and himself as many groans, then, without warning, he kicked her roughly aside.

"Go on, get out," he said, his voice strangely thick. "I'll see there's a measure of rum for you tonight."

"If you please, Dr. White, I don't want rum," Mary said, rising to her feet.

He looked sceptical. "Not sex? Not rum? What then?"

"Work."

His laugh was hard and humourless. "You must be mad to think I'd have a criminal about, and risk a scalpel in the ribs."

"Not by my hand, Dr. White." Mary touched her belly. "There's none experienced in midwifery on the ship, and if bad comes to worse, I might be needing you."

His cold grey eyes narrowed. "When did you conceive?"

"On the *Dunkirk*. Four months ago."

He leaned over and began to lace up his boots. "So you'll be popping about half-way. And puking from here to there."

Mary looked down at a small bald spot in the middle of his bent-over head. "I swear not, Sir. I've worked in a surgery before. It's the hold, and molesting by the crew that sickens me. Let me stay topside and keep this place clean. You'll not regret it, I promise."

"That's all you want? To muck about this butchery?" He gave her a suspicious stare.

Mary gazed straight into his eyes and said, "That, and extra victuals now and then."

"The Captain controls the rations," White snapped. "Which means you'll go hungry, like everyone else."

Mary's eyes remained on his, and her voice, when she spoke, was not pleading. "I've no fear of hunger for myself. But I've seen babes born to starving women. Them that survived never seemed right in the head. I could overcome the grief of a dead baby, but not of a dim-witted one."

Dr. White looked more closely at her. "You've got hard good sense, uncommon in a woman." He rose and turned his back on her. Then over his shoulder, flung the words she wanted to hear. "Work begins at daybreak."

"And you'll be wanting me to—"

White waved a hand at the blood-spattered mess around them. "Clean this pigsty."

In the weeks that followed, Mary cleaned as she had been taught by the doctor back in Cornwall, scrubbing every inch of the room where Dr. White worked. She was careful to keep her distance, though, for White let her know, with rough, unexpected shoves, that she was to stay out of his way. Much of the cleaning she did when he stepped out, or after he was done at night, so that when he returned, the room was as clean as salt water and muscle could make it.

When Dr. White attended a patient Mary paid close attention. She soon learned what instruments or bandages he was likely to want, and placed them in his hand as soon as—but never before—he asked. Within a week he was pushing minor cases—those with shallow cuts or a back that had been lashed with the whip—toward her with instructions to clean the wound. If he felt sympathy for the sick and injured, he never let it show. He treated the human body as if it were no more to him than the table upon which it lay. But for all his harsh ways, White was a good doctor, and Mary would never forget what she learned there, working by his side.

Privately, she wondered what cause he had for bitterness, and why he had chosen to practice his art aboard a ship, as neither his work nor the sea seemed to give him pleasure. If he appreciated Mary's help, he chose not to show that either—at least, not with smiles or kind words. Yet often, after he had gone out to dinner and left her cleaning up, when he returned to lock the surgery, he would hand her a bit of salt pork or some other morsel. That was their bargain. It was all Mary asked and all she needed from him.

Just before the fleet reached Río de Janeiro, an Irish convict, near death, was brought into the surgery by Sergeant Scott. The Irishman had been in irons for some months, and both legs were horribly infected.

He was delirious with fever, but one word running through his unintelligible mumbling was clear enough: "Colleen. Colleen."

Dr. White ignored the man's babbling and turned on the hapless sergeant. "If it's dead you wanted the man, Sergeant Scott, why didn't you fling him over the side to start?"

Scott took a step back and protested, "'Tis the rule, Sir. 'Fore ever we set sail, we catched him trying to creep into the women's quarters. What with him bein' a political prisoner and all—"

"And what the hell use will a cripple be in the colony?" demanded White. Seeing Mary staring at the man, he shouted, "Don't just stand there, woman. Clean out the pus!" To Scott he said, "No more irons, do you hear me? Let the wretch stay topside in good weather; God knows he's not about to creep anywhere now."

Mary set to work cleaning the rotted flesh where the too-tight irons had been fastened. After a moment the doctor pushed her aside and took on the task himself. "Bloody waste of time," he muttered. "The bastard's as good as dead."

"If you're planning to lay him topside," ventured Mary, "I could bring a convict women to tend him."

White stared at her for a moment. "Yes," he said. "Do that."

Mary all but fell into the hold, where she found Colleen lying listlessly in her hammock. During the first part of the voyage Colleen had spent every minute she could on deck, hoping for a glimpse of Johnny. But as weeks passed she had lost hope. Of late she lay in her hammock, not even bothering to scratch her fleabites; as if willing herself to death by immobility.

"Come, girl!" Mary jerked Colleen's hand so hard that she almost tumbled from the hammock. "There's an Irishman calling your name! It's your Johnny, I'm almost sure!"

"No!" Colleen gasp. "How—"

"They've had him in irons."

"Where?"

"In the surgery."

As Colleen lunged for the hatch, Mary caught the hem of her ragged gown and held her. "Colleen, you should know; it's bad."

Colleen's voice came out a whimper. "Oh God! What have they done to him?"

"It's his legs, Colleen. The doctor says . . . but the irons are off; at least there's that."

Colleen began to weep. "The bastards! The rotten bloody bastards!"

"Stop that ranting!" Mary's tone was as sharp as Dr. White's. "Go you up on deck and wait there, quiet. The doctor's wanting a woman to tend him. If you don't act the fool, that woman might be you!"

Mary planted Colleen at the rail and started for the surgery, but hung back when she saw Captain Phillip in the doorway, and heard angry words directed at the doctor.

"We're going to need every able-bodied man and then some, Sir. You tell me this one's as good as dead, and I tell you I'll not have one lost to a piddling irons infection it's your job to cure!"

The captain strode away, wearing the worried frown that perpetually darkened his countenance. Mary waited a moment, then cautiously entered the surgery.

"Well?" White demanded. "Where is she?"

Mary gestured to the deck. "Do you wish to see her now?"

"Now," the doctor mimicked sarcastically, "I wish to get this Irish arse out of here. Tell that woman, who-ever she is, that she brings some healing to bear or she'll feel the cat-o-nine tails herself."

Mary motioned to Colleen, who crossed the deck in a flash and saw the man whose face she had looked for in vain all the long weeks they had been at sea. Her gasp was audible. Mary jabbed her sharply in the ribs and said in a rough voice, "Help me get him out on deck, and mind you, hold him so his legs don't bear any weight!"

Dr. White did not offer to help. Few things repulsed him as much as injuries inflicted deliberately by hu-mans upon humans. White stepped to the door and motioned to the next patient who, he fervently hoped, would be suffering from a less revolting, more curable ailment.

Mary and Colleen laid Johnny flat on the deck. His feverish eyes were open, but he did not seem to see them and his babbling, as before, was pure nonsense interlaced with Colleen's name. Mary brought a basin of water and a rag from the surgery.

To Colleen she said, "Keep his face cool. A fever this

high can addle the brain. I don't know what else to do. I'll ask Dr. White later, when he's not so busy."

A hand tugged at her sleeve. It was the boy, Pip, his arm not yet healed from the grappling iron gash. "Miss Mary," he said, "I know somebody."

"Not now, Pip! Can't you see I'm busy?"

Pip appealed to Colleen. "There's a convict in the hammock next to mine what's a wonder with infections. He used to live in Africa and learned a-plenty from witch doctors. I seen him patch up lots on this trip that the doctor couldn't do no good for."

"Bring him!" cried Colleen.

Pip hesitated. "If he's sober. But he'll be wantin' rum."

"Bring him!" Colleen repeated with an authority which, Mary thought, would have sent any man, let alone a boy, off to do her bidding.

Pip soon returned with a hard-faced, bow-legged man with a mane of greasy grey hair.

"This here's Matey," Pip said.

Matey looked at Colleen with booze-bleared eyes. "Where's the rum?"

Mary said, "This man has been in irons. Can you —?"

"Where's the rum?" Matey interrupted.

"Tonight," Colleen whispered. "I'll bring it."

Matey grinned meanly. "They catch you, you'll get a flogging."

"There's my word, take it or leave it," Colleen snapped. She unwrapped the bandages. "What do you think?"

Matey squatted and examined the wounds. "I seen worse. Some of 'em lived."

"Tell me what to do," Colleen begged.

Matey peered into Johnny's half-conscious face. "Don't know what your chances are, lad, what with two sluts and a quack tending you. Myself, I'd rather be in the hands of the Devil." He squinted up at the sky. "The sun can do a lot of curing if you keep the flies off." The old sailor rose to go. "Whatever you do, don't let that butcher in there go bleedin' him."

"Is that all?" Colleen cried.

"All till I say more." As Matey sauntered away, he grumbled to Pip, "Sluts. Always whinin' for something."

"You should never have promised him rum!" Mary whispered to Colleen. Both of them knew that the only way to get rum was by trading one's body for it, as Cass, Florie and many other convict women did night after night.

Colleen flashed her such a look that Mary drew back. "Ye'll not tell me what I ought not," she hissed. "The only thing I ought not, and will not, is let him lie here and die! My Johnny shall live, do you hear me? He shall!"

By Dr. White's orders, Colleen cleaned Johnny's wounds and fetched him water and held his head in her lap day after day. She gave him most of her rations and applied the poultices Matey brought her. By the time the ship dropped anchor in Río de Janeiro's harbour, Johnny was on his way to recovery—not yet walking but sitting, smiling, and definitely alive.

To Mary's eyes, this Brazil was the most beautiful place she had ever beheld. While the *Charlotte* took on supplies, Mary stood at the rail listening to the voices of traders in small boats below. She heard Lieutenant Tench tell a sailor that the language spoken in this part of the world was Portuguese. Mary was sure she had heard its musical rhythms before, long ago, on one of the voyages with her father. But it could not have been here. Had she ever seen the great green hump of a mountain overlooking Río's harbour, she would have remembered. It called to her now, and she felt a powerful restlessness. She imagined disguising herself as a man and climbing down the ropes to one of the small trading boats. She imagined diving overboard and swimming to shore in the dead of night. She imagined following a trail up through lush vegetation to the peak of that humpy green mountain. Every stone, every clump of earth, every plant seemed to be calling her. But the weight of her belly held her where she was. Mary knew she would not climb the mountain that pierced the sky above Río de Janeiro, nor see it ever again, except, perhaps, in dreams.

The wind was with them on the crossing from Brazil to South Africa. By now everyone aboard—crew and convict, male and female—knew everyone else. There were even a few babies among them, for Mary was not the only woman to have borne the weight of a jailer's body during her time in prison. Most of the infants did not survive, and from what Mary saw of their scrawny bodies, it was better so. Normally babes were delivered in the hold, with women tending women, but in a few cases a woman in great distress was brought to the surgery. Mary would assist Dr. White, in hopes that the mother would live even if her newborn (more often stillborn) did not. White might have spared Mary that—the sight of women screaming in pain to deliver a babe who would not see the light of day. But he did not, and Mary stayed by his side and did his bidding. Afterwards, when there was a tiny blue body to be wrapped in sacking and dropped overboard into a watery grave, Mary would stare at him with defiant eyes which said, "This will not be the fate of mine."

In such moments the doctor would look at her with something approaching admiration. He had known hard women before, but Mary was not old enough for experience to have stolen the softness from her face. What he saw in her eyes was something else. If she had been a man, he might have called it courage.

The closer it came to Mary's time, the calmer she became. Her eyes were radiant, and her skin glowed. Such signs of health, rare among those aboard, owed much to the food White shared with her. While in port at Río, White had seen to it that she had citrus daily, and even cheese, but once at sea again, rations were thin. Once Mary tried to slip a tidbit into her pocket for Colleen to give to Johnny, but the doctor grasped her hand, took the bit from her, and shoved it into his own mouth. "I'm not about to feed the whole ship," he said angrily. "If you have no care for your baby, damned if I do."

Mary had almost wept with shame, for it was known that not even the officers had full bellies on this voyage, and if she had extra, it was because gaunt-faced Dr. White had given her some of his rations. From that time on, Mary gave no more thoughts to sharing, but before the doctor's eyes, wolfed down whatever he brought.

Pregnancy and what came of it was ever in her mind. Knowing Colleen had traded her body for rum to buy poultices from Matey, Mary watched her anxiously, as Colleen must have watched herself. But by the time they were nearing the southern tip of Africa, Colleen, as she held out her arm for Johnny to lean on, was able to pat her perfectly-flat belly and give Mary a reassuring wink.

It was more a wonder, Mary thought, that Florie had not conceived, for she lay under one sailor or another almost every night, all for the rum she craved. Mary asked Dr. White why more women were not with child, for he knew, as she did, that many convict women were used thus. She herself escaped the nightly harassment only because Cass's hammock swung between hers and the hatch. More than once, a drunken sailor heading for Mary had found himself dragged on top of Cass, who took his rum and his member with equal appetite and sent him reeling back the way he'd come.

Dr. White thrust a basin with the remains of a

mangled finger in Mary's hands for disposal. "Nature knows what she's about," he said shortly. "Starving women rarely conceive."

Thinking of this, and how it might explain why little Florie, thin as a flower stem, had not got pregnant, Mary emptied the basin over the railing. A mop swabbed round her feet, nearer than necessary. Will Bryant glanced up, pretending to be surprised to see her.

"Why, it's that Cornwall girl. The one that don't get sick at sea," Will teased. "When's the baby due?"

"Any day now," Mary said serenely.

"He'll be a sailor, sure."

"Sure she will," Mary retorted, and was pleased to see his blue eyes light with surprise and laughter. She might have stayed to chat, just to let his Cornwall accent caress her ears, but a patient had entered the surgery. Dr. White would be needing her, and she needed Will Bryant not at all.

On September 8, 1787, Mary, squatting as Cass had directed, and supported on either side by Colleen and Florie, pushed a slimy little body out of hers and into Cass's capable hands. Cass grunted with satisfaction and brought the babe close to Mary's face so she could see its sex.

"A girl," Colleen cooed. "A wee slip of a girl."

Colleen helped Mary into her hammock. Cass laid the infant in her arms. Florie put a cup to Mary's lips. "Here, love, have a sip of rum."

But Mary turned her face away, and slept.

59

A bare twenty-four hours later, Mary struggled through the hatch and made her way to the surgery. Dr. White looked up in surprise. Mary moved back the rag from the newborn's wrinkled red face for the doctor's inspection. Something—not a smile, but certainly satisfaction—softened his expression. But all he said was, "Ugly little brat."

Mary smiled. "She is that. But healthy, as am I."

"If you're thinking of coming back to work, forget it. I'll not have a mewing—."

Mary interrupted. "The woman, Colleen, who nursed the man they had in irons, she'll clean for you these next few days. Then we'll trade places. She'll tend my babe and I'll go on working as before."

White opened his mouth to contradict her, but his mind, quicker than his words, recognised the value of her plan. He bent to lace up his boots, then rose and left the surgery. He hadn't said yes, but he hadn't said no. Mary smiled. She knew that when Colleen appeared in the surgery next morning, Dr. White would treat her with the same feigned indifference he showed to everyone else.

During the few days of rest Mary took following the baby's birth, a great peace, interlaced with sadness, settled over her. The weather was fine and the ship sailed smoothly, allowing her to spend all her waking hours on deck.

"'Tis a pleasant sight you make, Miss Broad," James Brown greeted her as she sat in the morning sunshine nursing the baby. "How nice it would be if all on this voyage were as contented as your little one there."

Mary smiled up at him. "Thank you, Mr. Brown."

"What did you name her?"

"Charlotte, for the ship. Praying she'll be free, same as it, and can go home again."

James stood there, the silence both separating and connecting them. Finally he said, "A wee one she is, to be in the world without a father."

Mary said nothing. Again there was a silence, longer than before.

At last James cleared his throat. "The captain can perform marriages, you know."

Mary sighed. Although she and James Brown rarely spoke, she had often felt his gaze upon her. She had sworn to Florie that she craved no man, but something in his eyes caused a pang of hunger for some inexplicable thing. It was as if he had thoughts on many things, which, if she but had the confidence, she might ask him to reveal. However, the thought he now revealed was one she had guessed even before he got up his nerve to say it. She only wished she had known how to tell him to hold his tongue and spare them both their pride. Now that it was out, there was nothing for it but the truth.

"Ah, James," she shook her head sadly. "When I was a girl back in Cornwall, I was open as a flower for any decent man who'd bed me in marriage. But with all that's passed, I tell you straight, I am not fit to be a wife."

"Aren't I the one to decide that?" he asked stiffly.

"No, Mr. Brown, you are not."

"I see."

"I doubt you do. But 'twas kind of you to ask."

James stared long at her but she kept her eyes lowered, not wanting to see his shame, or him to see hers. She couldn't bear to reveal her sordid history and, if she did, what decent man would want her?

Nevertheless, James's words gave Mary reason to think on the matter of a father. She thought of the guard, Spence, on the *Dunkirk* who had planted his seed. And an eon before that, the vicar's son, Adam, whom she had eyed from behind her hymnal when she was a bashful teenager. Was it really so far-fetched to imagine that they might have married? Had not Adam, in riding off to university on his father's fine grey mare, tipped his hat to her in passing?

"You've eyes like your sweet daddy," she cooed to the baby. "No, yours are bluer than his. But you have the same long lashes. They lie against your cheek same as his, when his head was bowed in prayer."

Colleen's laughter burst behind her. "Bowed in prayer? What fairy tale are you telling that child, Mary?"

"That her father was a parson's son." Mary's voice turned wistful. "And might've been, had I not gone astray. Adam was his name. Adam Ash. He would've loved her so."

"You should be ashamed," Colleen chided, but her tone was more sad than critical, "to corrupt the innocent with lies."

Even as the fantasy faded from her mind, Mary tried

to hold it in her heart. "Some love in such a way, they say, as cannot die. Like you and Johnny."

"'Tis true," Colleen agreed. "But be a sensible lass. Never waste your time or hers with thoughts of what might have been. It weakens the spirit, and makes it that much harder to do what must be done in the here and now."

"I suppose." Mary sighed, and felt the dream slide away. "How is your Johnny?"

Colleen looked pained for an instant. Then she took her own advice and turned her thoughts away from what might have been. "His body will never be what it was, but at least he's alive. Oh, Mary, how can I ever thank you?"

"You could stand for my daughter."

Colleen laughed aloud. "Why, you're crazy! You know I'm Catholic."

"True," Mary smiled ruefully. "But Florie's never sober and Cass claims she's the Devil's own, so where's the choice?"

Colleen leaned down and kissed the baby. "I'll teach our Charlotte the religion of rebellion, I will!"

A month later they sighted the west coast of Africa, and dropped anchor at Table Bay. Lieutenant Tench told Mary that as soon as a priest could be brought aboard, her baby could be baptised. Mary had wanted to ask James Brown to stand for her daughter, along with Colleen, but she feared he would take it as an encouragement, and she did not want to hurt him with another refusal. After turning the matter over in her mind, she asked Dr. White. He looked at her as if she were mad.

"I am not a religious man."

"That's why I have chosen you," Mary persisted.

"I fail to follow your logic," he grumped. "Not that one expects logic from a woman."

Mary pinned him with one of her steady blue-eyed gazes. "Would I wish the man who stands for my babe to be one who teaches her, in years to come, what a sinner her mother was?" She saw that the doctor took her point, and added. "Better he is a non-believer who teaches her nothing, but lets her be. As you have let me be."

White made no reply. As he was wont to do when in agreement but not inclined to say so, he left the room. Mary smiled after him, and was not surprised, when the priest came aboard a few days later, to see Dr. White come stand beside Colleen. First Colleen in an amused voice, then White in snappish tones, took vows to act as the child's godparents.

Mary, mindful of Colleen's comment about how one so innocent was deserving of the truth, at the last instant christened the baby Charlotte Spence, thereby recording the true name of the man whose lustful blood flowed in her daughter's delicate veins.

During the fleet's stay at the Cape there was constant confusion as livestock and other supplies were loaded aboard. Mary, having just finished cleaning the surgery, heard Charlotte wail, and knew that she was hungry.

She went out onto the deck where Colleen sat tending her, and took the baby to her breast.

Will Bryant and a balding, middle-aged carpenter named Cox approached, lugging a heavy keg. Seeing the women, they stopped. Behind them, bow-legged Matey and a black man from Barbados struggled with a similar keg. The black man was forced to halt to avoid bumping into Will and Cox.

"Damn you, Bados, keep moving!" Matey swore.

Then he saw that it was Will and Cox who blocked the way as they stopped to chat with the women. "Wouldn't you know?" Matey muttered. "Bitches must be in heat."

Cox made an obscene gesture at the old sea-man, whose crime, it was said, was scavenging, then turned a hungry gaze on Colleen. Her red hair and blooming good looks had a way of catching a man's eye, but Colleen had eyes for Johnny alone, and never returned the men's glances. Florie though, responded to Cox's warmth as a cat to a hearth. "It's a nice day, isn't it, Mr. Cox?"

Will reached out to stroke the baby's cheek, not-so-accidentally touching Mary's breast. Mary flinched, and handed the baby to Colleen. "Dr. White's needing me", she murmured.

"Come, little one." Colleen lifted the infant high and smiled into its tiny face. "I'll teach you a bit of Irish brogue while your mum's back is turned."

At that moment a sailor bawled at them. Cox and Will picked up the keg and continued across the deck. Florie gazed after the carpenter wistfully. She had lain under any number of men and would have been glad to oblige Cox as well, though rare it was that a convict would have the wherewithal to bribe guards to let them visit the women's quarters. The wispy, worn-out girl knew instinctively that only Cox or someone like him could offer the protection she had never had. Like every person on this voyage, Cox had lost weight, but he was still a bigger man than most, and Florie longed to feel his bulk wrapped around her frail body.

The loading of supplies went on for nearly a month, for the fleet must carry not only enough to get itself across another great ocean, but enough to sustain more than a thousand souls for at least one year, until crops could be planted and harvested to feed the colony.

Mary stood in the door of the surgery watching hogs being driven aboard by Luke, an easy-going country man from the north of England. Pip was aiming to help, but the hogs kept trying to trample him, and sometimes succeeded. Will Bryant, who appeared to have no knowledge of livestock, was not much help either.

"Bryant, you dolt, its hogs we're moving, not a boat," Luke chided. "You got to do more than point them in the right direction!"

Cox shoved Will aside. "Out of the way, Bryant. One of these porkers goes over the side, it's our hide they'll fry. Scrapper, get behind and keep 'em moving."

Scrapper, a street bully older than Pip, gave the smaller boy a whack on the side of the head and, with the same stick, whacked the backsides of the hogs.

"You, Bryant," called Lieutenant Clark, "Over here." As Will hurried toward him, the officer asked, "Can you cipher?"

"Aye, Mr. Clark."

"Give Brown a hand with these kegs. I want a double count of every one that comes aboard."

"Yes sir!"

Will looked over Brown's shoulder at the list. "I say, mate, you got numbers running down that page clean as any clerk."

"Clerking is what I know. Here." James Brown handed him a paper and pen. "Check the size of each container against this list."

"It's a clerk you were? Where was that?"

"Canada," Brown replied shortly.

Mary listened to their exchange with interest. She had wondered from the first day she came aboard the *Charlotte* at James Brown's odd accent and learned handwriting.

"They say the Canadians are as bad as the Irish when it comes to mucking about in politics," Will jibed.

"Could be," James replied easily, "though they never caught me directly. Nailed for a missing case of cinnamon, I was, though that was none of my doing either." He pointed his pen at Will. "Mind you keep that tally straight."

James looked up and saw Mary watching him. He dropped his eyes and turned away. Mary felt a stab of loneliness, and again the certainty that this, the one man she had ever met who stirred something deep inside her, would not wish to touch her or be touched by

her if he knew her crime and how hard she had been
used by other men.

The warm spring month they remained in Table Bay,
there at the southern tip of Africa, was the closest
thing to a pleasant time that mariners and convicts
had yet experienced on the voyage. There was fresh
food and, for all the work, Captain Phillip saw to it that
his crew had ample leave. The sailors always returned
to the ship in high spirits. Mary listened to their tales
and thought it possible, amidst the confusion, to bolt.
But what back in Río had been the weight of a babe
in her belly was now the weight of a babe in arms. It
would not be easy to get from ship to shore with a
newborn, but there must be a way!

One day James Brown, who was much trusted by
the officers, was sent ashore on some errand. Upon his
return, Mary found an occasion to speak with him.

"Did you find your stay in Cape Town pleasant, Mr.
Brown?"

James looked at her curiously. Mary had not spoken
to him since the day of his proposal, and rarely took
the initiative in conversation with any man.

"The French have lately joined the Dutch in defend-
ing Cape Town," he said. "Their presence lends an air
of gaiety to this dour Dutch settlement."

"I have heard it said that some settlers have taken
Hottentots for wives," Mary ventured.

James must have seen where her musings had taken
her. She was thinking that if these European men were
so in need of a woman about the house, that perhaps

she, even with a babe in arms, might be taken in, if not as a wife, perhaps by a family wanting a servant.

"This Africa is a harsh land and, from what I've seen, these settlers are harsher than the land." There was caution in his tone. "The Dutch have brought with them uncommonly strict religious beliefs."

Someone called his name and he started to move away. Then he looked back at Mary and added, "Watch, when the Afrikaners bring supplies aboard, how they treat their oxen and their slaves. It is said that their women fare but little better."

Mary knew nothing of the Dutch religion, but she watched, as James had suggested. When she saw how the farmers flogged their animals, and treated their slaves as badly or worse, she knew it would be unwise to throw herself on the mercy of such men. If they had any kindness in them, she reasoned, they saved it for their own.

At last the First Fleet weighed anchor and set sail around the Cape of Good Hope. This would be the longest part of the voyage: sixty-five hundred miles across the Indian Ocean and to the opposite side of a great unknown continent, to a place Captain Cook had named Botany Bay. When they lost sight of the African mainland, Captain Phillip told his crew that it would be nigh onto three months before they sighted land again.

What he didn't tell them, but they learned soon enough, was that the monstrous swells in this new ocean would be unlike any they had known before.

Convicts who had overcome seasickness in the Atlantic now vomited until they retched bile from empty stomachs. The smell below deck was beyond bearing, causing Mary to stay on deck whenever she was allowed. Other women chided her for taking an infant into the night air, but Mary paid them no mind. More than a dozen prisoners had already died on the voyage, and for sure there would be others. Whatever sickness travelled aboard this ship, she knew it to be in the stinking hold, not borne on a fresh ocean breeze.

One night as she walked the deck with a fretful Charlotte in her arms, she encountered Will Bryant. Like Mary, Will was a trusted prisoner and allowed to move about the ship with a fair degree of freedom. Will pulled back a corner of the baby's wrap to look into its face. "A bit fussy, is your wee one. Might she be sick?"

"No," Mary replied. "Just restless."

"Like her mum." Will nuzzled the baby's face with his own, which, lying as it was on Mary's shoulder, put his breath into her hair. Mary's body shuddered away from him.

Will grinned. "I've got strong teeth, but I don't bite."

"Just don't—."

"Don't what?" Will lifted his arms as if to embrace her.

"Don't touch me!" Mary hissed.

"Why, what a funny —."

"Call a man's grasp funny if you like, but none's

brought me joy! I'll be over this rail before any on this ship has his way with me!"

Her vehemence so startled Will that he took a step back and held up his hand in alarm. "Hey there! What kind of talk is that for a girl with a babe in her arms? I was just looking for a bit of fun, and if it's no fun for you, why, one's no party."

"Just so you know," Mary said faintly.

Will's eyes softened. "I only crave to pass time with you because we're both from Cornwall." The sincerity in his voice was soothing. "A word now and then, why, it's like a breath of home. Be honest now. Don't you feel a teeny bit of the same?"

Mary hesitated, then replied, "I . . . I suppose so."

"Well then, there you have it. It's friends we are, with something in it for both of us. And now a good night to you, Miss Mary."

Will walked away, whistling.

Mary looked after him, pondering his strange remark. A man as a friend? She supposed she had counted some of the men her father had crewed with as friends, but that was when she was a child. As a grown woman she had had few friends, and none of them had been men.

Months passed. Those bright October days off the tip of Africa dwindled to a distant memory. There were some who felt sure that any time now, the ship would sail off the edge of the earth, and others who suffered so much they wished it would. But Mary remained in good health, and her child thrived. Baby Charlotte was five months old when the ship sailed into Botany Bay.

After the shouting and gawking that accompanied the first sightings of land died down, Captain Phillip put a party of men ashore. They returned to report that the site where Captain Cook had landed decades before was not well suited for settlement, so Phillip moved the fleet into a harbour just north of Botany Bay. He named it Port Jackson, but to the prisoners and to much of the world for years to come, the convict colony would still be known as Botany Bay.

Captain Phillip called the convicts to attention and took stock of the motley lot. A farmer by upbringing, he could not think what had possessed the Crown to suppose that raw land could be tamed and a law-abiding English colony established by rabble such as this. But Phillip was a man driven by duty, and his duty he would do.

"Convict men will go ashore at once," Captain Phillip informed them. "You will construct accommodations for officers, crew, women, and lastly, yourselves. How many masons are there among you?"

One hand went up.

"How many carpenters?"

Cox raised his hand.

"Sawyers?"

No one responded.

"Fishermen?"

Will Bryant and Bados raised their hands. Captain Phillip ignored the black man and nodded to Will.

"You with a trade, pick from the others as many as you'll be needing to do your job."

Will glanced over at Bados. "You African?"

"West Indian," Bados replied. "From the island of Barbados."

"Well, Bados, can you throw a net?"

"Sure can," Bados grinned.

Will turned to Luke. "What about you, Luke? Know anything about fishing?"

Luke smiled his slow, easy smile. "Dropped a line in a stream here and there. If there's more to it than that, why, you'd be the man to teach me."

"What about me?" Matey demanded. "I'm a tar through and through. Ain't nothin' on land that beckons me."

"Okay, Mate," Will said agreeably. "You're in."

Matey grabbed Scrapper by the arm and pulled him into the group. "What about young Scrapper here?"

Will looked at the young tough doubtfully. "Him? Why I doubt he can even swim."

"Who's needin' to swim lessen you sink us?" Scrapper shot back. "I lived around the docks all me bloody life, and ha'nt seen a net yet I can't mend. Sure and that's some use to a fishin' crew."

"So it is," Will admitted.

"Please, Master Bryant," Pip stood on tiptoe and called over Bados's shoulder, "can I come with you? I'm a good hand, and awful quick to do what I'm told; just ask anybody."

"It's men Bryant's wanting, not fish bait," Scrapper sneered.

"Come now, Pip's a good lad," Luke offered.

"Sure, bring him along," Matey seconded. "Every crew's got to have a mutt to kick."

Will, who had taken note of the fact that Pip called him Master and Scrapper did not, nodded. "All right, Pip." To Scrapper he added, "And you, lout, leave him alone."

Will and his fishing crew were assigned a dinghy. Soon fresh fish was added to the crew's diet. The leavings made good fish broth for convicts.

For days Mary and the other women leaned on the ship's shore-side railing and watched as men felled trees to construct insubstantial lean-tos, and hauled buckets of mud to make bricks for more substantial structures to come. Whatever terrors they had felt for this unknown land vanished in anticipation of setting foot on solid ground; something all of them, once or many times on the voyage, had thought never to do again.

Few convicts had any construction experience and the sailors who guarded them were equally unskilled. As shacks were thrown up, the impatient women remarked on the location of this one or the sideways slant of that one, noting preferences and dislikes. Mary, although she said nothing, did the same. That one at the edge of the woods, she thought, near those boulders. The stoop, should it ever have a stoop, would be shady in the afternoon and offered a fine view of the harbour.

At last Captain Phillip set a day for their disembarkation. The excitement of the women was like a fever, so starved were they for the feel of solid ground under their feet. But when morning light revealed a squally day, Captain Phillip delayed the move from ship to shore. He marched to and fro on the bridge, his face darkening as the clouds darkened. The wind was rising and the water had a nasty chop. When Lieutenant Tench asked if he should put the women in the rowboats before the weather grew any worse, Phillip snapped, "I didn't bring the wretched creatures halfway around the world to have them drown in the harbour."

"It's a fact that in this chop they'll get as wet as if they swam to shore," Tench agreed.

Phillip wavered between caution and the impatience he always felt when there was a job to be done. He did want the overwrought women ashore before the storm broke, for who knew how long it might last? They might be forced to remain aboard for several days longer. If that was not more than they could bear, he felt it certainly more than he could take of their clamouring, high-pitched voices. On the other hand, a sudden squall could easily swamp a dinghy, and it was unlikely that any of the women could swim.

All day Phillip paced and worried and could not make up his mind. Then, late in the afternoon, the sun broke through for just a moment. In that instant the captain gave in to the pressure of their collective long-ing and ordered the women rowed ashore.

No sooner were the women in the boats than it began to rain, but that did not dampen their spirits. Colleen saw Johnny waiting on shore, and leapt out before the dinghy could be drawn into shallow water. He waded out and took her in his arms. Oblivious to her lurching walk and his lopsided gait, they swung each other around and around in a joyful Irish jig.

Other women splashed ashore, sea legs which had not touched solid ground for a year or more causing them to stagger like drunks. More than a few fell down and pressed their lips to the ground, laughing hysteri-cally or weeping with joy.

Mary scooped up a handful of sand and held it out to Charlotte. The baby clutched at it, then tried to thrust a fistful into her mouth. Mary laughed and wiped it away. "Yes, my love, the earth's that sweet, but meant for your feet, not your face."

The sailors who had brought them pushed off, return-ing to the ship as ordered. Mary finished wiping sand from Charlotte's face and looked about. In the time it had taken them to travel from ship to shore, the sun had sunk below the horizon. Great dark clouds roiled across the sky. Any minute the light rain would become a downpour, turning dusk to darkness that much faster. Mary looked toward a hillside covered with lean-tos, which the sailors who rowed them over had said were for the women. Should she wait for an assignment, or would it be first-come, first-served?

Debating whether to be so bold as to simply go and claim the one she fancied, Mary glanced beyond the group of just-arrived women, to see who might be in charge. What she saw at the far end of the beach was a group of men, more than five hundred of them, clustered as if—what?

A chill went down her spine. There was something in the way the men milled about which reminded her of a herd of cattle she had seen once, moving in the same restless, pent-up way. As she and her mother had watched from the lane, the herd, without warning, suddenly stampeded down the hill as if driven by the Devil himself. They broke through a fence and trampled the whole of a neighbour's field before they regained their senses.

Suddenly there was a flash of lightning and a thunder clap which seemed to come from directly above. Rain poured down in torrents and a gale-force wind drove waves far up the beach. The women scrambled toward higher ground, toward the men, who were watching them from above. Mary felt rather than saw the danger. She turned and ran the opposite way, toward the little hut at the far end, near the edge of the forest.

Not until she ducked inside the doorway did she look back. The mob was moving as one, a mindless, stampeding herd. They collided with the sodden cluster of women, and screams such as Mary had never heard filled the air. The group splintered as the women fled in every direction. Some tried to reach the lean-tos, but few made it that far and those who did soon had cause to regret it. As men attacked the women, wind attacked the flimsy huts. In the last seconds before dusk was transformed into pitch black night, Mary saw thatched roofs lift and the poorly-constructed huts disintegrate as if made of straw.

Wind, or was it the Devil's own breath? What Dr. White saw from the ship, and later recorded in his diary, took his own breath away. As the women, skirts flung high by the wind, battled the drenching storm, convict men were upon them. Black dark descended, only to be split apart by jagged bolts of lightning. Each flash revealed women fleeing, women nude, women falling, men atop women. Many, many men.

For a full five minutes White gaped, unable to believe the scene unfolding in broken segments of brilliant illumination. Then a cry went up around him; no, not a cry, a howl. The crew was shouting, "Give us rum and give us leave! Give us rum and give us leave!"

Dr. White made his way to the bridge, Lieutenant Tench close behind. Captain Phillip turned to them, and in the next lightning flash, they saw the disbelieving look in his eyes.

"Captain!" Tench shouted to be heard over the storm and ruckus below. "I fear the men are near mutiny."

Darkness closed in again. Below them the men chanted, "Give us rum and give us leave. Would you deny His Majesty's mariners what wretched convicts have in plenty?"

White, who rarely felt sympathy for anyone, felt something close to sympathy for the conscientious Phillip, that his well-run voyage should end thus.

"There will be no mutiny on my ship," came Phillip's strangled voice.

For long moments the officers stood mute as the chant of the sailors grew louder and moved nearer to where they stood. White knew that Phillip must choose between protecting the women and holding his command. He did not know what choice he himself would make, but for a ship's captain there could be but one choice.

"Give them a ration of rum," Phillip ordered. "Lower the boats."

"Aye, Captain," said Tench.

He called out the captain's orders and heard them echoed by other voices in the darkness. The next lightning flash revealed a crew-turned-rabble downing their rations of rum and piling into the boats. White stood silent, incredulous. Had the storm caused the madness, or had it been aboard this ship all along?

Mary huddled in a corner of the hut. Through gaping cracks in the lean-to walls, she watched the nightmare unfold in dramatic bursts, illuminated by the worst lightning storm she had ever witnessed. Although men outnumbered women ten to one, it was the women's voices that dominated; every anguished shriek or sob imaginable, many scarcely seeming human.

"If they ever tell you Hell is a burning place," she whispered to the baby in her arms, "don't believe it. What it is is a wildness of wind and rain and thunder and lightning."

Perhaps for the sake of a daughter who must grow

up in a world of men, Mary did not speak of how men, as they appeared to her just then, seemed the most hellish element of all.

With each blinding flash of light Mary saw afresh the terror the men were inflicting on the women. There was Florie stumbling, falling. A heap of men tumbled on top of her, among them Cox the carpenter. And yonder Cass, on her knees at water's edge. Scrapper jerked her backward on the sand and began rutting between her legs.

The first boat load of sailors landed, and for a moment Mary imagined that the mariners had been dispatched to restore order. Then, before Scrapper was into Cass, a sailor was into him. When Mary realised what the crew's arrival meant, her horror doubled.

A few feet from Scrapper was a boy—Mary thought it was Pip—pawing at the sand like a burrowing animal to hide himself beneath an overturned dinghy. Close by, Colleen and Johnny stood back to back, each with a spade in hand, fighting a mob of convicts.

Luke galloped past the door of Mary's hut, one of several men in pursuit of a woman carrying an infant. One man tackled the woman about the legs. She dropped the baby as she went down, its screams mingling with hers. Luke stumbled over the infant and went sprawling. He sat up dazed, and crawled toward the wailing child.

"Damn me, if you ain't the noisiest little pup." Luke picked up the baby and stumbled along the beach. When Mary next saw him, he was shoving the baby beneath the dinghy. She almost smiled, wondering what little Pip would do to calm the squalling infant.

Charlotte whimpered. "Shh," Mary soothed. "It's scared you are, and aren't we all in this heathen hell. But by God's grace one babe's been saved, and so shall you, my little one."

As the roofing thatch was torn away, Mary crouched on the floor and folded her body to shelter the baby from wind and rain. A mighty gust of wind sent the last of the thatch sailing through the night air, and the frame of the lean-to collapsed around them. Miraculously, the slender logs fell in a criss-cross pattern, leaving a little space so that Mary and Charlotte were not crushed or even trapped.

Mary looked toward the forest, wondering if they would be safer there and whether to make a run for it. But another flash of lightning revealed chaos in that direction, too. She saw James trying to defend an old crone beset by a gang of sailors, until brought to his knees by a kick in the groin. The next blaze of lightning showed sailors competing for the poor old hag's withered body, and James on his hands and knees, vomiting. Just beyond, at the edge of the forest, stood a row of aborigines. They grinned down at the retching man, then turned their astonished gazes back to the clearing where each new flash of lightning provided them with another glimpse of white man's civilisation.

Bados squatted near the aborigines. When the next bolt of light came, an aborigine was standing before him with a naked girl. Bados, head down, seemed to be waving the offer away.

Mary remained where she was, in hopes that she would not be noticed amidst the debris of the tumbled-down hut. And she might not have been, had Charlotte not cried out. Two men halted a yard away. They stood there panting hard until another flash of lightning revealed woman flesh.

The sailors, Mary saw, were drunk, and none too steady on their feet. As they started toward her, she laid Charlotte on the ground, stood, and snatched up a hefty stick. She landed a solid blow on the jaw of the first one, but the other one grabbed the end of her stick, and then her arm. She bit the hand that held her as hard as she could, but the man's other hand struck her just as hard. There was a flash inside her head, and a moment of blackness, but she stayed on her feet. Suddenly she was released and, with the next illumination, she saw why. Will Bryant stood over the man, who sprawled unconscious at his feet. The other sailor stumbled away.

Mary bent over and picked up the baby. Will's arms wrapped about her waist and lifted her free of the lean-to's debris. He carried her into the darkness and forced her down on her back in a narrow space. Mary felt the scrape of stone on both her arms. Then she was in a crevice between two boulders, with Will's body on top of hers. Feet pounded by on either side, other men pursuing other women. Mary lay on the wet ground breathing hard, waiting for the inevitable. It took her a minute, or maybe two, to realise that Will's weight was not full on her. He'd left space for Charlotte, clutched against her breast. It took even longer for her to accept the incredible fact that Will was not attacking, but was sheltering her and the baby.

At dawn, Charlotte's nuzzling woke Mary. She lay un-moving, fearful of disturbing Will, whose body still rested on hers. But the baby's squirming had awakened him, too.

"She's hungry," Will whispered.

He reached down and exposed a breast. Mary moved the baby's mouth to her nipple. For a few minutes she only heard the rhythmic sound of the baby's suckling, and from not far away, equally rhythmic sounds of surf lapping against sand.

"How's her mum?" Will murmured into Mary's hair.

"A bit stiff, for sure."

As she spoke, Mary felt, with a rising sense of fore-boding, that the most manly part of Will Bryant was likewise stiff. But Will seemed disinclined to satisfy his urge at that moment. He moved his weight off Mary and pulled her into a sitting position.

"I got lucky," he grinned. "I had something mighty soft to lie on, and not even a hangover to show for the party."

Mary looked out across the beach, soft with first light. The area was strewn with naked bodies. "Soon they'll all be awake," she murmured. "Expecting you to've caught fish to feed every mouth."

"Yours is the first I'll feed." Will paused. "A wedding breakfast, if you please, Mary Broad."

When she did not reply, he added, with a hint of sulk

in his voice, "That is, if you've come to welcome my touch after all."

Mary looked again at the debris-strewn beach. Some women had begun to gather scraps of clothing to cover themselves. Others just lay there, quietly sobbing.

She turned her blue-eyed gaze up to meet Will's, and saw herself reflected in the blue of his eyes. "Yes," she said. "I do."

2

The Penal Colony, 1788—1791

Mary leaned on the handle of the wooden hoe and watched her toddler touching and naming the plants in the pathetic garden.

"Bean." "Onion." "Tado," Charlotte lisped.

"Po-tato," Mary corrected. "I wish!" Neither the sandy soil nor the drought-shrivelled plants resembled the lush garden her mother had cultivated back in Cornwall. Here the seasons were backward, the rain too much or not enough, the seeds brought from England too old.

And the colony too hungry, Mary thought sadly. On the side of the garden furthest from the cabin, she saw that just-sprouted onions had been bitten off clean, and knew the loss was not to insects or wild animals, but to some half-starved person. She must ask Will again about having someone to guard the garden at night.

But she knew already that he would only ask, with a mocking laugh, where she thought they might find a guard who could be trusted.

He would be right, of course, but it annoyed her that he appeared indifferent to the food she struggled to produce. Such was his pride in the bounty of fish which he and his mates brought in every day that he seemed not to notice how listless Charlotte became when there were no vegetables to add to the stew. Nor did he seem to have Mary's craving for fresh greens. His craving was for alcohol, and enough of that there was about. However little food there might be, Mary thought bitterly, men always found some that could be fermented, and judged it worth the transformation.

She knew that the stores that had come with the First Fleet had dwindled dramatically, and the colony's first year of backbreaking cultivation here on the shores of Botany Bay had been as unproductive as her own garden. The breeding livestock had fared no better. Their rations of meal and bully beef, skimpy enough from the start, had been cut in October. A ship had been sent back to Africa to purchase supplies, but no one knew when it might return.

The only food the colony had in reasonable quantity was the fish which Will and his crew netted daily. Within a week of their arrival Will had been placed in charge of all the fishing boats and, for his contribution to a colony which otherwise would have starved, he had been granted uncommon privileges. A sturdy house had been built for them; a cabin of rough logs and wattle, but roomier than the shacks most convicts called home. The hut had two window openings, one on either side of the door, that, when the wooden flaps were propped open, offered a fine view of the sparkling harbour. Because Will was out in the boat from pre-dawn to late afternoon on all but the Lord's Day, another convict, a man of about fifty named Joe Paget, had been assigned to turn up the soil for their garden. For these and other reasons, they were better off than almost any convict family in the colony.

Those "other reasons" were what fretted Mary. Back on the ship, when they were en route from England, Will had been given responsibility for issuing rations to the ship's male convicts and had earned the respect of Dr. White and others for being "strictly honest." However, Mary knew her husband was not that.

Even as she stood here in the slanting light of late afternoon, Will would be coming ashore with his catch, to be distributed to everyone according to his or her due, as determined by the authorities. Above and beyond the extra ration Will was given for his own family, there would be fish secreted in his rucksack or wrapped in a net which he claimed to be taking home to repair. The stolen fish would be sold in secret to any who had the wherewithal to barter or buy. Thus they lived well in comparison to their neighbours, just as Will had lived well in his days as a swashbuckling smuggler back in Cornwall. But for how long? Mary, bound to Will Bryant by Reverend Johnson's nuptial blessing four days after their landing, had risen in status as Will had risen, and would, she feared, fall when he fell.

Mary moved from the garden to an open-sided shed beside the hut where a pot boiled over the fire. She picked up the ladle, stirred, and looked down the path. Will was coming toward her in that confident, long-legged stride which pleased her eye and caused her body to feel uncommonly alive. She could tell by his satisfied expression and the weightiness of his ruck-sack that it carried more than their share of fresh-caught fish.

He swung the sack off his shoulder and, in a swift movement, dropped into the pot an already-cleaned fish twice the size of their rightful ration. Mary could not conceal her distress. "Ah, Will, I wish you wouldn't! It's but a week since they hanged that old woman for stealing a bit of butter."

"Are you calling me an old woman?" Will teased.

"I'm telling you to stop it!" Mary said sharply. "Before you lose us everything we have, and all the respect you've earned for yourself!"

"Respect?" Will scoffed. "What do I care for the respect of sour pusses like Governor Phillip and that hypocrite Reverend Johnson?"

He scooped up Charlotte and set her astride his shoulders. "Aye, but your mum's a scold today. Come, pretty. Let's poke into Cox's shop and see what him and Johnny is up to."

Grateful though she was for Will's attentions to Charlotte, Mary couldn't suppress resentment and a strong suspicion that he was using the child to give an appearance of innocence to his unlawful dealings. Charlotte looked back and waved. The glee on the toddler's face was enough to brighten Mary's own with a smile, making her appear happier than she felt.

Cox's carpentry shop was close by. Mary could see it clearly from where she stood. Will dropped his rucksack behind the workbench, and stood exchanging gossip with Cox and Johnny—Johnny having been made Cox's assistant because his crippled legs made him unfit for most other forms of work. A moment later Cox bent down, seeming to hunt for a tool. Mary knew this would be the moment that some agreed-upon amount of fish would be transferred from Will's bag to Cox's, probably in exchange for some agreed-upon amount of alcohol which Florie, who lived with Cox, would have acquired from Cass.

Mary was not the only one who saw. Bados, who had a knack for making fine things from wood, sat in the corner of the carpentry shed. He had no tools of his own, but was permitted to use Cox's, providing he did not carry them away from the shop. Some time back Will had commissioned Bados to carve a wooden comb for Mary to use for untangling her long hair. A gift it had been for her twenty-third birthday, which fell three months after their wedding.

Bados, sitting in a shadowed corner of the carpentry shop, was now showing Charlotte some new carving. From the way he held it to his lips, Mary surmised that it was a flute. He must have seen the exchange of contraband fish as well as she. She trusted Bados; he was, after all, a part of Will's crew. But if Will could be careless around him, how many others knew what he was up to? Like as not the whole colony knew, she thought bitterly, except for those in positions of authority.

She lifted the steaming fish from the stew and began picking out the bones. It was her scolding approach, she knew, that set Will on edge and brought out his rebellious nature. If she was to stop him taking such risks, she must come at the problem from another direction.

But what had she to give him other than herself, and what was there of her that he did not already have? Didn't she rise before sunup to cook his ration of johnnycake so that he never went off with an empty belly? Didn't she wash his ragged clothes, and mend them until her fingertips bled? And when had she ever denied him the pleasure of her body?

Just then she saw Cass coming along the path, staggering under a load of bricks. Carrying bricks was heavy work normally done by unskilled men and given to women only as punishment. Mary had lost count of how many times Cass had run afoul of the authorities. According to Florie, this time it was because Cass had come by some wild honey and had a recipe for the fermentation of something—Florie couldn't remember what—which would produce strong drink. The story was that Cass had cut a deal with a guard, but later, when the beverage was ready to sell, they had fallen out. The guard drank some, sold some, and stole some, leaving Cass with only enough to be used as evidence against her when he turned her in.

Mary supposed that Cass had drunk a goodly share

of her concoction as well for, like Florie—indeed, like most of the convict women—Cass was only sober when she could not find the means to be otherwise. Still, Mary felt affection for the old woman. She picked up a chunk of fish and walked out to meet Cass. Cass stopped, but was loath to put down her burden of bricks because of the difficulty of hoisting it onto her back again.

"Open," Mary said, holding the hunk of fish under Cass's nose. The old woman's mouth dropped open and Mary laid a morsel on her tongue. Cass swallowed it in a single gulp.

"Chew!" Mary admonished, as if speaking to little Charlotte. "You can't be so sure as all that that I've picked it clean of bones!" She placed a second bite in Cass's mouth, and Cass obeyed, if two or three snaps of her crooked yellow teeth could be called chewing.

When Cass finished the last of it, she said, "Don't do that again."

Mary stepped back in surprise. "What?"

"None of us is getting rations enough to feed a child," Cass growled in a low voice. "If you've got some to give away, it's because you've got more than your share. It's a capital offence, you know."

"But we're friends!" Mary exclaimed.

Cass adjusted her load and groaned. "Don't be a fool, Mary. None's got friends in Botany Bay."

Mary had been mildly depressed before, but as she went back to boning the fish, she felt herself bordering on despair. She looked across the way and saw Will watching her. If she let her feelings show, he'd stay over there all evening. And with good reason, she thought. Why should a man who has worked hard from before sunup have to come home to a carping wife? She forced a smile and held up two fingers close together to show him that dinner would be ready shortly.

Will hoisted Charlotte onto his shoulder again and started for home. As they approached, Mary scooped up a bowl of stew for each of them into rough wooden bowls. Will set the child down and, although he must have been ravenous, put an arm around Mary and breathed into her hair, causing her skin to prickle with pleasure.

During daylight hours, Will hardly seemed to notice her body, though much was revealed in the skimpy burlap shift which she and all other convict women were compelled to wear now that the meagre clothing they had brought with them had fallen to rags. But at night, when they lay together on their bed of eucalyptus leaves, Will had a way of burying his face in her hair, drawing in its scent and releasing hot breath into it that caused the muscles of her belly to tighten with pleasure. From the start he had taken care with her, stroking her slowly and watching with satisfaction as she relaxed under his touch. Little by little his hands had erased her body's memory of other men. Within a few months, she was able to enjoy their intimacy. She could not have asked for more, not then. But afterwards, ah, afterwards.

Will always fell into sleep afterwards as swiftly as a man dives into water. Mary would lie there listening to his even breathing, curled close against him but far away. Half-conscious memories carried her back to earliest childhood and how it had been with her parents: how rustling, tussling sounds from their bed gave way to murmured endearments and soft conversation. Those murmurings and the slap of water against the hull of the ship had lulled her to sleep as a child. When she was older, and she and her mother slept together in their Cornwall cottage, they too talked softly, sleepily, far into the night. Only when her father returned from his voyages would Mary be sent to her own cot on the far side of the room, for, as her mother had explained, husband and wife were meant to share a bed whenever they could. Once again, and for however long her father remained at home, their intermingled whispers would become Mary's lullaby.

Little Charlotte fell asleep to no such sounds. Between Mary and Will no endearments were exchanged, no secrets shared. Night after night, tired though Mary might be, the long black silence kept her awake. So vast was the silent blackness of Botany Bay that Mary felt herself a castaway in the midst of a great dark ocean with no land or light in sight.

"Will," she whispered on one such night, repeating his name twice before he roused himself. "Do you ever think of sailing your little boat out of the harbour and away?"

"No, love," he yawned into her hair. "I'm much too young to die."

"Maybe we're dead already."

"Silly girl! Give me one year past emancipation and I'll have you dressed in silk."

"It's not silk I hunger for; it's home."

"Here is home," Will murmured, and disappeared into sleep again.

Although the longing remained inside her, Mary had little time to dwell on it. Charlotte was an easy child, but at an age where she required constant watching to keep her from doing damage in the garden as she tried to emulate her mother's weeding, or from wandering into the bush, which was filled with all manner of biting, stinging, poisonous creatures. As often as possible Mary took her down to the shore for, in February's midsummer heat, it was cooler there.

While Charlotte dug in the sand, Mary searched for shellfish among the rocks. Shellfish had been plentiful at first, but as convicts, guards, and officers scoured the shore seeking something to supplement their meagre rations, just about everything edible had been taken. Mary was pleased to find, in one overlooked crevice, two small shellfish to add a bit of variety to their fish-stew supper.

She tried to pick up Charlotte to carry her home, but the child would walk. Mary took her hand and slowed her own pace to match the toddler's. They had almost reached the cabin door when she heard running footsteps bearing down on them. She turned and saw James Brown. The look on his face bespoke disaster.

"Mary!" he shouted. "Mary, come quickly."

Mary had seen James often enough since their arrival; indeed, as he had been placed in charge of distributing rations from the government stores, it would have been impossible not to see him on a near-daily basis. But he had always maintained an attitude of stiff impersonality toward her. Never had he called her by her given name.

"It's Will!" she cried. "He's drowned!"

"No! Caught selling fish!"

Mary snatched up Charlotte, but James pulled the child from her arms. "Don't take her! They have him on the triangle."

By the time Mary reached the settlement centre, she felt out of breath and mind. What little remained seemed to leave her when she saw the scourge wielding a whip. Governor Phillip and other officers looked on.

Mary closed her eyes and covered her ears but could not block out the awful sounds. It seemed as if the count of one hundred would never be reached and as it drew near, again she held her breath. Pray God it was only one hundred lashes and not the five hundred others had got—that is, those who weren't hanged when caught stealing food. The scourge stopped on the hundredth lash. Will had been spared, Mary knew, because he was the most experienced fisherman in the colony. But for him, all would have starved by now.

Mary pushed through the crowd to reach him, but Luke and Bados got there first. The thongs binding Will's wrists were untied. The men caught him as he fell. Assisted by Pip and Scrapper, they created a sling of their own oar-hardened arms and carried Will through the crowd, face down.

Governor Phillip gave Mary a grim look and spoke

the first words he had ever directed toward her. "Next time, Madam, your husband will hang."

Mary looked up into the governor's face, hardened by sun and perpetual worry, and said, "There will be no next time, Sir."

As she followed the men carrying Will along the path to their cottage, Colleen put an arm around her and whispered, "It was that scum Joseph Paget who testified that Will forced him to act as go-between to move stolen fish."

"What? The Joseph they sent to clear the ground for our garden?" Mary had liked the man, who was close in age to Cass and, Mary suspected, often shared the older woman's bed. Joseph had entertained both her and Charlotte, reciting rhymes and singing sea shanties as he hacked away at soil that had never known a hoe.

"The same, may the bastard rot in hell," Colleen swore. "They caught him first and let him off for naming who on the fishing crew done the stealing. Then they grabbed Will and found his rucksack stuffed with fish."

Mary thought nothing could be worse than watching her husband being whipped, but Will's screams, when Matey marched into the cottage and poured a bucket of salt water over his flayed back, were like a knife piercing her own chest.

"Don't," Will gasped. "Not again. I'd rather die."

"And die ye will, or take forever to heal," Matey

said with no show of sympathy for the agonising pain which he himself had felt more than once.

"Matey knows about healing," Pip reminded them. "Remember the good he did for Johnny."

"Right," said Luke, "and he's done all the good that's needed for now. Get out and let the poor devil rest."

Matey marched off, mumbling about snivellers. Luke, Pip, and Scrapper went, too, but Bados lingered by the door. When the others were out of earshot, Bados said to Mary, "The blacks have something they use for cuts—crushed leaves, and what else I can't say. But Baneelon would know."

"Go talk to her," Cass urged Mary. "I'll sit with Will till ye get back."

"Where's Charlotte?" Florie asked.

"James took her," Mary said, distracted. "I don't know where they went."

"I'll find them," Colleen said. "And I'll give Charlotte supper and keep her with me tonight, so she'll not be upset by his cries."

Mary stumbled out of the house then, away from Will's agonising moans, which she herself could hardly bear.

She searched for over an hour but never found the aboriginal woman who had been brought to the colony, with her brother Bennelong, to live. However, she came upon another native woman down among the rocks, cracking shellfish for her three children. Because Will and Mary's cabin was near the edge of the forest, they saw the aborigines often, even those who were shy about coming into the settlement. The natives' shyness had not lessened with the passage of time, for many had fallen ill and died of diseases brought by the Europeans, against which they had no natural tolerance. When the naked woman saw Mary coming, she made as if to leave.

"Wait!" Mary cried. "Please! Help me!"

Although some of the natives understood a few words of English, it was most likely Mary's tone that stayed the woman when she so obviously wanted to run away.

"They've taken the cat-o-nine to Will. Whipped him bad, they did! I need your help!" It occurred to Mary as she said it that she must have been mad to ask for aid from this wild black woman who spoke no English.

To her astonishment, the woman understood. She picked up a stick and pretended to whip the back of her little boy, then opened her mouth in something like a howl of pain.

Mary swallowed her amazement and nodded. "Yes, they whipped him like that."

The woman's eldest boy pointed across the bay. Mary came to where he stood and saw that from there the settlement's main square was distant but visible, as was the now-empty triangle where Will had been whipped.

Mary grasped a handful of leaves from a bush and began rubbing them on the back of the child whom the woman had pretended to whip. The woman gave her a gap-toothed smile, shook her head vigorously and took off at a trot that left Mary trailing behind, barely keeping up. At last the long-limbed black woman came upon a tree. She said something to the boy in her own language. He climbed the tree with remarkable agility and began picking leaves. His mother shouted something up to him and he moved further out onto the branch—dangerously far out, Mary thought—to reach for new leaves. He dropped them as he picked. The two smaller children raced about collecting and bringing them to their mother. At last the woman called her child down, and began walking swiftly in the direction of her camp.

Mary tried to follow, but the woman shook her head and pointed in the opposite direction, toward Mary's house. Mary made as if to take the leaves. At this the woman made a frightful face. Forceful words in her own language made it clear that Mary was not to follow. Mary hurried home through the tangled, brushy woods, praying that this woman, whom she understood so poorly, had at least comprehended what she was asking, and would not simply wander off and forget their whole exchange.

It was hours later, well after dark, when the woman appeared. She did not knock but walked into the hut as if it were her own. She carried a large shell filled with a stinking, dark green paste. She squatted beside Will and smeared the foul mixture over lash marks that had turned his smooth tanned skin into raw meat. When the woman was done, she gave Mary another of her gap-toothed smiles. She fingered a few objects, one being the comb that Will had had made for Mary. Mary closed the woman's hand around it, indicating that she should have it. She seemed pleased with the gift, but a moment later dropped it on the floor and pointed to a wooden bowl. Mary handed her the bowl. The woman took it and went away.

Will slept little that night, and Mary, not at all, although she surely would have tried had she been able to foresee the day that awaited her.

It began at sunrise with a thunderous banging on the door. Will moaned, and Mary hurried to the door, fearing it would splinter before she could get it open. Sergeant Scott stood on the stoop, brows beetled.

"Out!" he said, and, looking over her shoulder, bellowed at Will, "Up and out, ye theivin' bastard! You and your kin can make do as best you can in that shack down yonder." He jerked his head in the direction they were bidden to go. Seeing that neither Mary nor Will comprehended, he added, "Where them Irish bolters lived afore they went missin' and got 'emselves lost and starved to death."

Mary knew the derelict hut. It was half the size of their cabin and surrounded by head-high brush. Will got to his feet, swaying and muttering oaths, not at Scott—he dared not do that—but at his ragged clothing as he tried to dress without causing himself more pain.

Two men under Scott's command began flinging the family's meagre possessions out the door. Along the path, convicts and their mariner guards, already on the way to work, paused to watch the Bryants' fall from grace.

Scott noticed Cass among the gawkers. "That old

hag still a friend of yours?" he asked Mary. Mary hesitated, fearing that to say yes might cause Cass some trouble. "You'll be needing somebody to stay with anything left behind," Scott barked. "Else they'll be pickin' you clean whilst your back is turned."

At that, Mary nodded. Scott motioned to Cass who, not being close enough to hear what he had said to Mary, approached with a kind of defiant fearfulness. "You a friend of this here family?" Scott asked again.

Cass likewise hesitated, lest the wrong answer carry some unknown penalty. But at last she mumbled, "Aye, Mr. Scott."

"Then stay by their goods till all's removed, and keep the vultures off," Scott ordered.

"Aye, Sir." Cass took up a stance between the Bryants' things and the gaping crowd.

"Thank you," Mary said, her words meant for Scott and Cass alike. Both were hard as iron and considered overt signs of sympathy to be a kind of weakness. But neither was given to inflicting pain and, when they felt they must do so for duty or survival, took no pleasure in it.

Will was struggling to move a heavy chest, one which on a normal day he'd have hoisted onto his back, but this morning could not. He had paid Cox to build the chest. Except for three stools he had whittled himself, it was their only furniture. By standards in the convict community, where most had no furnishings at all, these things were seen as luxuries. No one in the crowd offered to help carry the heavy chest, so Mary took one end. Together she and Will staggered down the path to the derelict shack to which they'd been demoted.

It took only one more trip to move what little more there was. Cass came with them on the last trip, lugging the cast iron cooking pot. When she saw the holes in the reed roof of the shack, she shook her head. "Drafty is what it is," she cracked. "Until that's repaired, you might as well be sleeping outdoors."

"It wouldn't be the first time we've done that since coming ashore," Mary replied.

"Aye." Cass grimaced. "Most anywhere I've been, I could always say 'I've seen worse.' But I ain't heard none say that about bloody Botany Bay."

Cass trudged off, leaving Mary alone with Will. He had collapsed on the floor, though it had not yet been swept and was covered with leaf debris and the droppings of small animals.

"They've given me the one day," said Will weakly. "Tomorrow I'm to work again."

"Then you'd best get some rest. I'll go back to the garden and see what I can find for supper, if it hasn't been stripped already. I doubt we'll be getting a ration of fish today."

When Mary returned from the garden with a head of cabbage and some immature beans, she saw that rocks had been arranged for cooking and a fire already laid. She looked around for a bucket with which to go and fetch water—a much further walk it would be to the stream from this cabin—and saw that it had already been filled. She was touched that Will had done those chores in his condition, when it was not normal for him to do them at all.

When she had a small fire blazing, water set to boil, and vegetables washed, Mary went inside the dilapidated hut. Two logs left behind by the previous tenants still remained, squared off with the corner of the room to form a sleeping area. It was now filled with fresh eucalyptus leaves, topped with dry grass. The grass was less fragrant than the leaves but not so harsh to lie upon. Will sprawled face-down on the makeshift bed.

"You went for wood and water and bedding," she said gently. "I daresay all that moving about in the heat has worsened the pain."

"'Twas Johnny. He done all that. Damn me, if I ain't a mess to have a cripple looking after me."

"You'd have done the same for him," Mary said, although she was fairly certain that it would never have occurred to Will.

"That woman came from the bush, too, and smeared some balm on my back." Will grinned weakly. "Had to hold my breath while she was squatted down here, such a rank smell she's got."

"You smell pretty rank yourself," Mary retorted with a near smile. "I can't imagine what besides leaves she puts in that mix that it gives off such an awful stink."

"Don't matter to me how it smells, long as it does the trick. And that I can testify. The pain went down right away."

"I guess the natives feel the same. If rancid fat keeps

off the biting bugs, smear it all over they will, and not mind about the smell."

Mary sat down on the chest, the first chance she'd had to sit all morning. But her body was made tense by thoughts moving in several directions at once. She must go for Charlotte soon, and look to their meal. Breakfast, lunch and dinner rolled into one—the only food they would have this day—simmered over the fire. Then she must collect more wood and bring more water.

She thought Will had fallen asleep, but when she looked toward him, his bloodshot blue eyes were open, watchful. "What puts that look on your face?" he asked.

"What look?"

"A jumpy look, I'd say it was."

"Oh that. Just counting the things I've yet to do, the ones that can't wait till the morrow."

"What else?"

She didn't like this interrogation. It wasn't like him, and anyway, she had no ready answer. She went to the door and looked out. Scrub was thick around the shack, either never cut or grown anew since the Irishmen bolted and met with death. She could not see the harbour from here, the glittering blue and green harbour, which was the one truly beautiful thing in this forsaken place.

"I was thinking," she said slowly, although it had just come into her mind, "how it was one year ago today that we landed here."

Mary went out then, telling Will that she must go

get Charlotte. He had not responded to her remark about it being the anniversary of their landing, nor had he made mention of the fact that in a few more days it would be the anniversary of their marriage. If indeed he thought of himself as married. She had heard others in the colony, particularly those inclined to change partners, claim that none of what Reverend Johnson had called "nuptial blessings" were lawful marriages, because no banns had been published.

However, her legal status as wife was of no more concern to Mary now than it had been the previous year when she and other couples stood before Reverend Johnson for words he was pleased to call a blessing. Foremost in her mind was the thought that, hard as the past year had been, Will's actions ensured that the year to come would be infinitely harder.

What would he have said to that, she wondered angrily, then felt her anger sag into depression. Being angry with Will was like being angry with a small child. He acted impulsively, without care for consequences, then regretted his folly so bitterly that, despite her best intentions to hold him accountable, she felt the urge to comfort rather than to scold him.

Mary walked back toward the settlement, head held high. She met the gaze of those she passed on the path so that, rather than them being able to stare at her in pity or condemnation, they were forced to drop their eyes and either mumble a greeting or pass in silence. Thus she met all her convict neighbours until she reached the square and saw coming toward her the person she least cared to see. She tried to pass him, looking at the ground, but Joseph Paget stopped, blocking her path.

"I'm sorry," he mumbled. "I had no choice."

Her head came up at that, and she spat anger at him as if she were a viper and he had trodden on her tail. "No choice? Was it some other who ran tattling for the pleasure of seeing my husband beaten half to death?"

"If he was half beat to death, what do you think they'd have done to me? Five hundred lashes, they said, if I didn't speak the truth which they well-knowed already!"

"You hung him there!" she shouted, pointing at the triangle on the far side of the square. "You, with your flapping mouth."

"It wasn't me what gave the order to carry off them fish and fetch him back his rum!"

"As if you got no part of it!"

"That I did, but didn't I tell him time and again we ought to call it quits? I knowed we was being watched, and he knowed it well as me."

Paget stood there twisting a rag of a cap in his hand, waiting for Mary to acknowledge his point. When she said nothing, he added in a defeated tone of voice, "'Twas love of rum that got him them licks, Miss Mary, and I ain't no better. When a man's got a need for drink, there's precious little he won't say or do."

Mary's anger against the man should have lessened then, but it did not, for he had said to her face what she did not want to hear or know. Instead of admitting that he spoke the truth, she stared at him with scorching fury: her anger at his betrayal fuelled by some greater anger she felt toward Will, and on top of both, a blazing hatred for God or Fate or whatever it was that caused her to suffer the consequences of their wilful ways.

Then, like a flame that has run through kindling and has nothing left to burn, her fury turned to something as insubstantial as ashes. Paget must have seen the change in her face, for he said, "I'm sorry, Miss Mary. I never meant to bring hardship on you and the little girl."

With that he stepped aside, and Mary walked on. Ahead of her loomed the triangle. It made her want to vomit, but she drew her feelings in and, by force of will, blocked out the horror of Will hanging there. He had not been the first and would not be the last. As hunger in the colony grew, there would be more lawbreakers in the year to come than there had been in the one just past.

Her destination was not Colleen and Johnny's house, not yet. She was headed for a small office in the side of the warehouse where all the colony's provisions were stored.

James sat working on inventories of what supplies remained. He did not look up at once to see who blocked the light, thus giving Mary time to watch his long tapered fingers move a quill pen across paper, leaving behind a trail of beautiful script. Mary had known few educated men, and she marvelled that one of her acquaintance should have such skills as James possessed.

When James reached the end of the line he looked

up. For one unguarded instant Mary saw in his eyes the pleasure he derived from her mere presence. Then he shielded his feelings from her and said, with his usual formality, "Mrs. Bryant! How is your husband?"

"No better, no worse, than could be expected. I came to thank you for letting me know. And for keeping Charlotte away."

She turned to go, for being so near to James nudged longings in her that she must not allow to grow. As she had suppressed them on shipboard so she would suppress them here, where they were even less appropriate.

He remained seated at his desk, but his voice reached out and held her in the doorway. "Will you be all right?"

"Yes." She paused. "But perhaps you could tell me—that ship sent for supplies four months ago, when might she return?"

"Six months hence, at best.

"Six months! Will we not all have starved by then?"

"You think the Crown cares?" James exploded. "If they really wanted the colony to survive, they would have replenished our supplies six months back. What does it matter in London if hundreds of convicts starve, and scores of mariners perish with them? Will there not always be more where we came from?" He moderated his voice. "Why do you ask?"

"Will must be back at work by morning, but you can be sure our ration of fish will be cut. The garden is lost due to our having to move. The shore is all but stripped of shellfish, and now that the birds have all been slaughtered, there are no eggs to find."

"Is it not the same for all of us?" James said, the tiredness in his voice reminding Mary that in handing out the daily rations, he heard whines of hunger hundreds of times a day. "Who among us is not starving, little by little?"

Perhaps it was his hopelessness that challenged Mary to answer back. "My child", she said with quiet intensity, "shall not starve".

Another man might have sneered at such bravado, but James Brown did not. He cocked his head in a thoughtful manner, and asked, with interest, "Do you have a plan?"

"Not . . . yet," Mary admitted. "Live with the natives if need be. I don't see their children starving for lack of supplies from England."

James smiled, not in humour but in admiration of her will.

"Have you thought of working?"

Mary snorted. "What is it you think I do all day long? Why, I've not sat for so much as a cup of tea yet today!"

"Begging your pardon, Mrs. Bryant. I meant working out of the home."

Mary shook her head. "I've no schooling, Mr. Brown, and what I can do, so can every other woman in the colony."

"You were a great help to Dr. White on the ship coming over."

"Then he was alone. Now he has the help of doctors from other ships in the fleet."

"And all are overburdened for, as you well know, with increasing hunger comes increasing sickness."

Mary considered for a moment, then said, "There's no harm in asking, is there?"

"No." James hesitated. "Unless your husband objects."

"I shall not tell him it was your idea." She smiled grimly. "And having brought his family to this, he would do well not to put stones in my path."

Mary's next stop was Colleen and Johnny's cottage. In size and construction it was as pathetic as all the other convict huts, yet certain details gave it a homey feel. There was a rough wooden bench on either side of the door, and cut-off stumps for sitting and visiting. There was a garden, too, better tended than most. It even had flowers, which Colleen had found in the forest and transplanted here to add a little brightness. For all they were Irish, and political prisoners at that, once the work day ended, their yard was usually full of friends.

As she approached, Mary could hear Charlotte's laughter and wondered what Colleen or Johnny might be doing to make her solemn child so happy. She came around the corner and saw Colleen dancing with Charlotte in her arms while Johnny jigged about, pretending to play music on a twig broom. Where under heaven, Mary wondered, did they find the energy—and Johnny with his bad legs at that! She felt a flicker of envy to see her child giggling in Colleen's embrace, or perhaps it was guilt, for this was the kind of simple pleasure Mary's mother had so easily created for her. Before anguish at her own limitations fully pierced Mary's heart, Charlotte saw her, gave a squeal of delight, and held out her sun-browned arms.

Johnny dropped onto the other bench, and Colleen, breathless, fell into his lap. "Mary!" she gasped, "How's Will?"

"Resting," Mary replied, and to Johnny, "Thank you for all you did."

"'Twasn't much," he said with a dismissive wave. "I'm sorry I couldn't do more."

"There's only the roof," Mary said. "I'll gather reeds for it, and Will can repair it on Sunday."

"Forget the roof and do a garden," Colleen advised. "It's food you need, and nothing grows overnight."

"I'll start clearing the weeds this afternoon."

"Just a small clearing," Johnny suggested, "Leave tall bushes all around as a barrier against prying eyes."

Colleen leapt from his lap and went around to the shady side of the house. She came back lugging a burlap bag. "Look what Johnny did."

Mary peered in. "Why, these are half-grown plants. Surely you didn't take them from your own—."

"Not from our garden, no. I dug them from yours not an hour ago. You've worked hard to bring them along this far; no point in losing them now. Some won't take, of course, but if you work the soil till it's fine and free of stones, and keep the plants watered, some should tolerate the move."

"Oh, Johnny, Colleen! What fine friends you are! However can I repay you?"

"Easy," Colleen flipped, "Just make us a present of this wee dancer." She leaned over and kissed Charlotte, who puckered her own lips and made a smacking sound in the air.

As soon as Mary got back to the shack she gave Charlotte and Will their thin soup, then went to work in the garden. She cleared a tiny square and got some plants in the ground. By noon the next day the rest of the plants were in. She spent the afternoon carrying water. The distance to the creek was so far that she didn't know whether to pray for rain to save her carrying bucket after bucketful, or to pray for the rain to hold off until they'd time to re-thatch those gaping holes in the roof.

It took a good three weeks to get the garden up and growing. By then the rains had come, so she could leave off watering every day. She had also gathered the reeds needed to mend the roof, and helped Will make the repairs—although not before they had been soaked through three times.

Their food and fish ration was scantier now, as Mary had expected it would be in retaliation for Will's greed. She managed as best she could, and put off going to Dr. White until three things occurred which reminded her of how desperate life was becoming, not only for her family but for everyone in the slowly starving colony.

First, an old lady, Dorothy Handland, hanged herself. It might have been confusion, for she was said to be eighty-four years old. Or it might have been that she could bear the hunger no longer; she had, after all, been transported in the first place for stealing a hunk of cheese.

Then, in early March, seven mariners were hanged for stealing food. Governor Phillip had announced at Will's flogging that henceforth, no matter one's standing in the community, any who stole food would hang. Still, there were those who took the chance.

The third thing that put a fright in Mary happened one day when she was roaming the forest looking for anything she could find—sweet tea, wild spinach, or a nest of birds' eggs. She came upon a native encampment and saw five aborigine bodies scattered about. They did not have the starved look of the colonists, but they were dead all the same.

Mary scooped up Charlotte before the child could toddle into the camp. "Sleeping," she lied, in a shaky voice. She fled back to town and straight to Dr. White's office.

White was alone in his surgery, resting after the morning rush with all its decisions as to who was truly ill and who was malingering. Mary set Charlotte down to play in the dirt and went inside. As usual, the doctor had kicked off his boots. Without bothering to say hello, Mary knelt down, lifted one of his feet into her lap, and began to massage.

White groaned with relief. Then, in his usual cranky tone, demanded, "What do you want this time?"

"The same as before," Mary smiled. "Work, here in the surgery."

He pulled his foot out of her lap. "And where would I get money to pay you?"

She picked up the other foot and drew it to her, noting that there was no real resistance from him. "It's not money I need, Sir."

He let her continue massaging for a moment, then planted both feet firmly on the floor. "Rations are harder to come by now than they were on the crossing. And what would you do with Charlotte? I won't have her here, not with the amount of sickness that's about."

"I'll ask Colleen to look after her, like before. It needn't be very long. Just until my new garden is producing." She hesitated. "I had thought to spend time with the natives, and pay more attention to what they find to feed their children, for most are fit enough. But today I came upon a group of five, all dead."

"How close did you get?"

"Not close enough to touch them."

"Stay away from them and any others you come upon," White ordered. "And yes, there are others. They're dying in droves and it's hard to know why. From what I've seen, their diseases are no different from ours, measles and the like. But we do not die so readily."

He pulled on his boots. "I can't help you this time, Mary. Why not ask among the officers to see if any need help about the house?"

Mary shook her head. "They've long since found

servants they can trust. And besides, those here without their wives and most in need of a woman to cook and clean will be wanting more than that."

She reached for the laces to do them up but he pushed her hands away. "Will you stop fussing over me?" Jerking at the laces with what seemed like anger, he snapped, "Don't you know we're done for, girl? The breeding livestock has all died or been poached, and garden sprouts are jerked out and eaten before they're an inch high. Birds that, a year ago, covered the shore with nests have been slaughtered, and shellfish have been stripped from the rocks all around the bay. And where the hell are the ships sent for supplies, which should have returned long ago? Starvation's in store for all of us."

He stood and Mary stood, staring at each other as if they were adversaries. Mary said, in a voice as hard as his own, just what she had said to James: "My daughter shall not starve."

When White made no reply she said, "I'll speak to Colleen this afternoon about looking after Charlotte."

Mary worked mornings at the surgery for the next four months. As White had warned, what extra food he found for her was even less than on the ship. However little it was, she took it gratefully and carried it home to Charlotte. Once White chided her, pointing out that if she let herself starve to death, there was little chance of her child surviving, but Mary only gave him a look, and he never spoke of it again.

In early December, as the summer heat was bearing

down, Mary marched into the surgery one morning with an attitude that made White give her a second glance. Her first task was to make tea for them both, to which he usually added a piece of hardtack. Mary had learned back on the ship that the more unobtrusively she performed her tasks the better he liked it, but this morning she seemed not to care. She poured them each a cup of tea, then plopped herself on a stool and glared at him accusingly.

"Did you not say that Nature knows better than to put starving women in a family way?"

The tea, half-way to his mouth, sloshed a little. White set it back down and looked her over. "What I said was that starving women don't conceive as readily as healthy ones. But when one's been underfed, and then begins to fatten—."

"Do I look as if I've fattened?" Mary screeched.

Although White had once thought her pretty, malnutrition had pared her to such thinness that her body retained hardly any womanly curves. Her light brown hair was still streaked with gold from spending so much time out of doors, but under sun-baked skin her complexion was sallow. She was as upset as he had ever seen her.

"The garden you planted is producing, is it not? And screened as it is by brambles, you said yourself that there has been no thieving from it. Then there's the fish—you weren't cut off entirely. And this." He laid a piece of hardtack between them. "On the whole, I, or rather, Nature, would say you're better off now."

"I am *not* better off!" Mary shouted, then put her head in her hands and wept.

White sighed. "How far along are you?"

"I don't know. Two months or so."

"Cheer up. Maybe it'll be stillborn. Most are now. Or you might miscarry. Especially if you keep up that bawling."

"If I thought all it took was weeping, I'd fill this teacup with tears," Mary choked, but she made an effort to stifle her sobs.

White stared into his tea. After awhile he said, "I've ridded women of brats before, but I'd not do it for you. There's a great danger of infection, and I can tell you, it's a horrible way to die."

Mary choked back one last sob. "When I was a girl my mother told me that women have no say in the matter; that men decide when to plant and God decides whether or not there'll be a harvest. And neither gives a farthing for a woman's feelings."

"I've not seen much attention from the Almighty to any manner of human suffering," the doctor said shortly and, as if he had lost all interest in her plight, he rose and opened the door.

The usual line of mariners and convicts had formed outside. He looked at their wasted bodies and said aloud what might have been a plea to God, but more likely was a taking of the Lord's name in vain. White himself couldn't have said which it was, so bothered was he by all that awful hope collected in their eyes. Why should they suppose he had the power to ameliorate their pain? For that matter, why should he even bother to try when, day after day, God reinvented their suffering, and every other known to humankind.

⊕

Emanuel was born on the afternoon of April 3, 1790. He was a tiny infant and it was an easy birth. He slid into Cass's capable hands, and didn't yowl until she splashed him with cold water to wash away the slime. Will was out on the boat, but Cass allowed Charlotte in right away. Charlotte watched the infant with intense interest, but warily, as if it were an unfamiliar wildlife specimen she had come upon in the bush. It appeared to be gnawing on her mother's breast, but she didn't seem to mind, so perhaps it wasn't as bad as all that.

Colleen and Florie came in next. Florie, as usual, was a little drunk and, because she was so, Cass pushed her back from the bed. Florie retreated to the corner like a small dog and, from that distance, watched mother and child. Soon she slipped into a doze. Colleen hovered over the birthing bed, her green eyes filled with a longing that almost broke Mary's heart. She would never give up her newborn, but if she had had the power to grant Colleen this second pregnancy she would gladly have done so, knowing how much she and Johnny craved a child of their own.

That evening, as Will fussed and chuckled over his son, Mary marvelled at how oblivious he seemed to what might well be the fate of both their children. If he thought of the possibility of starvation, it never showed. He and his crew were again bringing in an abundance of fish. Not all their previous privileges had been restored, but Will had regained some status in the colony. Back was his cheerful confidence with its careless edge. There was just one difference. With increasing frequency, he lapsed into a dark mood. It was usually coupled with his arriving home late, reeking of liquor. On some of those nights he had pawed at her body, heavily pregnant though she'd been. Now that the baby was out, she dreaded what was to come.

Emanuel had been born near the end of a summer drought. The colony's food stores were lower than ever and still no ships came. The burning sun had killed or stunted most of what was in the garden. Mary racked her brain for other means of getting enough food to nourish her family and herself for, unless she had milk, the baby was as good as dead. Everyone was in the same situation. Between them—nearly a thousand souls in all—the area around Botany Bay had been scraped clean. She could not leave both the baby and Charlotte with Colleen, so that put an end to her work with Dr. White. All Mary could do was tend her drought-stricken garden and fragile children, protecting both as best she could.

At last the winter rains arrived and, in June 1790, the long-awaited ship hove into view. Every soul in the colony ran down to the shore, shouting for joy or weeping with relief. It was an English ship, *Lady Juliana*. But if she had been named for a lady, that lady must have been a witch. Her cargo was not food but two hundred and twenty-two convict women.

These new arrivals had dressed themselves as well as they could under the circumstances in preparation for landing. Pathetic though that was, they cut a fine sight compared to the women of the colony, whose few garments had long since disintegrated, leaving them dressed, as Mary was, in simple shifts made from burlap bags which had been used to transport tapioca and other supplies on the voyage out.

The women convicts from *Lady Juliana* were rowed ashore in weather as unsettled as it had been that day the women of the First Fleet had arrived two-and-a-half years earlier. Blustery winds drove black clouds across the sky, and a cold rain fell intermittently. There was an ominous rumbling. Mary recognised it for what it was: the same male animal growl for sex that had turned the night of her own landing into a living hell. She looked across to where Governor Phillip and his officers stood, and felt reassured. Although the mariners gazed upon the newly-arrived women with the same lechery as their convict brethren, she sensed that this time discipline would prevail.

While mariners and male convicts salivated at the sight of so many women, Phillip's face held an expression of disbelief. He looked at his officers and they back at him, unable to conceal their dismay. How could the colony possibly feed so many extra mouths when it was already on its knees with hunger? No way could these wasted, sea-weary females support themselves. The only hope was that the *Lady Juliana* had also brought food.

Mary had similar thoughts, but was glad to see the women all the same. She felt that the presence of more women in the colony would deflect pressures created by the ten-to-one male-to-female ratio. Also, there would be news from home. The women of the colony ran among the newcomers, plying them with questions. Mary started toward them, too, but a hand gripped her arm and held her back.

"No," said Dr. White. "There is all manner of sickness on a ship such as this, not to mention the vermin. Stay away from them for now."

So Mary did not mingle with the new arrivals, but watched them from afar. After a while she took her children and returned to their hovel, there to await news, second hand, from her neighbours and from Will.

Will was late getting in that evening, for he had taken advantage of his position to gossip with members of the *Juliana's* crew.

"They say they have aboard but a little flour, not even enough to feed these wretches they've dumped on us, let alone to replenish our stores," Will reported angrily.

Mary could scarcely believe it. "Surely there are other ships? The *Lady Juliana* sailed not alone, did she?"

"Three ships in this Second Fleet," Will confirmed. "More than a thousand convicts they set sail with, men coming on the other two and like to arrive any day."

"How can we feed a thousand more when we can't even feed ourselves?" Mary ranted.

Will mopped the last drop of broth from his bowl with a bit of johnnycake and jammed it into his mouth. "Won't be no thousand more. *Lady Juliana*'s crew claims half perished on the voyage, and them that survived are worse off than the ones that landed today."

"How is that possible?" Mary gasped, shifting Emanuel to her other breast.

"Is your memory of the crossing so short then?" Will asked crossly. "All's needed is a handful of sick ones to start, and from what I heard, they set sail with more than that. Some thieving contractors, and a captain in league with them and vile as a slaver to boot." He paused. "Them contracting bastards tried to cheat the First Fleet, too. And would've got away with it if Old Phillip hadn't been such a stickler. I don't know that he cared a fig for the convicts, but he wasn't ready to see his crew starve or die of some ship-borne plague."

"We were lucky," Mary murmured. "You think it is as bad as it can get, but in truth, there is always worse to be."

It would be some time before the full extent of the Second Fleet's tragedy was confirmed. Of one thousand and six convicts, two hundred and sixty-seven had perished at sea during the eleven-month voyage, and another hundred and fifty had died soon after landing. That was not quite half of those who had set sail from England, as Will had been told, but for the stunned colonists and skeletal survivors, it was close enough.

Those who had come with the First Fleet had had their share of sufferings but, like Mary, admitted amongst themselves that their lot couldn't hold a candle to the abuses suffered by this wasted cargo of human bones.

Vermin-ridden sick and dying convicts were not the only horrors the Second Fleet delivered. It had also brought more soldiers, especially recruited to act as guards in the penal colony. The Botany Bay Rangers, as they were called, were a vile lot, most with histories as criminal as the convicts they had been sent to control. They mingled freely with the convict population, and what they wanted, they took. Mary and other women spoke in whispers of what might lie in store for them. Up until now those among them who were married—and nearly all were—had been subjected to the whims of only one man and felt reasonably well-protected from the others. They had no assurance at all that things would remain that way.

Cass and Florie were unkempt wenches with missing or rotting teeth, more likely to offer their bodies for booze than to have a man demand sexual favours from them. But for Mary and Colleen, the danger was great. Colleen, who had always walked with pride beside her Johnny, took to covering as much of her body as she could with filthy rags as a means of escaping notice, and hunching like a hag when compelled to go out in public.

Mary, for her part, stayed in her bush-concealed hut with the children, only going out as necessary to get their daily ration. She used a rag to cover her sun-bleached hair, and smeared herself with filth, even leaving some of Emanuel's faeces on her person to add to the repellent smell. She sometimes felt James's eyes upon her as he recorded the rations doled out, and burned with shame. But what other defence did she have?

Fetching water was another daily chore, but that was less of a problem. Because Will must be down to the dock at first light, Mary rose early to make breakfast. When he was gone, she went for water while her children and most of the colony still slept.

Although it was spooky to tread the path to the stream before the sun had risen, those moments of solitude had their value. Pausing on the return to rest from the burden of water she lugged, Mary would look out to sea and recall the freedoms she had known there as a child. Or she would watch clouds being blown across the sky in a stiff morning breeze and imagine sailing away from Botany Bay.

Florie, in drunken moments, dreamed of finding buried treasure with which to buy her liberty, and Colleen, even when she was sober, spoke of returning to Ireland with Johnny to lead a revolution. But when it came to fantasies, Mary had not changed since she was a girl. However improbable her dreams, she sought to ground them in the possible. Her imaginings took her ever to ways and means. It was this that engaged her mind the morning she encountered James Brown upon the path.

It was a foggy morning, and she started when she saw a man's shape emerging out of the gloom. But an instant later he spoke, having recognised her before she recognised him. "Good morning, Mrs. Bryant," he said in his usual formal way.

"Ah, good morning, Mr. Brown," she exclaimed, relieved that it was a friend. "What brings you to fetch water so early in the morning?"

"I'm busy all the day," he explained. "The stream is less stirred up of a morning than it is in the evening. And you?"

Mary lowered her voice. "'Tis avoidance of the Rangers, who stir up more than mud in this colony."

"A sad truth you speak," he acknowledged. "Is this why I see so little of you these days?"

"Yes," Mary admitted, pleased that he had noted her absence. "That is also why, when I go out to fetch our ration, I exaggerate my filth and seek to appear as a hag."

"A difficult task for you, Mrs. Bryant," he said gallantly.

Sensing that the conversation was skirting the edge of intimacy, Mary picked up her pails and made to go. Then, as James stepped aside and she was about to move past him, she suddenly set her pails down again, and spoke. "Sir, might I ask you a question?"

Surprise showed in his eyes. "Most certainly. Anything at all."

"I was wondering . . . how long is your sentence?"

"Twenty years. I have seventeen yet to go."

"Twenty years!" Mary exclaimed. "For a crime you didn't commit!"

A smile played about his lips. "And how do you know that?"

Mary blushed. "On the crossing I heard you say the charge was a case of cinnamon gone missing, which was none of your doing. I'm sure you spoke the truth."

"Indeed, that was true. It was not I who stole the cinnamon, but some acquaintances who required the means to buy arms. In seeking to throw off the yoke of the British Empire, we Canadians are little different from our Irish brethren."

"Ah," Mary said. "But your connection to the rebels was not known?"

The smile vanished and the brown eyes turned serious. "Had it been known, I would have hanged. And had I claimed innocence and pointed a finger at them, I would have been set free. That was the bargain they offered. Thus I was given twenty years, not for the cinnamon, which they knew well I did not steal, but because I denied any knowledge of those who did."

Mary nodded thoughtfully. "Colleen says it was like that for her and Johnny. Had they been willing to name names, their sentences would have been shortened."

James shrugged. "Not that it matters. Once transported to this blasted place, what chance have any of us of ever earning passage back to England?"

"This of which you speak is ever in my mind," Mary confessed.

"And in mine," James said, with a piercing gaze which seemed to say much more.

Mary held his gaze for a moment, trying to glean all that was being said without words. Then she took up her burden of water again. "Good day, Mr. Brown. I must go now, for the children will waken soon, and I'd not want them to find me gone."

One winter day in August, as Mary squatted by the fire cooking a johnnycake for herself on the flat of an upturned spade, Colleen came up the path in a rush. Mary thought, as Colleen hurried toward her, that the dirt the Irish lass had deliberately smeared on her person had done little to conceal her loveliness. A frizz of curls surrounded her face like a copper halo, and her white teeth flashed in a radiant smile. Instinctively Mary glanced at Colleen's breasts, saw how full they had become, and guessed the news before Colleen could blurt it.

"Oh Mary, I am, I really am!" Colleen held the burlap shift against her belly which as yet showed no trace of swelling.

"Bless you!" Mary said, although she secretly wondered how anyone could feel good about bringing a child into the wretched uncertainty of this place. "What does Johnny say?"

Colleen face was suffused with hope and joy. "He says seeing how this baby will be born free, as soon as it draws breath, that part of him that's in our child will be free as well."

"He's a lucky man, your Johnny is." Spontaneously, Mary lifted the johnnycake off the upturned shovel and thrust it toward Colleen. "Here. You have it."

Colleen put her hands behind her back. "Don't be daft, Mary!"

Mary caught one of Colleen's hands and shoved the

johnnycake into it. "It's my present for the baby. You cannot refuse."

Almost involuntarily, Colleen brought the hot johnnycake to her mouth, holding it barely a second to cool before she swallowed it down. "Ah Mary," she whispered, "how can you bring yourself to share when there's so little?"

"Friends share," Mary replied firmly.

Colleen gave her a troubled look. "Cass says none are friends in Botany Bay."

"Cass is wrong."

Hunger in the colony was mitigated in October with the return of the ship *Supply*, which the governor had sent out six months earlier. The *Supply* came laden with rice and salted meat, plus news that a Dutch ship had been contracted to bring an additional three hundred and fifty tons of food.

The mid-December arrival of that Dutch ship, the *Waaksamheyd*, caused shouts of joy to ring out from every part of the settlement. When Will came in that evening, he could hardly eat for all he had to tell. "Ah, Mary, if you could see what she carries! Barrels upon barrels of rice and pork and beef and sugar. 'Tis a vast amount more than what came on the *Supply*."

"This is what you've heard?" Mary found it hard to contain her own excitement.

"This is what I saw with my own eyes, when I was ordered out to deliver fresh fish for the crew that stayed aboard."

As they lay in bed that night, Mary was aware that Will had not, as was his custom, fallen directly to sleep. She turned toward him to let him know that she too was still awake.

"Did any among the crew speak English?" she asked.

"Aye, one chap. He told me of a mutiny."

"What? On their vessel?"

"No, no. An English ship. The *Bounty*. A year and a half ago, off O'Tahiti. The mutineers set the captain adrift in an open boat, him and eighteen others. What a brutal bunch they must've been!"

"They've caught and hanged them, have they?" Mary questioned.

"Nay. The story's more fantastical than that. The mutineers made their getaway with the ship, and ain't been seen hide nor hair of since, except for putting into O'Tahiti to carry off some women. That you can believe, can you not?"

"Sure, mutineers would think like that," Mary agreed.

"What's hard to believe is this. That old sea-dog Captain Bligh made it all the way to Timor, upwards of four thousand miles from where they started out."

"Four thousand miles in an open boat? How many survived the journey?"

"Every man, save one killed by savages on the first day out, when they was trying to make landfall on an island."

"Don't you think it's a bit too fanciful to be true?"

"This mariner who told the tale said he heard all about it in Timor, when they put in at Kupang. That's where Bligh and his men fetched up, this being June before last, some sixteen months back. In Kupang they got taken on by a whaler, and was all of them back in England in sight of a year."

They said no more but neither did they sleep. What each pictured was more improbable than the story just recounted, but they did not share their thoughts; not Will, because his were yet to be fully formed, and not Mary, because hers, formed long ago, wanted refreshing.

A thin moon lay on the shoulder of the night sky, putting Mary in mind of a stray curl from her golden-haired infant. For days she had waited for this night, with just enough light to make her way down to the boats but not enough to be seen by a sentry from far down the beach. She waded into the dark water and untied the line of the smallest rowboat from her husband's larger fishing boat. She pointed it seaward, gave it a shove away from shore, and pulled herself up and over the side. Using an oar, she poled until she could no longer reach bottom, to avoid any sound of splashing. Then she sat straight, took both oars in hand and rowed hard for the *Waaksamheyd*. The heavy work she did day in and day out had given her strong arms, and she was along side the Dutch ship in less than a quarter hour.

"Permission to come aboard, if you please," she

called up in a clear voice that gave no hint of the terror she felt.

A response came in Dutch. Although she did not understand the words she knew the meaning, for any watchman on any ship would have asked the same question: "Who goes there?"

"A woman, with a message for Captain Deter Smit."

Again the watchman responded in Dutch. As his footsteps echoed away, she surmised that he had gone to fetch someone who spoke English, or possibly the captain, as she had pronounced Smit's name clearly, the way Will said it was spoken by the crew.

Mary waited for what seemed an eternity before she heard footsteps returning, this time the heavy tread of two men.

A foreigner's voice, speaking accented English, called out in a tone that was neither gracious nor friendly, "Who are you, Madam, and what do you want?"

"Mary Bryant, Sir. A moment of your time, if you can spare it. May I board?"

There was a silence, then a gruff response. "As you please."

A rope ladder was thrown down. Mary fastened her rowboat to it and climbed swiftly up. It was long ago that she had last performed such a feat, and she was pleased to find that, like many skills one learns in early childhood, this one had not been forgotten.

Upon reaching the deck, she entered a circle of light cast by the watchman's lantern. She stood straight and still (and clean, for she had bathed fresh and combed her hair before coming), and appraised the two men as they appraised her. By the watchman's deference, she presumed the second person to be not the English-speaking seaman Will had mentioned, but Captain Smit himself. He matched Will's description of the Hollander as not a young man nor a very tall one. Mary further noted that nothing about this captain looked soft.

Of course he would be accustomed to traders, including women offering themselves. The word "no" seemed ready on his lips, but she could tell that he had a curiosity that wanted satisfying. He might be wondering how a landlubber could stand with bare feet so confidently planted on his deck. Or what reason a woman clothed in a burlap shift might have to smile with the joy she was feeling at this moment.

"Well, Madam?" he asked sharply.

"'Tis the feel of the ship, Captain Smit," she said, offering first the why of her stance and her smile. "My father was a seafaring man, and many a time I went with him. Sometimes I feel like a fish on land, not able to get enough air."

"If you have come to beg passage as a stowaway, don't waste my time," he snapped. "No convict shall put to sea on this ship."

He started to walk away, but turned when she spoke. "I'm looking for nothing of the kind, Captain Smit. I have a good husband asleep over there, and two children who'll find me making johnnycake in the dawn. But between now and then, is there not time for a landlocked girl to listen to the talk of a man who's sailed the world?"

For a long moment he stared at her, lantern-light reflected in his eyes so she could not tell their true colour, or what thoughts might lie behind them. Then he said in the same gruff voice, "Your father spoiled you, Mary Bryant. That much I can see. Come."

She followed him across the deck and along the corridor to his quarters. As she stepped inside, the terrible anxiety that had gripped her during the planning of this excursion, and the horrors she had imagined should the captain choose to report her rather than receive her, fell away. As a man grows calm when he lies upon a woman's breast decades beyond the time when a mother comforted him there, so Mary was calmed by the captain's quarters, much like the ones where she had been welcomed and entertained as a child.

"Sit," commanded the captain. "What will you drink, Madam?"

"Tea, if you please, Captain Smit."

"You are the first I have met in this place who does not beg for rum," he remarked.

Mary did not reply, nor did she sit. Instead, she moved to the wall and examined the chart pinned there. "Do show me where you came from, Captain Smit, and all the places you've been."

Behind her, she heard the captain give a command to the cabin boy in Dutch, to have the tea brought, she supposed. Then Smit stood beside her, a smile of derision on his lips.

"So this cheeky convict reads navigational charts, does she?"

Mary ignored the sarcasm. "Charts I learned to read at my father's knee, and read better yet than books."

Smit gave her a second glance, then turned his gaze to the map. "We took on stores in Batavia, and came down this way." He ran his finger down the west coast of Australia.

"What of this route?" Mary asked, running her own forefinger across the top of Australia and south along the east coast to Botany Bay. "Is it not smoother sailing?"

"Smoother, perhaps. But the Coral Sea's a tricky one. Natives who live along the coast have a knack for navigating through the reefs, but few white men have lived to tell of such a voyage."

"How do they do it? The natives, I mean. Do they know the reef so well?"

There was a tap on the door and, at Smit's bidding, the cabin boy entered with tea and biscuits. Smit said, in a slightly peevish tone, "Did you not hear me tell you to sit?" Without waiting on Mary, he sat himself.

"Aye, Captain," Mary said, and scooted into her seat like a child scolded for dallying.

As if she were a child, Smit poured the tea for them both. He leaned back in his chair and said, "The Great Barrier Reef is a thousand miles long. No man could know it all." He blew on his tea, and went on, thoughtfully. "No, I think it is something else. Some knack for looking past the surface and seeing—well, seeing is not the right word either. Maybe they just feel the coral rising up to bite a hole in their boat, and they turn aside in the nick of time."

Mary gazed across at him, wide-eyed. "Have you ever felt such a thing, Sir?"

Smit laughed. "Me? No. I depend on these." He waved at the charts strewn about the room. "And keep my distance from reefs that bite."

Mary nodded, and sipped her tea. "How came you to be a seafaring man, Captain?"

As she set her cup down, the Captain refilled it, and laid two biscuits on her plate. Then he leaned back and told a story of a merchant's son sent to sea at a tender age, for having failed to apply himself at school, and for what his father perceived as the advantages of having a seafaring trader in the family. Mary never interrupted his recitation, but answered what questions he put to her; questions that she saw were designed to determine the truth of her claim to have sailed with her father. If he paused too long, she would ask something more to keep him going.

At last, when the teapot was drained and the biscuits he had placed on her plate consumed, Mary rose. "What a story, Captain Smit! You've made me forget the time!"

He rose as well. "As have you, Mrs. Bryant." He picked up the tin of biscuits, which had lain open between them the whole of the evening. No doubt he had left it so in a spirit of generosity, not knowing what force of will had been required of Mary to not grab and gobble the contents. "Here," he offered the tin. "A small token of your visit."

She hesitated, and shook her head. "I cannot, Sir.

With so much hunger in the Colony, the smallest morsel gives rise to envy."

Smit eyed her body. "You look better fed than most in this port."

"At the cost of a hundred lashes for my husband, when he was caught holding back a few fish from his catch to feed his family!" Mary exclaimed bitterly.

Smit's mouth twisted in disgust. "And the English fancy themselves civilised! Will you take a meal with me then, before you go?"

"I cannot this night, Sir, for I have no more time." She turned around to the chart on the wall. "It would comfort me, though, to have one of these to feast my eyes on when my heart's sore for the sea."

He eyed her narrowly for a moment, then asked, "Which will you have?"

"This one," she said, pointing to one that showed the north and east coasts of Australia, with its little-known Coral Sea, leading down to (or away from) Botany Bay.

"That one, eh?" Smit stirred among the cache of charts. "Yes, I have a second one of those. In any case, it is not I who will ever sail the impossible sea." He turned back to her, rolling the chart as he spoke. "You do know that your great Captain Cook himself ran aground on a reef there? It was not then, nor has it yet, been truly charted."

"I shall remember that," Mary said, looking straight into his eyes.

He walked her out to that part of the deck where her boat was secured. As she reached for the rope ladder, he said, "We shall not be sailing for at least two months. Perhaps you would care to come again."

"'Twould be a great pleasure, Captain Smit," she responded, and moved hand under hand down the ladder with a great, floating sensation of relief.

Upon reaching shore, she re-fastened the rowboat and trod on silent bare feet across the beach and along the path to her hut. Will lay sleeping deeply as he always did. This she knew by his gentle snores, although it was too black inside the hut to see even the outline of his body. She slid the rolled chart under the leaves that served as their bed, and lay down beside him with a sigh as deep as the gulf that separated their life from that of Captain Smit's.

It was but two nights later, while the moon was still small, that Mary went again to visit Smit. Again the watchman bade her wait while he informed the captain. The watchman returned alone, and called down to Mary. She did not understand what he said, and feared that she was being told to leave. Then he leaned over the side and, speaking sharply, repeated the command, this time waving her up. Lantern swinging, he led her across the deck and along the corridor to the captain's quarters. There was a single knock, and the door opened. Smit's expression was as dour as it had been on their first meeting, and his command to enter was just as curt. But once inside, when they were alone and the light was better, Mary saw in his hazel-coloured eyes some satisfaction that she had returned.

The conversation began with stiff formality, and Mary wondered that he did not order tea. Had she offended him perhaps, by refusing the biscuits on her previous visit? The mystery of his seeming lapse of hospitality was soon explained. A tap on the door was followed by the cabin boy, who laid the table for two, then went away, and returned twice bearing trays of food. Overcome, Mary bowed her head.

"Do you pray?" queried Smit.

Mary looked up. "My mother did. And I was taught as well. But I have come to believe that the kindness of God, like the kindness of men, is kindled not by need or gratitude, but within the heart of the one who gives." Her eyes slanted with humour. "For all I know, Sir, it may offend Our Lord to have mortals giving Him advice as to where His charities ought be placed."

Smit chuckled. "What a little heathen you are, Mary Bryant."

He piled their plates with food then, and the Hollander's conversation flowed easily, as he spoke of the ports of call where he had acquired this delicacy or that.

When the meal ended, he rose and went to the sideboard for a bottle. Mary followed, but showed no interest in his selection of alcoholic beverages. Instead, she picked up a quadrant.

Holding a bottle over the lip of a glass, Smit asked, "Will you have a touch of brandy?"

Fiddling with the quadrant, she asked, "How does this work?"

"If I show you how it works you'll be wanting me to give it to you," Smit grinned.

"That is true," Mary admitted.

He poured a brandy for himself, sniffed it, and sipped. Then he set the glass down and took the quadrant from her.

"It's for measuring angles, you see, and altitude."

Mary's third visit to the *Waaksamheyd* followed the pattern of the second, except that this time, after the cabin boy had cleared away the remains of their meal, Smit got up and locked the door behind him. Mary knew what this portended, and sought to delay it by distracting him into conversation. "Tell me of this Captain Cook, who sailed the Coral Sea and lived to tell of it. What did he say of the journey?"

"Let's see." Smit lit a cigar and seemed to search his memory. "He said that in some ports the natives were friendly, and in some they posed a danger. Captain Bligh reported the same, when he arrived in Timor last year."

"What was Captain Bligh's route?"

Smit reached for a chart, and spread it on the table between them. "He came this way. It took him about four months, I believe, to reach Kupang."

Mary leaned close, following his finger across the map. Smit broke off suddenly, and ran his hand over her breast.

"It's a rough weave you're wearing, Mrs. Bryant. And if rough to this old paw, it must be painful to your young skin."

"One grows accustomed," Mary said, ignoring the liberty he had just taken.

Abruptly, Smit rolled up the chart and crossed the room to a sea chest at the foot of his bed. From it he removed a piece of scarlet cloth. He brought the fabric and laid it in her arms. Mary sighed, for the feel of it evoked in her memory a kerchief made of fabric such as this—silk it was—that her father had once brought home from a voyage for her mother.

"It is a gown of the sort they wear in India," Smit told her. "Will you put it on?"

Mary unfolded the fabric in puzzlement. "It looks to be but a length of cloth, Sir. I cannot see how it might be worn."

"Remove your garment, Mrs. Bryant, and I will teach you." With that, Smit turned his back on her.

For Mary there was no decision to be made, for that decision had been made before she ever set foot aboard the *Waaksamheyd*. Whatever a man might need of a woman—and she knew men to need a great many more things than sex—sex they would have. And should have, she believed, if she was to get what she wanted in return.

When Smit turned to look at her again, she stood naked, faced away from him. He took up the sari and began to wind it around her. The sensuous way it flowed over her skin was almost more than she could bear. "I've never felt the touch of a thing so gentle," she murmured in ecstasy. "Why, it's lighter than the very air!"

"Then you shall have it."

Mary fingered the fine fabric, running her hands from where it covered her breast down her thighs and back again. Then she said simply, "I'd rather have a compass."

Smit narrowed his eyes. She saw in him then the trader that he was; tough in his dealings, but with enough decency to strike a bargain he deemed fair to both. "Very well," he said gruffly. Grasping the silk with one hand, he placed the other hand on her shoulder and turned her round and round, unwinding the sari. When she stood naked before him he said, "Give me a bit of comfort, Madam, and you shall have your compass."

First light was but two hours off when Mary reached shore and tied the rowboat to Will's fishing boat. Seeing the beach empty, she scurried across the sand. She had just started along the path leading to her hut when she heard a footstep behind her. Before she could turn her head to see who it was, a hand came out of the darkness and grabbed her by the hair.

"Now where might you have been, my Mary, that you come back in the wee hours with your hair stinking of tobacco?"

"Shhh!" Mary said, relieved that it was Will and not a Ranger.

With one hand tangled in her hair, he raised the other and backhanded her across the face so hard that she fell to the ground. "Don't shush me, you slut! I'm your husband!"

Her lips, where he had crushed them against her

teeth, oozed blood into her mouth. She hardly felt the pain, so great was her fear that they might be heard. Still on her knees, she grasped his wrist and laid the compass in his hand.

"A compass!" he gasped. "You stole it from the old fart?"

"He gave it to me," Mary whispered, and staggered to her feet.

"Arrrg!" The sound was more beast than human. "His hands on your body! It makes me want to puke!"

Facing him, she said in a low, cold voice, "It would profit you more to ponder your own body's freedom, Will Bryant, than to fret about the comings and goings of mine."

He slapped her again, this time with the flat of his hand so she did not feel hard knuckles as she had with the first blow. And this time, having seen it coming, she did not go down. She turned and walked up the path. Will scrambled after her.

"You think I'm some crazy Irishman, to go running north with a notion of China just across the river?" he hissed. "A compass is no good at all without a chart."

"We have a chart."

He spoke not another word to her, but in the blackness of their cabin and before she could remove her shift, he shoved her down on their bed of leaves and pushed hard into her.

Although Will's hunger for her body had not diminished in the three years of their marriage, his way with her had changed. The teasing tenderness he had shown in the beginning had all but disappeared. Initially, she thought her pregnancy had changed him, but she soon understood that it was the rum. With passions fuelled not by affection but by alcohol, he seemed to forget the ways in which he had given her pleasure in the beginning. He went at her with clumsy jabs which were of minimal value to him and none at all to her. What was there for either of them in an act which, by reason of drink, was left incomplete or forgotten by morning?

Mary had tolerated the change without a murmur, not because she feared her husband but because she feared pregnancy. In a sloppy drunken state, if he did manage to stay atop her long enough to get relief, she could ease him out of her so that the flow came onto her belly. He would fall heavily on her, not sober enough to know or care. Although there was no pleasure in it for her, neither had there been any violence, until this night.

This night, though, Will drove into her as if he wished he were a stake nailing her to the ground. She made no sound and did not lift a hand—not to restrain him during the aggression nor to comfort him afterwards, when he rolled to the side and sobbed.

Less than an hour later, the first grey light shone through the cracks of their hut. Mary rose, as she always did, to build a fire and make a johnnycake to tide her husband through the day. When the miserly amount of food was ready she held the upturned shovel out to him. Will snatched the bit and stuffed it into his mouth. He picked up his rucksack as if to be off, but continued to stand there, shifting his weight from foot to foot.

At last he said, in a low, uncertain voice, "I beg your pardon, Mary."

She responded, dully, "You've done no wrong, nor I, but what was wrung out of us by this miserable place."

"'Tis hard," he said. "For a man, a hard thing, this."

Mary turned away, bitter in the knowledge that he imagined the choices she had made to be harder on himself than on her.

The summer lay on Botany Bay, hot and dry. Mary had not many more opportunities to slip across the bay to the Dutch ship, but those she had, she took. On each visit thereafter, she first shared a meal with Captain Smit, and then she shared his bed. On one visit he gave her a leather tobacco pouch that might be worn on a string about her neck. That night and on every other visit, it was stuffed with tidbits of meat and cheese for Charlotte. As for the baby, what filled Mary's belly also filled her breasts. Thus while the *Waaksamheyd* lay at anchor in Botany Bay, she and the children thrived.

On the matter of supplies to the colony, Captain Smit sought to drive a hard bargain, and Governor Phillip drove back just as hard. Wrangling between the two was fierce, and dragged on day after day for three full months. By night, Mary and Smit engaged in barter as well, but it was of a softer nature, and led to a closeness neither had anticipated.

As she lay naked beside him on a night she judged

to be their last, Mary admitted as much. With a sadness she had never expected to feel, she murmured, "Ah, good Captain! When I look across the harbour and see your great ship gone, I shall be lonelier than before."

Smit was silent for a very long time. At last he said, "Perhaps there is room aboard for one small convict after all."

Mary turned neither toward him nor away, but lay as she was with her head on his arm, pondering the proposition. She knew something of the life of womenfolk who went to sea with their men, so she could imagine how her days with Smit would be spent—how cold and dismissive he would be by day, followed by tenderness at night in proportion to the pleasure she gave him. Weeks of sailing would be interspersed with times when the ship lay at anchor in some exotic port. There they would be fêted by governors and enticed with exquisite goods such as the silken sari which Smit, for his entertainment, still sometimes bade her wear. Barring storms at sea, it would be a peaceful life.

Mary believed that, were she as innocent as she had been back in Cornwall, she could be happy with such a life, had even dreamt of it as a girl. But that was before she carried the guilty weight of her mother's lonely passing. That weight alone she might have borne; indeed, had borne these four years since. But she felt that she had not the strength nor enough forgetting in her to live with the memory of children abandoned as well.

Captain Smit was watching her now, by the light of

the lantern which he would have burning even when they lay together. Like a little boy, she thought, he wanted to see the thing that amused him, and which, when he had satiated his sexual desire, he petted and stroked like a kitten. Mary sat up. Pulling her knees to her chest, she looked over at Smit with a smile. "If I had the provisions I might have eaten on this voyage, I'd make use of them on another."

Smit sighed. "You have the manners of a child, Mary Bryant, but the body of a woman." He squeezed one breast, hard enough to make her wince. "And by what whim of God I do not know, you have been given the mind of a man. Why not come with me?"

Mary glanced sideways at him and saw in the hazel eyes a longing she had not glimpsed there before. She caught the hand that clutched her breast and kissed the tough-skinned palm. "If I sailed with you my husband would howl, and would have a new wife in six months' time. That I would not regret. But it would sadden my little girl forever. And likely my son would die."

Smit lay beside her a moment longer, then abruptly rose from the bed and pulled on a robe. He stepped outside the cabin and gave a string of orders. Then he returned to the bedside and said, "If the weather be fair, we sail at dawn on Monday next."

She understood that he meant the remark both as farewell and a repeat of the invitation to join him if she should change her mind. She felt it only fair to let him know that her mind was made up. "I venture that the night to follow will be without a moon."

"How would you know that?" he asked in surprise. "Among the convicts are there any with an almanac that shows phases of the moon?"

"Not that I have seen," Mary admitted. Although it caused her to blush, she explained, "My monthly flow comes with the full of the moon. From that I count the days, to know when the moon will be small or early set." To cover her embarrassment, she reached for her burlap shift and slipped it on.

Smit watched her movements and shook his head. "In all my travels, Madam, I have never met a woman such as you."

"Am I the only one, then?" Mary tried to sound a playful note, but his reply mattered to her, as he must have guessed it would.

"Most surely, Mary Bryant. The only one."

He walked her across the deck, as he always did. When they reached the railing where the rope ladder was tied, he said, "You will find provisions in the boat, along with a musket and ammunition, well-wrapped against the wet."

She was astonished by his generosity, and by how completely he comprehended the plans she had not spoken openly of until this night. "I don't know how to shoot, Captain."

He smiled. "Perhaps someone less dangerous than you can find a use for it. Have you chosen a vessel?"

"I have," Mary confessed.

"And is it swift enough?"

"The swiftest in port, once yours has sailed."

Smit gazed across the harbour until his eyes came

to rest on a six-oar cutter, broad of beam and a good thirty feet long. "The Governor's own boat?" he exclaimed incredulously.

Her cool smile told him he had guessed correctly.

"Madam, Madam!" He shook his head. "A man with your qualities would be an admiral. Or a buccaneer."

Smit might have forced one of his hard scratchy-whiskered kisses on her then, as he often did at their parting. But on this last night he only raised his hand in an oddly military salute and said, "Godspeed, Mary Bryant."

She caught the hand as it fell, and used it to wipe her tears. "Godspeed, my Captain."

⊕

As she approached the shore, Will waded out, grasped the rowboat's line, and fastened it to his fishing boat. Mary handed over six bags of provisions.

"Damn me," he muttered, "if he's not given you everything but the boat itself!"

"We have a boat," Mary whispered back.

Will stared at her. She pointed to the cutter, tied a short distance down the beach. "There's but one thing to be done, and that's to find a crew, for we cannot sail her alone."

Will made no reply, nor had Mary expected one. She had yet to see him plan for anything that required thinking more than one step ahead. She revealed to him her plan to take the Governor's boat only because it was now necessary for him to think that one step ahead, and to help recruit a crew.

By the time they were in the hut, Will's mind had travelled in the general direction she wanted it to go. "My fishing mates," he whispered, as they crouched together, stuffing the things Mary had acquired into a hole he had hollowed out beneath their bed. "They're strong at rowing and accustomed to long hours on the water. And Cox, for he's got tools to make repairs along the way."

"Yes," Mary agreed, as she covered the opening of their hiding place with poles. "Cox and your mates, except for Matey."

"Leave Matey?" Will exclaimed. "A foolish thing that would be. Why, Matey's the best boatman of the lot!"

"He's a drunk," Mary said flatly, not voicing her greater concern, which was that Matey had a knack for inciting Will to drink with him.

"Matey's a lifer," Will pointed out. "It'd be cruel to leave him."

"A life sentence is too good for a man caught red-handed luring ships onto the rocks. Scavenging is one thing; drowning folks for profit is something else," Mary said vehemently.

"Getting a little priggish there, my girl," Will sneered. "Anyway, even with Matey, there's room for one more. Johnny? He's a lifer, too."

Mary rocked back on her heels and thought it over. "Johnny's a good man, for all he's a cripple. But he'll not come without Colleen, nor would I ask him to make such a choice. Leave Matey behind and we can bring both of them."

As she spoke, Mary knew that this was unwise. Johnny, besides being crippled, worked in the carpentry shop, so had neither the strength nor the rowing skills of the men on Will's crew. Even Pip, youngest and smallest of the crew, would be more useful.

And then there was Colleen. It was time for her baby to be born, but the exact day could not be foretold, nor how difficult might be the birthing. The night of their bolting was equally uncertain. If a storm blew in, it could delay the departure of the *Waaksamheyd*, and their departure would have to be delayed as well. What if the child was newly birthed, or born in the boat a few days out? Colleen might even be locked in labour at the very hour best for sailing! One thing was certain: Colleen could not pull her weight, even if she and the infant managed to survive conditions so raw, and perils that were sure to come their way.

Both Mary and Will were silent for a moment, as they heaped dry grass and leaves over the poles which covered their cache of provisions. When it again had the appearance of what passed for a bed in the colony, Will rose. "I will not leave Matey behind. And that, Madam, is that."

"Very well." Mary rose and faced him. "I ask only that you do not speak to him of it until the very day. For when Matey drinks he blabs, and his tongue can hang us all."

"And what shall be that day?" Will asked.

"Let us wait and see," Mary equivocated. "Tell them to be ready, and we will see."

"And the last passenger?"

"James Brown."

Will's mouth dropped open in surprise. "The Canadian? Are you daft, woman? Why, he's naught but a clerk!"

"He has keys to the government storeroom," Mary retorted. "Where else do you suppose we'll find provisions to feed eleven mouths on a voyage of so many months?"

Will turned and left the hut. He had not given assent, but Mary knew she had won her point. She looked longingly at their pathetic bed of grass and leaves, for she had not slept an hour that night and could easily have dozed all day. But there was already a streak of grey in the sky. It was time to build a fire, cook breakfast for Will, then make gruel for Charlotte and give Emanuel her breast. After that, and before the sun grew too blazing hot, there was the garden to tend, wood to gather, rations to claim, and the evening meal to make.

Also, between Will's leaving and the children's waking, there was the water to fetch. She had seen James almost daily since their conversation, along the path to the stream. Their eyes spoke volumes to one another, but no words beyond brief and proper greetings had been exchanged. This morning, though, she would put the proposition to him.

Mary was always the first to draw water from the

stream, for few had reason to rise so early, nor much desire, given how many in the colony were prone to pass part of the night in drunkenness. She filled the heavy pails, then walked back toward her hut, pausing where she usually stopped to rest, on a rise which gave a view out to sea. She had not waited long before James appeared. "Good morning, Mrs. Bryant," he said with his usual formality.

"Good morning, Mr. Brown," she said, matching his formal tone. But instead of dropping her eyes as she normally did, she put out her hand to touch his arm. That stopped him in his tracks. She tried to speak, but the words caught in her throat. James was highly regarded in government circles. The risk she took in revealing their plans to him was great. She trusted him implicitly, but could it be that the completeness with which she gave that trust was a sign of her own foolishness?

"There is something you wish to ask me?"

Mary nodded, still mute.

He waited, and when he saw that she could not speak her mind, he said, "There is a question I have for you as well. Something personal."

"Please!" she said, relieved to have a moment of respite from the fear generated by her self-doubt. Her blue eyes searched his brown ones. She saw that what he wanted to ask was of great importance to him. "Ask what you will," she encouraged, "and I will answer you truly."

He stared into her eyes a moment longer, then posed his question. "On the ship coming over, you never gave Will Bryant the time of day. Yet you chose him over me. I have often wondered why."

Mary looked at him in surprise. "Do you not know? Will and I are here for crimes we committed; we're of the same class. But you—you're no criminal, James! Educated as you are, why, we're no match, you and I!"

James sighed and shook his head. "Mary, Mary! If you think we're no match only for the reasons you give, then you have done us both a great wrong."

"In what way?" She was puzzled, for she had only voiced the obvious.

"It is not education that counts, or even intelligence, but the nature of one's mind. Early in our voyage, I perceived you as a woman apart, whose actions were never frivolous, but always thoughtful. Are we not alike in this?"

Never had a man looked so deep into her and no one, with the exception of her now-dead mother, had ever recognised her propensity to thought. It was as if he had unveiled her innermost way of being, measured it against himself, and found it not to be less.

Mary's response, barely audible, was choked with emotion. "'Tis a pity you did not speak to me thus before we reached Botany Bay."

"You gave me no encouragement," he reminded her with a trace of bitterness.

"How was I to know?" she whispered.

James lapsed into hopeless silence and looked away, at the harbour view she herself often sought for solace. At last he said, "A while back you asked about my sentence. Why?"

"I was wondering . . . if a group was preparing to bolt, and asked you to join, what would you say?"

"If you were among them, I would say count me in."

"I am. As are my husband and my children."

He looked her full in the face and not only in the face, but taking in all of her, surface and what lay beneath; a woman exposed, perhaps not even to herself, but taken in by him.

"There are certain things . . . the smell of a pine forest, the music of a violin, the flight of a bird . . . one can love without possessing."

"Certain things, yes," Mary agreed, loving the romanticism of his remark but thinking it more than a little foolish. "But can a man feel thus about a woman?"

"Perhaps. Once in a lifetime."

It was as if each of the phrases he uttered opened a little wider some door into himself, until now, with his heart wide open, Mary saw the full extent of her loss. Tears filled her eyes. Then she blinked back those tears and looked away. Nothing could destroy her well-laid plans quicker than allowing herself to dwell on the mistakes of the past and on what might have been. Such thoughts would only clutter her mind and cloud her judgment. For that reason she permitted no response or show of emotion to his declaration of love.

James waited a moment for her reaction and, when there was none that he could see, he asked, "Does your husband know I am being ask to bolt with you?"

"Yes."

"Then it is settled."

Contained again, dry of eye and cool of voice, she said, "We shall be nine, eleven with the children. Some supplies we have, but not enough."

"And the time?"

"On the tide that follows the sailing of the *Waaksam-heyd*, if no storm is brewing and the night be black enough."

"A fair plan," he said. "I shall await your notice."

Later, when Mary was back at the hut nursing the baby, she recalled the conversation. It came to her then that James had asked nothing about how they intended to accomplish what was planned; what they meant to use for a boat, whether they had a compass or chart; indeed, even if they had those things, who in the group knew how to use them. For all James knew, she might be luring him into a mad adventure that was doomed from the start. Yet he trusted her—or loved her—enough to say yes with no reassurance as to practical matters. The only thing that seemed to matter was that she wanted him with her.

She had told Will only a partial truth when she said she wanted James along because he had access to government stores. She wanted him with her because she knew, had always known, that he was a man she could trust. What she now knew was that he trusted her as much.

The danger came, as danger so often does, from a direction least expected. Mary was on her hands and knees in the garden, pulling weeds and looking for any vegetables that might be harvested to add flavour to the evening broth, or dried to carry with them, when Colleen came flying up the path. Mary saw at once that Colleen was in a state. Her eyes were as wild as her long red hair, and her belly, now great with child, heaved in an alarming way.

"Colleen!" Mary cried. "Are you—?"

"You bitch!" Colleen screamed. "And you call yourself a friend!"

Mary's mouth dropped open, but before a word could come out, Colleen had hold of her shoulders and was shaking her like an empty sack. "Was it not I who wiped your brow the night they brought you in? Does it count for nothing that I am Charlotte's godmother and we treat her as our own? What is this coldness in you, Mary, that you can think of leaving us behind?"

Her fierceness terrified Mary, for it gave a glimpse of the freedom fighter Colleen once had been, and an Irish temper that captivity had not diminished. Mary steadied her voice, if not her pounding heart, and tried to sound reasonable. "Come, Colleen. Do you want this baby or not? No newborn could survive such hardships as every bolter faces."

Colleen let go of Mary's shoulders then and held out her hands in supplication. "Then take Johnny. Please, Mary! I beg you!"

Mary wiped sweat from her forehead, her earth-soiled fingers leaving a trail of dirt in the roots of her hair. "You know Johnny would never leave without you!"

"I'll force him to go! Johnny's got a life sentence! I've got but eight years more. If he got away, he could be waiting for me over there! We could start all over again!"

"There's no room, Colleen. Not on this voyage."

Colleen must have heard in Mary's voice a determination that matched her own, because for a moment she seemed at a loss for words. Then she reached out and grasped a handful of Mary's hair close to the scalp. Mary felt as if it was being pulled out by the roots. Colleen drew her forward until their faces were only inches apart, and hissed, "You'll not go without him. I shall see to that."

Then she turned and left by the way she had come.

That night, Mary said nothing to Will of what had transpired, but neither could she sleep. She longed to slip away to the *Waaksamheyd*, eat a hearty meal, then lie in Captain Smit's great bed and pay the price he asked for passage, hers alone, away from this hellish place. She tried to weigh the risk of making one last trip out to the Dutch ship to save herself, against the risk of waiting to see what Colleen would do. If the woman held her tongue they might get away. But if she carried out her threat to inform—and that, of course, was what it was—all of them were doomed.

In the end, it was not how the risks balanced against each other that caused Mary to stay the course. It was the responsibility she felt for the children who slept soundly beside her, and one other who had never shared her bed, but who trusted her just as much.

As heavy as the fear was Mary's sadness at having

lost the friendship of the one woman in all of Botany Bay whom she truly admired. It was, after all, Colleen's determination to keep Johnny alive that had shown Mary what power a woman can have when she sets her mind to a task. When Mary declared to Dr. White, "My daughter shall not starve," who was she emulating but Colleen? Had she not proven herself to be just as strong? But now? What would happen when their two wills clashed, the one as driven as the other?

The following day, walking to the centre of the settlement, Mary did not follow the path that led past Cox's workshop, for next to it was Colleen and Johnny's hut. Normally, she would have stopped there to rest and visit. But now, knowing she would not be welcome, she took a less-used trail that ran along the back.

She was just a little past the workshop when she looked back and saw that Charlotte was no longer meandering behind but had turned aside, her attention captured by the activity of some insect or another. Mary walked back to get her rather than calling out, because she could hear voices inside the shop, and did not want to draw attention to the fact that she had chosen to go by the back way.

As she retraced her steps to get Charlotte, the voices from the shop became more distinct. Cox was saying, "This here plane's come to fit your hand better than mine, John-boy. I want you to have it."

And Johnny's reply, short and bitter, "You don't have to buy my silence."

"If there'd been room for one more—," Cox began, but Johnny cut him off.

"The fisher-boys would have picked an Irishman? Not bloody likely!"

"'Twas Mary's choice who'd go," Cox protested.

At the mention of her name, Mary gave up pretending that she wasn't trying to hear the conversation. Johnny replied, quick enough. "So my wife says."

"And Florie tells me that wife of yours is scheming to inform on us. If you let her."

And Johnny's retort: "Something you wouldn't know, Cox. Back in Ireland 'twas Colleen who headed up our bunch. No man living ever told that lass what to do."

Cox voiced exactly the question that popped into Mary's mind. "Then how come you got transported for life, and her only ten years?"

"They wouldn't believe the deeds we done was led by a woman. The judge had it in his mind she was just a doxy. She would have gone scot-free if she'd been willing to name the ones that wasn't caught."

"You're saying she won't inform?"

"I'm saying Colleen will do what she bloody well pleases. She always did."

There was then the sound of other voices coming into the shop. Mary took Charlotte by the hand and led her onward in the direction they had been going.

So Johnny knew, as well as Colleen. Mary had surmised as much, and worried afresh. But what she heard in the settlement next day brought a surge of fear, and certain dread that they would never make it out of Botany Bay. It was from Dr. White that she got the news.

"Mary!" he called sharply as she passed by his surgery. She moved toward the door with the children, but he pushed Charlotte back outside and bade her wait for her mother there. Once the door was shut he wasted no time telling Mary what mischief was afoot. In a low voice, he said, "It is known that Will's crew is planning to bolt."

So, Mary thought, Colleen has informed already. But why had the authorities not come to search their hut and seize the provisions secreted there?

Mary tried to affect a laugh. "Will Bryant bolt? And leave behind his wife and children? Why, his sentence is practically up!"

"It's not known if Will is in on it," White admitted. "Matey was heard bragging about it to some others. Fool that he is, he implied he was the ringleader. But when the authorities searched his hut they found nothing. He whined and said it was only liquor talking; that every convict in the colony harbours such a fantasy, with no means or intention of realising it."

"So what has that to do with us?" Mary asked, feigning annoyance to cover her fright. "I grant you my husband spends more time drinking with that scum than—."

"That is precisely what it has to do with you," White snapped. "No one in authority is fool enough to believe that any besides Bryant is smart enough to organise this thing. So the lot of them are being watched. None more closely than your husband."

Mary tried but failed to smile. All that came out was a shaky, "Thank you, Dr. White. I shall see to it that, come nightfall, my husband is at home, with nothing more incriminating in his arms than this child I hold, or that one playing out in the yard."

Mary had known from the start that secrecy was the key to success, and had likewise known that with so many in on the plan, secrecy was nearly impossible. Now there was Colleen shouting in her face, Johnny speaking of it in the shop, Matey bragging about it to other convicts, and even the authorities alerted that something was afoot. Who in the colony *didn't* know?

A short time later, Mary stood in line with the others and collected the day's ration of food from James. He must have noticed her paleness, for he took a second look at her face, and his own showed concern. Of course they could not speak, not till tomorrow morning when she and he went for water. By that time they might already have been seized. As things stood, the only flicker of comfort she could take in the situation was that no one, not even Will, knew she had actually invited James, and that he had agreed to join them.

In that desolate state of mind, Mary stumbled in the direction of home, following Charlotte, who ran ahead on their usual path. Up ahead, Mary saw Colleen seated on a bench in her tiny garden. Florie was approaching along the path from the opposite direction.

Florie waved at Mary, and turned into the garden.

"Hey, Colleen," she spoke in a wheedling tone. "Might you have a nip of rum about?"

Colleen, the one who was always laughing, singing, and inviting neighbours to come sit a spell, now leaned back against the wall of her hut, great belly protruding, and snapped, "What do you need more for, when you're so sotted you never know half of what's going on?"

Florie ignored the insult and seated herself on the bench on the opposite side of the doorway. "I know my Coxie's leaving," she said sadly. "Are you going to see he's brought back and hanged?"

"They've got no right to take Cox and leave Johnny behind!" Colleen barked.

"Johnny's not the man he used to be, Colleen. But he's man enough to stand by you. That's more than I can say for Coxie."

Colleen tossed her head. "I don't want Johnny standing by! I want him on that boat and myself as well, or the lot of them can hang!" She glanced in Mary's direction, letting her know she had seen her coming, and meant for her to hear.

Mary walked steadily toward her, for in her mind, they were as good as caught already. It was what Florie said next that caused her eyes to widen in amazement.

"Sad it is to think of what a child is going to suffer in this colony, with all knowing his dear old mum curried favour with the authorities by informing on her friends."

Colleen gasped. "Who would tell such a thing?"

Florie turned her thin hands palms up in a gesture of helplessness. "Why, Colleen, you say yourself how my tongue wags at both ends when I drink."

"Florie, you are a pig!" Colleen shouted.

"So Coxie says. But he hardly ever hits me," Florie said complacently. Then she called out to Cass, who was striding toward them, "Hey Cass, come sit a spell."

"What, Johnny's got two women doing for him, and needs a third?" Cass jibed in her rough mannish voice.

"No, it's Colleen," Florie drawled. "She's looking for a way to lose her baby, and die in childbed, and see Johnny hanged for bolting."

Cass leered into Colleen's face. "Smells like murder to me," she cackled. "A nice game murder is, for them that's not afraid to burn in Hell."

"Witch!" Colleen muttered, but said no more, for just then Charlotte dashed into the yard. The child clambered onto the bench next to Colleen, caught her face in her hands, and turned it to her own for a kiss.

Mary had not thought of what she would say to Colleen. All that came to mind as she stood before the hugely pregnant Irish woman, was, "I do what I must, Colleen. And so must you."

"I shall," Colleen said coldly. "Now take you off to talk to Cass and Florie, and give me some time with my little Charlotte, whose life means more to me than yours."

Mary moved to the other side of the yard and sat down with Cass and Florie. She had no notion what Colleen might do and, at this point, felt that it hardly mattered. By the others' worried looks, she could tell that they thought the plan doomed to failure as well.

"You'll not catch me out on that wretched ocean again," Cass stated flatly. "I'd not endure another crossing if they gave me free passage back to England."

"Free passage indeed!" Florie scoffed. "The only thing that comes free in this miserable place is misery itself."

Cass nodded, and muttered under her breath to Florie and Mary, "She'll feel a lot better, our Colleen will, once the brat pops out. If she hasn't gone and killed her friends by then."

The three sat quietly then, listening to Colleen's clear alto voice raised in song. The lyrics spoke of the one thing they, who had lost so much, still had left to lose, that being hope itself.

As Will was about to leave for work next morning, Mary said, "If the *Waaksamheyd* sails out of the harbour today, as I expect it will, come directly home when your work is done. Tell the others to come here as soon as it is black dark, bringing with them such provisions as they can muster."

"Tonight?" Will asked with some surprise. "I thought we'd linger a few days, till the Dutch ship is far gone."

"We have no time to linger," Mary said shortly.

When Will had gone off down the path to the harbour, Mary took her water pails and went to the stream. On the return she paused to wait in the usual place, on the rise that gave a view out over the harbour. When she saw that the *Waaksamheyd* had already weighed anchor and was moving toward the narrow neck of the bay, Mary had trouble holding back her tears. Smit was not a man she had loved, but he had been more than a friend. He had offered her two chances at freedom; one on his terms and one on hers. The first was lost forever. Whether she could grasp the second would be known by tomorrow's dawn.

"Mary?" James's hand curved lightly around her waist. "Are you alright?"

She turned to him. There were still tears in her eyes, which she did not try to explain. All she said was, "Will and his crew are being closely watched. The risk is greater now than when I spoke to you before. You've no need to throw in your lot with us, for I have revealed to no one that you consented to come. Draw back now and none will be the wiser."

He studied her for a moment. "Tell me I'm not welcome and I shan't come."

"That would be a lie. What I do not welcome is the thought of your death on my conscience, along with all the others, if we are caught."

He gave a slight squeeze, so that she noticed for the first time the intimate place his hand rested. "I am man enough to be responsible for what I do. Come Hell or high water—and I expect we'll face some of both—my decision to go with you is altogether my own."

"At dark, then," she said, and picked up her pails of water. "With what provisions you can lay hands on."

He might have kissed her then; she would not have resisted. But he must have sensed the absence of desire, for he did not, and she was grateful. She could not have explained that the absence of passion had nothing to do with him. It was that these past days of ever-rising fear, the quarrel with Colleen, and the departure of Smit, taking with him the freedom that she now doubted she could win by her own design—these things had simply drained her.

The daylight hours were fraught with tension, as Mary went about her usual chores in a show of normalcy. Much of the time was spent in her garden where she harvested every edible thing, scrubbed soil off potatoes and turnips, and laid in what stores she could. Will returned at nightfall, and they ate in silence. Then darkness descended and there was nothing to do but wait. There was no clock tower in the settlement, and none among them had a timepiece; thus they had no way to set an exact hour for gathering. Each man must choose the time of least risk for leaving his hut and for hurrying to Will and Mary's hut.

After removing all the provisions they had collected from the hiding place under the bed, Mary put the children down to sleep as if it was a normal night. She and Will then bundled the supplies in preparation for transport to the beach.

Matey, with rum on his breath, was the first to arrive, Scrapper in his wake. Next came James, leaving some provisions and going back to get more. Luke and Bados appeared shortly thereafter, followed by Pip. Will sent Pip back out to stand watch a little distance up the trail. Pip had a piercing whistle. If anyone not of their group should approach, he was to whistle a warning.

As there was no back door to the hut, it was unsafe to wait inside. They crouched in the yard, fully aware that if a warning whistle came from Pip, there would be a scramble for the bushes and it would be every man for himself.

"What's taking Cox so long? And that Brown," Will muttered. He fingered a hatchet, freshly sharpened. "If the Canadian clerk turns out to be a snitch and has in mind to fetch the Rangers, I'll see he never lives to brag about it."

"Must you think such evil thoughts?" Mary scolded in a whisper. "You'd do better to feel gratitude for the provisions he has donated to our cause."

Will might have answered her back, but just then James, laden with all he could carry, slipped into the clearing. As he set down his load, Will asked, "Did you see anything of Cox?"

James squatted between Will and Mary and whispered, "Two Rangers are hanging about on the path in front of his shop. I don't think he can leave without being seen."

"Shall we go without him?" Will asked, in a low voice.

There was a babble of whispered opinions, most in favour of not risking a longer wait. But Mary said, "We have a fair bit of darkness left, more than enough to get down to the boat and out of the harbour before daylight. We will wait as long as we can."

They fell silent then, and waited.

At last the sound they were straining their ears for came: the footsteps of two people hurrying up the path. Cox burst into the clearing, followed close behind by Pip.

"Sorry, mates," Cox gasped. "My tools was still in the shop, and I was loath to come without them. I thought them bloody Rangers was never going to go on by."

Everyone leapt to their feet and scrambled madly to get their provisions together, on their backs or in their arms. "Follow Will," Mary instructed, lest they assume they would be taking the fishing boat and throw their things in it. Will was the only one—she hoped—who knew that it was the Governor's cutter they intended to use for their getaway.

As the others plunged down the trail leading to the beach, Mary stepped inside the hut and took the two sleeping children in her arms. Emanuel, just a little shy of his first birthday, was no weight at all to lift. Charlotte, although she was three-and-a-half, was a slight child, too, whom Mary could easily rest on the other hip. Apart from the children, all she carried were the chart and quadrant; those two things and one more she trusted to no one else. The leather tobacco pouch which Smit had given her for bringing tidbits of food to Charlotte, hung about her neck. In it was the compass.

When Mary reached the beach, the others were already at the cutter, some handing provisions in, others trying to stow them in such a way as to leave space for men at the oars. Mary laid the chart and quadrant on a rock to protect them from the wet, then waded into the water and passed the children up to Will. Then she returned for the navigational instruments.

Just as she bent to pick them up, a figure burst out of the bushes, followed closely by a second, taller one. The shape of the first, as it turned sideways for an instant to speak to the one behind, revealed itself as Colleen. For one heart-stopping instant Mary believed Colleen was as good as her word and had led the sentry to them. Then they were upon her, and she saw that the taller one was Johnny.

"Mary!" Colleen whispered urgently, and grasped Mary about the waist with a hug that pushed the breath out of her lungs. "Here, take this!" She thrust a packet into Mary's hand. "Sweet tea! 'Tis the only gift I have."

Mary all but collapsed with relief onto her friend's ample bosom and belly. "Colleen, you've given me a gift more precious than this! The love of the sister you are to me, the only one I've ever had."

Then Will was at Mary's side, tugging on her arm, and Johnny took hold of Colleen. Being drawn in opposite directions, they nearly pulled each other off balance before it came to them that they must let go.

Mary ran down to the water and, with chart and quadrant held above her head to keep them from getting splashed, waded out to the boat. It was hard to find space in the cutter, so cluttered was it with provisions which had been thrown aboard helter-skelter. Scrapper and Pip, being the smallest, sat at the first set of oars. Next came Bados and Luke, with Matey behind them, the seat next to him reserved for Will. Cox and James would ride in the stern until they were well away. Later, when there was time, they would be trained on the oars.

Mary was taken up into the bow of the boat next to where the children had been bedded down, and Will took his place next to Matey at the back. The men gave their all to the oars, with not a word spoken. That had been agreed upon before, for the neck of the harbour was narrow, and it was said that the sentries never slept. It must be approaching midnight, Mary calculated, but she could not be sure. The sky was overcast, making the night very black. Only faintly could they make out the deeper blackness of rocks that lined the neck of the harbour.

Then the first swell of the open ocean lifted the cutter and they sailed into the vastness as silently as a bird takes to the sky.

3

Freedom

The Coral Sea

So great was their fear of discovery that silence reigned even after they were past the neck of the harbour and far out to sea. The men at the oars pulled hard, with little conversation beyond an occasional murmur. They kept their ears tuned to the sounds of the surf because, on this moonless night, it was hard to discern exactly how far they were from shore. All were relieved when dawn greyed the sky and the outline of the land and its rocky points were clearly visible.

It was Will who finally broke their self-imposed silence by announcing, "Come broad day, we'll start looking for a harbour to put in and rest."

Mary, who had curled up in the bow next to the sleeping children, raised her head and called back to him, "Better we row on through the day and not stop until nightfall. If no safe place be found then, we should go on through another night."

A mild grumble went up from the men, and Will opened his mouth to contradict her. But before he could speak, Mary rose and said to the group at large, "Or have you forgotten how many bolters were caught on their first or second day out and brought back to hang? All because they stopped to rest, and the mariners, who well know the region around the settlement, were able to overtake them?"

Will's mouth closed in a grim line. Mary unrolled the chart and studied it. Taking the compass from the leather tobacco pouch, she turned to the sea and set a course. Except for when she was tending to the children, she remained thus throughout the daylight hours, and would do so for many days to come. Although she faced away from the men as she pointed out the direction they were to go, they were not even one day out when she began to feel the respect her knowledge of navigation inspired in them.

She likewise felt her husband's coldness toward her and realised her error in countermanding his order. The crew had a great liking for him, and respected him for his boating skills. It would not do to be at odds with him, not when they needed every scrap of ability each of them had if this reckless adventure was to succeed.

Turning from her vigil in the bow of the boat to nurse Emanuel, Mary covertly studied the men. At the back sat bandy-legged Matey; next to him, Scrapper, one cheek disfigured by a knife scar so close to the eye that one wondered that he had not been blinded in that particular altercation. Scrapper practically lived in Matey's shadow, either for the protection the older man afforded him, or because there was, between them, a genuine bond of affection. Mary had no liking for either, but watching the strong and perfect harmony with which they rowed, she saw Will's wisdom in insisting that both be brought along.

The centre seat was occupied by Luke and Cox. Luke's freckled face was creased by a grin as he endeavoured to teach the carpenter to handle the oars. "It's the hat," Luke teased, pointing to the rag Mary had hung over Cox's bald pate to protect it from the blazing sun. "Too bad we ne'er thought to swipe Old Phillip's topper. What with a brain so blistered, you keep forgettin' it's an oar and not a hammer you're swinging."

"You got enough hair for both of us there," Cox shot back, casting a glance at Luke's reddish, shoulder-length strands, banded back with a twist of rope. "Whyn't you chop off the bottom half and hang it over my poor fried dome?"

As Luke trained the carpenter, Will, seated on the foremost bench, instructed James, who sat beside him. The two were about the same size, just under six feet tall. But in other respects they differed greatly. Will's deeply tanned torso rippled with muscle, while James's office job had rendered him so pale that he dared not remove his shirt for fear that the sunburn beginning to redden his face would spread fire across his upper body.

When James lifted a hand to wipe sweat from his

brow, Mary saw that his palm was raw with broken blisters. The bleeding hand returned to the oar and James continued to pull without complaint. Will must have seen the hand as well, but showed no sympathy. He needled James by reminding him that all his book learning and jiggling of numbers were now the most useless of skills. "A fine burden you'll be till you learn to pull your weight," Will gloated. "If'n you ever do." And a few minutes later, "Now didn't I tell you don't do like that? You keep making a mess of it, don't expect me to stop these other boys from flinging you over the side."

Not at the oars just then were Bados and Pip. They were engaged in hoisting the cutter's single sail. They did so efficiently, Bados' being the biggest man in the group, and experienced at sail-rigging. Pip, although small, was nimble of body and quick to follow Bados's instructions. This last, Mary noticed, was not something others on Will's crew would do. Mary surmised that Will had observed as much and that was why, when there was a job requiring two men, he regularly teamed Bados with the boy. In this way he could make use of the black man's abilities without evoking the kind of dissent that might have occurred had he tried to put Bados in charge of a white man on his crew.

As Mary took stock of her companions, her main concern was their thinness. She had gained a little weight during the three months of occasional feasts at Smit's table, but the others had not had that advantage, and the years of malnutrition had pared them to the bone. Of all the disasters that might befall them, the one Mary dreaded most was the thought of slow starvation.

She had known at the outset that they would likely be sailing for at least one night and day, and maybe a second one as well, depending on how far they travelled and where they found to come ashore and rest. A river mouth was the most desirable, for they would need fresh water soon. Despite the necessity of conserving supplies for the long journey ahead, with uncertain sources of food along the way, she had prepared balls of rice and beans and baked potatoes that could be eaten by hand as they travelled. She thought it unwise to have the men weaken at the outset, when survival depended on putting as much distance as possible between themselves and any parties sent out to fetch them back.

A little after midday, she held up a tidbit of food and motioned Will to come forward to have a word in private. He hesitated a moment, then called for Bados to take his oar.

When Will came to her, Mary asked in a low voice, "Do you think the governor has sent a boat after us?" She handed him the bite, and waited to get the answer she expected.

"Sure he'll be fool enough to do that," Will chuckled. "Useless though it be, when we've got the swiftest boat in the colony and my men at the oars. There's not one among the mariners who can match the least of my crew when it comes to rowing!"

"Yet if he sends a party overland by some shorter

way, might not they be lying in wait for us at some likely river's mouth?"

Will considered this possibility a moment, then as Mary had expected, nodded assent. For he was not stupid, her husband. It was simply his disinclination to think a thing through. Mary saw that this gap in his thinking was hers to mend, and sooner rather than later. If she waited too long and then showed herself to be at odds with his decision, as had happened this morning on the issue of whether they should take the first river mouth they came to or continue rowing through the day, conflict was sure to follow.

Thus, early in the afternoon, she planted in Will a good reason for continuing through a second night, and waited to see if it would take root. As it happened, two things occurred which supported what she knew to be the safest course. First, no good landing place presented itself, in part because she had charted a course due north. This put them some distance out from the shore, which curved to the west just above the neck of the Sydney Cove. Second, as the sun dipped closer to the horizon, the wind came up and blew in such a way that they were able to use the sail and give the men a rest from rowing. Thus, when Will informed them that they would continue on through the night, and begin at daybreak to skirt the coast in search of a river mouth where they could take a good long rest, all could see that this was a right decision—and not see that Mary had any hand in it.

They could hardly have been luckier in their choice of

a place to put ashore than the small river where they harboured late on their second day out—this after more than forty hours of rowing and sailing. They encountered no natives who might have objected to their landing, and they were able to help themselves to what the area offered, which was, in fact, an abundance of many foods which they already knew and valued.

Will sent two men down to collect shellfish, and took three others with him to cast the net for fish. Mary asked Cox to chop a cabbage palm and peel it, layer by layer, down to its delicate, edible heart. James she directed to gather wood and build a fire, for however limited his other skills, this was something any man would know. Then she asked him to pick leaves from sarsaparilla creepers among the rocks, these being familiar to all in the colony for the sweet tea they yielded.

By the time Will and his men returned, two kettles boiled, one for tea and a second one, with a handful of rice and a little salt thrown in, awaiting the fish that they brought back. Mary handed each man a bowl of tea to hold them while the stew simmered to readiness.

Mary used her own tea time to nurse Emanuel, then went to check on Charlotte. The three-year-old sat near Bados, who was showing her how to draw designs in the sand.

Luke, sprawled on the ground nearby, peered at Bados's sand drawing and asked, "What's that supposed to be?"

"A palm tree like grows back home, in Barbados," Bados explained.

"Barbados, eh? I heard tell it's a pretty isle." Luke clicked his tongue in sympathy. "Bet you're sorry you ever set foot in England. What got you transported?"

"Cucumbers," the black man replied.

"What's 'cumbers?" Charlotte wanted to know.

Bados made a rough sketch in the sand. "Looks like a fat green stick, and good to eat. Stole seven of 'em from a kitchen garden. A year I got for every one."

Luke sighed. "Nothing I've missed like fresh vegetables. Last good meal I had was a big vegetable stew with a couple of poached rabbits tossed in."

"You got transported for poaching?" Mary asked in surprise.

Luke grinned. "More because I riled the gamekeeper. But he riled me first."

"How's that?" Bados asked.

"He caught me with the rabbits fair and square. Said he wouldn't turn me in, but was gonna keep my rabbits. It was him standing there, fat as a squire's hog, saying how much he was gonna enjoy them rabbits roasted. And me fair hungry, with two kids at home who hadn't had a scrap of meat for weeks. Got me in such a rage I knocked his block off and took me rabbits home to the wife. Was just finishing the meal when he come with the law."

They all laughed at Luke's audacity, if not at the outcome. Their talk of food reminded Mary of how hungry everyone was. She laid Emanuel down to nap on a scrap of canvas in the shade, told Charlotte to sit beside him, and set about ladling bowls of stew.

Once and twice over, Mary filled the bowls, with

the men allowing as how it was the finest meal they had ever eaten. Mary felt deeply satisfied, and not only from the food. The ingredients in the stew had been commonplace in the colony, if never so plentiful as this. The richness they tasted—she knew, for she tasted it, too—was the flavour of freedom.

She was about to refill her own soup bowl when she noticed that one filled previously still remained. She looked about to see who might be missing.

"Where's Cox?" she asked.

"Yonder," Will said, jerking his chin toward the shore.

Mary saw him sitting on a rock, bald head slumped on his chest like a man condemned to die. She picked up his bowl of fish stew and walked down to where he was.

"Are you not hungry?" Mary asked, supposing that his sunburn had given him a fever.

Cox shook his head, and made no move to take the bowl she held out to him.

"What is it, Coxie?"

He let out a sigh which was more like a groan. "'Twas bad of me to leave like that, Mary, without a word to Florie, no goodbye nor nothing."

"She knew you were going, Coxie. I know she did."

"Don't that make it even worse? Her sitting there sad as a whipped puppy, waiting for me to do whatever I was gonna do. Florie's mind's been fuzzy, you know, ever since that first night the women came ashore. I was the fifth or sixth bloke on her, and I saw she was right off her head."

"That's two years past, Coxie, and you did look out for her all the time since," Mary reminded him gently.

Cox choked on a sob. "But who's looking out for my Florie now?"

"Come, have some stew," Mary urged. "When you get to England you can write to her."

"Yes, damn me, that I'll do. Florie would like that," Cox conceded, and did not resist when Mary lifted his big paw and placed the bowl of stew in it.

They stayed in that place two days, long enough to dry fish to add to their provisions, and to stow the supplies in a more orderly fashion. Then they sailed two days more, and again went ashore. The second spot they chose for rest and replenishment was even more pleasant than the first. Just a little way back from the beach, they found a shady glade and a place where the river formed itself into a pool, ideal for fishing and bathing.

"'Tis fitting," Mary told Will with a smile, "that your son should celebrate his first birthday in such a perfect place."

"Aye." Will took the baby from her and tossed him aloft, to Mary's consternation and to the child's delight. "Had we a bottle of rum, we'd toast you in style, my boy!"

Mary for her part thanked all the stars in the firmament that there was no rum to be had. Nor could she understand, when she watched the group take its ease after another plentiful meal gathered from their surroundings, what Will and his companions felt might be added by inebriation. Back in Botany Bay, yes, she could easily understand why one might wish to drink oneself into a forgetful stupor. But in an Eden such as this?

Looking about, it was hard not to compare this place to the colony, and to feel that in less than a week they had travelled from Purgatory to Paradise. Music from Bados's flute floated on the air. James sat with his back against a tree, writing in his journal. Matey was at work repairing a sail, while Scrapper mended a hole in the fishing net—until Luke challenged Cox to an arm-wrestling contest, and the others stopped to watch and cheer.

Mary wandered over to the fresh-water lagoon where Pip and Will were playing with the children. She sat down on the bank and dangled her feet in the cool, clear water. Will, with a mischievous glint in his eye, handed Emanuel to Pip. Grasping Mary by the ankles, he pulled her laughing into the water. This she would recall later as the one and only time they ever joined in play. And play they did, the children splashing around them, all through the hot afternoon of Emanuel's first birthday. Not till the sun went down did they drag themselves out and return to the fire, which James had kept burning, to feed the children again, and to help themselves to more of the plentiful stew.

Then each person curled up on whatever bedding they'd had the wits to bring and fell asleep, except for Bados, who stayed awake for a time, playing his flute.

Again they sailed a full day and straight through the

night. Mary stayed in the bow of the boat with the children, and used the compass to determine their north-westerly course. They followed the shore (but not too closely), slowed by a current which flowed in the opposite direction, but often aided by the wind, which let them make full use of the cutter's single sail.

Mary was always glad when dawn came and, compass in hand, she could determine that they were on course. But if dawn was a relief, the heat of the day, when the sun fell full on them, was not. During their first week out, both Cox and James, unaccustomed to working out of doors, suffered terribly from sunburn. At stops along the way, Mary gave them cooling poultices made of leaves and fat, but the burns already inflicted they could only endure. By the end of the second week they were as brown as the others; a fortunate thing for, as they travelled north, the intensity of the sun increased.

One late afternoon, they landed in a likely-looking cove and sighted, just beyond the trees where they had put ashore, a curl of smoke indicating a native encampment. Will took the musket, which was their only weapon, and the men approached cautiously, by twos, a little spread out. Mary waited with the children back at the boat, to see what the situation might be. It was only a couple of minutes before she heard Will shouting for her to come. With Emanuel in her arms and Charlotte by the hand, she made her way along a well-worn trail until she emerged in a clearing. There were a few crude huts and, in front of several of them, smouldering fires with meat roasting atop. But not a soul in sight.

"Is no one about?" Mary asked.

"None we've spied," Will told her. "What you see is what we seen when we got here."

Matey grabbed a hunk of meat off some aborigine's fire. "Looky here, boys! The wogs have laid on a party for us!" the old sailor chortled. He flipped the meat from hand to hand to cool, then set to gnawing it like a dog.

"Will, do you think—?" Mary was about to ask if he thought it was wise to go thieving from the natives, who might not have run away so far that they couldn't come back and attack. But it was already too late. Others were now doing as Matey had done, running from fire to fire, snatching up and squabbling over whatever was cooking there. Only James held back, along with Will, Mary, and the children. But he too must have realised that there was nothing to be done.

"Shall we camp here, then?" Mary asked. "Or back on the beach?"

Will squinted at the sky. "Here, I reckon. If it rains, we can shelter in these huts."

"Then I'll go back for the kettle and other needs," Mary said.

"You do that," Will said, and then, seeming to notice that she had a baby in one arm and a toddler clinging to her skirt, said, "You, James. Lend her a hand."

It would have been easier to leave the children there, but Mary sensed that it would not do for her to go alone with James, for if Will did not notice now, he might remember at some time in the future and hold it against her then. Thus she, James, and the children made their way back to the boat. They did not speak, nor did Mary feel it necessary.

James had said before, when commenting on how he had observed her mind at work, "Are we not alike in this?" She still felt a kind of amazement that he should have recognised the seriousness of her thoughts, and judged them to be in any way equal to his own. But there were moments such as this, as they walked in silence to the boat and back again, when she did indeed feel them to be joined in similar thoughts—or in this case, a similar foreboding.

At dusk a light rain began to fall, so they took shelter inside the crude huts. Mary suggested to Will that perhaps he should post a watch. He agreed to send Bados to sleep in the boat, but scoffed at the idea that a watch was needed in the camp.

"They ran like rabbits," he pointed out. "Scared plumb out of their wits. Probably never seen civilised folks before. They didn't attack us by day, sure and they'll not risk it by night." With that, he rolled over and fell asleep.

Mary said no more, but had Bados carry all of the cooking pots back to the boat rather than leave them lying about. Then she lay down inside a hut with her children and, uneasy though she was, soon fell asleep.

She woke sometime in the night. Through the doorway of the hut, she saw an aborigine woman soundlessly collecting things left behind. Other shadows flitted through the camp. Before Mary could make up her mind whether to awaken Will, they were gone.

Mary rose at dawn, for by then the weather was so warm that it was better to do whatever needed doing during the cool of the morning. Emanuel and Charlotte were awake as well, and James, when he heard her murmuring to the children, roused himself to collect wood and build a fire. Bados appeared soon thereafter, bringing the things she needed to make breakfast. The rest slept on. With no one to order them about, only the smell of cooking food would entice them to rise.

Mary had only taken the first johnnycake from the fire and handed it to Charlotte when she heard Scrapper shout. She looked up to see him dragging Pip violently from sleep by the hair of his head. "Who took my shirt? Were it you, twerp?"

"No, I swear!" Pip grabbed hold of Scrapper's hands and tried to disentangle them before the hair detached from his head.

Then a shout from Cox. "What the hell? My knife was in the log, right at my hand. I know; I felt it in the night. And now it's gone!"

James looked around sharply. "The abos must have come back for their stuff, and picked up a bit of ours in the bargain."

"They wouldn't have the nerve!" Matey retorted.

"I saw them," Mary said, holding out a johnnycake to her husband.

"Saw them?" Will snatched the food from her. "Why the hell didn't you wake us up?"

"They were many," she said quietly. "I thought it better they come and go in peace, for if they had set upon us, who knows what might have happened? We might have driven them off, but some of us, sleeping as we were, might have been wounded. I thought you would not want to risk that, when we're needing every man at the oars."

Will chewed on her words and on the johnnycake for a moment, then, as she went back to cooking, turned away. She heard him order the others to pack up, saying that they would not spend any more time in this blasted place, but would sail on.

That was not a decision Mary would have made, for she believed the aborigines desired conflict no more than she. Although there would have been some risk to remaining, she saw by the sky that a squall was coming, and thought it the greater risk. But by then they were on their way, as Will had commanded.

It soon began to rain, no longer the light drizzle it had been the night before, but hard now, accompanied by a rising wind. Mary forced the children to stay in the cramped but covered space under the bow of the boat, for, in a continuing rain such as this, she knew how quickly one could become chilled. Emanuel cried and Charlotte fretted but Mary was firm, only allowing them out when the baby needed to nurse, or Charlotte had to be held over the side to relieve her bladder and bowels. Then she dried them as best she could, and tucked them back into the covered bow. As the squall worsened they sailed close to shore, looking for a place to shelter. But it was a wild, rocky coast, and each time they approached, they saw it would be dangerous to attempt a landing. On the third such attempt, rocks loomed up so sudden and close that no one had to tell the crew to veer seaward.

But the sea, in this squall turned to gale, was hardly less threatening. The boat rose and plunged over range upon range of watery mountains. The men at the oars struggled to keep it headed into the waves, while the rest bailed for all they were worth.

The storm raged for nearly a week. The men rowed, fought the mountainous waves, and bailed out the water that poured in on top of them. Before the ordeal was half over, they had become like mechanised skeletons, barely able to lift the oars and keep up with the bailing.

It was on the morning of the seventh day that Mary awoke to sunshine glittering on a still-choppy sea. She took out the compass. The boat was drifting south. Now it was possible to set a course and sail, but who had the strength? The men lay collapsed over their oars or curled in the stern, sleeping the sleep of the utterly exhausted.

"Will!" she called out. "Luke! Scrapper! James! Come on, Coxie. Here, Matey. Pip? Would you row to your last breath, or die without trying?"

Of all the crew, Pip was the frailest, yet his eyes opened first. Responding to Mary's voice, he dragged himself up and took an oar in hand. One by one, five others moved to the oars. At Mary's direction, they brought the boat around and headed it in the north-westerly direction. Will and Matey set the sail, which allowed the men to spend more time recovering as the wind pushed the cutter forward.

After sailing northwest for a full day, and still no sighting of land, Mary realised that the storm had blown them far out to sea—how far, she could not calculate. She only knew that they must make landfall soon. Despite days of drenching rain, they had little water in reserve, for the simple reason that most of their containers were unlidded. Whatever fresh water they had collected had either been spilled or had been contaminated with salt water in the heavy surf. She lifted a slim brown arm and reset their course due west, hoping that they would strike land by the following day.

They did not sight land, not that day nor the next. From the chart and others Mary had studied in Smit's cabin, she knew that there was a point at which the eastern coast of the continent bulged out. Beyond the bulge, it angled toward the west. If they had been blown past that bulge then the distance to land was even further than she supposed. The coastline had been mapped by both Captain Cook and Dutch sailors before him. But the treacherous Coral Sea, which they must sail through to get there, was as yet uncharted.

Another day passed and still no sight of land. Beneath the light of a crescent moon, Mary picked up a whimpering Emanuel and put him to her breast. He nuzzled, sucked, and nuzzled. The whimper became a weak cry. Mary laid him back in the bow, knowing he would soon fall asleep.

A little while later, Will crawled forward and curled up against her.

With tears in her voice but not her eyes, for she was too dehydrated, Mary told her husband, "I have no milk."

Will clutched her hand, and laid his head on her breast. Perhaps she should have been comforted, but all she felt was one added burden. What she sensed in his embrace was not the strength of a man aiming to console but a frightened boy needing consolation. Perhaps the warmth of her body did console him, for he soon fell asleep. Mary did not sleep. How could she, when she knew that in the bow of the boat two emaciated children lay, not sleeping but dying?

Mary woke to find the children silent and men collapsed all along the length of the boat. She hardly felt it worthwhile to move herself. They had been out of sight of land nigh onto two weeks, she calculated, first with days of storm, followed by more days of endless blue sky and sea. However, after lying there a few minutes, she forced herself into a sitting position and scanned the horizon.

A speck? A speck! Could it be land?

"Land!" she cried hoarsely.

"Land?" Will whispered, staggering to his feet.

Suddenly the boat was alive with shouts of, "Land!" "Dear God!" "Land ahoy!"

There was a scramble for positions, and six oars smacked the water. With what strength each rower had left, he pulled for the saving shore.

The speck Mary had sighted proved to be not the mainland but a mere spit of sand. It supported a few scraggly bushes but, as far as they could see, no animal life at all. They paddled around the tiny island, seeking a break in the reef where they could ease the boat through into protected water. Once anchored, the men crawled out of the cutter and dragged themselves to shore.

The children lay crumpled in the bow and did not move. Will started to lift them out but Mary stopped him. "Leave them here where they have a bit of shade. I'll bring them out later, when we've found water and something to feed them."

Will staggered to shore and fell onto the sand alongside the others. Mary, barely able to stand herself, caught hold of him and urged him up. "Please, Will! Look for water!"

As he stumbled off to do her bidding, she went from one man to the next, pleading. "Matey, do you want to die of thirst? Get up and help Will search for water! Luke, go see if you can find some small animals to snare. Come on, Coxie, we need food. A bird's nest would be right handy. Bados, won't you throw out a line and see if you can catch some fish? Pip, Scrapper, be good lads and see what you can net. James, do find some driftwood and make a fire. We've a bit of rice left, and if water's to be had, there's soup at least."

One by one the men rose and began to stagger about the tiny island, so small that the whole of it could easily be viewed from end to end. James found enough driftwood to build a fire, but Mary was loath to use their last sips of fresh water to make the promised soup.

Will and Matey, who had circled the island in opposite directions and then criss-crossed it, returned with discouraging news. "There's not a drop of sweet water to be had."

"No cabbage palms, nor any other edible plant neither," Cox offered on his return.

"Not one of these bushes got a bird's nest in it," Luke announced gloomily.

"I saw some small bright fish, but they scooted away," Pip reported.

"I seen 'em, too," Scrapper added. "We got no net fine enough to catch them."

Suddenly there was a shout from Bados down on the beach. Heads turned to see him half in the water, half out, struggling with something. The men rushed to his aid and, in a few minutes, they returned carrying a turtle so large that it took both Bados and Will to lift it.

"Here you are, Mary," Bados grinned. "Work your magic!"

Will let go of his side of the turtle so suddenly that Bados, who was holding it by the opposite flipper, was almost jerked off balance.

"Since when do you call my wife by her given name?" Will snarled at the black man.

Bados dropped the turtle and walked away. The eyes of the men slid past Will uneasily. Then they did what men do: they turned their attention to the turtle to prevent its escape, and pretended the incident had never happened.

Mary handed Will a knife. "Catch the blood," she said coldly.

She walked down to the shore and past Bados, who stood staring moodily out to sea. She climbed into the boat and lifted Charlotte from the bow. "Give me a hand, please, Bados," she called in a weak voice which revealed how little strength she had left.

Bados hesitated, then waded out to the boat. As he took the starving child from her, she said softly, "If my babies are to live, Bados, 'twill be your catch that saved them."

Without looking at her, Bados replied, "I think that turtle come on the beach to lay eggs. Same as they do back in Barbados."

"Pray you find some," Mary said. Then she lifted Emanuel from his nest, slipped over the side, and splashed through the water to shore—a woman so emaciated that she seemed no more than a child herself, carrying a small, limp doll.

Bados laid Charlotte in the shade of a bush and walked away. Mary put Emanuel next to his sister, and collapsed beside the children.

When she next opened her eyes, James was kneeling beside her, holding a wooden bowl. "It's the blood. Here, Mary. Drink."

"The children—" she began, but he interrupted.

"I have already given them as much as they can take. Here. You must."

Mary closed her eyes and forced herself to drink.

She wondered, later, whether Will had deliberately sent James with the blood, rather than serve her himself. Not that it mattered. What mattered was that they had food, some part of it in liquid form. Within the hour, all had eaten as much as they could manage after coming so close to starvation.

Mary fell asleep. When she woke, she saw that the children needed to be moved in order to keep them in the skimpy shade cast by the bush. Both woke and, although they did not become active at once, it was clear that they felt revived.

Glancing round, Mary noticed that Will and the men were cutting strips of turtle meat and laying them out to dry in the sun. Will must have noticed her moving about, because he soon wandered over.

"Is that smiles I see on them little faces?" he asked jovially.

"They're ever so much stronger," Mary agreed. "And in so short a time! Turtle blood must agree with them."

Beyond Will, she saw Bados approaching. He did not come near, but called out, "I find them eggs. They yonder, by the fire."

Will whirled sharply, but Bados had already turned away. This time the black man had not used Mary's name, but neither had Bados directed the report to Will by name. Will scowled after him, then stalked off in another direction.

All through the afternoon, Mary gave the children such sips of blood as she could persuade them to drink, and allowed each a sip or two of water as well. On the morrow, she judged, their tiny shrunken bellies might be able to tolerate eggs. She herself drifted in and out of sleep, not bothering, for once, to busy herself with cooking for the men. Let them get hungry enough, she thought with grim satisfaction, and they'd be perfectly capable of feeding themselves.

The sun was near to setting when she woke to find Charlotte gone. She looked about and saw her sitting at the edge of the gentle surf. Will lay dozing nearby. Mary went to the child, who was playing in the sand. Charlotte looked up at her with bright blue eyes, much too large for her tiny face.

"I make a house," she informed her mother.

Mary sat down beside her and took a handful of wet sand, which she dribbled onto Charlotte's heap, giving it turrets. "Now we have a castle, like they build in England," she said.

"Is this England?"

Mary smiled at the absurdity. "No, precious. This is not England."

"Where is this?" Charlotte wanted to know.

"Very far from England, my love. And far from Botany Bay."

Mary and James had exchanged few words on the voyage thus far, and then only when a task at hand required it. Mary might say, "I will have the fire built here, if you please, Mr. Brown." Or he, "Thank you, Mrs. Bryant," when she doled out his share of the food. So James looked up quickly from writing in his journal when she approached him next morning.

"Mr. Brown," she said stiffly. "I wonder if you might possess a timepiece."

"Regretfully, Mrs. Bryant, I do not." He smiled ruefully. "And have not since the day of my arrest. Have you need of one?"

"Aye, sir. For you see, I have a quadrant, and some slight knowledge of its use, but no means of determining high noon."

"And none of the others in our company have a timepiece either?"

"Indeed, several do." Mary's eyes slanted with humour. "But as in your case, I expect their timepieces are being maintained by jailers or some other they have encountered since they were taken into custody."

James smiled, and then ventured, "You could use a stick."

"A stick?" Mary gave him a blank look.

"Stuck into the sand. When its shadow reaches the shortest point—or ceases to exist—there would be your exact midday."

"Ah. I was not aware of that!" Mary exclaimed. "Would you be so kind, Mr. Brown, as to tend to this for me, and to inform me of the moment? I shall be ready with the quadrant, and perhaps can determine our latitude."

"I should think our longitude would be more important," James remarked. "That we might know how far we are from the coast."

Mary gave a small shrug. "Of course. But the instruments I have do not provide that information. All we can know for sure is that the mainland lies to the west.

If we sail in that direction, I hardly see how it can be missed."

James did promptly inform her of high noon, as near as could be determined by stick and shadow. When Mary had finished calculating the latitude, she saw, as she had suspected, that they were north of the bulge in the continent's eastern coast. This was a favourable thing, indicating that, due to the storm, they had travelled much further north than she would have imagined possible in so short a time. But being so far north was also a disadvantage. The mainland now angled away from them, so it would take even longer to get there.

They left the sand spit the following day, for little good it did to have a bounty of food when there was not a drop of water to drink, apart from a few sips Mary had held back for the children. There was no doubt in her mind that the tiny atoll where they had rested was indeed in the Coral Sea, or as Captain Smit had called it, "the impossible sea." Her calculations as to latitude confirmed it, and coral was often in evidence, either as small islands like the one that had saved them or, more ominously, as reefs just below the surface. She stood in the bow, her eyes constantly skimming the water. Occasionally she raised an arm to signal a turn to left or right.

"Starboard," she would say quietly, and behind her Will would echo loudly, "Starboard!" The rhythm of the oars would shift to change direction, then steady again. Mary's eyes never left the water.

There was no reason for Will to resist the instructions she gave, but as was his wont, he could not long abide being directed by someone else. This Mary knew, but knew not how, with coral all about, things might be done differently. She only hoped that when the moment came that he must rebel, it would not cost them too dearly. But of course, it did.

She had just spoken, as she had dozens of times before, "Port." But instead of passing the instruction to the rowers, he leaned forward, squinted over her shoulder, said, "I don't see—"

"PORT, HARD!" she screamed.

The boat spun at her command. Too late. There was a scraping noise against the bottom.

"Goddamned thing came out of nowhere!" Will exclaimed.

"I heard some splintering," Cox called from midship.

Mary turned around. "Jump over and take a look, Coxie."

The carpenter hung his head shamefacedly. "Ah, Mary. Big old ox like me, I'd sink right to the bottom."

Mary grasped that the man couldn't swim, and said, "You then, Scrapper. Swim under and see what the damage is."

"I ain't no fish, and I don't float, neither!" the young tough called back indignantly.

James lifted his hands with a smile that said sorry, but he was also a non-swimmer.

"I can paddle about a bit," Luke offered, "but doubt I can hold my breath long enough to see the bottom."

Pip's petrified expression said he would take the plunge if Mary required it of him, but he did not expect to survive the ordeal.

Will said nothing, nor did Mary turn to him. Truth be told, she did not know whether her husband could swim, and she thought it unwise to humiliate him again if it happened that he could not.

Matey solved the problem by standing up and throwing off his shirt. "Damn me if I ain't stuck at sea with a bunch of lily-livered landlubbers!" With that he dove overboard and swam under the cutter. A minute later he popped to the surface. "It ain't clear through, but she'll need caulking pretty quick."

Matey was hauled aboard. Men picked up the oars and began to row. The tension of sailing through these claws of coral showed on every face, except Mary's. As if in a trance, she pointed to the left, then straight, left again, now right. With no further hesitation, Will, standing behind her, called her signals to the rowers.

Mary had become as tanned as the men. The hunger endured during the week they had battled the storm, and the week of near-starvation that followed, had pared away her curves, leaving her with a hard leanness that was more that of a boy than a woman. Will caught the long braid of sun-bleached hair hanging down her back, and held it briefly in his hand. Mary felt the gesture, and in it the longing, which she understood. She supposed that the softness of her hair was the only thing about her that seemed feminine, in the old way.

At long last the mainland came into view. The very sight of it in the distance gave the rowers a renewed energy that bordered on the jolly. It was dusk by the time they approached close enough to see how rugged this part of the coast was. Mary scanned the shore, looking for a place of sufficient calm where they wouldn't be thrown against the rocks. Will, standing behind her, motioned for the men to row parallel to the shore, as he looked for a likely spot.

Cox called, "We got to make land, Cap'n. She's seeping bad."

"Yonder," Will pointed. "Between them rocks."

"Won't be easy," Matey allowed, not willing to admit himself afraid.

"I've landed in worse, and on darker nights back in Cornwall," Will said confidently. "There, men!" He pointed again.

The oarsmen followed his lead. The boat rose on the crest of a wave and came down frighteningly close to the rocks. There was a momentary calm when all saw the small, sandy cove Will had sighted, where they could land safely after all.

Suddenly, out of the twilight, a lance sailed past, just inches above the bow of the boat. What Mary saw in that instant made her scream. Dark bodies perched among the rocks on either side of the tiny cove, spears poised and letting fly. Many fell short, but more than a few struck the boat. Every oar swung to a single side, forcing the cutter to turn tail and plow into a wave. For the next few minutes there was no time for anything but pulling on the oars and bailing. At last they were past the breakers, exhausted. And night was upon them.

"The bastards!" Will howled in frustration.

"Next time I'll have a bloody musket in me hand!" Scrapper boasted uselessly.

Matey guffawed. "You fancy you could hit something at that distance? You make me laugh!"

"I could hit you at this distance, needing nothing but a fist," Scrapper threatened, rising and half turning around in his seat.

Matey grabbed Scrapper by the throat and squeezed until the boy gagged. "And a bit of air, maybe?" Matey grinned evilly.

Cox rose and interposed his bulk between them. "Bless me, boys. That's enough!"

Mary ignored the ruckus and turned to face the open sea. "A little to starboard, there. That's it," she said quietly.

Pip leaned forward. "Can you see in the dark, Miss Mary?"

"The coral is not something you see, Pip. You feel it," she said in a low voice, for she knew no other way to explain it.

Charlotte whined, and the baby wailed. Will said, "They're needing something to eat."

"Then they must be fed," Mary said, without taking her eyes from the black water. Raising her voice to be heard further back, she said, "Easy to port. Slowly. There." And lowering her voice again, to speak to Will, "Give them a sip of water first."

They made it safely through the night, although by what magic or miracle Mary herself could not have said. Dawn found them sailing smoothly between the coast and a string of off-shore islands. A little after sunup, they came upon an island with a likely-looking cove, into which flowed a freshwater stream. As there were no native boats or signs of encampment, they deemed the place to be uninhabited. To everyone's relief, Will announced that they would lay up there for a few days, long enough to repair the boat and replenish their supplies.

After the boat had been dragged into the shallows and overturned for caulking, Bados was sent to fish and look for turtle eggs, and Luke sent to set snares and explore the area. In mid-afternoon, Luke returned with a dozen small animals.

Charlotte watched with fascination as Luke cleaned them and showed her the young that came out of their little pouches. But she set up a wail when she learned that she could not keep them as playthings for, being separated from their mothers, they were as good as dead already.

"I never saw creatures such as these, with pockets on their bellies, and young ones inside," Luke admitted. "But it seems like they ought to be edible. There's only vegetable matter in their innards, so I can't see they'd be much different from rabbits and squirrels like we have back home."

"I'll spit them over the fire," Mary decided. "That should make them tasty enough."

"Get 'em warm and we'll eat 'em, no questions asked," Cox called from where he and the others were at work caulking the overturned boat.

"I et monkey before, in Africa," Matey offered.

"What took you to Africa?" James queried.

"Jumped ship there, back in '75," Matey responded. "Stayed ten years. A hell hole, it was, but better'n being keel-hauled for kicking the bosun in the nuts."

"I et a rat once, in London." Pip, sitting atop the boat's upturned bottom, nodded at the skewered meat Mary had just placed over the fire. "Cooked it just like that."

Scrapper, who sat facing him, looked closely at Pip. "Thing about eating rat," he dead-panned, "it makes you look like one. Twitchy little nose, just five or six whiskers stuck in around the mouth—."

Pip flung a handful of caulking at his tormentor. Scrapper gave him a shove that sent him sliding down the side of the boat onto the sand. Pip sat up, unfortunately in line with Scrapper's foot, which kicked him square in the face.

"Aye, but you're a mean bastard, Scrapper!" James exclaimed.

"That I am," Scrapper said complacently. "But I don't look like no rat."

Pip crawled across the sand to Mary, wiping blood from his nose.

"Get back over here, boy," Will commanded. "The job's not done."

Pip hunkered down between Mary and Luke like a cowering pup.

"Leave him be," Mary said shortly.

Before anything could develop between husband and wife, Luke stood and said easily, "I found a nice little spring a ways up yonder, Cap'n. Tasted mighty sweet. Mind if I take the boy with me to fetch back a few pails?"

Will gave a curt nod and turned away, letting it pass. Mary understood that the others were aware of the tension between herself and Will. It saddened and shamed her, but there was nothing she could do except, like Will, let it pass.

Over the next few days, as they enjoyed an abundance of fresh food and clean, clear water, small annoyances faded and a sense of camaraderie returned. Mary asked that Pip be regularly assigned to attend to Emanuel, for fear that when she was occupied in cooking and drying meat and fruit for their onward journey, he might crawl into the sea and drown. Will saw the need and readily agreed.

Mary herself, when she had time, took Charlotte in hand and taught her to swim in the clear lagoon, as she herself had been taught to swim at about the same age. When Mary was busy preparing food, Charlotte trailed after Will, or hung around with whoever was doing something the child deemed of interest.

One day, as Will stood examining the caulking done the day before, Mary went to him and spread her chart

on the sand at his feet. "We're here, I judge." She pointed to Cape York's eastern coast.

"How much further to Timor?" Will wanted to
know.

"Maybe fifteen hundred miles."

James came to stand next to Will. He pointed to
New Guinea. "There is nothing here?"

"I don't think so," Mary replied. "That is to say, nothing that would attract a European ship that might get
us home by and by. Once we get round this point," she
touched the northernmost tip of the Australian continent, "we'll be out of the coral and the sea will be safer.
But the land may still hold hazards. Captain Smit says
natives to the north are cannibals."

At the mention of Smit, Will snatched up the chart,
rolled it, and walked away, slapping it irritably against
his thigh. "Matey! Scrapper! Bados! Luke! Come on,
mates. The tide's come in. Let's get this tub floating
again."

Mary followed him, put her hand round the chart
next to his, and said quietly, "Here, let me take that so
it doesn't get in your way."

He gave her a hard look, but her eyes were mild and
non-confrontational. He let go of the chart, and went
on gathering his men about him. Mary understood
the mention of Smit to have been an indiscretion on
her part, and vowed not to be so careless again.

But that evening, when all were bedded down on
the sand, and quiet, so that Mary fancied only herself
and the stars were conscious, resentment welled up
inside her. It was too much, she thought, to do all that

she was expected to do and, beyond those burdens, to mould her every word in such a way that none gave offence to Will. Although her husband slept on one side of her, and her children on the other, she felt an ever-deepening sense of loneliness; an emptiness that needed filling with the presence of the only person, since the death of her parents, who made her feel understood, and less than totally alone.

A few days after leaving that place, and finding themselves forced toward the mainland by coral, they came to a river and rowed up it a ways, looking for a place where the boat would be sheltered near a likely spot for camping. But the vegetation was altogether strange, denser than any Mary had ever seen. Seemingly impenetrable greenery grew right down to the water's edge—and hung over into it; trees, bushes and vines, as thick as could be. Birds in number were disturbed by their approach; and butterflies, some so large that they might be mistaken for birds, fluttered over the water. They steered toward the middle of the river, although the current was stronger there, to avoid being swatted in the face by branches that reached out from either shore.

"'Tis eerie," Mary murmured. "I've not seen such as this before. Why, look yonder." She pointed to a spiky plant growing in the fork of an overhanging tree. "It's like there's not enough ground, so you've got plants growing right out of trees, and vines hanging from both."

"We've come into the tropics, that's what we've

done," Matey announced. "I seen the likes of this, I have, over yonder in Africa, down south of the Canaries."

They paddled the better part of an hour until they came upon an opening in the trees, a muddy bank backed by mashed-down vegetation. "There," Luke motioned. "Might that do?"

Suddenly Bados, who had spoken scarcely a word since Will's reprimand back on the sand spit, half-stood in the middle of the boat and shouted, "No! Turn round! Turn round!"

Startled, the others gaped at him. He was pointing at the far end of the muddy bank.

"What?" asked several voices. "What you on about, Bados?"

Mary's gaze followed in the direction he pointed, and at first found nothing. Then, what she saw all but stopped her heart. It was a creature lying in the mud, and close to the colour of it. The snouted head alone was nearly three feet long, and the length of its body she could not guess. They were still fifty yards off, but now that she had spotted it she could see the huge jaws, slightly parted, from which protruded great fangs.

"A dragon!" Pip squeaked.

"No sir!" cried Bados. "That's a crocodile! They got them in Barbados, too. We need be taking ourselves back the way we come!"

"Where's that musket?" Will cried. "We'll put an end to that monster!"

"No!" Mary said sharply. "'Twould be a waste of ammunition. For, dead or alive, there may be others! We'll not stay the night here with such beasts as this about."

"Turn round!" Bados begged again, his voice hoarse with terror. "A crocodile takes a place to be his own, he won't think twice to come after us!"

"Fine by me!" Scrapper yelped. "This whole bleedin' place is givin' me the willies!"

He dug an oar into the water to bring the boat about, and the others, without waiting for a command from Will, did the same. Once turned around, the rowers pulled hard for only a moment, then eased off and let the current carry them swiftly back the way they had come.

Mary dipped a hand into the water, tasted it and, finding it sweet, began to scoop up fresh water to refill their containers. Will, although he was not at the oars, declined to help. Plainly in a snit over having been countermanded by his wife, he lapsed into moody silence.

Matey clapped him on the back. "Doubt you could've taken him with one shot anyway, Cap'n. Was one croc I knowed of in Africa that got to grabbing natives when they went down to the river for water. They asked a Frenchman what had a gun to come and kill it. He told me later that the first three shots barely fazed it. 'Course he got it in the end, and I helped him skin it. When we got a look at the hide, you could see why it wasn't easy for a musket ball to sink in. Like a kind of armour is the hide of them beasts." Matey paused, and added in an awed voice, "And the one I skinned wasn't near the size of the one back there."

As they approached the sea, Mary called back to Bados. "What more do you know of these creatures, Bados? Will we be safe on the beach, or ought we to travel on, away from the river's mouth?"

"Them we have in Barbados, they live in murky places like back yonder. But I tell you same as Matey, I never in my life seen one so big as that. The ones we got at home, they more the size of a man. That one, why, he be long as any three."

They floated in silence for another minute, then Bados spoke again. "They make a track, a smooth-like place where they drag that big tail. We might get ourselves some little way up the beach from this river, then look around for tracks, to know if it's common for them to come down to the beach. Them back home, though, they don't do that."

"Once we find a likely looking beach out in the open," Luke put in, "Bados and me can scout the area for tracks."

They did find a safe place further along the beach, although none truly felt assured of safety, even after Luke set up a line of snares at the edge of the forest to catch anything that might come creeping out to molest them in their sleep. "Ain't nothing I got that can hold one of them monsters," Luke admitted. "But if one gets snared, it might thrash about in breaking free enough to wake us."

They all agreed that that was a reasonable plan and, nervous though they were, made a show of normalcy. The men went off to fish and hunt, except for James, whom Mary sent to gather firewood, and Pip, who was now regularly assigned the job of tending the children when they were on land. Charlotte, after being long confined in the boat, had a great need to run about, and little Emanuel, when he wasn't creeping across the sand, liked to walk upright with someone holding his hands.

Luke soon returned, but with only a single small animal he deemed edible. He went off down the beach to see what luck the fishers were having, and Mary set to chopping the flesh of the animal into small pieces to add flavour to the day's soup. James returned with an armload of wood, and came near to Mary to lay a fire.

Any keen observer with an understanding of human nature would have guessed that these two were in love, not by longing looks sent to each other—for there were none—nor by the time they spent together, since they approached one another only when the task at hand required it. Rather, it would have been apparent from the way they avoided each other's eyes. When they were in close proximity, their movements became stiff and guarded, as if not trusting their own bodies to keep the secret of their hearts.

However, no one else was about, so James, as he arranged the wood and put flint spark to the kindling, spoke to Mary. "When you were at the quadrant, I saw that we have likely crossed over the Tropic of Capricorn."

"I am quite sure of that," Mary confirmed.

"And your chart shows Kupang to be only ten degrees south of the Equator." James glanced up at her for confirmation.

"That's right," Mary nodded, for by now she had a map of their route well established in her mind.

"Then it is as Matey said: we have reached the tropics. I venture to say that the rest of our journey from here to there will be in this clime, and with vegetation such as we encountered today."

Mary glanced toward him with a wry smile. "And with creatures such as that monster we saw today? Was it your intention to comfort me with such knowledge, James?"

James laughed. "Not knowledge, Mary. Just a guess, based on books I read when I was a boy back in Canada. I had a fascination with the tropics and hoped some day to visit." His smile faded, and he added, "But of course, with no notion then of the circumstances that would bring me here."

"Do you regret coming with us?" she asked, stopping her work long enough to look directly at him.

"Coming with you," he said quietly, "is one of the few things in recent years that I shall never regret." With that, he rose and moved away.

They sailed north for many more days, past white sand beaches lined with swaying palms and grey sand beaches interrupted by rocky outcroppings. Sometimes there was no beach, just mangrove swamps swarming with insects which tormented them even on the boat. As they were now sailing between the coast and a string of offshore islands, the sea itself was turquoise and smooth. Its transparent quality made it easy to see the coral, providing one's eyes were focussed on what lay just ahead of the boat, and were straining to see beneath the surface every minute. As Mary's were, day after day. At times images rose up in her mind, most often of Colleen, Dr. White, and other friends she had left back in Botany Bay. Soon, though, she found that she could not allow the images to linger, but must keep her mind empty of thought. For when memories filled her inner vision, she could not sense the coral, or see the subtle change in the colour of the water which forewarned her that coral lay in their path.

One afternoon they came to a great wide river backed by rolling green hills. Will wanted to spend some days there, for it offered fine shelter, and the land around did not seem quite so wild. But Mary insisted that they continue north. "Such a place is sure to have a settlement of savages about, and it might be a large one," she reasoned. "We've got but the one musket. If they came at us in numbers, we couldn't be certain of driving them off."

So they travelled on, and camped instead on a beautiful island to the north, with forested slopes rising up from a crystal clear lagoon. Small streams sent sweet water trickling musically over pebbles and cascading down rock faces covered in soft green moss. To Mary's eyes this was the most enchanting place they had yet come to on their journey. As she stood silently absorbing its beauty, there was a moment when she failed to understand the compulsion, shared by all, to press on.

That evening, as James laid the fire and he and Mary had their usual moment to exchange a few words in private, he said, "The aborigines around Botany Bay were peaceable enough. Have you reason to believe the ones here in the north are more like those who attacked us?"

Mary glanced around. Although no one except Pip and the children were in sight, she lowered her voice. "Captain Smit told me what Captain Cook wrote of the area when he passed this way some twenty years back. By the last reading I took of our latitude, I believe that great river we passed two days ago may have been one where Captain Cook put in. He stayed a good long time to make repairs to his ship after it ran aground. According to his log, there were many natives in the area, and they were friendly."

"But you did not want to chance them treating us as well?"

She gave him a wry, sideways smile. "I did not want to chance our men not treating *them* well. According to Captain Cook's report, he and his men made friends with the locals by offering them gifts—not the hurting end of a musket."

James gave an admiring chuckle. "An amazing mind you have, Mary, that you can see the shoals of human character that lie just below the surface, which are as likely to threaten our progress as any hidden reef."

By now Mary judged them to be coasting the most northern part of the continent, a region which her chart showed as Arnhem Land; so named, Smit had told her, after the ship of a Dutch captain who had discovered it a century before Cook's voyage in these same waters. Days were stressful for, despite the translucent beauty of the water, coral shoals lay thickly beneath the surface, affording Mary hardly a moment in the day of looking away. And sailing by night to avoid the heat was far too dangerous.

They had travelled some distance north from the river where Captain Cook's ship had laid up for repairs, and well beyond the beautiful island where Mary's imagination had teased her with the notion of remaining ever after; thus her eyes kept scanning the west, searching not for land but for a watery passage across the top of Arnhem Land.

Finally there came the jubilant day when Mary's quadrant calculations informed her that they had reached that latitude. Thus did they leave the Coral Sea and, sailing westward between many small islands, approach the Arafura Sea.

The Arafura and Timor Seas

Cape York to Timor

The wind was with them and very fair that day, so that the men, although seated at the oars, were able to take their ease. Will motioned James to take his place, and came forward to look at the chart Mary had spread on the bow.

"With luck, we should make Timor in a month," Mary said, tracing what she believed to be their route between the islands that dotted these waters.

"A thousand miles in a month?" Will asked sceptically.

Charlotte, clinging to her father's leg, said, "'Nother boat." But neither of her parents heard her.

"We have done at least two thousand already, in just eight weeks," Mary pointed out.

"'Nother boat," Charlotte repeated, pulling hard at her father's shirt, and pointing.

Will glanced back, and gave a start. A war canoe as long as the cutter, but sleeker and with much more sail, was coming up on them fast.

"For the lova—pull, mates! Pull for your life!" Will shouted.

There was a stunned silence as each confirmed with a backward glance that his words were no mere figure of speech. Oars hit the water with force. Scrapper was the paddler nearest Will. Will pulled the boy from his seat and took the oar himself, for he was much the better rower.

By then the great war canoe was close enough to see its occupants: a dozen naked war-painted men, spears aloft, relishing the impending slaughter—or so it seemed to Mary. She grabbed Charlotte up in her arms as if to flee, although of course there was no place to go. What should she do if they were taken? Dive overboard, choose drowning to butchery—or worse? The choices were so terrible that her mind could not compute the odds. She stared hard at the savagely-painted faces, trying to judge the men to whom they belonged.

Scrapper made a dive past Mary's legs to where her things were stored in the bow, and rose up with the musket in hand. As he stuffed it with powder and shot, the gap between the two boats continued to narrow.

Mary could now clearly see the face of an old chief, sitting in regal fashion, surrounded by his warriors. He smiled broadly, perhaps for the same reason his warriors smiled. But little Charlotte could not know that. Secure in her mother's arms, she smiled brightly back at him, and waved her tiny hand.

Scrapper took aim, and yelled, "Hey, you bastards! Here's a bellyful of—"

"Wait!" Mary shouted. For in the same instant she sensed a change in the intent of their pursuers.

Scrapper appealed to Will who, on the foremost oar, was rowing for all he was worth. "Whose bloody musket is it anyway?"

"Mine," Mary said. Her hand closed on the barrel of the gun. "Give it to me."

Reluctantly he relinquished the gun, perhaps because by then it was obvious to him too that the gap between the boats was widening. The war canoe had given up the chase.

Mary put Charlotte down and, with both hands free, rolled the oilcloth back around the gun and replaced it in the bow.

Will, likewise gauging the danger to be past, rose and motioned to Scrapper to retake his place at the oar. Then he and Mary stood in the bow together, neither meeting the other's eyes as they watched the war canoe recede into the distance.

Later, remembering Charlotte's smile and wave to the old chief, Mary would always believe that the innocent childish act had saved their lives. The children overall had been less trouble on the trip than she had anticipated. Except for the week of stormy seas, and the one to follow when they had nearly died, and an incident when a jellyfish brushed Charlotte's arm and left her wailing for hours, the children had been hardly any trouble at all.

Emanuel was always within easy reach, in Mary's arms or tucked into the bow of the boat. When the weather was good and the sea calm, Charlotte would clamber between the rowers to the back of the boat, where whichever two men were not at the oars would be resting. Next to Will she favoured Bados, who had found a bit of bamboo on one of their stops, carved a little flute for her, and taught her to play simple tunes. Charlotte also liked to sing, and learned the words to most of the shanties which Matey led. He knew many from his days as a mariner on sailing ships, and adapted them to the rhythm of their rowing.

Once, when they were camped on a small island, Will came upon Charlotte bellowing out words in no way fit to come from the mouth of a child. He chuckled behind his hand, but scolded Mary for allowing it, and said she ought to serve up a punishment that would prevent the little girl from ever using such foul language again. Mary agreed to talk to Charlotte, but said that if any punishment was to be meted out, it belonged to Matey for singing songs with lyrics a child ought not be learning. Will did speak to Matey about it, and thereafter, Matey limited himself to songs appropriate to a ship that was homeward bound, and not likely to land a child in trouble for learning. For uncouth as Matey was, he had no desire to see the little girl grow up rough. He went so far as to explain to her that shanties belonged on the sea, and one never should sing them on land.

Mary liked the shanties Matey led, for it helped the men to keep the rhythm of rowing, and created a sense of harmony among all aboard, whether at the oars or not. Bados, when he was rowing, joined in on the shanties in a deep rich baritone. But when the sail was up and the men were not at the oars, he occasionally turned to singing of a different type. Slow and mournful songs came from deep inside him and rolled out across the water. All up and down the boat, men, children, and Mary fell silent.

The songs he sang created a sense of closeness, but of a very different quality from the physical rhythms called forth by Matey's shanties. Bados's songs bound them together in a mood of aching loneliness, even as their minds travelled to different places in an effort to claim, in memory at least, what it was they longed for, or had lost a long time ago.

Once when Bados was singing such a song, Mary turned around to see Cox, on the most forward seat, with tears streaming down his cheeks.

She touched his hand and said, "I'm sorry, Coxie," although she had no idea what might have caused the tears.

"She's gonna perish there without me," he choked. "Same as that other girl back in Londontown that I treated so bad, drinking up all my wages while she was dying of consumption, and brawling to boot, so fierce as to land me here on this far side of the world! Ah, Mary!" he agonised, "if I knew how to go back to my Florie, by God, I would do it."

Mary was amazed by the confession. She knew from

a previous conversation that Cox felt bad about leaving Florie, but had no idea that he had grown so fond of her as all that. It occurred to her that whatever each person was missing, or wherever they would like to be at that moment, Cox was the only one who longed for something back in Botany Bay.

During the first days of sailing across the Sea of Timor, there were frequent native sightings. In many places that seemed uninhabited they saw crocodiles, which precluded camping there. There were nights when, although land was at hand, the proximity of unfriendly natives and fearsome beasts put them so much on edge that they felt compelled to anchor offshore and sleep on the boat.

However, by now all the men were skilled at the oars and in excellent physical condition. That, combined with favourable winds, made it a near certainty that they would reach Kupang within a couple of weeks. One day, as they were congratulating themselves on the success of their escape, James broached the subject of a story.

"A story? What do you mean?" Cox asked.

"We can't just walk in and say, 'Good day, Governor. We're bolters from Botany Bay looking for passage on a ship back to civilisation,'" James explained. "We must have a story."

"We'll say we're shipwreck survivors," Matey said complacently.

James turned to him. "What ship? Sailing under what flag?"

"English, for sure," Will laughed. "Seeing how we don't speak nothing else."

"That much is certain," James agreed. "But if one calls the ship by one name and one another, and we give different reports as to where she went down or who the captain was—you see what I mean?"

"'Tis understood," Mary said, speaking for all of them. "A story we must have. You lay it out, James, and we'll learn it together so we don't give ourselves away."

By Mary's calculations they were within a week of Kupang when they came upon a small island with a fine little cove, waterfalls tumbling down a rock face, and no boats about to suggest human habitation. The cutter was again in need of caulking so, after exploring the island to confirm the absence of natives and crocodiles, they decided to spend a few days there, resting and repairing the boat.

It proved a good choice. Both fish and game were plentiful, requiring no great effort to feed themselves. On what Will had decided would be their last night before pushing on, the men sprawled around the fire, their muscular, sun-darkened bodies relaxed and their bellies full of food. Bados picked up his flute as he always did of an evening, and began to play a tune. Mary moved a little away from the fire to bed down the children, because the music soothed them as it soothed her. Luke rose and added wood to the fire. It blazed up, lighting the faces around and adding warmth to the moment.

"Ah, that feels good," Cox sighed, holding his hands out to the fire.

"Like to stay here a bit, I would," Pip said wistfully.

"Good island, this 'un," Matey agreed. "No bleedin' blacks to creep up and cut your throat."

Bados laid his flute aside and stared moodily into the fire.

"Like to get my hands on one that tries," Scrapper boasted.

Luke gave him a playful punch on the shoulder. "You should've said so sooner. We could've let you loose on those big fellers back there in the war canoe."

"With a musket in me mitt, you better believe it!" Scrapper yapped.

"A musket and no bleedin' woman winkin' her eyes at the cannibal bastards," Matey carped.

Will sprang to his feet and gave Matey a kick that sent him sprawling. "Mind your fucking mouth!" he snarled.

Matey picked himself up, a grin on his face but with a look in his eyes that Mary had seen before. She dreaded what it might portend. Feigning an apologetic demeanour, Matey slapped Will on the back and said, "Ah, man, I meant no disrespect. Why, Miss Mary's the best captain I ever knowed. Ain't she, boys?"

The others murmured agreement. Will looked around like an animal at bay, then drew back his fist and punched Matey square in the mouth. Matey went down again, but this time he came up with the nearest weapon to hand: Bados's flute. He smashed it against Will's face.

In a flash, Bados was on Matey, choking to kill. Not until Mary's hands grasped Bados's wrists did the big West Indian seem to realise what he was doing. With a half-sob, he scooped up the broken flute and ran toward the beach.

There was a stunned silence. Matey threw an arm around Will's shoulder and made a show of concern for the bruise he had made on his cheek. "Sorry, Cap'n. Reckon I been too long without a bottle. Beginnin' to wear on my nerves, it is."

"Ah, you're just a wore-out old salt," Will growled, choosing, for his own reasons, to minimise the incident by responding with an insult instead of his fists.

The rest of the men glanced at one another and away, none wanting to add to the conflagration, or to be seen taking one side or another.

Nor did Mary speak. She picked up the wooden bowls scattered about, placed them in the empty stew pot, and trudged off toward the surf to do the washing up. Pip, whose job that usually was, followed at a distance, perhaps understanding that she wanted to be alone and was only using the chore as a pretext for getting away from the men.

If it was solitude Mary sought, she did not find it on the beach. There was Bados sitting on the sand, knees drawn up to his chin, sobbing. She knelt beside him and laid a hand on his arm. She wished she had the words to express what a solace his strong, silent presence, coupled with the music, had been from the start. She knew that his nightly melodies helped not only her and the children, but the men as well, to mitigate fear and loneliness each time they laid down to sleep in a strange and dangerous place. But as this had to do with emotions which she was unaccustomed to putting into words, she remained silent, hoping her hand on his arm would convey all that.

Little by little his sobs quieted. At last he spoke. "I tell you Mary, I feel real bad. I vex before, but never so I want to kill a man. You leave me now. I don't go with you no more."

"If you stay here, Bados, you'll never get back to England. Nor to the West Indies."

He took a breath and let it out in a long and hopeless sigh. "Day I left Barbados, everybody say how I be a free man now, I gonna make my fortune and buy all my family out of bondage. But my mama, she just look at me and say, 'Son, you been a joy.' She done seen the future and know I never coming back." He paused, and added with sad finality, "I ain't no fool, Mary. This fair island, it be the closest I ever get to home."

Mary recalled the island off the coast of Arnhem Land where she had briefly fantasised spending the rest of her life. She understood something of his attraction to this place, but now as then, she considered the practicality of such a course. "'Twould be impossible to stay alive here with nothing to start you out, Bados. Timor is but a few days further. Why not go on that far with us? Lay in some supplies and then come back."

Bados was silent, and she could tell he was considering her suggestion. His question showed that he recognised the sense of her suggestion, as well as its flaws. "How'd I find my way back?"

"I'll show you how to read the chart and use a compass. Once we arrive, we'll not need them anymore. Nor the boat."

He sat there fingering the pieces of his broken flute. "I got no schoolin', Mary."

"Nor I, Bados. But charts are easier to read than books, and the compass easier yet. I give you my word—"

"Miss Mary!" Pip's squeak of alarm caused Mary and Bados to look up. Silhouetted against the firelight, they could see Will walking toward them. Both rose. Bados faded into the shadows. When Will arrived, Mary was alone, scrubbing the stew pot in the surf.

"Taking a long time to wash up, ain't you, girl?"

"I was talking to Bados. He wants to stay here."

"So let him stay. We don't need him," Will boasted, but frowned as he spoke. Mary could tell that he was visualising the next day, thinking that one step ahead, which he rarely did. "Though none's stronger. Damn lucky he was at the oars when them savages bore down on us."

Mary scrubbed at the iron pot with a handful of sand, then rinsed the bowls and placed them inside. Over her shoulder she said, "Our chances are better if we stick together."

Will laughed, bitterly. "Sticking together, are we? Sure and you'd see it that way, having them all at your beck and call."

Mary sighed and got up off her knees. She handed Will the cast iron cooking pot to carry back to camp.

He stared at the pot moodily, then bellowed, "Don't

get uppity with me, Madam. I'm not your goddamned manservant!" He flung the pot at her feet and stalked off down the beach.

Again Mary knelt on the beach and, in the darkness, began to search for the wooden bowls which had scattered onto the sand.

Pip came to help her. "You go on back, Miss Mary," he whispered. "I'll rinse 'em off again."

Mary gave the boy's shoulder a grateful squeeze, then picked up the heavy pot and trudged back to camp. Tired though she was, she knew that she would have trouble falling asleep, for anger burned within her. It was fed by feelings coming at her from many directions; among them this reminder that her circumstances were such that she could not even give and receive words of kindness unless they were whispered in secret.

It was the first morning on the entire journey that Mary woke not in the grey light of dawn but with morning sun blazing full in her face. She automatically threw out an arm to touch her children, but they had already left the nest. She sat up and looked about. Some of the men were still asleep, which informed her that Will had decided not to sail that day after all; else he would have wakened them early. She saw him down on the beach, checking over the boat. Charlotte was at his side. Pip was a little way off, holding Emanuel by the hand, as the child had begun to toddle.

A fire had been built, waiting, she supposed, for her to make breakfast. Neither James nor Bados were among those still sleeping. She wondered if Bados had acted on his intent to leave the group, and had disappeared into the forest for good.

She rose, poured water into the kettle and, while it came to a boil, cleaned some still-flopping fish which lay nearby in the net that had dragged them in. When the fish were cooked she moved the simple stew off the fire to cool. She picked some broad leaves from a nearby plant and used them to wrap two of the cooled fish. Then she went over a small rise and down to the beach, not where Will and the children were, but further along, where they would not see her go. She had no chance of finding Bados if he chose not to show himself, but she thought that if he saw her walking along the beach, he might come to her.

She stopped frequently to see what shells lay on the sand and what creatures might be in the tide pools. By moving so slowly, Bados, if he saw her, would have time to come out from wherever he might be hiding in the forest. She had walked about a quarter mile along the seaweed-strewn beach when she saw a trail leading into the forest. She was wondering where it might go when she glanced up and saw Bados sitting on a high bluff, staring out to sea. He gave no sign of having seen her, and indeed, was looking off in another direction. She began to climb, supposing that the bluff had been used as a lookout by others and that was where this trail must lead.

She walked slowly, pausing to look about. It was possible to see only a few feet into such dense forest. Remembering the snakes Luke had reported lying up in trees, she paid close attention to her surroundings. She used her ears as well and so knew, before the person behind her appeared, that someone was following.

It was James. He did not speak but, as she turned, he simply reached out his arms to her. And she to him. Standing as he was, a few inches lower than her on the trail, their lips, level with each other, came together naturally. They kissed as if they had done exactly this a thousand times before.

Perhaps James had, in his imagination, but Mary had never allowed herself that secret thrill. In the whole of her life she had been trained, and had trained herself, to not dream of the impossible. She had first supposed James's love to be impossible by reason of his being better than she. When he denied that and she realised her mistake, she had continued to suppress such fantasies, judging any form of intimacy, even in her imagination, to be too great a danger.

Yet they stood now in just such danger. So passionate was their embrace, and so little attention did they give to anything else, that it might have resulted in death at the hands of their own kind as readily as from the fatal bite of a serpent. However, it was not such a horrible fate that finally parted them, but the act of two wills, accompanied by silent, gasping laughter at their own audacity.

"Did you expect that of me?" Mary asked.

"I did," James admitted. "Because in my heart I know you."

"I don't know you so well," Mary conceded, and

added longingly, "But I look forward to a time when I can learn."

"And this is not our time." He said the words before she could, so she only nodded.

"Then let us continue on the way you were going. To see Bados, were you?"

"To persuade him to stay with us," Mary acknowledged. "But perhaps it's better that you go alone."

James looked doubtful. "How do you propose to persuade him?"

Mary lifted the tobacco pouch containing the compass from where it hung between her breasts. "With this."

"I don't understand."

"I told him that if he would go on as far as Timor, I'd give him the chart and compass, so he can find his way back."

James looked surprised. "Surely he cannot read?"

"No, but he can learn to read a compass. And perhaps one of us can teach him to read the chart. It's only a picture of land and water. Even Charlotte understands the representation of a trail in the sand."

"Why not let him stay? England is not his home, and has treated him more than a little harshly." James grimaced. "Seven years transported for stealing seven cucumbers!"

"We could," Mary acknowledged. "But I would like to have him with us till we reach Timor. Which of us might now be dead if he hadn't spied that enormous crocodile?"

"True," James admitted. "And to leave him here

alone, and with no flint for making fire, no line to make snares, no fishing net, no musket or ammunition, what chance would he have?"

"I have spoken to him of this already, and of how, once we reach the Dutch colony at Kupang, we won't need these things anymore." Mary took the compass from the tobacco pouch and laid it in James's hand. "Go now. Convince him that he can learn how to use it, then bring it back to me. It's confidence he's wanting, nothing more. Ah, and this." She gave him the leaf-wrapped fish. "Two bites of breakfast, one for him and one for you."

James tucked the fish into one pocket, the compass into the other, and asked, "What about Will? He said we would sail on today."

"Take your time," Mary said firmly. "We shall not leave this island until Bados is ready to come with us."

They kissed again, long and hungrily, hands roving each other's back and pressing hard to bring their bodies close, then making space for his hand on her breast, hers on his hardness. The clothing between them intensified the ache until at last they pulled apart, both of them hurting as lovers do when parting in advance of a long separation. It went without saying that between now and their arrival in England, the opportunity to be in each other's arms was not likely to present itself again.

It was as if Will had guessed Mary's determination to stay until Bados agreed to rejoin them, because he made no mention of sailing that day or the next. The

233

others must have suspected it, too, and were glad for any excuse to stay longer on an island where food was plentiful, and molesting insects were not as bad as they had been in most places. It passed without comment when, late in the afternoon of the second day, Bados appeared and joined the others for supper. No one needed to be told that on the morrow they would leave.

They sailed due west just to the north of Latitude 10° south. Timor, when they sighted it, brought a thunderous cheer. This, their dreamed-of destination, was so beautiful it took their breath away. Rather than the jungle-covered mountains which they had found so fearsome, here were green rolling hills which, had they not been graced with palm trees and fringed with broad golden beaches, would have reminded them of home. Mary picked a distinctive rock outcropping and steered them toward it, having already got Will to agree that they would rest here for another few days before coasting around the tip of Timor to the city of Kupang, which lay on the far side of the island. The reason, she had explained to him, was to give them more time to practice the story James had laid out for them.

Another reason, although she kept it from Will, was her desire to give Bados time to get his bearings. During their three-day rest on the eastern side of Timor, she found an occasion to speak to Bados alone, explaining that he had but to mark this point well. There would be no more to navigating the return than coasting back around to here, then following the compass reading due east until he reached the island where he hoped to settle.

During that final rest stop, and again on the boat as they coasted toward Kupang, they practised the story which James had devised. Time spent on the *Charlotte* during the voyage to Botany Bay had given all a clear idea of how mariners and officers addressed each other. Prior to that, Matey had crewed on a whaler, and was able to provide details about the workings of such ships, so it was decided to pretend that the ship from which they'd been cast adrift had been a whaler. Each person was assigned a role, which they practised with a diligence that caused Cox to laugh and claim that they were good enough to perform for the King.

"Yes," James said with serious smile. "But our act must be of longer duration, and, if any should fail, the consequences will be more than boos. It could be as it was in days of old, when those who brought displeasure to their King risked being removed from the stage of life."

The Dutch East India Colony—
Kupang, Timor

June-September 1791

They sailed into Kupang Harbour with a well-earned sense of pride. And yet so long were they from the shores of civilisation that they couldn't help but gape in wonder at the bustling port. By the time the oarsmen brought the cutter dockside, a crowd had gathered.

Will, standing tall and confident despite bare feet and the rags he wore in place of shirt and pants, stepped off the boat first, and shook the hand of an official who introduced himself as Bruger.

"William Bryant, Master's Mate on Her Majesty's ship, the *Dunkirk*, what went down in a storm some twenty-one days ago," Will announced, borrowing the name of the hulk they had been imprisoned on back in England, which, if that wreck had ever managed to limp into the open sea, surely would have sunk. "A whaler she was, Mr. Bruger. God willing, some others from our ill-fated ship made landfall here already?"

"No sir." Bruger, a stout man whose eyes, Mary judged, did not miss much of what went on around the docks, skimmed the cutter's passengers and looked back at Will. "This is the first ve have heard of this unfortunate thing."

After a few more questions, which Will handled with aplomb, the cutter's passengers were placed in a cart and driven for some distance along a street lined with solid colonial buildings. Most of the edifices were squarish, two or three storeys of unadorned stone in the Dutch colonial style. However, the governor's residence to which they were conveyed was differently designed. Perched on a rise in the centre of a rolling green lawn, it was a two-storey mansion with wings stretching out on either side of the entrance, and verandas which encircled the house, upstairs and down. They dismounted from the cart, but Bruger bade them wait in the courtyard while he went inside to announce their arrival.

They had been standing there several moments when Mary noticed that they were being observed from an upstairs veranda by a man with a visage as stern as a Calvinist minister. Unconsciously, she moved her children so that Charlotte concealed her bare legs from the man's gaze, and Emanuel, whom she held in her arms, hid her skimpily-covered breasts.

A short time later Bruger returned. "The gouverneur vill allow you to draw upon the Crown's credit such necessities as you require," he told Will brusquely. "Two changes of clothing complete he has ordered me to issue to you and your men. They are to be quartered in the barracks." He paused, and said, "Gouverneur Wanjon extends an invitation for you, Sir, as an officer, to lodge here as his guest. With your family, of course."

Will's mouth dropped open in surprise. "He don't want to meet us first?"

"He vill vait until you have been restored to an appearance befitting civilised men," Bruger said shortly. "After you have been barbered and clothed, all in your party shall return here, at the sunset hour, to take refreshments with the gouverneur."

"Even . . ." Will slightly inclined his head, "the darky?"

"As you have arrived together, so vill our gouverneur take his first measure of you—after you have been restored to your decent selves, of course," Bruger said, speaking with such stiffness that Mary suspected he too found it shocking that the governor's invitation included a black man.

Still addressing only Will, Bruger said, "You, Sir, vill accompany me to sign for the clothing issued to your men. Your vife and the *kinder*, they go with Mira." He half-turned, and motioned to an Indonesian girl waiting on the steps of the mansion. "She vill show them to the quarters Gouverneur Wanjon has designated for your family."

Mary had never in her life glimpsed the inside of such a house. The floors were of hardwood so highly polished that they reflected every foot that crossed them. The furniture was likewise smooth and heavily polished. Yards of exquisite fabrics draped the windows, and candles in heavy brass holders were set about at frequent intervals. Certain details of the decor reminded her of Captain Smit's quarters so that, despite its grander scale, the place was not quite so intimidating as it might otherwise have been.

She followed Mira, a petite and perfectly-formed girl who could not have been more than sixteen, along a corridor to a wing of the house which seemed very little used. The Indonesian servant opened the door into a room more spacious than their hut had been back in Botany Bay. It was furnished with not one but two large beds. Fat cushions and patterned rugs were scattered about. Mira crossed the room and threw open a door containing many small panes of glass. Mary stepped out onto a veranda, partly to take in the view of a well-tended lawn and flowering trees, and partly to get past the strangeness of being shut up inside after so many weeks in the open air.

"Come," Mira said, motioning to Mary with delicate hands. "A bath we make ready, first for the *kinder*, then for you, Mevrouw."

Thus was Mary introduced to the first in-the-home bath she had ever seen, which was filled, at Mira's command, by another servant bringing pails of warm water from a distant part of the house. The children splashed happily in the tub, not overly impressed by a body of water so much smaller than the beaches and lagoons where all their previous baths had been taken. Soap was unfamiliar to them, and of course they got it in their eyes, and set up such a howl that servants came running and fluttered about, trying to console them.

By the time Mary and Mira had fished them out and got them dry, a large Indonesian woman, whom Mira called Siti, arrived with plates of food. Siti herded the children to a small table out on the veranda, and proceeded to feed them food which, except for the rice, was entirely unfamiliar. The children did not object, perhaps because so much of what they had eaten in recent months was altogether strange to them. Siti pushed a few bites of food into Mary's mouth as if she were one of the children, then shooed her away. Mira tugged her back to the bathroom, where, to Mary's astonishment, Mira proceeded to bathe her! Mary protested that such a service was for invalids and she was no such thing, but Mira had her instructions (as Mary later learned), and scrubbed her from hair to toenails.

Out and dried off, Mary reached for the rags she had been wearing, but Mira snatched them from her, and handed them to another servant whom she addressed in Indonesian. A wave of the woman's hands left Mary with the clear impression that the instruction was to burn the clothes.

"No!" Mary cried in alarm, for although Bruger had indicated that the men were to have new clothes, he had said nothing about clothing for her. "I have no other!"

"Come, Mevrouw," Mira soothed, wrapping her in the towel and leading her back to the bedroom. "We have other." Mira ran her hands down her own outfit, which was similar to the sari Captain Smit had often had Mary wear, although of sturdier material. "Like this for you, but more special."

Mira sat Mary in a chair and began to comb and braid her hair. Through the open veranda doors, Mary could see the children cheerfully consuming the food that Siti offered. Charlotte ran in several times to stick tidbits of food in her mother's mouth, then went out again. Mary realised that just as she as a child had learned to trust the kindness of sailors on shipboard, so her own children had become accustomed to being passed from kindly hand to kindly hand on the voyage away from Botany Bay. Nor did the strangeness of this place seem to frighten them, for had not every day of the past ten weeks brought them into novel surroundings? At last Mary began to relax and, following her children's example, let members of the governor's household take charge.

Once Mary's hair was in braids, Mira wound them round and round her head and pinned them in place. Then she held up a looking glass. Mary had never seen herself in a glass before, although of course she had some idea of her image from having, on a few occasions, gazed into a reflecting pool. The face in the mirror interested her as might the face in a painting, for it possessed many details which she would not have attributed to herself; most notably, the deep clear blue of the eyes and, thanks to constant exposure to the sun, skin quite as dark as that of the Indonesian girl. By contrast, the hair, bleached by that same sun, was much lighter than she imagined hers to be.

The image was, in fact, that of a beautiful woman—more beautiful than Mary had ever been in her life or would likely ever be again. But this above all she failed to register. As a child she had been attended and pampered, much as Charlotte had been on their voyage, but no one had ever spoken of her appearance, at least not in her hearing. Nor had it been a topic of conversation between her and her parents as she grew older. At home as on shipboard, it was her quickness to learn that they remarked on, or her skill in performing a given task. She had never been courted or even had girlfriends during her youth, so the comparisons and competitions that permeate those circles were unknown to her. Physical attentions foisted on her after her arrest seemed a factor of male lust, unrelated to physical charms. In the colony, with so few women about, even hags like Cass and others much more worn out were constantly in demand, suggesting that the only attribute that mattered was the fact that they were female. Will himself had never offered Mary a single compliment beyond one on the crossing, when he had told her her Cornwall accent helped assuage his loneliness.

Certainly Mary's self-esteem had grown in the past

two months, fostered by James's open expressions of admiration, by the respect of the others, and by her own assessment of an escape well-planned and executed. But in no instance had any of that to do with her appearance. Thus it was hardly surprising that Mary neither registered the mirrored image as that of a lovely woman nor would have given it any importance if she had.

However, she had no time to reflect on her reflection, for yet another servant arrived with a garment which appeared to be a simple tube of light cotton fabric. The dominant colour was burnt umber, with intricate designs woven or dyed into it.

"This *kain panjang;* you wear now," Mira announced.

Mira helped her don the long sarong which, when firmly tied above her breasts, left her shoulders bare. Back in England Mary might have felt immodest to have so much of her upper body exposed, but after three years of wearing skimpy shifts made from burlap bags in which rice or flour had been transported to the colony, a gown of simple design and so well-suited to the heat of the tropics felt perfectly natural. Still, recalling the frown of the man who had stared down from the upper balcony as they waited in the courtyard, Mary wondered if the costume covered enough for European sensibilities.

As if reading her mind, Mira draped a gaily printed length of light cotton fabric around Mary's shoulders. "*Seledang,*" she called the garment. "This you wear for meet the gouverneur."

"What about . . .?" Mary pointed to her feet. Her only pair of shoes had fallen apart at least two years ago. Although her small feet had not widened as a result of going barefoot, the soles had grown as tough as leather.

"Ah, I forget!" Mira clapped a hand to her forehead. Then, sizing up Mary's feet and judging them to be about the same as her own, she stepped out of her slippers. Giggling like a schoolgirl, she placed them on Mary's feet. Mary herself began to laugh, partly from pent-up tension at being in such strange surroundings and confronted with so many unfamiliar customs, but also because she sensed in Mira something of what Colleen had been to her: a fellow female conspirator; a sister.

Mary had some misgivings about leaving the children, but Mira insisted that they remain with the servants, which they seemed happy enough to do. Mary followed the girl back along the corridor, up a broad stairway, and out to a balconied veranda. A tall black-suited man stood with his back to her, watching the sun drop toward the horizon. Mira slipped away, leaving Mary alone, wondering how she should announce herself.

Perhaps the governor sensed her presence, for he turned and, giving a slight start, said, "Mevrouw Bryant. I am Gouverneur Wanjon. Velcom to Kupang."

The words were kind although the face above the tight collar was not particularly so. He had the pallor of a man who spends little time out of doors, with skin stretched so tight over his cheekbones as to suggest a struggle with ill health. His eyes and the lines around them put Mary in mind of Governor Phillip's back in Botany Bay. They were those of a man for whom there is no end of worry, and rarely a reason to smile.

Having had no training whatever in formal behaviour, and too few contacts with those from classes above her own to know what might be expected of her, Mary simply spoke her heart. "Oh, Governor Wanjon! How kind you are to welcome us so. My children went to your Siti straightaway, and ate everything she gave them."

"I am glad you approve, Mevrouw. Some say the natives cannot be trained, but my *babus* are as fine as any servants to be found in Amsterdam. They speak Dutch, and vhen castaways from the *Bounty* were *mit* us two years ago, Mira even learned English. Goot vhen ve have visitors from the British Empire such as yourselves," he said stiffly.

"And how often is that, Governor? That British ships call in?"

"Vell now, many Dutch vessels stop in Kupang, but not so many from your country."

A servant approached with a tray of drinks. Wanjon motioned toward them and asked, "Vill you take refreshment, Mevrouw Bryant?

Mary smiled up at him. "I do not drink liquor, Sir, and your Mira served me tea but an hour ago. I am content to drink my fill of sweet evening air, if this would not offend you."

Something close to approval softened the governor's judgmental gaze. "Indeed, Mevrouw, the drink you speak of is my own favourite at this hour—." He broke off and turned his attention to the doorway as Bruger led the men from Botany Bay onto the veranda. "But perhaps the men in your party vill prefer something stronger."

Mary stared at the men, or more particularly, at her husband. Will stared back at her with equal amazement. Neither had ever seen the other so well-dressed, barbered, and combed. Will moved quickly, possessively, to Mary's side. Bruger followed and made the introductions.

"Gouverneur Wanjon, this is Master's Mate Bryant. Mr. Cox, Mr. Morton, Mr. Lucas, Mr. Butcher, Master Pippin, and," motioning to Bados, who remained in the background, "Baxter Walker from the West Indies. All were members of the *Dunkirk*'s crew. Mr. Brown here is the only civilian."

Wanjon's eyes moved down the line of men as Bruger spoke, and settled on James. "How came you to be on this ill-fated vessel, Meneer Brown?"

"As an accountant with the firm, Governor, sailing for the first time on one of our company's ships," James replied. "It was only by God's grace that I fell into the sea in reach of a boat."

Wanjon gave what might have been a sympathetic nod, and addressed his next question to no one in particular. "And your companions, did they go down mit the ship?"

Matey stepped forward. Bowing his head in a way meant to convey both sadness and respect, he spoke in a broken voice. "I 'spect they did, Sir. Quick as she sank, there wasn't no time to lower the boats. Our'n had scarcely touched the water 'fore the deck tilted and I meself was flung into the sea."

"Vhat a tragedy! Do you think your captain vas to blame, Meneer Bryant?"

"Oh, no, Governor," Will said with a fine show of loyalty. "'Twas the heavy seas, with nothing more to be done than what he'd done. When lightning hit the mast, well, that was that. Master Pippin here was cabin boy, and the last in our bunch to see the captain."

Thus cued, Pip spoke with trembling emotion. "He gave a compass, chart, and quadrant into me hand and said to me, go into the boat with the Bryants and their children. I barely had time to do as I was bid 'fore the ship slid sideways and them not already in the boat went falling every which way."

"These worthy seamen," Will cut in, motioning to Luke, Cox, Matey, Scrapper and Bados, "got washed from the deck close at hand so we fished them out. What with the wildness of the sea and the night so black, 'twere no more we could do."

Wanjon nodded, seemingly satisfied with the recitation, and motioned to the servant to come forward and serve the glasses of cognac. Mary darted a quick glance at James and saw that he was pleased with the way the men had delivered the lines he had taught them.

"Tell me, Meneer Bryant," the governor addressed Will. "Are you villing to vork vhile you vait for a ship to England?"

"Yes, indeed, Governor," Will assured him. "Cox

here was ship's carpenter, and a fine one he is. I'm a seafaring man myself, but I know fishing. If you could supply us with nets and such, I'll take these other boys and we'll bring in a right good catch."

"I vill do it," the governor said, looking sternly pleased. And to James, "The accountant of the Dutch East India Company took sick three months ago, and is not yet himself. Perhaps you vould care to assist in his office?"

"With great pleasure, Governor. I would be most grateful for the opportunity."

Wanjon's gaze moved to Bados. Apparently seeing nothing amiss in the fact that Bados had not been served a drink, he asked, "Vhat about you, boy?"

"I fish, Sir," Bados replied in his deep, rich voice.

"Our men are never idle when there is work to do," Mary attested quickly.

"Indeed, Mevrouw. No one is idle in this colony," Wanjon said coldly.

Although a simple statement of fact, Mary took it as a rebuke. Wanjon had conversed with her readily enough when they were alone, but she sensed his displeasure at her speaking up now that there were other men present, and so she said nothing more.

Wanjon spent barely half an hour with them, his grey-blue gaze falling first on one and then another. Mary noticed that when a comment or gesture satisfied him, the stern look was often accompanied by a slight nod of approval, and when it did not, the eyes narrowed with skepticism or displeasure.

"On the morrow," he said to the group at large,

"Meneer Bruger will accompany First Mate Bryant to acquire the supplies needed to outfit your boat for fishing. And you, Meneer Cox, if you are so inclined, might go with him to a carpentry shop where you will be offered work."

Apparently satisfied by the nods and murmurs of agreement, Wanjon ordered a servant to have the cart brought around to take the men back to the barracks where, he informed them, dinner would be served in due time, to supplement the hastily-prepared meal they had been given upon arrival.

As James started for the door with the others, Wanjon said, "Perhaps, Meneer Brown, you vould care to join First Mate Bryant and his good vife at my table tonight, that ve might have an opportunity to discuss your interim employment with the Dutch East India Company."

It was not put as a question, any more than his instructions to the others had been. James understood as much, and responded diffidently, "It would be an honour, Governor."

After Wanjon left the room, Bruger further clarified what was expected of James by adding, "Dinner will be at eight o'clock, making it not worthwhile to return to the barracks. Perhaps you would care to visit with the Bryants in their quarters until the appointed hour."

So James went with Will and Mary along the corridor leading back to their bedroom. Mira greeted them at the door with a finger to her lips, and pointed to the children, curled up like kittens and fast asleep in one of the great beds. Then she slipped out, saying she would return to let them know when dinner was served. Mary motioned to the men to pass through the room and out onto the veranda, so as to not disturb the children.

"Ain't we done well!" Will gloated, as he flopped into a chair at the small table on the veranda. "The governor's a sour old puss, but that's the way with all them high mucky-mucks. Amazing generous he is for a Hollander."

"Let's hope we don't have to spend much time in his company," James said in a worried voice. "Did you notice how he judged our men by the way they handled their liquor?"

"How's that?" Will asked in surprise. "Why, wasn't nothing served but them wee glasses filled one time over. My Emanuel could handle that much!"

"It was not how much they drank, but how," James explained carefully. "A well-brought up person would sip slowly, savouring the smell as well as the taste, and smiling a little, to show some appreciation. The lower classes, and heavy boozers of any class, gulp it down the way Matey did. Chances are the governor will not mix with them socially again, but you might warn them to not guzzle in public, even if they are given the chance."

"Aye, I better do that," Will agreed.

Mary said nothing, but she recalled how Will, while not downing his drink in a single gulp like Matey, had polished it off in a couple of swallows, and that had caused a narrowing of the governor's eyes. Thus she understood James's warning to be not for the men but for Will, who would shortly be dining with the governor.

Talk then turned to conditions where the men were quartered. They had been fed immediately, Will told Mary, then taken to a large room in the barracks. There were cots covered in clean linen, with a small chest along side for each man's belongings—not that any of them had much to call his own.

"I left the musket and ammunition, and some other stuff in the boat for safe-keeping," Will informed Mary. "I was afeared that if I brought it out, Bruger might take a mind to confiscate it. As it stands, he promised the cutter will be well-watched, and none allowed to set foot on her without my leave."

"That was a wise decision," Mary agreed, although she knew, perhaps even before the thought occurred to her husband, that he might one day decide to sell or trade the gun for rum.

A similarly wise decision she herself had made for, in the small bundle she had brought with her, which contained her own and the children's rags, she had concealed the quadrant, chart, and compass. Unbeknownst to Will, they were now hidden under the bed, and would remain there until she had an opportunity to slip them to Bados.

It was full dark when Mira appeared, announcing dinner and saying she would sit with the children until Mary's return. As they walked along the corridor behind the servant sent to guide them, James murmured to Will, "Don't forget, when we are to be seated, to pull out the chair for your wife."

"What?" Will chortled. "These fine clothes made it so she can't do for herself?"

James gave a good-natured laugh. "You didn't notice how heavy the furniture is around here? No three-legged stools will we find at the governor's table. Sure any woman can pull out her own chair, making a horrible racket and gouging the floor in the process. Weak old men do the same. But a man with good muscle under his sleeves makes that known to other men present by lifting the chair and moving it out quietly for any lady standing nearby."

This was as much news to Mary as to Will, and caused in her a mounting tension. If they did not know the rules for so much as how to swallow a drink or sit down at the table, how much more had life's experiences not taught them, which might inform the governor of things about their origins that they needed to conceal?

Mary was spared the strain of making conversation during much of the meal, for Wanjon was more interested in the men. From Will he elicited a credible description of the captain of the ship presumed to have been lost, it having been previously decided that the fictional captain would be modelled on Captain Phillip, whom they had had plenty of time to observe on the crossing. Then Wanjon turned his attention to James, with a discussion clearly meant to determine just how accomplished an accountant James was. It was not until the end of dinner that the governor directed a question to Mary.

"What part of England do you hail from, Mevrouw Bryant?"

"Cornwall, Sir. As does my husband. We are both of us from seafaring families."

"No doubt they will be overjoyed to hear of your survival of this recent disaster."

The comment caused such a rush of emotions in Mary that she blanched, and for a second or two could not speak. Then she gathered herself together and said, "My father was lost at sea some seven years ago, and my mother passed away five years back."

"I am so sorry to hear that." Wanjon frowned as if something about her statement puzzled him, and asked, "Your father was lost at sea, and yet you did not fear coming abroad with your children on a voyage of long duration?"

Mary laid down the spoon with which she had been stirring sugar into her coffee, and said, carefully, "My father died at sea, and my mother fell ill on land. I did not take it to be the sea or the land that killed them, but rather, that their time had come." She paused, and when the others remained silent, she added, "A few weeks ago I thought our time had come, but" she smiled across the table at the governor, "here we are."

As with their earlier meeting, when the governor was ready to conclude the dinner, he said a stiff good-night and left it to the servants to show them out. One went to bring up a cart to take James back to the barracks. Mary and Will lingered with him, discussing the evening in low tones.

"I think he was favourably impressed," James said.

"But I would not want to endure this ordeal every night!"

"Neither would I!" Will muttered. "Why, the victuals they served up to us in the barracks when we first come in was three times as hearty as this one!"

"Once I see how things are done at the office, I shall try to arrange to work evenings, thus making it inconvenient to dine with him at his accustomed hour," James decided. "And you, Will, might want to claim that the crew members are still distraught over the loss of the ship and their mates, and they need you around to steady them. Or something like that."

Will nodded. Then, as if on cue, both men turned to Mary.

"I'll use the children as an excuse," she said. "I can say that, although they're cheerful enough by day, the night gives rise to nightmares related to the wreck."

"Perfect," James approved. "Wanjon doesn't strike me as a very sociable character, and probably prefers to maintain his established routine. Our excuses will relieve him of any obligation he might feel to dine with us on a regular basis."

A horse-drawn conveyance—not the cart in which they had been brought earlier, but a fine two-wheeled buggy—rolled up the circular driveway and stopped at the foot of the steps. James climbed in and disappeared into the darkness, leaving Will and Mary to return to their room. Leaving Mary to face the moment she had most dreaded since their arrival.

She waited until Mira had said goodnight and she heard the girl's footsteps fade away. Will was already pulling his boots off. "Damned things put a blister on my heel and I ain't walked a mile in 'em yet," he complained. He looked up at Mary with a gleam in his eye. "How come you're not here along side me already, woman? Never had such a bed as this, now have we?"

"It does beat that wet sand where we spent our first night in Botany Bay," Mary smiled. Then sobered. "But you'll have this bed to yourself, Will, whilst I sleep with the children."

The boot he had just removed dropped to the floor with a thud. He stared at her in astonishment. "What might you be meaning by that, my girl?"

"I think you understand," Mary said quietly. "I made half the crossing with a child inside me, gave birth on the high seas, and landed to an uncertain fate with a baby in my arms. I'm not going through that all over again on the way back, not with two already to tend."

"What about me?" he howled. "Have you given no thought to what I been through without no woman for nigh on to three months?"

"I have." Mary bowed her head. "And I am truly ashamed to withhold that comfort from you, my lawful wedded husband. But I tell you straight, this trip is using all the strength I've got. I can't be taking on one burden more."

"Lawful wedded husband! Ha!" He jerked off his second boot, dropped it on the floor, and flung himself onto the bed. "Where'd you get that notion? Ain't none in Botany Bay ever got wedded in the law! How could they've been, with no publishing of the banns?"

He glared a moment, waiting to see how she took the news. Mary flinched, but held her tongue.

"Ain't you got nothing to say to that?" he demanded.

"I'd say we might leave this aside for now, seeing as how we've got to keep up the appearance of man and wife to maintain our freedom. I'd say it's been a long and wearing day. I'd say you might be wanting to get some rest right now, as you're due to meet with Bruger soon after sunup."

With that Mary snuffed the candle and stepped out onto the veranda. The warm night air held the scent of unfamiliar flowers and just a little of the sea's salty smell. Thoughts ran through her head, so tangled with emotions that she had trouble sorting them out. She did not love Will, had never loved him, but she felt an enormous sense of obligation. Not because they were married—if they were—but because he had saved her on the night of their landing. Was her engineering their escape from the penal colony payment enough for that, or did she owe him the rest of her life? And if she did, what was that life worth to her? For she knew full well that she had refused to lie with him not only to protect herself from pregnancy, but because she preferred another.

As she stood there in the tropical night air with a breeze caressing her skin, another thought surfaced which so surprised her that she turned it over in her mind a few times to determine its validity. She had expected Will to be violently angry, even to the point of taking her by force; an act against which she had no defence. Now, replaying the moment in her head, she realised that although he had been angry, he had accepted her decision with surprising acquiescence. His only retort, really, had been that bit about not being lawfully married. Offensive as it was, it had come as no shock. Back in Botany Bay, Will often bragged that as soon as his time was served, he expected to become a wealthy man by selling fish in the colony. The boast included a declaration that once he acquired some wealth he would be a man about town, not bound to any one woman.

Was this, then, where Will imagined himself to be? That, having vaulted into freedom, he was now poised on the brink of becoming an affluent businessman, if not in Botany Bay, then here in Kupang? In going about the city with Bruger, had those beautiful Indonesian women caught his eye and ignited his fantasy?

Exhausted as she was from the day just ending, which had brought more changes of scenery, more encounters with strangers, more new customs and new experiences than she might have had in a year back in Botany Bay, Mary suddenly felt her emotional turmoil subside. Marriage vows or no, Will's possible lack of commitment made her own longing to be free seem less shameful. She tuned her ear to the bedroom. Hearing Will's even breathing, she slipped out of her sarong and slid into the other bed beside her children. Within seconds she was sleeping as soundly as he.

Mary woke to a tapping. The children stirred beside her. Will was nowhere to be seen.

"Mevrouw?" It was Mira's voice, coming from beyond the door.

Mary called out that she was awake and Mira came in, followed by a servant bearing a tray of food. As before, it was carried out to the little table on the veranda.

While the servant took the children in hand and got them into their clothes and to the table to help themselves to whatever caught their fancy, Mira helped Mary do up her sarong and brought a basin of water for her to wash her face.

Mary had known of servants who cleaned, as she herself had done for doctors, but in her experience, personal services such as Mira now insisted on providing were limited to what mothers did for small children, or what one might do for an invalid. She tried, as she had the previous day, to persuade Mira to let her do for herself, but Mira would have none of it.

At last, in a small struggle for the comb over who should do her hair, Mira cried out in frustration, "Mevrouw, please! Gouverneur Wanjon orders me do for you as for his wife! One who disobeys our gouverneur is punished!"

It was only then that Mary understood that the Indonesian girl was acting under orders. And that Wanjon had—"A wife?" Mary echoed. "Where is this wife?"

"Ah, the fever took her three years ago," Mira explained. "Gouverneur Wanjon have no more wife."

Thereafter Mary did not protest the personal services which Mira felt bound to provide. Having no knowledge of the lives of the upper classes, she did not know it was commonplace for ladies to require such attentions of a maid and, had anyone told her, she would not have believed it. Personally, she found the fussing excessive, and supposed it to be the result of Mira having been trained to look after an invalid woman. But she did not want to interfere with the girl's training or get her in trouble with her employer, so once again she adopted the compliance exhibited by her contented children, and let Mira do as she wished.

What Mira wished that day was for Mary to come with her to town to purchase fabric to make new clothes for the children. This Mary was thrilled to do, for her children had never owned any garment made from fabric not previously used, first for transporting supplies to the colony, then as clothing for one of their parents. Only when that had gone to rags would the material be patched together into some sort of garment for one of the children.

As Mira guided her along the bustling commercial district, Mary's head swivelled from side to side, eyes wide with astonishment at all the things on offer. When at last they entered a fabric store and Mira told her to select what she wanted, Mary simply shook her head and said, "You must choose, Mira. I cannot."

This delighted Mira, who conducted the whole

transaction in her own language. When Mary asked about payment, Mira explained that "the King of England would pay." This was her understanding of charges drawn on the Crown on behalf of the shipwreck survivors.

As they walked further along the street, Mary heard her name called. She turned and saw Cox smiling from the doorway of a carpentry shop, a dusting of sawdust down the front of his new shirt.

"Don't you look the part of a native!" he greeted her. "But for that crown o' golden hair wound around your head." He lowered his voice, and said, "I'm to get a little pay for this work above and beyond my keep. I'm thinking to buy my Florie one of them kind of gowns." He gestured to the sarongs Mary and Mira were wearing, his eyes settling on Mira. "She's about her size, wouldn't you say?"

"Yes," Mary agreed, and explained to Mira, "Cox has a wife the same size as you. He wants to take her a dress like yours."

"Kain panjang," Mira corrected, beaming at the compliment. "You take her two, one for working wear, one for holidays."

"Right you are," Cox laughed, and added, with a wink at Mary, "Can't you see my girl on her way to church of a Sunday morning, rigged out in one of these South Seas outfits?"

Cox was called back into the shop, and the women walked on. Mira pointed to an upstairs window in the largest building on the street and said, "Mr. Brown, he working there."

Mary looked up and saw James's head bent over his work, but he did not glance out the window to notice her passing.

Mary told Mira that, because the wreck had happened at night, the children were having nightmares and she did not wish to leave them after dark. She asked Mira to explain this to the governor, and apparently she did, for that day and each day thereafter, meals were brought from the kitchen and served in their quarters. Mary did not see Will from dawn to dark, and presumed he was taking his meals with the men in the barracks. By the time he came in at night, she was in bed with the children, either asleep or pretending to be.

Once Mary had finished sewing decent clothing for the children—sewing being a skill her mother had taught her well—she spent a good deal of time with them out of doors, letting them run about, climb trees, and frolic on the lawn. She occasionally saw Wanjon observing them from an upstairs balcony, as he had on the day of their arrival. He seemed to confine himself to the opposite wing of the house from where she was, leaving it only when a carriage was brought round to take him into town. Thus, without going out of her way to avoid him, a whole week passed when she but occasionally glimpsed him.

She became increasingly comfortable in her new surroundings, bothered only by the lack of anything to do. Toward the end of the first week she discovered the kitchen and took to spending a good deal of time there, curious to see how the cook, aided by Siti, prepared her exquisite concoctions, often with ingredients which Mary had never seen before.

On one such day, as Mary sat in a corner of the kitchen with Emanuel in her lap, eating from a plate of delicacies the cook had given her to share with the children, she heard suppressed laughter and conspiratorial whispers approaching from outside. A moment later Pip and Mira burst into the kitchen. Mira snatched a fried shrimp from a plate at the cook's elbow and popped it into Pip's mouth. He grabbed her by the wrist and pretended to eat her fingers as well, causing them both to dissolve into giggles. They did not notice Mary sitting in a dimly-lit corner, perhaps because they had eyes only for each other. Mira had just turned to steal another shrimp for Pip, when Wanjon's voice came through the open door.

"*Acht*, Mira, there you are! And you, Cabin Boy, you are here too? Vhat do you vant?"

It was a question that Mary might have asked, had she had the opportunity. She held her breath, hoping Pip would have a good answer. His frightened look and suddenly stiff posture suggested that he might not. But she had underestimated the boy.

Drawing up to his whole small height, Pip said, "I was wanting to help in your kitchen, Sir. I am very good about the house, Sir."

"Ve don't use vhite boys for such vork," Wanjon said bluntly.

"I can do most anything," Pip persisted. "If my captain was here he would vouch for me. Why, I did everything about his cabin, and in the galley, too, whatever he bade me do, Sir, on account of what I don't know how to do, I'm fair quick to learn."

"Is this so?" Wanjon said. Then, without waiting for Pip to answer, he said, "You make a good pot of tea, maybe?"

"Oh, aye, sir, I can make tea," Pip fairly squeaked with relief. "That I can do."

"Vell, this my Siti has not mastered, not like the English. Mevrouw Bryant, I think she vould like good tea." To Mira he said, "As the hour approaches, you will ask Mevrouw Bryant to join me for tea. If she accept, you, Cabin Boy, make this tea, and Mira, you vill mind the kinder."

"Aye, aye, Sir! Right away, Sir!" Pip's voice followed the sound of Wanjon's steps echoing away.

It was only then, as Charlotte dashed forward and flung herself around one of Pip's legs, and Emanuel toddled over to grab the other, that Pip realised Mary was in the room.

"Oh, Miss Mary!" he exulted, picking up Emanuel and giving him a great hug. "Did you hear that? Can you show me how to make tea in the right English way? I never done such a thing, and me mum died so long ago, I don't remember how she did it."

Mary rose, laughing, from the bench where she'd been sitting. "The same as Siti makes it, only be sure the water is boiling hard. Rinse the pot and the cups, too, with boiling water. Then put in the leaves and boiling water, and serve it that very minute. It's waiting about that turns the tea cool and bitter."

"He'll think I knew all along!" Pip crowed. Again his hand went out to touch Mira as if her presence was some sort of miracle, and physical touch was needed to confirm that she was not a mirage.

Tea was served on the upstairs veranda about an hour before sunset. Mary had dreaded again sitting across the table from the governor, and her apprehension grew when she realised that it would only be the two of them. But conversation proved less difficult than she expected. She adopted the child's trick of asking questions, which had worked so well with Captain Smit, thereby guiding the conversation toward subjects which did not require her to reveal or invent a great deal about herself and her companions. Wanjon responded to her questions with long-winded commentaries on the history of the Dutch East India company, and descriptions of various places he had served. Just prior to coming to Kupang, he had been in Batavia, which he called "a virtual cesspool of disease." Mary knew from Mira that it was his wife's ill health that had caused him to petition the company for a transfer to the more healthful city of Kupang. But either the move came too late or the illness was too strong, for here his wife had been buried.

As clouds along the horizon flamed with sunset colours, Wanjon rose and invited Mary to stand at the railing and watch the sun slip into the sea. The view from the balconied veranda was indeed breathtaking.

"'Tis like a prayer," Mary murmured. "If there be such a thing as a prayer without words."

Wanjon frowned, perplexed. "In what way does it resemble prayer?"

When Mary made the statement she had not been prepared to put the notion into words, and struggled to find a few which approximated what she meant. "Well, there's the feeling of gratitude that wells up in one's heart, that such beauty exists. And a sense of wanting to make oneself worthy. Is this not something of what we're meant to feel in prayer?"

Wanjon did not respond, but turned again to stare at the multicoloured sky. Mary could not know what he was thinking, and hoped she hadn't offended him. It seemed she had not for, when he adjourned their hour of sociability, he invited her to join him on the morrow at the same hour. Thus began a ritual of afternoon tea several times a week. It was stressful for Mary at first, but became less so as the weeks wore on.

They had been in Kupang almost two months when Will came clumping into their room one evening a little earlier than usual, just before Mary snuffed the candle. He did not greet her, but went directly to his own bed and began to undress. With his back to her, he asked, "You got any notion where that darky's got to?"

"Who? Bados?" Mary responded in surprise. "Why, didn't he show up to go out on the boat today?"

"Not today nor for a whole week gone by," Will informed her.

"A week!" Mary exclaimed. "Has no one seen him about town?"

"Would I be asking you if they had?" Will retorted grumpily. "Cox is right there in the middle of everything, and James can see for a good long ways from where he sits. Said last they seen of him was more'n a week ago. Not that they been looking. Figured him to be out on the boat with Matey and Scrapper and Luke and me."

"Does he not sleep in the barracks with the other men?"

"Nay, not from the beginning. The Hollanders wouldn't have a black amongst them, so he was put somewhere else, out with some natives. Don't none of them speak English, nor the Hollanders either, but for Bruger, and I didn't want to say nothing to him. Not yet, anyway."

Will flopped onto his bed with an exasperated sigh. "You'd think Bados would be more dependable than that, after we went and brought him with us. And Pip, too, the pipsqueak. I asked him where he got to and he told me the governor's put him to work here in the house. I can't hardly put up a fuss, saying as how Pip's part of my crew and I'm needing him on the boat, not if the governor's taken a mind to put him into service here. Though why he'd want the boy hanging around here I can't imagine, when the old fart's got natives all over the place hopping to his beck and call."

Mary said nothing to that, although she knew full well the use to which Pip had been put. When she had mentioned to the governor over tea that Pip had assisted in looking after the children during their long and difficult voyage as castaways, the governor had set him the task of minding the children as well as preparing their afternoon tea.

Mary assumed that the governor had done this because Mira, although she continued to provide personal services for Mary according to her own sense of what was required, was also relied upon by Wanjon for a variety of other services. He probably did not want her tied up with childcare all day long. It wasn't that the children were difficult, for they were generally quiet and easily satisfied. But as Mira had made clear at the very beginning, they, or more accurately the area in which they played, must be watched carefully, for Kupang was home to many poisonous snakes. Given that warning, Mary welcomed Pip's help with the children, and they, of course, were happy to have him inventing and sharing in their games.

"You don't really need Pip and Bados, do you?" Mary inquired of Will. "Naturally it's easier to have a man for each oar, but you and the three you've got, you're the best of the lot."

She knew as she spoke that this was not strictly true; plausible only in the case of Pip, who was small for his seventeen years, and not as strong as the men. Bados, though, was as strong as any two, and had rowing skills to match his strength. Will had guessed as much at the beginning, which was why Bados was selected for his fishing crew in the first place. But Mary was fairly certain that Will would never admit to the black man being a better sailor than himself, Luke, Matey, and Scrapper.

"'Course I don't need them," Will huffed. "I just expected some loyalty, I surely did, after all I done for them."

"Maybe the governor gave Bados some other assignment, the same as he did with Pip," Mary suggested, "and he had no choice in the matter."

"Aye," Will replied, sounding somewhat mollified. "That could be what happened. It's not like I can go questioning old Sour Puss. Even Bruger acts like I'm speaking out of turn when I remark this or that to him. Capt'n Phillip, when he got to be governor of the colony, never acted so high and mighty as that Bruger does when he's out and about the docks."

"Well, with a little luck we shan't be here much longer," Mary said, and blew out the candle.

"Prayin' to God that's our luck!" Will echoed the sentiment. Then added, as an afterthought, "I bet Bados turns up quick enough when an English ship puts into port."

"Very likely," Mary said, although she did not think it likely at all. But it seemed even less likely that Bados would have left Kupang without the navigational tools promised him.

The next day, as her hair was being braided, it occurred to Mary that Mira was often sent to town on errands; so she might have seen Bados or would know where he was staying.

"You remember the black man who arrived with us?" Mary asked

"Yes, Mevrouw."

"Have you seen him about?"

The hands stopped, and for a moment held taut the braid without moving. Then, "No, Mevrouw."

"Have you heard anyone speak of him? Someone who might know where he is?"

This time Mira let go of the braid entirely, picked up the hand-held looking glass, and said, "Maybe today we make the braids go a different way, loops by ears, and not over the top?"

Mary took the looking glass from the girl's hand and laid it back on the dressing table. "Mira," she said. "I have something that belongs to Bados. It is very important. If you know where he is, you must take me there."

"Maybe I find him, I take things," Mira suggested brightly.

"No, you take me to him," Mary insisted. Then added, "Don't worry, Mira. If Bados doesn't want anyone to know where he is, I won't tell. But he is my friend. I must see him."

Mira hesitated, then shrugged, and said, "Tomorrow we walk to town. Maybe we see somebody who know him. Maybe not."

Although Mary repeatedly suggested that they walk to town to look for Bados, Mira kept finding excuses until Mary hinted that she might ask Governor Wanjon to find someone else to accompany her. Mira immediately agreed to go with her, confirming Mary's suspicion that the governor had told Mira from the start to accompany her to town whenever she wished to go.

Pip was left in charge of the children and they set

off. They were about halfway along the crowded main shopping area when, far up ahead, something caught Mira's eye. At first Mary did not know who or what it was, but after a quarter hour of being sometimes hurried along and sometimes slowed down as Mira appeared to dawdle, she realised that they were following someone. The person was a statuesque Indonesian woman. Her height, added to by a basket on her head, made her easy to see at a distance. She soon left the main street and followed a narrow side street which, at the edge of town, became a mere trail.

Mira and Mary continued to follow at a distance, often losing sight of the woman. But as they were now on the trail, which wound through dense vegetation, the direction she had taken seemed fairly definite. Mary, like Mira, hiked up the skirt of her sarong in order to walk faster, for keeping up with the athletic stride of the taller woman was no easy matter.

At one point Mary, drenched in perspiration and totally out of breath, begged Mira to stop and let her rest. Mira complied, saying only, "I see now. We go to the lagoon."

Mary took that to mean that Mira had figured out where the woman was going and no longer needed to keep her in sight. "Who is this woman we're following?" she asked.

"Inah. She fisher woman."

After resting a moment, Mary walked on. Now ahead of Mira, she kept her eyes on the narrow trail, for the vegetation was thick and she was mindful of the venomous serpents said to inhabit this region. She looked up only when a brightness indicated a clearing ahead. As the last low branches parted to give her a view of the open area, she stopped so suddenly that Mira stepped on her heel. The girl murmured an apology which Mary scarcely heard.

A turquoise lagoon glittered in the late morning sun. On the near side was a crescent of white sand, and on the far side, a small hill topped by two or three native huts. The same sort of forested, vine-trailing tropical vegetation through which they had been walking surrounded the area. However, all of those details escaped Mary's notice. Her eyes were riveted on the woman, standing with her back to them, about twenty yards away. Basket, sandals, and sarong now lay on the sand. For a few seconds the woman stood there, every curve and muscle of back and buttocks highlighted in the sun. Then she flung herself forward in a shallow dive and began to swim toward a dugout canoe floating in the lagoon.

A man in the dugout stood, untied a loincloth wrap from around his hips, and likewise dove into the water. In the second he stood there with his naked, muscular body exposed to Mary's view, she registered his colour—not copper like the woman, but ebony. Bados, of course. The two swimmers came together in the water and, taking hold of each other, began to play, bringing their faces together, sinking below the surface, rising, caressing, and kissing. After a few minutes of intimate frolic, they swam alongside the dugout, one on either side, and began drawing it toward the shore.

Mira whispered, "We go now. Come another day!"

"Yes!" Mary exclaimed, and turned to follow her back down the trail.

But their movement must have caught Inah's eye, for she called out sharply, in Indonesian. Mira stopped in her tracks and stood for a moment, trembling. Then she turned around, walked out into the clearing, and called to the woman. Mary heard her name in the conversation that followed, and so came forward to stand next to Mira.

"Bados!" she called. "I've come to visit. Do you want us to come back another time?"

Bados's rich deep laughter rolled across the water toward her. "No, you stay, Mary. But maybe you turn round for a minute, give me time to cover my middle parts."

Blushing, Mary did as he suggested, and waited till he called her name before turning back to face him. By then, Bados stood on the beach, wearing a wrap-around cloth which covered him from waist to thigh. Inah came out of the water quite naked and, hand on one hip, let loose a torrent of Indonesian at Mira.

As Mira responded, Inah picked up her sarong from the sand, shook it off, and proceeded to dress. Mira rushed forward to help her tie the sarong, but Inah brushed her hands away as if they were bothersome insects.

"So this is where you've been keeping yourself, Bados!" Mary exclaimed.

"You not be giving me away to the others, will you, Mary?"

"Of course not!" Mary assured him. She glanced

toward Inah, whose conversation with Mira seemed somewhat unfriendly. "What is she saying?"

"Can't tell," Bados replied. "I don't know Timor talk, just a few words. And Inah speak no English. But she my woman now."

"Is that so?" Mary laughed. "If you don't speak the same language, how do you know she's your woman?"

"Is true," Mira confirmed. "Inah say me she keep this big man."

"Inah be coming with me to that island, Mary. I need the chart and compass."

"Do you remember how to use them?" Mary asked.

"I remember everything James showed me. I take them, I take the boat, and Inah and me, we go back to that island."

"Are you sure she understands what you have in mind?" Mary asked doubtfully. She looked at Mira. "Ask Inah. Does she understand Bados wants to take her to a distant island?"

There was another rapid-fire exchange in Indonesian, then Mira translated to Mary. "She say if he has a big boat, she go with him wherever he wants to go."

"You know Will's using the boat for fishing," Mary reminded Bados. "And just the two of you, when there are six oars to manage—are you sure you can handle it?"

"I take that boat." Bados repeated stubbornly.

"Inah has many brothers," Mira explained. "Brothers have wives. Some tired of these Dutch, make life in Kupang so hard. Their boats small, like that." She motioned to the dugout in the lagoon. "Can't go far. But in a big one . . ." Mira shrugged.

"I see. All right, Bados. I'll bring the compass and chart as soon as I can. But you be careful when you take that boat. It's well-guarded at night, and if they catch you—," Mary's voice and eyes reflected her concern.

"Don't you worry for me, Mary," Bados interrupted kindly. "I already know what they do to a black man when he go stealing cucumbers from a kitchen garden. Nobody have to speak about how short my life be if I get caught stealing that boat you already stole. But they'll not catch me this time. I be getting back to that island or death take me in the act."

Inah spoke sharply to Mira again in Indonesian, and again Mary requested translation. Mira, looking more frightened than before, said, "She said we must not tell that Bados is here. If we do, she will put a spell on us and we will die."

Bados laughed and wagged a finger at Inah. She caught it and bit it playfully, but with enough force to let him know that she was not intimidated.

Mary was not bothered by Inah's threat, since she had no intention of telling anyone. What concerned her was the realisation that perhaps too much had been said already in Mira's presence. She gave the girl a worried look. "You will not speak of this to anyone, will you, Mira?"

Mira shook her head. "No, Mary. I want no spell on me. But this talk," she drew a circle with her finger to include all of them, "very dangerous!"

Bados nodded, then did a surprising thing. He took Mira's hand and Mary's, and laid one on top of the other. Then he reached for Inah's hand, which he put on top of Mira's and Mary's, and finally he placed his own hands, top and bottom. Mary knew no custom such as this and, by the puzzled looks on the faces of the other women, surmised that they did not either. Still, the message was clear: that they were together in this conspiracy, and must trust one another.

Given that some in this little circle were virtual strangers to others, she did not know how much trust there could be. But it did not seem that they had any choice.

Mary and Mira walked back to town more slowly than they had come. Despite shade cast by the dense forest, the heat was stifling. Although Mary tried to banish images of Bados's and Inah's nudity from her mind, they lingered and thrilled her. She had once seen a picture that depicted Adam and Eve in the nude, eyes downcast, hands covering their private parts. The painting conveyed neither Eden's paradisiacal qualities nor the couple's pleasure at being there. Yet the unashamed nudity of Bados and Inah had conveyed both paradise and pleasure, along with a sense of freedom. And all of it as far removed from her own life as a return to the Garden of Eden.

They had reached town and were passing through Kupang's commercial centre when James leaned out the window of his office, and called, "Mrs. Bryant, a moment if you please, that I might have a word with you."

Mary stood in a slim strip of shade cast by the building, and waited with apprehension, for she had caught something of anxiety in James' voice, and knew it must be serious for him to hail her in public.

When James reached her side, he glanced at Mira in a way which indicated a desire to speak to Mary in private. The girl tactfully wandered a few yards away to gaze into a shop window, although, Mary suspected, not so far that she couldn't overhear what was being said.

"I am sorry to convey bad news," James said hurriedly. "But Will has been brawling down at the docks, in plain view of everyone."

"When was this?" Mary asked in dismay.

"Yesterday. As I heard the story, they came in with a good catch and were unloading it when Matey started drinking from a bottle of rum he had stashed on the boat. Will ordered him to wait until the fish was delivered, and they got into a fist fight in front of a crowd there on the dock." James drew a breath. "That's not the worst of it, Mary. Apparently they screamed obscenities at each other which included references to Botany Bay!"

"Oh no!" Mary gasped. "And word of this has spread already?"

"I don't know how much was understood by the bystanders," James admitted. "Bruger, of course, speaks English but he wasn't there, and got the story second hand. I heard him later, in the hall outside my office, reporting the incident to Wanjon."

"What did he say?" Mary asked, her chest tight with apprehension.

"Only that the fight was broken up by Luke before the *gendarmes* arrived. Bruger asked Wanjon if he should take further action, but the governor said that would be awkward, given that you and Will are guests in his house. Then—and here is the part that alarmed me, Mary—Bruger said that Bryant and his men have more knowledge of lowlife than seafaring. So their rough ways have been noticed! Wanjon brushed that off, saying, 'All Englishmen are lowlife. Such as Bryant would never be an officer in the Dutch navy.'"

James paused, and added, "There was one more thing, Mary, and you can take pride in this. Wanjon said that the wife—meaning you—'is very gracious.'"

Mary was silent for a minute, mulling over what he had told her. "I suppose I haven't made any serious missteps in his presence. But what about Matey? What shall we do?"

"I don't know. Will could put a stop to it, but he won't. Once the day's catch is in, he matches Matey drink for drink." James took a deep breath. "It is a certainty that from now on all our men will be watched. When Bruger asked if he should take any action, Wanjon said, 'We will wait. A fool is never a fool only once.' I shudder to think what might happen if they get rowdy again, or loose-lipped."

"I will speak to him," Mary promised. "But I doubt it will do any good." She hesitated, and added, "We are, in a sense, estranged from one another. Will leaves before I wake in the morning, and rarely returns before the wee hours."

"I understand," James nodded. "But do try. I will talk to Matey, for in drink it is he who sets the pace. Will, and Scrapper, of course, follow his lead, and Cox is a hard drinker as well. Then Luke is not to be left out, so he goes along with them. Bados and Pip are the only ones I've not seen around, drinking to the point of foolishness."

Mary glanced toward Mira with a slight smile. "Pip has been otherwise occupied. Bados as well."

"Ah yes." James' eyes slanted with humour. "I saw Bados following a magnificent Indonesian woman a few weeks back. Come to think of it, I haven't seen him since."

Mira wandered back toward them, and Mary guessed, from the overly-innocent look on the girl's face, that she had overheard at least some of their conversation. "Mira," she asked directly, "Did you know about my husband's fight on the boat yesterday?"

"Yes, Mevrouw."

"Did the governor speak of it to you?"

"No, Mevrouw. He does not speak of such things to me." Mira hesitated, then added, "I think he does not want trouble for your husband."

"The governor is a kind man," Mary acknowledged. "I'm sure he would not make trouble for us. What I am afraid of is that my husband will make trouble for himself."

Mary did not talk to Will that night, as she had promised to do, because he did not return to their room. This she discovered when she woke from a dream, a dream in which it was she, not Bados, standing in the canoe, feeling freer than she had ever felt before and not concerned about her nudity, not even aware that she was nude until she was in the water with James, wrapped in his skin as he was in hers.

She woke damp, but it was the salty wetness of her own perspiration, not that of the lovely lagoon. Dawn had already greyed the sky. The coverlet on Will's bed was smooth, as the maid had left it, which indicated that he had not returned. Mary slipped out of bed and went to stand on the veranda, watching the sunrise. She ached with longing for the kind of freedom Bados and Inah seemed to have, and she envied Mira, who could at least share touches and laugher with the man she loved. Yet she, who had brought them this close to their dreams, still languished oceans away from the fulfilment of her own.

Mary saw Bados once more, about a week after her first visit. This time she found him sitting on a bench next to one of the huts across the lagoon. He was playing his flute—a newly made one, Mary noticed—while Inah accompanied him on a stringed instrument that resembled a lute. The pair continued to play as Mary and Mira approached, and laid aside the instruments only when they were standing before them. Mira applauded delicately. Mary unwrapped the navigational instruments from her seledang and handed them to Bados.

Bados turned to Inah. "You see. I told you she would bring them." He motioned to Mira. "You tell Inah, Mary is our friend."

Mira made the translation, then said, shyly, "I also your friend, Bados."

He grinned. "If you didn't tell anybody where I'm at, I guess you are."

"More friend than that," Mira insisted. "Pip and me, we want to go with you."

"Go where?" Bados asked in surprise.

"To that island," Mira said, and repeated the request to Inah in her own language.

Bados looked thoughtful, and opened his mouth to give what Mary judged to be a positive response, but Inah interrupted sharply. Mira hung her head in shame.

"What's Inah saying?" Bados wanted to know.

"She said I am nothing, just house girl. Not strong for work, not smart to learn," Mira confessed. Then added hopefully. "But my Pip, he is very smart, yes?"

"Pip's a good boy," Bados agreed. "But he's a white boy. He'll be wanting to go back to England with the others."

Mira seemed to give up on Bados understanding, and appealed to Mary. "Pip want to marry me, but Governeur Wanjon will not allow," she said hopelessly.

"Have you asked the governor?" Mary wanted to know. "Maybe he—."

But Mira was shaking her head. "I cannot go. I his babu."

"What's a babu?" Bados asked. "That mean you his slave or something?"

"His babu," Mira repeated, leaving them still unclear as to the extent of the governor's control over her life. She spoke again to Inah, and Inah nodded, a bit more sympathetically this time. Mira made a prayerful motion with her hands, and Inah shrugged.

"We think about it," Bados said finally. "Pip's little, but he can row like a man. And you," he grinned at Mira. "You'd be worth something to tell me what my Inah's saying when we're not grasping each others' meaning."

⊕

It was now early August, two full months since their arrival, and still no European ship had called in at Kupang. Mary did not see James again, but guessed that his talk with the men had not done much to modify their behaviour. Will, when he came back to their room at all, stumbled in late at night reeking of rum. His arrival was not particularly quiet, and she could only hope that it did not wake Governor Wanjon in the other wing of the house.

Mary had a great deal of time on her hands. She had no responsibilities other than tending her children, and even that pleasant chore she could discharge onto Pip whenever she wished. Not since she herself was a small child had she had the luxury of so little labour and so much time to muse and meditate. The experience worked strange spells on her. Sometimes she would wake in the night filled with longing for James, and slip out onto the veranda where she could gaze at the stars and imagine him beside her. Often the fantasy placed them in Cornwall, gazing at this very same sky albeit with stars in very different alignments. Or she might imagine them aboard a ship bound for Canada, where yet another life awaited them.

Then there were nights when she woke in terror from a dream, remembered or not, in which she and her children had seemed in great peril. In those frightening moments she would turn her head to listen closely to the breath of first one and then the other of her children, stroke back the hair from their foreheads, and run her hands along their small, smooth limbs. Reassured that they were safe and sweetly asleep, she herself might fall back to sleep. Or she might not.

Three things lurked in her mind like great crouching beasts. There was the fear that Bados would get caught trying to steal the boat and be hanged before her very eyes, for which she would surely hold herself responsible. There was the fear that Will or one of the others in their drunkenness would spill out who they really were. And there was the fear that she herself might make some slip which would reveal to the governor that she was not the wife of an officer at all, but an impostor, a convicted criminal.

These things tormented Mary, not only at night but sometimes in the bright light of day. Wandering around the beautiful grounds of the governor's home, dressed in yet another of the exquisite sarongs Mira provided for her, watching her well-clothed children frolic about on legs that had grown plump, fear stalked her even during those languorous hours.

Little wonder that she sometimes rose at night and slipped out onto the veranda where the flower-perfumed darkness aided her in conjuring a fantasy of loving James in the flesh as well as in her imagination. Only then did the crouching fears back off, allowing her something approximating peace.

Fears and fantasies alike she put aside when Mira came with an invitation from Wanjon to join him for tea. Mira was always on hand, as she had been that first day, to ensure that Mary was bathed, dressed, combed, and braided before the appointed hour. All Mary had to do was climb the stairs to the second-floor veranda, where she would find Wanjon waiting.

It was on such an afternoon at the very end of August that she sat down to tea with him with a sense of actual pleasure, for she had learned to read his moods and could see that on this day he was much at ease. To a casual observer it might seem that nothing had changed during the two months he and Mary had been taking tea together. He continued to adhere rigidly to the single hour before sunset, that hour ending after they stood at the balcony railing to watch the red ball as it touched the horizon and melted into the ocean. Given that they had by now engaged in this ritual a dozen times or more, it was hardly surprising that there had been modest changes, both in the content of their conversation and in their appreciation for each other's company. They talked more easily now; Mary, because her confidence in her ability to give acceptable responses had grown, and the governor because he had discovered that Mary was genuinely interested in the subjects upon which he chose to discourse. On this day which, unbeknownst to her, was the last time they would share this pleasant hour of sociability, he said as much.

"The nautical adventures of Europe's great explorers, crime in the colonies, the difficulties of Dutch traders—you are the first lady I have met who converses on such subjects, Mevrouw Bryant. Tell me, vere did you gain your knowledge?"

Naturally Mary had made good use of the things she had learned from Captain Smit, but she had not been aware that these were subjects about which most well-bred women would be ignorant. The truth, or part of the truth, was as good a reply as any. "Perhaps men discuss serious matters more freely in the presence of ladies on shipboard, where they cannot escape," she told Wanjon with a smile.

The governor laughed—not something he did easily or often—and Mary felt encouraged to continue. "And the conversation of wise men interests me," she confided, aware of the flattery implicit in her words. "Perhaps I listen more than I should."

Immediately the governor grew serious. "It is no vaste of time to listen ven one does so intelligently, Mevrouw Bryant."

Mary was trying to formulate an appropriate response to the compliment when a racket from downstairs attracted their attention. Will's voice and heavy tread rose above a clamour of servants' voices and— was that James, trying to cajole him into going to his room? But the voices came closer as the footsteps moved ominously up the stairs.

By the time Will stood teetering in the doorway, Wanjon was on his feet. His face was a mask of disapproval, but he spoke with stiff, and probably feigned, cordiality. "Gentlemen! Just in time for tea, is it? Or something stronger perhaps? Normally I vait for the sun to set, but a little earlier, I see this is no problem for you, Meneer Bryant."

"Thank you, Governor," James responded quickly. "But Mr. Bryant has a fierce toothache. He—"

Will, speaking in a slurred voice, interrupted. "One little nip to tide us over till dinner would be welcome, Gov'nor, an' I thank ye kindly. A pleasure 'twould be to sit me down with me little wife and such a gentleman as yerself, Sir. A man likes that sort of thing after a hard day's work, he does."

Mary rushed to Will's side, exclaiming over her shoulder, "You must excuse us, Governor! I believe the rum my husband took for pain makes us not fit company. I must do what I can for his comfort."

Will cast the governor a triumphant look and beamed down at Mary. "As ye say, little wife. We'll be off to see what you got in store for me comfort."

James and Mary managed to get Will turned around, down the stairs and along the hall. As they reached their room, Mary realised that Mira was following anxiously behind.

"Mira," she whispered urgently. "Tell Pip to keep the children outside or down in the kitchen as long as he can! Time for my husband to fall asleep!"

"Yes, Mevrouw!" Mira replied, and scurried away.

By the time Mary entered the room, James had Will seated on the bed, and had knelt to unlace his boots.

"A fine flunky ye make, Jamie," Will chortled. "A gentleman's flunky I'd say. But ye needn't go to such bother. I been in the hay with this 'un," he waved his hand in Mary's general direction, "with me boots on before."

James cast Mary an anguished look which she read too well. It said that he did not want to leave her alone with Will, but neither did he want to remain, knowing that his presence only intensified the humiliation she was already suffering.

"Go, James," she said firmly. "I can manage."

"Righto," Will chortled. "We're wanting it to be just the two of us now, we are. Whyn't you go finish slopping down tea with Gov'nor Sourpuss?"

Reluctantly, James moved toward the door, but went out only when Mary urged him. Jerking her head toward Will, she closed her eyes in a gesture of sleep. James nodded with understanding, and said, "Good evening, Mrs. Bryant. And a good evening to you, too, Will. See you on the morrow."

Will did not respond for he had fallen back on the bed. His feet, clad in unlaced boots, still rested on the floor. Within minutes he lapsed into a drunken snore.

Mary slipped out and down to the kitchen, where she found the children being fed. To avoid offending the cook she ate a little herself, although she had no appetite. Then she took the children back to their quarters, explaining on the way that their father was sleeping and they must be very quiet when they entered the room. She tucked them into bed and climbed in beside them without bothering to undress them or herself.

They were soon asleep, but Mary was not. After a while she got up and tiptoed out to the veranda, where she tried and failed to conjure a fantasy that might bring her peace. The beasts of fear that skulked at the edges of her mind were more present now than ever. Even that first day when they were yet unpractised at passing themselves off as shipwreck survivors, with the governor's sharp ears and eyes judging every word and gesture, she had not been in such a state of anxiety as this. It was as if the night-time darkness that had closed in around her was the thing to be feared. As with so many of the dangers she had faced, there was no way to run from it. No place to go.

There was a flicker of light behind her. Mary turned with a start and saw that Will had wakened and lit a candle. He staggered to his rucksack, which had been dropped on the floor, and from it took a bottle. Uncorking it, he sank down in a chair and began to swig. To Mary's alarm, she saw that it was more than half full.

She stepped back inside the room. Will lowered the bottle and looked at her with a crooked grin. "Come here, Mary, and sit upon me knee."

"Will," she said quietly, trying to keep scold and anxiety out of her voice, "you must stop drinking."

She reached for the bottle but he held it away from her, and deliberately took another long gulp. Then he wiped his mouth and sneered, "Since when do you tell me what I must, Madam? Since you become a lady and started taking tea with the gov'nor?"

"Will, please," Mary pleaded. "Can I refuse when he offers me a cup of tea? We are his guests. We cannot rile him!"

"I cannot? I cannot? Why, surely I can. I got you to keep him sotted, just like you sotted that old Dutch bastard back in Botany Bay!"

As he spoke, Will lurched to his feet, jerked the top of Mary's sarong to her waist, and grasped one of her breasts.

"No!" she whispered, backing away, and thought him put off when he tipped the bottle again and gulped several times more.

Then, carefully, he set down the bottle, and without warning, slapped her across the face with the hard-knuckled side of his hand. She dashed out onto the veranda, but Will was right behind her. There he caught her and hit her again. Then, half-seated on the veranda rail, he tried to pull her to him. Mary gave him a shove with all her strength. He toppled backwards over the rail, landing on the lawn with a thump.

"You whore!" he bellowed. "You'll answer for this!" He got to his feet and reached for the railing to haul himself back up onto the veranda.

"You come over that rail, Will Bryant, and I'll scream to bring every soul in the house! You're the one who will answer—to the governor." With that Mary fled back into the bedroom, locking the door behind her.

Will stared through the veranda railing at the locked door. "Bleedin' bitch. Gonna rat on me, is she? Wants me out of the way, that's what. Well, we'll see about that!" Off he staggered, either to the front of the house to be let back in, or to the barracks to spend the night.

Hoping he had headed for the barracks, Mary blew out the candle and climbed into bed without undressing. In the darkness she heard, not for the first time, the plaintive tinkle of a piano coming from Wanjon's wing of the house.

Will heard the sound, too, and followed it, although Mary learned this only later, when Mira related what had transpired. Mira said that, despite her efforts to prevent Will from going unannounced to the governor's quarters, he barged right in. Outraged by the intrusion, Wanjon rose from the piano and roared, "Bryant! I do not invite you here!"

To which Will responded, in what Mira described as a very impertinent tone, "Beggin' your pardon, Gov'nor. Not up to snuff, am I, for private chit-chat? My lady wife, now, bet you'd be glad enough to have her pay you a little visit."

"You are drunk, Bryant. Go to your quarters at once."

"Now, Sir, if it's my wife you're wanting, you can have her. Not for free, mind you. Old Captain Smit back in Botany Bay give her a chart and a compass and a musket to boot for spreading them bonny legs. If she's doing the same for you, why—."

"*Godverdomme!* Sit down, Bryant!" the governor commanded. Then he told Mira, hovering in the doorway, to fetch Bruger at once with a contingent of guards—a command which, being in Dutch, Will apparently had not understood.

As the governor was instructing Mira, Will was saying, "You not being an Englishman, I can see how you mighta been fooled. But 'tween you and me, Gov'nor, our Mary ain't the lady she makes herself out to be. 'Twas for stealing a cloak she got transported, with one brat born on the crossing long before she hooked up with me. I was all for staying in Botany Bay. My time's now up, y'see. I'm a free man. I woulda done well there. But Mary was set on getting out, and laid such plans as you wouldn't believe could be worked by a woman's mind. Never knew a doxy with such a talent for having her way with men."

Mira understood something of the slurs being made against Mary's character, but did not know the meaning of Botany Bay, thus did not grasp that Will had confessed to their being bolters. Had she understood this, she would have gone to warn Pip. But she recognised only Wanjon's anger at Will for invading his privacy, and never guessed the disaster those words portended for all of them.

Mary, as yet knowing none of this, heard the piano music break off abruptly. She feared that Will had created some sort of ruckus on the other side of the house which had caught Wanjon's attention. It required no prescience on her part to know that the beast of human error which she had so long feared was about to pull her into its maw. She stood looking down at her sleeping children, wishing she had the courage to end their lives and her own at this moment. If she could have done that, she felt that she would be able to endure whatever afterlife awaited her for the crime, knowing that her children had died in sweet innocence, having spent the last months of their life in peace, plenty, and freedom.

As for herself, she felt the impulse her father must have felt that night he pointed his little boat into the storm and shouted, "At least I'll die a free man!" Except that he had known freedom and she had not; at least, not as her mother had known it, free to come and go as she pleased, in her own cottage or on shipboard, free to go wandering in the woods or along the shore. Free to lie in the arms of a man she loved.

The bedroom door burst open. Mary turned to see Mira, tears spilling off her face in every direction. "My Pip, Mevrouw! They have taken him! And your husband! And now to the barracks for the others!"

Instantly Mary knew that, incredible as it seemed, Will must have revealed that they were not shipwreck survivors, but escaped convicts.

"I thought the guards came only to take Meneer Bryant, so angry was the gouverneur with him for entering his room," Mira wept. "I did not know they would take all!"

"You must run fast to Bados!" Mary ordered the girl. "Tell him what has happened!"

"No, no! It is night! I am afraid!"

"You must!" Mary pleaded. "Or he will be taken, too."

"But what of you, Mevrouw? And the kinder?"

"We are in no danger," Mary assured her. "We have done no wrong."

"Ah, but you do not know—," Mira stopped herself, as yet unable to tell Mary what Will had said about her.

It hardly mattered. Mary guessed—not Will's exact words, but close enough. She stepped out onto the veranda, wondering whether she could find her way across the city to the trail leading to the lagoon. She saw shadows moving about on the lawn, and realised that guards had been posted around the house. Already she was a prisoner.

Mary turned back to the Indonesian girl. "It is the last great favour I ask of you, Mira. If you can bring the news to Bados, it may save his life. I will return the favour by asking the governor to pardon Pip, for he is but a boy."

Mira gave Mary a wide and wet-eyed look, then ran off down the corridor. Mary did not know whether the girl would carry the terrible news to Bados or not.

The fact that she was not taken into custody that night, and Siti brought breakfast trays as usual the next morning, gave Mary a slender ray of hope. She did not know Wanjon well, but she knew him well enough to be sure that he was mulling the matter over, perhaps even praying for guidance, as he was a very religious man. Had Will told him how and from whom she had acquired the navigational instruments? And if so, what effect would that have on his decision? Would he damn her for having traded her body for the items needed to facilitate their escape? Or, knowing a fellow Hollander to have been involved, would he be more lenient? Would James, having proven useful to the Dutch East India Company, be treated differently? Would her speaking up for Pip have any effect? And what lay in store for the children?

All day these and other thoughts tormented Mary. When the children grew restless, she walked out of doors with them, as was her custom. No one stopped her, but soon a servant approached and said that by the governor's orders, Mary must return to her room. Mary obeyed, expecting Wanjon to send for her at any moment. But he did not. Nor did Mira appear that day. Dinner trays came at the usual hour, delivered by servants who spoke no English, so Mary had no way of finding out what had happened to the others. Night had fallen and the children were already asleep when Bruger himself came to fetch her.

He led Mary, not to the upstairs veranda where she had always met the governor before, but to a study lined with books. Wanjon, seated behind a desk of dark polished wood, did not rise when she entered, nor did he invite her to sit. Although he was not looking down from a high bench like the judge who sentenced her to be transported, his countenance was much the same.

Mary grasped at once that Wanjon was about to sit in judgement on her.

She stood before him as she had on that first afternoon, dressed in the sarong Mira called a kain panjang, with a simple seledang around her shoulders for modesty's sake, long golden braids encircling her head like a crown. Wanjon glanced up when she entered, then dropped his eyes to a page of notes on the desk before him.

"Your husband has informed upon you, Mevrouw. Have you anything to say?"

Mary took a deep breath. "I ask but two clemencies of you, Governor, and neither for myself, for I am indeed a bolter from Botany Bay. I would ask only that you be lenient with the boy Pip, for he is but a child who had no say in the matter of coming with us. And I beg mercy for my children, who have committed no crime. Pray let me leave them in your care."

Wanjon continued to stare at the papers on his desk, for the longest time not speaking. At last he said, "I do not vant persons in this house who remind me of—." He swallowed hard, and when he looked up at her, his eyes were sad. "No, Mevrouw Bryant. The Bible tells us that the sins of the parents vill be visited upon the children. It is the vill of God."

Mary had mentally practised her plea for clemency, and had hesitated only slightly before delivering it. But the governor's use of the Good Book, which her mother had revered, to justify his own lack of compassion so outraged her that words she never should have spoken rushed hotly out of her mouth.

"A God who punishes the innocent is no better than ourselves!"

Wanjon's eyes bulged with shock. "For shame, Mevrouw!" To Bruger, who lingered in the doorway, he called a rapid command in Dutch.

Mary was marched out of the governor's office, down the corridor to her room. "Take your kinder," Bruger told her. "It is to the dungeon you go."

Mary stared at him in disbelief. "My children are condemned to prison? For what? The crime of innocent sleep?"

"I am so ordered," Bruger informed her stiffly.

Mary turned to look at her children, sleeping peacefully in the great soft bed. The thought of taking them up from there and laying them down on a cold dungeon floor was almost more than she could bear. Bruger must have envisioned a similar contrast because he said, grudgingly, "If you take a pillow for the kinder, I think it vill not be missed."

Mary looked longingly at the many eiderdown cushions scattered about the room. Any one of them would have made a comfortable cot for a child. But pride intervened, coupled with an irrational anger over which she had no control. Speaking in a voice as cold as her blood was hot, she said, "Had the governor offered the cushions as charity for my children I would have accepted. But I will not be accused of stealing, even for their sake. You are my witness, Mr. Bruger, that we leave this room with only the clothes upon our backs, which the governor did kindly provide us. If they are not our own, but only on loan, do inform me and they shall be returned on the morrow. And we shall go forward more naked than when we arrived. As your governor pleases."

With that she hoisted the children into her arms. Charlotte whimpered and Emanuel began to sob, not a common thing for either of them to do when wakened. No doubt they had felt the extreme tension that had permeated the household during the previous twenty-four hours, and perhaps they had not been sleeping so peacefully after all. Even Emanuel, as he dropped his drowsy head onto Mary's perspiring shoulder, must have smelled her fear and fury.

Bruger assigned two guards the task of escorting Mary to the fort. As no conveyance was provided, it was a long walk and a slow one. With Emanuel in her arms, Mary matched her steps to Charlotte's as the sleepy child stumbled along beside her. The guards, perhaps feeling a small degree of regret for the duty they were forced to perform, did not hurry them.

It was a bright and windy night. As they approached the waterfront, Mary saw, far out, a boat. A dark sliver on the water, it raised a sail which had the same shape as the one on the cutter which had brought them here. The sail crossed a path of moonlight and disappeared from view.

Mary tightened her arm about Emanuel, and squeezed Charlotte's hand. "Look at the moon, darlings. It's on its way to England."

4

Of Men and Mercy

A flicker of lantern light crept into the dungeon when the jailer opened the door, but Mary barely had time to glimpse bodies strewn about before the door clanged shut, leaving them in the clammy blackness.

"Mummy," Charlotte spoke in a small frightened voice. "I don't like this place."

Then Pip's voice, close at hand, "Hey, Charlotte. I'm here, too. Come, sit by me."

Charlotte took a step forward, being guided, Mary surmised, by Pip. Mary held onto the little girl's hand and moved forward with her.

"For the lovagod!" It was Luke's voice. "The bastard's gone and shut the babies up in this hell hole, too!"

From the other side of the room came a hoarse sob. Then Matey's voice, "Shut yer mouth, you bleedin' graft, afore I shut it for you."

And Cox's: "Shut up yourself, you rum-soaked ass. You think he would've blabbed if you hadn't got him so drunk he couldn't stand up?"

And Scrapper's: "I been drunker than that plenty of times and it never drove me to squeal on me pals." He added in a mutter, "Wouldn't have lived long if I had."

"Wasn't drink that drove him to it," Matey snarled.

"Don't go saying more, fellas, not with the little ones here," came Pip's plea.

There was another retching sob, then silence as absolute as the darkness.

A man's hand touched Mary's shoulder and slid down her arm. She knew that touch, for palm and pressure alike, it was the softest she had ever felt. How many nights had she lain awake remembering the feel of James's hands during that brief moment of intimacy they'd had back on Bados's island? How many daylight hours had she dreamed of them touching her like that again and forever, in how many different settings? But never in a place such as this.

She felt herself being pulled down by Charlotte, who must be seating herself next to Pip. Mary lowered herself onto the cold stones, and moved Emanuel from her shoulder onto her lap. He whimpered a bit, then slept. James's hand found hers and brought it to his lips. Mary might have lain her head on his shoulder and wept, but what would have been the use of that? He was the man of her dreams, but this was not her dream. She held her body stiffly erect, resisting not the loving touch but the brutality being done to her dream of love.

Mary was awakened by an assault upon her senses, vile smells coming from two slop buckets filled with discharge from men's bladders and bowels. She moved Emanuel from her lap to rest his head against his sister, and struggled stiffly to her feet. She needed to relieve herself, and as the darkness had faded to grey gloom, she figured that this was the nearest thing to privacy she would have until night returned. None of the mounds of humanity bestirred themselves as she crossed the room. She did her business, and returned to the place between Pip and James where she and the children had passed the night. Soon she fell into a doze again, and did not waken until the jailer's key rattled in the lock. Two guards stood by as he opened the door and passed in a kettle of gruel. He indicated to Mary that she should have the tin cups he had brought for her and the children.

She rose quickly and took them from him. As she did so, she pointed to the buckets. "Please allow us to empty our slops," she beseeched. The children would be awake soon, needing to relieve themselves. She saw no way to hold her children above the brimming buckets to urinate and defecate without causing the filth to splash out onto them and her.

The jailer seemed to understand, for he nodded. She went to bring the buckets, but before she could grasp the handles, James was there, his hands on her waist to move her aside. Then he took the slop pails up himself. He staggered to the door with the foul weight and was let out into the corridor to carry them away.

Mary went to the kettle and dipped cups of gruel for the children, and one for James, in case the others should scrape the kettle clean before he returned—which in fact they did. Will was the last to claim his share, and small enough it was. The others, without so much as saying a word, seemed to have determined that this was how it would be.

When James returned, Mary handed him his cup of gruel. She then crossed the floor with her children to help them relieve themselves before the pails should fill up again. Emanuel accepted this strange new way of making his toilet, but Charlotte resisted, whined for her chamber pot, and begged to be allowed to go back to their room and get it from under the bed. At length Mary gave up and led her back to sit next to Pip, knowing that when the pressure of her bladder grew strong enough, the child would give in to nature's demand.

Mary calculated that by now it must be broad day, but the dungeon remained as dim as dusk. The only light came through a slit in the stone wall high up near the ceiling, with a lesser amount coming through a small barred window in the door that led out into the corridor. She started to rise, to walk to the door and see what was visible through the bars. James must have sensed her intent, because he quickly stood and offered a hand to help her to her feet.

It was then that one of the formless shapes across the room lunged forward and Will snarled, "Havin' trouble keeping your hands to yourself, Brown? Seems like this whole damned morning you're finding reasons to handle me slut of a wife."

James whirled round and let fly a fist that smacked Will square in the jaw. Will crashed backwards, falling over Scrapper who, with an oath, shoved him roughly aside. Then Will was up and would have gone for James, probably to devastating effect, for although they were the same size, Will was much the stronger due to the physical nature of his work. But Luke was quicker, and got to Will before he could make good on his intent to beat James senseless.

A hammerlock hold around the neck brought Will gagging to his knees. Into his ear, Luke growled, "The only one likely to get beat is you, you bloody snitch. I'd stomp you to death myself for what you done, except it would deprive us all of the only thing we've got left to look forward to, and that's the chance to see your arse hanged." With that he flung Will back against the wall, amidst shouts of approval from the other men.

Until the ruckus, the children hadn't known that Will was in the room. When Charlotte realised he was, she gave an ecstatic cry. "Papa! You're here!"

"Papa!" Emanuel echoed, and toddled after his sister as she crossed the room to Will.

At that, the others fell silent. The only sounds were those of Charlotte pleading with her father to take them out of this dark place, and Will's sobbing, inarticulate responses.

Some hours later the jailer came again and called Mary out. She started to collect the children but he indicated that she should leave them behind. Grasping her by the arm, he propelled her along the corridor and up many stone steps to the tower. He knocked, and when a voice bade them enter, he opened the heavy door and shoved her forward.

Mary judged it to be the office of whoever commanded the colony's military brigade, but the only person present besides herself and the jailer was Wanjon. He stood, his tall spare frame slightly stooped, hands clasped behind his back. The pale skin on his face was drawn, except about the neck where it hung loosely, attesting to the fact that his youth was well behind him. That skin, hanging as it did above his black suit, recalled to Mary a vulture, and caused her to think dark thoughts about how this must be his true nature, for was he not using his power to turn them all into carrion?

Mary was aware that the dungeon's stink hung about her and her sarong had not benefited from contact with the filthy floor, but she determined not to show shame for circumstances that were not of her own making. She fixed him with a questioning gaze.

Clearing his throat, he said, "Mevrouw Bryant, your companions say you reached Kupang mit a chart, quadrant, and compass. Ve do not find these things. The boat is missing also. And the neeger. Do you think he took them?"

Mary looked down, not wanting Wanjon to read in her eyes the sudden elation that filled her heart. "What use would an illiterate man have for navigational instruments?"

"I believe you taught him to use them," he said in an accusatory tone.

The lowered eyes flashed up. "What else do you believe, Governor? That I, who lately supped at your table, am now so dangerous that I must be caged like a beast?"

Wanjon was taken clearly aback by her sarcasm. "You have powers over men," he snapped. "In that respect, yes, Mevrouw, you are dangerous."

"You jest, Sir, and cruelly so! Do I not sit in this prison by your will? Once again in a man's prison where I suffer every violence men can do to a woman?" Mary raised her bare arms in exasperation. "What powers do you imagine that I have?"

Wanjon's thin lips tightened. "The neeger got clean away, Mevrouw. I think this vas your doing."

"Is that my crime?" she demanded to know. "Allowing myself to feel mercy? What does your Bible say of mercy, Sir? That it belongs to God alone? That we mortals are meant to measure goodness by the weight of vengeance we heap on one another?"

Never had Mary spoken to any man in such a daring way. It startled her, and appeared to frighten him. "You play, Voman! Mit words and men's minds! I vill not interview you again!"

"As you please, Sir." She swallowed, her throat tight with anger and sadness. "For my part, I shall remember you as you were, when you were merciful and we were friends."

"Friends? Friends?" he repeated sarcastically. "No

doubt you hoped ve might be more than friends, Mev-rouw Bryant."

"Was it I who thought thus, Governor?"

"Who knows vhat you think, you, a common crimi-nal!" he shouted.

"What I think is that you condemn me not for my thoughts but for your own," she said bitterly. "Do you not suppose that God knows those thoughts as well as I?"

His gasp was audible. "You dare pretend to know a man's thoughts, even as God knows them? Acht, but you are a vicked voman!"

So flustered was Wanjon that he roared for the jail-er three times over, although the man was standing right near him. With a furious flapping of hands, the governor emphasised the speed with which Mary was to be returned to the dungeon.

The anger loosed in Mary during that interview did not dissipate, but swelled to encompass the whole of mankind. Back in the dungeon, she huddled on the stinking stone floor, filled with a hatred of men. She could not even bear to look at James, but turned her eyes away when she felt his gaze upon her. Thus she remained for the next three days, overcome by emo-tional storms such as she had never known.

During all the abuses suffered during her previous imprisonment, she had blamed only herself. She ac-cepted that she had brought it upon herself and, once recovered from the shock, had taken it as her own responsibility to do whatever she could to better her situation. But now things were different. She was different. Perhaps it was because this incarceration was not the result of her own actions. Perhaps it was because her children had been damned as well. Or because she had recently felt the respect of others, and had come close enough to freedom to imagine its reality. The blow, so swift and unjust, wounded her sense of reason. Equilibrium lost, she hunkered down on the cold stone floor and hated.

During the few days that Mary lay under that leaden cloud, the children gravitated to Will. Most of the time he responded gratefully, for they were the only ones in the room who would approach him. When he lapsed into brooding self-pity, they circled the room and were kindly treated by men who had been like family to them during the voyage from Botany Bay. When they grew tired they returned to Pip, cuddled next to him like kittens, and fell asleep.

There was much discussion during those first days as to why Bados had not been arrested, too. It was Matey who advanced the theory that, "He mighta made a run for it." With a meaningful glance in Mary's direction, he added, "Like if somebody got word to him that we was gettin' grabbed."

"Could be," Cox allowed. "He did have a woman."

This brought a babble of disbelieving commentary, but Cox stood by his story. "I seen her myself, I did. Was right soon after we got here. Bados showed up in the carpentry shop and wanted to borrow a whittling knife to make another flute. I let him do, like before, long as he didn't leave the shop. So there he was sitting, working away, when down the street comes this woman. A big woman she was, dang near as tall as Bados. And bosoms, oh my! They stuck out in front of her like lanterns on a carriage!"

Cox waited for the men's guffaws to die down, then continued his story. "Blinded our Bados, they did. Why, he was up and out of that shop before I could say a word, and off down the street after her. I was right put out, 'cause he didn't take time to lay down that whittling knife and I was afraid the master of the shop would blame me for it going missing. But two days later Bados was back, grinning like a man fully satisfied. He said he was sorry about going off with the knife, on account of he plumb forgot he had it in his hand." Cox chuckled. "Then he crossed over the street where this same woman was bargaining her fish with a stall keeper. Bados lifted the basket off her head, which must've weighed half as much as a man, because it was a strain for him to lift, and you know how strong he is."

"So you reckon this woman or one of her people got wind of what was afoot and sent word to him?" Scrapper asked.

"I 'spect so," Cox concluded. "Seems like these locals got a certain amount of bitterness about the way they're getting treated. I figure any chance they get to stick it to the Dutch on the sly, they'd take some pleasure in it."

Mary contributed nothing to the conversations about Bados. She roused herself only once, when a quarrel broke out over who would handle the daily chore of dumping the slops. Some insisted that Will, who had brought this misfortune upon them, should have sole responsibility for the disgusting task, while others felt Pip could be forced to do it, as he was the weakest and least able to defend himself.

At length, tired of the quarrel over who would empty the slops, Mary rose and shouted, "You will take turns!" She pointed a finger at each, and named the order in which they would go. The jailer, who was probably sick of the bickering as well, ordered the men to comply, beginning with Will, whom she had indicated should go first.

A few days after Mary's meeting with Wanjon, Mira's anxious face appeared at the small barred window. Pip ran forward and, fingers to fingers and lips to lips between the bars, they touched as best they could. The jailer allowed them two or three minutes, then ordered Pip away from the door and motioned Mary to come forward. The door was opened and two cushions were shoved in.

"Gouverneur Wanjon give for the kinder," Mira explained.

Although Mary longed to refuse the gift, she did not. Angry as she was, she suspected that the governor's conscience was bothering him, and he was trying to prove his humanity, at least to himself. She also understood that her challenging manner and bitter hatred toward him had accomplished nothing. It was time she took herself in hand and set a different course.

"Give the governor my thanks for this small kindness," Mary murmured to Mira. "And tell him this: The eighth day of September is nigh upon us. That being Charlotte's fourth birthday, perhaps he will see fit to grant her God's own gift of a breath of fresh air and a few rays of sunlight."

"I will tell him that," Mira promised. And to Pip, "Tomorrow, my Pip, I come again."

Mira did come on the morrow, and each night after that. Once she brought a cushion for Pip taken from her own bed. Mary only had to look into the girl's eyes, and see the smirk on the face of the jailer, to know the price Mira was paying for those nightly visits.

On the seventh of September, when they had been confined a week, Bruger brought news of a welcome change. Henceforth, he said, Mary and the children were to be allowed out from dawn to sunset, providing they stayed in the vicinity of the fort. The men would be allowed out, three at a time, for half a day each. They were to receive this privilege, Bruger said, for as long as they remained in the governor's charge.

James, who had always had a cordial relationship with Bruger, asked how long that might be. Bruger said that the governor would consider his responsibility discharged upon the arrival of a British ship. Then they would be turned over to English authority, as represented by its captain.

When James reported this to the group, they muttered uneasily. Some were of the opinion that they would receive better treatment from their own countrymen, but others, recalling the conditions of their imprisonment back in England, felt that the opposite might be true. It was Cox who voiced the underlying dread which haunted them all.

"Don't make much difference, do it? We'll be travelling back as prisoners same as we come, and lucky if we get a captain as square as Phillip. And what'll we see of merry old England once we get there, but the inside of another gaol? Leastways till we come to trial."

"Then what?" Scrapper asked fearfully.

Cox gave him a sorrowful look. "We're bolters, ain't we? Reckon we'll be sentenced to hang. Or else transported back to Botany Bay."

That bleak truth clouded the cheer they had felt upon being told that henceforth they would be allowed out each day to take exercise. Still, they had something to look forward to on the morrow. James reminded the others that it was Mary's sending word of Charlotte's impending birthday that had resulted in this privilege.

"'Twas Mira's doing," Mary insisted, and knew that to be the truth. She had had two interviews with Wanjon and had gained not one concession, as her flaring anger had only made him more intransigent. It was Mira, trained to be sweet and subservient even when she was bitterly unhappy, who managed to elicit mercy from the dry old man.

Despite Mary's disclaimer, the men cheered her. Then Matey led off with a rousing birthday song for Charlotte, which the others joined in. It was then that Mary noted a change in the men's attitude toward her. During the voyage of escape they had shown her respect, but had done so in subtle, even secretive ways, to avoid offending Will. Their loyalty was to him, and reasonably so, given that he had captained the fishing crew, and Cox, although not on the crew, was his boon drinking companion. James was the only outsider, and he, like Mary, had known that cohesion of the group depended on acknowledging Will as leader.

But if there had been reasons to feel or fake loyalty to Will then, there were none now.

That much James had made clear the morning Will called Mary a slut. And Luke had backed James up. Mary had been too deep in her own darkness just then to read the mood of the men. But now, as they praised her for having found a way to ease the discomfort of prison, the message was plain and public: she, not Will, was their leader.

But where was the value in that, Mary wondered despairingly, now that they were confined, with no place to go, nor any way to get there?

The following day, as soon as the jailer came with their gruel, Mary asked that she and the children be let out, and Pip as well. Pip, although he was seventeen, looked to be no more than twelve, his growth having been stunted by a lifetime of hunger. The jailer took Pip's measure, and, as the governor's instructions had been to allow Mary and the children to roam free in the vicinity of the fort for the better part of the day, he supposed that included the boy who, as far as he knew, was also one of her children.

Coming up from the dungeon, the brilliance of the sun at first so hurt their eyes that Emanuel buried his face in Mary's shoulder and cried. But when Pip went cartwheeling across the meadow, Emanuel squirmed to be put down and went toddling after Pip and Charlotte. Soon all three were racing about like puppies let out of a box, and even Mary was smiling.

On the far side of the meadow surrounding the fort, Mary found a rivulet wending its way out of the forest and meandering toward the sea. There she was able to wash herself and the children. Then she laid down in the sweet-smelling grass and waited for the sun to dry her skin and sarong.

She had been there about an hour, listening to the children's voices as they played nearby, when she opened her eyes to see Will looming over her. She sat up quickly and saw, some way off, Matey and Scrapper as well. Will immediately began to berate her for the misfortune that had befallen them.

"You're like the rest of them," he mocked. "Putting it all on me and my drinking. But what was the reason for me taking to drink, if not you selling your twat to another old Dutch geezer? Last time a compass, this time for naught but a cup o' tea. Gettin' cheaper all the time, you are."

Not wanting the children to overhear, Mary jumped to her feet and tried to walk away. Will, already in a fury generated by his own thoughts, became angrier still. He grabbed Mary by the braid and slammed her against a tree. She screamed, and saw by his startled look that he had not anticipated that. Apparently he had expected her to accept his abuse in silence, as she always had in the past.

Not only was she not silent this time, she began to put up a fierce struggle. Before Will could figure out how to hit her when he needed both hands to hold her, Matey and Scrapper came dashing up. With the natural cunning of a street tough, Scrapper dragged Will behind a stand of trees, for the guards, having heard the scream, were already looking their way.

"Give 'em a wave," Scrapper instructed Pip, who had likewise come running. "So they'll think it was one of the young'uns. We don't want them wandering by whilst we're having a private chat with Old Blabber-mouth."

Scrapper got one of Will's arms twisted behind him in such a way as to put him down on his knees. Matey clicked his tongue in mock sympathy. "Will, ya poor devil, didn't I tell you way back on the crossing that a slut is never worth the grief she's gonna bring you? But you wouldn't listen, would you? Now, by God, she's gone and made you lose your reason."

"That ain't no excuse!" Scrapper shouted. "Ain't I been duped by plenty of floozies in me life? You never saw me go bonkers and run off at the mouth in such a way as to land my pals in the pokey!"

Matey picked up a dry stalk of bamboo and smashed it across his knee, leaving the broken ends splintered and sharp as shards of glass. Holding it before Will's face, he said, "The boy's right, you know. You keep running that mouth of yours, by reason of being drove crazy by a woman, I'm afeared I'll have to quieten down that tongue, like what I seen done to a blabber in Africa, using a splinter of bamboo what weren't no bigger than this."

The old man poked Will's face with the slivered

bamboo, increasing the pressure until Will begged for mercy. "You're right and don't I know it! 'Tis help I need, man to man, to keep me on the straight. Come on, boys. Give me a chance!"

"I don't mind to do that," Matey said in an agreeable tone that belied the pain he was causing Will with the bamboo splinters. "But we can't be havin' you kicking up no more stink with our Mary here, y'understand?"

"I'm done!" Will gasped. "Done with her I am. Lemme go and I'll be getting as far from her as I can."

"There's a smart 'un," Matey grinned approvingly, and signalled to Scrapper to release his hold on Will. But just to make the point, he turned around and called to Mary, who had remained on the other side of the trees. "You let us know, Captain Mary, if he gives you any more grief, and we'll come settle the rest o' this score." The word Captain being thrown in loud and clear because, as Matey had known all along, giving the title over to her caused Will more pain than bamboo splinters.

Charlotte and Emanuel came running then, having wanted to come before but being held back by Pip, who suspected some violence might be taking place behind the bushes. When Charlotte saw blood on Will's face, she took him by the hand and insisted he come to the stream where she could wash it away. He went with her, mumbling sulkily as to how a child not his own had more loyalty in her smallest finger than all the others put together.

Mary was not surprised that Will, who had done them all the most grievous harm, should imagine himself to be the one betrayed. He had always been inclined to act on impulse without thought to consequences and, by the time the consequences came home to roost, he had already forgotten that he was the one who had brought them about.

She turned to Pip and said in a low voice, "When Will comes out for exercise each day, see that the children go to him, for it will cheer both him and them. But if he begins to ramble of dark things, bring them away at once, or call me to come get them."

"I'll do my best," Pip promised, and added, somewhat gloomily, "even if Will beats me half to death for interfering."

"I think Will has done the last beating he's likely to do of anyone," Mary said grimly. "For if you and I can't stop him, it seems that the others will."

This set a pattern to be followed for all the mornings for the rest of the month. Will would play with the children, teaching them games which Mary did not know, having not had that kind of childhood herself. Pip hung about until Will, supposing this to be an indication that the boy was loyal to him, urged him to join in playing hide and seek or ring around the rosy.

Scrapper and Matey stayed close to Mary, fancying themselves her protectors, which in fact they were as long as Will was on the loose. This self-assigned duty made it unnecessary for them to admit to themselves how much they needed her company.

Around noon, the three men were ordered back to the dungeon. Soon after that Mira arrived with a parcel of food, sent on the sly by Siti. She and Pip stole a few minutes of semi-privacy behind a stand of bamboo, then Mira ran swiftly away to attend to other errands. Mary watched the young babu go, seemingly so free. And yet what woman anywhere was truly free?

Mary climbed a nearby knoll where she could look out across the Timor Sea, sparkling in the sunshine. The view of sky and ocean was not so different from the one she had enjoyed back in Botany Bay, or the many she had seen from the deck of the *Charlotte*. Hundreds of hours she had spent gazing at the horizon, imprisoned in all but spirit. To have come so far, only to find the view so little changed, and freedom not even as close as that distant horizon, came near to breaking her heart.

Painful as that knowledge was, it did not incapacitate her as had the rage which poisoned her mind and rendered her incapable of thought in the first days after her arrest. But now that she had regained the capacity to think, her thoughts were bleak. The scenario offered by Cox—confinement here for an unknown length of time, to be followed by at least six months of imprisonment on the return voyage, then a cell in Newgate until it was decided if she was to be hanged or transported back to Botany Bay—this was her future.

Mary heard a shriek of laughter from Charlotte, and turned around to see the children sitting in the small, ankle-deep stream where they had earlier bathed, flinging handfuls of water at one another. For the second time in as many weeks she wished she had a way of ending their time on earth in this moment of tranquillity, rather than see them endure the agonies which would soon wreak havoc with their little lives.

And then it came to her that this was their life—and hers. Charlotte and Emanuel could laugh because they enjoyed the ignorance of the very young. They could revel in whatever pleasing sensations the moment provided because they had no knowledge of what was to come. She herself could not escape that knowledge, any more than Adam and Eve could.

And was this the knowledge that first couple had been given there in the Garden, she wondered? Knowledge that the same God who created the beauty and bounty of the world had an equal capacity for destruction and cruelty? What could be more cruel than being allowed to know that the future held all manner of suffering, without being permitted to know how it would unfold, and whether one could reasonably expect to survive?

How to survive—that was the question. Even as Mary brooded, she searched for ways and means. Some moments passed before she realised that she was staring at what might be the only survival tool at hand. She must follow her children's example and revel in every small delight the moment provided. For if one reached a point of being unable to take any pleasure from life, what would keep death at bay? *I must search for happiness,* she thought. *Just as I searched for food when we were starving back in Botany Bay. A scrap here, a scrap there . . . might be enough to keep one alive until the situation improved.*

This realisation was just taking shape in Mary's mind

when she saw that James, Cox, and Luke had been re-leased from the dungeon to take exercise. Without any notion of what she was about to do, she walked across the field to where they stood. Cox and Luke waved, but James only stood there. Little wonder. Although she had sat next to him for a week, and he had often held her hand, it was as if she had not been aware of him at all. She saw him now only because the shroud of fury that had bound her so tightly inside herself had fallen away, to be replaced by an attitude which, if not wiser, was certainly softer.

She walked straight to James, laid a hand on his shoulder, and stood on tiptoe to kiss him on the lips. It no longer mattered who knew she loved him. It only mattered that he should know. When at last she moved her lips away from his, he laid his head on her shoulder and wetted it with tears.

"I didn't know if you would come back to me," he whispered.

"I wanted to love you when we were free," she said. "But this is all we've got. Perhaps all we will ever have."

Looking past James she saw Luke's look of astonish-ment, and Cox's mouth hanging agape. Their surprise was proof of how well she and James had concealed their secret up to this moment.

"Don't you be afeared, Mary," Luke said quickly. "We won't be saying nothing to Will about your private af-fairs."

"Like to rub his nose in it myself," Cox blurted. "Han't he told me a hundred times, from way back in

Botany Bay, how he warn't no married man, on account of there being no publishing of the banns?"

"I think," Mary said with a faint smile, "that Will did not consider himself to be a married man, but he considered me a married woman. I'm not quite sure how he matched those points of view."

Luke and Cox guffawed, albeit more out of nervous relief than humour.

"In any case," Mary added, "what Will and I were in the past has little bearing on what we are now. It's prisoners we are, and as you yourself said, Mr. Cox, we are likely to be that for the rest of our lives."

Keeping one hand on James's arm, she reached the other out to include Cox and Luke. "Come, boys. There's a fine little stream over where the children are playing, if you'd care to lap up some cool sweet water and wash off some of that dungeon stink."

As they walked toward the rivulet, Mary linked arms with James and said, "What we have right now is not what we had our hearts set on, but you can see for yourself," she waved a hand at the meadow around them, the grasses sweet-smelling and slightly bent by a breeze coming off the bay, "it's not all bad."

James said nothing until they reached the stream. Then, as the other two went down on their knees to drink, he took Mary's face in his hands. Looking at her in that way he had of seeming to see things inside her that even she had not discovered yet, he said, "What I have right now is more than I dared to dream of back in Botany Bay."

Thus passed three weeks which were among the happiest yet of Mary's life. Which is not to say they were easy. Most difficult was the effort required to block out thoughts of what was to come. Mary usually managed to do this during the day, but at night, horrors that ranged from rape to hangings often haunted her dreams. All she could do was to wait for morning and, once out in the sunshine, try again to chase the nightmares away. By afternoon, when James was given his turn outdoors, Mary would be in a mental attitude which allowed her to take pleasure in his company as they walked and talked, their fingers and minds lightly entwined.

By unspoken mutual consent, what lay ahead was rarely mentioned. Yet it hung about the edges of their conversations, and occasionally crept in.

"I feel like Eve in the Garden," Mary once said. "Having brought knowledge to you which will lead to unknown suffering in some cast-out place we've yet to see."

James, who was lying in the grass beside her, raised himself on one elbow and studied her with a serious smile. "Do you suppose Adam had no hand in the decision to eat of that fruit of the tree of knowledge?"

Mary shrugged. "He did put the blame on Eve."

"But did God? Would you say that God blamed Eve?"

Mary smiled ruefully. "Maybe more than Adam.

After all, He sent her out to face the same hardships as Adam, with childbirth thrown in."

"That's true," James admitted. "But did you ever wonder whether they regretted doing what they did?"

"What do you mean?" Mary leaned forward to brush one of his long brown curls back from his face.

"There is nothing in the story to say they repented. That may well have been the thing that made God angriest, the fact that they valued the knowledge they had gained so much that, given a choice, they would have done it all over again."

"And would you?" Mary asked, for this was what the whole conversation had been about.

"Yes," he said simply. "And you?"

Mary was a long time in answering. Finally she said, "That's hard to say, not knowing what will become of my children. But I am fairly sure of this: I would rather see them dead than live a life of degradation in Botany Bay."

When thoughts of the future slipped into their musings, one or the other would turn the conversation in another direction. James was inclined to seek some small pleasure in the moment, to speak of the sweet taste of the water in the stream, or to point out to Mary a rainbow caught in the slanting rays of late afternoon sun. Mary was more likely to ask questions about things she did not understand, for she had a greater sense than ever before of all she did not know, and now, perhaps, never would find out.

When they were alone, they talked mostly of themselves and what they meant to each other. In this, Mary was more plain-spoken than James for, having had little social life as a girl, she was unaware of all the things a woman ought not mention. She and her mother, shy and inarticulate around most people, had spoken to each other of whatever came into their minds. Later, in prison, Mary had conversed with other women who likewise voiced their intimate thoughts. Thus Mary did not know what was considered inappropriate, and spoke to James as she would to anyone she trusted, of whatever was on her mind.

One day, when Pip and Mira had disappeared into the forest rather longer than usual, and emerged with languorous looks which made it clear that they had been engaged in the most intimate way, Mary turned to James and said, "I recall that you were once hungry for me in that way. Has it passed?"

James gave her a bemused look and said, "I recall that you once seemed hungry for me in that way. Has it passed?"

Mary laughed. "Your asking such a question tells me that you cannot see into my soul as well as I thought, for rarely is it empty of such dreams." Then she added, seriously, "But it is normal for a woman to hold passion in check, is it not? Not so for a man, if passion he has."

"Have you reason to doubt that I am a passionate man?"

Mary pondered this a moment. "You're not like other men."

James, who had been lying in the grass, sat up and

looked at her, puzzled. "Surely you don't mean—that is, you never supposed I favoured men over women?"

Mary shook her head. "I remember the night of our landing in Botany Bay. That was the first I knew that some men could be as lustful of men as of women. But you, I recall, were pursuing neither. I saw you attacked by a mob when you were only trying to protect poor old Dorothy Haggart. After that, well, I don't remember."

"I don't remember much after that either," James said. "But I do know that I was in that area looking for you."

"Had you found me, the outcome might have been no better, for I had problems of my own," Mary recalled, then continued to make her point. "But what I meant was, well, during all that time in the Colony, you never chose a wife."

"The woman I loved was taken," he said simply. Then added, with a teasing smile, "Had the *Lady Juliana* brought another Mary Broad, I might have married her."

"No doubt that would have been a wiser choice," Mary said sadly. "In the beginning I did not believe you could love me, and now that I know you can, I'm sorry for it."

"How can you be sorry when I am not?"

"How can you not be, when you've paid so dearly, and without once an intimacy such as Pip and Mira enjoyed not an hour ago?"

"Is that what you want? Here and now?"

"It is what I want but not here, not now. I had in

mind to wait until we were free, but seeing that we'll never be . . ." Sorrow overtook her, and she could not finish her sentence. She looked off into the distance, where she could see the children playing tag with Pip, and tried to get back to that place where it was the joy of the moment that filled her heart, not dread of the future.

"We aren't free, but we aren't dead yet either," James pointed out. "I would gladly make love to you here in the sunshine, and all night long in the dungeon as well. But I agree that, just as our fleeing Botany Bay was no time for merging our bodies, neither is imprisonment. And another thing." He laid his hand on her belly. "Have you given no thought to the hardship of pregnancy on the voyage home, under circumstances we have yet to know?"

"Indeed I have!" Mary exclaimed. "Why, 'twas over that very thing that Will and I quarrelled during our last night together. It was for my refusal, and for locking him out after he struck me, that he informed upon us. But it amazes me that you would think of that! I mean," she laughed, "most men don't. Sometimes I'm not sure they have any notion that what pleasures them for a few minutes can lead to suffering or even death for the woman!"

"Most men seem not to consider the consequences of any of their actions," James noted, a bitter reminder that they were where they were for just that reason. "But I am a person who tries to look ahead, and I noticed long ago that you do the same." He paused, and smiled. "But just because I was first drawn to you by what I observed of the workings of your mind doesn't mean I haven't hungered mightily for the rest of you."

Mary smiled back, only half-believing. "I suppose you speak the truth, but I have never known any other man who tempered his lust out of consideration for a woman."

"And you?" James asked. "What have you known of a woman's lust? Or temperance?"

The audacious question gave Mary pause, for it was not something she had ever considered before. "I think," she began hesitantly, "that this woman has not had much experience with personal lust, apart from a few minutes back on that island, when you held me in your arms and a weakness came upon me such that I could hardly stand. But before that . . ."

"Before that?" James prompted gently.

"One can hardly feel lust when one is being battered, as I was in prison," Mary said sharply. "'Twas terror pure and simple, same as for every woman on the night of our landing, when nearly a thousand men let their lust run rampant."

She paused, searching her memory, for she did not wish to deceive James with a dishonest history. "There in Botany Bay did I voluntarily offer my body, first to Will in payment for his protection, and later to Captain Smit in exchange for the compass and chart. Captain Smit and Will, too, for a time, were both kind to me. I repaid them out of my body, for it was the only thing I had that either of them wanted. It wasn't passion I felt but gratitude, and a desire to be as kind to

326

them as they were to me. There was some pleasure to be had in that."

"And is there something you want from me?" James asked, kissing her palm. "For which you would be willing to offer your body?"

Mary, who had been sitting beside him all this time, folded herself across his chest and kissed him. "Yes," she said. "What I want from you is you."

"Have you not enough of me already?" he teased. "Or must I take you into the forest to find the warm spot left by Pip and Mira?"

"That part of you I'll wait for," Mary said earnestly. "To have only when we've found our way to freedom. Or not at all."

"You have my promise," he whispered into her hair. "We shall finish this thing we have started in freedom or not at all."

⊕

So passed many hours that September spring, days in which dread and joy were so co-mingled that Mary gave up trying to sort them out. Not every moment with James was spent in conversation, for the children were often with them, begging for a story or falling asleep in their laps. At other times Luke, Cox, and Pip joined them and they talked of many things, mostly of friends left behind in Botany Bay, or recollections of adventures on the voyage. If anyone began to speculate on what was to come, that person was quickly shushed. Charlotte was old enough to understand,

and Mary did not want fear added to her other dis-
comforts.

The men were ordered back to the dungeon each day after only three hours of liberty, but Mary, Pip, and the children did not have to present themselves at the fort until the sun was about to set. Return to the dungeon was always difficult, made more so by the fact that it was required at precisely the time of day when Wanjon had often invited Mary to stand by his side and watch the sun slip into the sea. As she followed the jailer down the steep stone stairs, careful that she and the children not lose their footing as they descended into the gloom, it was all she could do to suppress her fury. But having learned how incapacitating that kind of rage could be, she contained it as best she could.

When the cell door clanged shut behind them, she stood still in the darkness until she felt James's arms come about her. Then they moved slowly to the wall and laid down together, Pip and the children on their pillows, and she and James in each other's arms. She tried not to think of anything else, although this was as difficult as suppressing her anger. All her life she had looked ahead, seeking some reasonable path to a better future. It was not easy to change that way of being, nor was she altogether successful in living for the moment, with no thought as to where the river of time was taking them.

The dungeon, dismal as it was, was not as bad as it might have been. Indeed, everyone in the room, save the children, had suffered more on the hulks and in gaols back in England. "This ain't the worst I knowed," Cox commented one evening. "Leastwise the floor stays still and you don't have everybody puking on everybody on account of rough seas."

"The food's not as bad as it was on the crossing neither," Pip put in. "And more of it than I got most days back in Botany Bay."

This was true. They were brought a pail of gruel each morning, and at night, a pail of soup. The soup was made from fish heads, potato peels, and other kitchen scraps, but it wasn't thin and it had plenty of nourishment. During the first week, when Mary had been indifferent to what went on around her, the men had quarrelled over who got what, once so violently that the soup was spilt on the floor and nobody got anything. But later, when Mary had regained her reason, she would go to the door herself to take the pail from the jailer. Then she would dip a cup of soup for every person, beginning with the children, just as she had done on the journey. There was always at least one full mug for each person, and sometimes enough for a second round, so they soon stopped complaining.

The remarks made by Cox and Pip demonstrated to Mary that the best way to pass the time was not to compare their present situation with the luxuries Wanjon had provided before their arrest, but to remind themselves of how much better it was than what they had endured during other periods of incarceration. From that moment on, she added this to her understanding of how bitterness might be kept at bay.

The worst days were when it rained, because on

those days they were not let out for exercise, and thus had no sunshine to lift their spirits. "Don't know how much more of this I can take," Scrapper muttered when they had missed two days out in a row on account of foul weather. "Might be next time I set foot outside I won't be comin' back."

"And how far do you think you'd be getting, afore the governor's troops catched you?" Matey sneered. "Didn't you see when we coasted round the point how many live hereabouts? Reckon they wouldn't rat you out in a minute when they caught you stealing stuff from their garden? And how'd you keep from starving if you didn't?"

"Bados got away, didn't he? If a nigger can do it, I surely can."

"Don't be counting on that," Matey came back at him. "When I jumped ship in Africa, I near about starved. And would've for sure if some bush black hadn't took pity on me and got me eating grubs and the like till I come back to the land of the livin'."

"Besides," Pip put in. "Bados had a boat."

"What? One of them tippy little dugout canoes like what the locals make?" Scrapper scoffed. "Couldn't nobody take to sea in one of them."

"No," Pip informed Scrapper. "Him and his woman took the cutter. Mira said 'twas on account of the cutter gone missing that the governor sent a search party all around the coast. They ain't found them yet, nor heard a word about them."

"Our cutter?" Will was incredulous.

"I think it was Governor Phillip's cutter," Mary remarked dryly. "If you mean the one that fetched us here."

"Can't no one man and one woman sail a six-oar cutter!" Will scoffed.

"I wouldn't say that for certain," Cox put in. "You know Bados was the strongest rower in our bunch, and from what I seen of his woman, she could've rowed for two."

Matey began to sing one of the sea shanties which they had often used to keep the rowing rhythm on their voyage.

"Not that one, Matey," Charlotte piped up. "You said that one's only for the sea, and it's different ones we sing on land."

"Right you are," Matey chuckled, and began to sing one of the land songs he had taught Charlotte, which she and the others soon joined in.

This gave Mary an idea, which she implemented forthwith. As soon as the song wound down and the group fell back into a depressed silence, she whispered to Charlotte, "Ask your papa to tell you a story of when he was a daring sailor back in England, and how he escaped the men who wanted his hide, and made a good living doing it."

Charlotte ran to Will and put the plea to him. Although he pretended to be reluctant, he was soon recounting stories of narrow escapes from the authorities during his days as a swashbuckling smuggler—leaving out the story of the one time his tricks didn't work and he ended up in gaol.

Scrapper followed with a tale from his own career

as a pickpocket. He had a gift for mimicry, and his imitations of an upper class lady when she discovered her purse had disappeared set them to howling with laughter.

Pip, with a little urging, recalled a dog he had once owned that he had taught to steal food from vendors' stands. "That dog knew to wait till a man's back was turned, and, even if they saw him, wasn't none could catch him," he bragged. "I'd lay in hiding a block or two away, and wait for him to come a-running. Whatever he brought, cheese or apple or tart, I always give him half. Like brothers we was, that pup and me."

After Pip had his turn at story-telling, Mary turned to James. "Come, James, you're a well-read man. What stories might you recount to keep our minds away from dark thoughts?"

"I do know a good story, about the travels of one Mr. Gulliver," James acknowledged. "It is a long tale, though. I haven't the voice to tell it all in one sitting."

"Very well then," Mary encouraged. "Tell it in pieces, day by day."

And so he did, beginning right then and carrying on for many days to come.

Mary often followed with a story from the Bible, for as she explained, "'Twas the most beautiful thing you ever saw, that great leather-bound book with gold leaf on the cover. Given to my parents on their wedding day by my father's best friend and owner of a ship upon which we sometimes sailed. It was the one and only thing of value my family ever owned."

She thought for a minute, trying to recall stories her mother had read to her as a child, which she had not thought of for many years. "Here's one you'll like, Matey, about how a strumpet teased poor old Samson into losing his hair, and all his great strength as well."

So began the habit of telling yarns to help them pass the time. The children listened with rapt attention to all that was told, but no stories delighted them quite so much as Luke's. His incredible tales were always about the doings of fairies and elves. He claimed that these wee, mischievous beings were numerous in the woods where his own family lived, and he swore he had personally encountered them on any number of occasions.

Only Cox would not tell stories, claiming he knew none to tell. But when pressed he would sing, in his deep rich baritone, ballads such as *Barbara Allen, Lily Lee, Henry Brown,* and *Bring Mary Home.* Although the tales thus told in song invariably ended in tragedy, they had an oddly comforting effect on the group, seeming somehow to draw them together. Often it was to Cox's sad songs that they fell asleep.

It was in mid-September, on a day they were confined inside due to pouring rain, that Mira came rushing down the steps, hair streaming with water and her sarong soaked through. Pip ran to the small window to greet her. She stuffed a dozen small bananas through the bars, so quickly that he could not catch them all and some fell to the floor. Breathlessly, she told him, "More Englishmen come!"

"A ship?" Pip asked excitedly.

"No ship. No clothes. Like you they come."

The jailer arrived just then, and, instead of allowing Mira a few minutes as he usually did, he shouted at her in Dutch, grabbed her by the arm, and dragged her away.

Pip turned around and repeated in bewilderment what the others had already heard. "Englishmen? No clothes?"

They did not have to wait long to discover the meaning of Mira's cryptic message. Within the hour they heard the tread of many men coming down the dungeon stairs. Mary went to the small barred window to see what she could out in the corridor. James came to stand behind her, his arm about her waist. The others crowded around, hoping to catch a glimpse of the newcomers. The first to pass by was the turnkey. He was followed by a group of men, heavily manacled, starvation-thin, and utterly naked. One, who looked no older than Pip, passed close to the barred window. Glancing in, his startled blue eyes met Mary's.

Several English-speaking guards followed. With blows and other forms of brutality, they drove the naked men into a dungeon room on the opposite side of the corridor. Next came the clanking sound of iron against iron, which suggested that, in addition to the manacles on their hands, these prisoners were being chained to the wall or floor. No one spoke until the guards' steps echoed away. Then James called out, "Hello there! Are you English?"

"Indeed we are," called back a rumbling voice. "Late of His Majesty's armed transport *Bounty*. And you?"

"Bolters from Botany Bay," Luke called.

"The *Bounty*?" Matey exclaimed. "By God! You must be mutineers!"

"Convicts!" came a voice from across the way. "I'd have no dealings with this lot!"

"Dare you imagine yourselves better than we?" Mary shot back. "Why, not one among us has such a crime as mutiny on his conscience!"

"By Jove!" exclaimed a boy's voice. "It was a woman's face I saw!"

"Aye," Matey told them. "'Tis Mary Bryant, our captain."

"Captain?" The word was followed by a chorus of disbelieving laughter.

"If Mary's not our captain then we have none!" Cox shouted defiantly.

Others, save Will, who crouched sullen and shame-faced in the far corner, echoed confirmation. Their declaration was greeted with more derisive laughter from across the corridor.

"Laugh if you like, scoundrels," Luke told them. "But the lass navigated us safe from Botany Bay to here, and upon my word, we arrived in better shape than you. Mutineers! Ug!"

"Withhold judgement, if you will," suggested one of the newcomers. "You know no more of us than we of you. We were not all mutineers, and it could be said that those who were had reason."

"All of us to a man refused to go with First Mate

Christian after he seized the ship, and we asked to be left on O'Tahiti," explained the deep-voiced man. "There we remained for two good years. Our troubles began when Captain Edwards came searching for the mutineers. He made no effort to distinguish between those who had known of the plot and those who were its victims, and confined us all in irons aboard the *Pandora*."

Another voice picked up the story. "This same Captain Edwards ran the *Pandora* on a reef about a thousand miles to the east of here. There were then fourteen from the *Bounty* aboard, but four drowned, along with a good number of the *Pandora*'s crew."

The *Bounty* men called out their names: Joseph Coleman, William McIntosh, William Muspratt, James Morrison, John Millward, Charles Norman, Michael Byron, Thomas Burkitt, and two boys, Thomas Ellison and Peter Heywood.

"You can't imagine what it was like crammed in an oven of a box on the *Pandora*'s deck and manacled hand and foot," one of the men recounted. "Five months we was, wallowing in our own sweat and vermin. Now looks like more of the same, minus the sweat. How long did you say you'd been chained up in this godforsaken hole?"

"We're not chained," Matey called back, drawing a chorus of cries from the other side about the injustice of common criminals being better treated than His Majesty's loyal mariners.

By the next day the rains had passed, and things went on as before, with Mary, Pip and the children out all day, joined by Will, Matey, and Scrapper in the morning, and James, Luke, and Cox in the afternoon. The *Bounty* prisoners, though, were not allowed to leave their cell. This was a puzzle to all of them, until Mira recounted to Pip what she had overheard.

"Captain Edwards not want prisoners take exercise," she whispered. "Gouverneur Wanjon tell Bruger this Englishman have no compassion."

Upon hearing this, Mary's dread deepened. That a man who did not hesitate to imprison small children considered Edwards to be deficient in compassion bespoke a future too horrifying to contemplate.

Several days later, each of the Botany Bay bolters had an opportunity to form their own opinion of Captain Edwards. The day began ominously, when the turnkey did not come as usual to let Mary and the children go outside. An hour or so later, two guards appeared and ordered Will to come with them. There was considerable speculation as to what this might mean. It was Matey who guessed correctly.

"Edwards is wanting information about us," Matey surmised. "Who'd be the likely one to ask but the one what blabbed before? Could be he'll have questions for the rest of us, too."

"What ought we to tell him?" Pip asked fearfully.

"We might as well tell the truth, as Will has probably done already," James advised. "Inventing stories that don't agree will only incur his wrath."

"With one exception," Mary interjected. "I propose we tell him that Pip and Scrapper, being just boys, didn't know that a bolting was planned, and were brought along without their consent, on account of being on Will's crew and needed for the rowing."

"Why let them off the hook?" Matey grumbled. "My neck don't fit a hangman's noose any better'n theirs."

"There's no way we can escape responsibility for our deeds," Mary argued. "What's the harm in trying to save the ones we can?"

Although her words rang of charity, and the others agreed to stick by that story, Mary's motives were not selfless. Once back in England, there was every chance that all would hang, herself included. If that was her fate, Charlotte and Emanuel would be left alone in the world. But if Pip and Scrapper could be presented as innocent victims, they might be spared. Pip truly loved her children, and Scrapper, out of gratitude, might act as their protector on London's harsh streets as well.

James was the next to be taken out, and after that, Luke, Matey, Cox, Scrapper, and Pip. Apprehension grew, as none were returned to the cell, so the others had no way to know what lay in store for them. Eventually, Mary was alone with the children, pretending calm for their sake. Nevertheless, Emanuel seemed to sense how frightened she was and began to cry. When at last the cell door swung open, she tried to take the children with her but the guard would not permit it. There was nothing to do but put the sobbing toddler down on his pillow and tell Charlotte to sit beside him and tell him a funny story.

Charlotte looked up at Mary, blue eyes wide in her thin little face, and said, "All the ones I can remember are scary."

Mary would have reminded her of some of the humorous tales Pip had told about his clever dog, but the guard shoved her roughly to hasten her along.

Why the hurry Mary failed to see because, when she reached the upper level, she was kept waiting out in the corridor a good long while. Voices coming from inside were those of Wanjon and, she surmised, Captain Edwards. At first she could not make out what they were saying, but as the conversation continued their voices rose. She soon gathered that they were discussing the information gleaned from the men.

"Impossible!" came the Englishman's voice. "Only a fool would believe such a story."

Wanjon, perhaps taking this as an oblique reference to his having believed the bolters' lies to start, and not pleased to have his credulity called into question a second time, gave a reply just short of a taunt. "Who then, Captain Edwards? They all say she vas at the helm the whole three thousand miles. That is three times the distance of your own open-boat voyage. Nearer that of Captain Bligh's, ya?"

"Sir!" snapped Edwards, his voice rising. "Common sense tells us that if both Cook and I ran upon the reefs crossing the Coral Sea, no ignorant wench of the criminal class could have navigated the whole length of it."

"Perhaps," Wanjon replied coolly, "you vill form a different opinion once you have interviewed her."

"I am not in the habit of reforming my opinions," Edwards asserted, and called out, "Bring in the prisoner."

Mary scarcely registered the indirect compliment paid her by Wanjon, so alarmed was she by Edwards's apparent rigidity. *Here is one who lacks the power to think, thus seizes upon a single notion and uses it like a stick to beat all who would disagree*, she thought as she was led into the room.

Edwards was a smallish man with smallish eyes and a rosebud mouth already puckered with contempt. Wanjon stood a little apart, thin lips faintly curved in a cynical smile. Although Mary did not glance his way, she sensed that he took some satisfaction from watching two people whose nationality he detested, and whom he had come to loathe, in an exchange which was likely to result in the humiliation of one or the other. She stood mute as Edwards looked her up and down.

"Well, woman, what have you to say for yourself?" he demanded.

"What would you have me say, Sir?"

"I will have you tell me what became of the navigational instruments purloined in Botany Bay," he snapped.

Mary met his stare directly, and said, "They were not purloined, but freely given."

"Ah yes." Edwards smiled sarcastically. "Bryant claims he traded fish for them. Of course, he gave Governor Wanjon a completely different account."

To this Mary said nothing, although she was surprised to hear that Will had changed his story. Perhaps, once sober, Will decided that it was less humiliating to claim that he had traded fish for the instruments than to admit he had traded his wife. Or allowed her to trade herself.

"Well?" Edwards said impatiently. "Where are they?"

"I do not know."

"Your companions have confirmed that these instruments were in your keeping always. That you wore the compass in a bag about your neck, and both chart and quadrant were always within your reach."

"They spoke the truth," Mary said.

"Well then. Governor Wanjon tells me your room was thoroughly searched, and nothing of the kind was found."

"This would surely be true," Mary replied. "As well as the governor's suspicion as to what became of them."

"That you gave them to the African? That is absurd!" Edwards snapped. "What use would he have but to sell them for drink?"

Mary shrugged. "Perhaps he did."

"Ve do not think so," Wanjon interjected. "Every merchant and marine in the colony vas questioned, and these things have not been seen."

Mary hesitated a moment, thinking through the implication of her words, then spoke carefully. "In my experience, the governor of this colony is very thorough. As he has more information than I, and his word carries more weight than mine in every particular, perhaps you are wasting your time with me. I cannot tell you what I do not know."

By Mary's calm demeanour, no one could have guessed the struggle going on within her. Fear of the interview had vanished before she entered the room, blotted out by a rising tide of rage. It was that rage she battled now, knowing that, for all their sakes, she must not incur Edwards's wrath as she had Wanjon's. And yet, never having been taught how to behave around those who presumed themselves to be her betters, she offended unknowingly by looking Edwards straight in the eye and by making suggestions that implied that he was not likely to achieve his ends by the method he had employed. That, and her failure to show fear, greatly annoyed him.

"Perhaps your memory will improve when you face a hanging judge," Edwards said menacingly, and motioned to a guard standing nearby to take her out.

As the door closed behind her, and as the guard was exchanging some information with another assigned to escort her to the dungeon, Mary overheard Edwards say, "You can see as well as I, Governor, that the strumpet is a thoroughly hardened criminal. It is an astonishment to me that you allow them to leave their cell."

"It is to prevent pestilence that ve see to the health of our prisoners," Wanjon said reasonably. "Our doctors say a little fresh air is useful." There was a pause in which he appeared to consider the matter. "Of course, these are English prisoners, now under your jurisdiction."

"Just so, Governor, and confined they shall be until I acquire a vessel to transport them to England."

"As you please," Wanjon said stiffly.

The door opened and Edwards stepped out. Seeing that Mary was still in the corridor, awaiting an escort back to the dungeon, Edwards said loudly, no doubt for her benefit, "What they suffer here is but a foretaste of what awaits them on the gallows, and beyond."

From inside the room came Wanjon's cold question, "And the children, Captain?"

"Bad seed, Governor. Bad seed. With luck they will not survive the voyage."

And so it was that during the final ten days of imprisonment at Kupang, all of the captives, including Emanuel and Charlotte, were confined to the dungeon. Deprived of fresh air and exercise, their spirits sank lower by the day. Mary realised that the need for diversion in the form of song and stories was greater than ever, but it was not easy to persuade the men to continue, or, indeed, to go on herself. Depressed as they were, they might not have made the effort had it not been for encouragement from the *Bounty* men. Once they heard the singing, and learned of stories being told, they begged the teller to stand by the small barred window that faced into the corridor, and to speak loudly so that they too might have some relief from the interminable boredom.

Scrapper honed his skills of mimicry and that comic genius became a great favourite with both groups. Will, Matey, and Pip, who had started out telling stories which were more or less autobiographical, began to drift from the truth for the sake of improving the drama or showing themselves in a more heroic light. James finished *Gulliver's Travels*, and embarked upon Shakespearean plays, sonnets, and poems, even though of the latter, the only one he could remember word for word was *The Phoenix and The Turtle*. Mary's Bible stories continued to be popular, although never so much in demand as Luke's intricate tales of elves and fairies. Soon everyone knew the words to the mournful ballads Cox favoured, and they sang or hummed along with him as, one by one, they drifted into troubled sleep.

The Java Sea

Kupang to Batavia

In early October, on as beautiful a day as ever seen in Kupang, the prisoners were brought up from the dungeon and marched to the dock. This was the first chance Mary and her group had had to see the men from the *Bounty* in broad daylight. They marvelled at the intricate tattoos the mariners had got while marooned in O'Tahiti. Morrison, a man with flowing black hair, had a star of the Order of the Garter on his chest. Millward had an emblem of O'Tahiti tattooed across his stomach. Seventeen year old Ellison had his name on his arm, and Heywood, only sixteen, had tattoos all over his body, including one on his leg which he told them had been taken from the design on a coin from his home, the Isle of Man.

One of the *Bounty* men, Michael Bryn, was so blind that he could not have been a mutineer had he wished. He said he had been taken on the voyage by Bligh solely to play the fiddle. When Pip remarked timidly that it would be nice to have the good cheer of fiddle music, Morrison remarked bitterly, "Good cheer ye'd have aboard the *Bounty* when that fiddle played, or ye'd have been wise to pretend. Once when two of us refused to dance, the captain had us flogged." Indeed, a welter of criss-cross scars like those that marked Will's back was proof that Morrison, Burkitt, Millward, and the black-bearded Muspratt had all been flogged by the *Bounty*'s captain for one reason or another.

Once on the dock, their attention turned to the ship they were to board, which bore the name *Rembang*. Seeing it was crewed by Hollanders, James whispered to Mary, "Edwards must have leased this vessel from the Dutch East India Company in order to transport himself, his mariners, and all the prisoners back to England."

"Will Edwards be the captain in charge, or does the ship come with its own?" Mary wondered. But no one knew the answer to this.

Whatever powers Edwards exercised on the ship he had acquired, one thing was obvious: he had ensured that the conditions they would endure on the *Rembang* would be vastly worse than any they had suffered before. Mary gasped when she reached the hold in which they were to travel and saw a long iron bar fastened to the floor. To it were attached sliding shackles—one for the ankle of each prisoner.

"Bilboes!" moaned Matey. "Damn me, but it don't get no worse than this!"

As the metal cuff was locked around her ankle, Mary fervently hoped that none of the men had ankles thick enough to cause the flesh to rot as it had on Johnny's legs during the months he had been shackled during their transportation. Only one detail in the horror of their new situation gave Mary a sliver of relief: the children were left unfettered because there were no shackles small enough to confine their tiny ankles.

At first they made an effort to keep up their spirits with the kind of singing and story-telling that had sustained them during the final days of imprisonment in the dungeon. To this end, the *Bounty* crew members, who were shackled in the same hold, joined in with tales of their own. Those from Botany Bay listened with great interest as they described the mutiny in detail, and their part—or lack of part—in it.

Most claimed they had been uninvolved. Muspratt and Millward feared that because they had deserted earlier and been caught, brought back to the ship, and flogged, Bligh was likely to suppose they had supported the mutiny and would see them hanged for it.

"I participated," admitted Thomas Ellison. "I woke from my hammock and went out to hear what the ruckus was about, and one of the mutineers shoved a musket in my hands. I went topside, understanding that a mutiny was under way, but more observer than participant, for I had not yet grasped where things stood. Then I saw that they were putting Captain Bligh overboard, along with as many others as the boat could hold, until he asked that no more come in, for fear of sinking them all."

"I begged leave to go with the captain," said Morrison. "But at his order we had no choice but to remain with the *Bounty*."

"I was taken into Christian's confidence," confessed Burkitt, "so I knew mutiny was afoot. But later I regretted having thrown in my lot with him. When we reached O'Tahiti to pick up women and supplies, I and some others asked him to put us ashore there."

"Ah, but life was good in O'Tahiti," reminisced Ellison. "A more beautiful isle with more beautiful women does not exist on earth."

There were sighs all up and down the line of shackled men as they imagined the beautiful island with its beautiful women described in loving detail by those who had been marooned there.

"Sure weren't nothing like that in Africa where I got marooned," Matey grumbled. "If O'Tahiti was all that fine, how come you let Edwards grab you? You knowing the island from living there two years and him a stranger to it, seems like you coulda give him the slip."

"Greater fools than that we were," moaned Morrison. "We dressed in what was left of our uniforms and rowed out to meet him, expecting to be received like honourable men."

"Don't I rue the day I decided not to go with Christian after all, but to stay in O'Tahiti," Burkitt groaned. "Edwards disbelieved every word we told him, and clapped us in irons from then till he sunk the ship in the Coral Sea."

"How got you from there to Kupang?" James wanted to know.

"An armourer's mate risked his life to set us free. The ship was already on her end, so we fell into the sea. Over the next few hours we were picked up by one of the ship's boats. On account of Edwards intended to use us as slaves, I s'pose, 'cause that's what he done," Morrison explained. "There was a sand spit not more than two miles off, but with scarce a sprig of vegetation, mind you."

"We was stranded on one like that for a few days," Pip remarked. "It wasn't so bad."

"Maybe not for you," Ellison shot back. "But Edwards made it hell for us. The ship's sails that were salvaged he had spread in such a way as to give shade for him and his men. But we who'd been shut up in *Pandora*'s hold already five months, our skin was white as the dead. During the day he worked us like slaves and wouldn't allow us any shade. All we could do, when we had the chance, was bury ourselves up to our ears in sand to keep from cooking to death. We suffered horribly from sunburn in that first week."

Coleman picked up the story. "Once the captain organised what supplies could be salvaged from the wreck, he took the two boats he had and made the run for Kupang. Us *Bounty* boys what survived the wreck got brung along so Edwards could put us to the oars. And that he did, with treatment brutal as any slave's ever been dealt."

The *Bounty* sailors continued for some time, recollecting the horrors they had endured at Edwards's hands, tales which sobered every prisoner for what it portended about their chance of arriving alive in England.

James endeavoured to change the subject by asking for news from Europe, but the mariners had little, since the *Bounty* had departed Portsmouth in 1787, just six months after the *Charlotte*. All they had to pass on were scraps picked up from the *Pandora*'s crew, about upheaval in France that had led to a mob storming the Bastille to gain weapons and free some prisoners, plus other riots before and since.

"I heard how French women even marched on Versailles in October of '89," Morrison chuckled. "On account of there being a shortage of bread."

Mary smiled grimly, recalling that it was in October 1789 that she had first rowed out to the *Waaksamheyd* and offered herself to Smit—that action also prompted by hunger, along with the certainty that if she remained in Botany Bay her children were going to starve.

"Them on the *Pandora* what deigned to talk to us said that at the time of their departure from England, Louis the Sixteenth was still on the throne but not expected to stay there long. And what's troublin' the royals ain't half the price common people are paying, for they're in the thick of it all," Muspratt commented.

"What chance of the chaos spreading to England?" James asked.

"They said there was some talk going round," Burkitt admitted. "But King George is doing his utmost to make sure them radical notions about taking away the rights of king and clergy don't find a following at home. Mostly, it's just talk."

At that they lapsed into silence, because in point of fact, it was all "just talk," and bore no more relation to their present situation than Luke's tales of the doings of fairies and elves.

They had not even begun to adjust to the discomfort of their new situation when things grew even worse. They suffered not only from being shackled and forced to lie on bare boards in their own filth, but within a week of casting off, all were struck down by diarrhea. Mary was caught between giving her children as little as possible of the slop they were fed, to spare them the terrible stomach cramps that followed, and knowing that if they did not eat, or at least drink, they would die of starvation and dehydration. The cramps, which she herself suffered, were so bad that in the end she let the children do as they would, eat if they desired or lie listless and starving if they lacked the strength. She never expected them to survive until they made port in Batavia, but somehow they did. This was due in no small part to the fact that they were not in bilboes. They wandered up and down the line of shackled prisoners, where they were treated with tenderness by all who were not themselves too sick to respond.

The *Rembang* was a month on its northwest run

through the Java Sea from Kupang to Batavia. By the time they anchored in the harbour of that fetid capital in November's midsummer heat, all were down to skin and bones, the children most pathetic of all. However, it was not one of the children but Matey, whom Mary believed to be as tough as the sea itself, who lifted his head one day and, eyes burning with fever, begged for water in a piteous voice. James, shackled in such a way as to be unable to aid the man, called out to Mary to pass a cup of water to him, if any be left in the bucket. She stared at him blankly and did not respond.

"Charlotte, Emanuel," James urged. "Get hold of your mother. Get her to stand up."

The children, weak though they were, began to pummel Mary until she lifted her head.

"Mary," James pleaded. "I think Matey is suffering from fever. We must get help or we'll all die right here."

"What can I do?" she asked dully.

"That you, Mary?" Will called from the other side. "Oh, Mary!"

"Pick up the cup," James urged. "Get some water and pass it to Matey."

She picked up the cup and in an automatic gesture, dipped into the bucket. The only sound was the scrape of metal on dry metal. For a moment she stared at the cup as if she had no idea what its purpose was. Then, propelled into action by some inner demon, she began to bang it against the bars. It was as if that noise wakened more of her, because she set up such a clanging one might have thought there were ten demons on the loose.

Shortly a Dutch sailor appeared, "Godverdomme! Ssush!" he shouted at her.

"I will speak to the captain," Mary shouted back.

The sailor spat through the bars and turned away. Immediately Mary started banging the cup again. Up and down the line, other prisoners, both from the *Bounty* and Botany Bay, began to do the same.

"Tell him Mary Bryant says it's for the safety of his ship," she called.

"Dutch captains do not need vomen to tell them how to make safe their vessels," sneered the sailor.

"Tell him yourself, then," Mary retorted. "There's fever down here."

It was as if she had turned into a spectre before his eyes. "Fever?" he repeated in terror. "The doctor mit Captain Edwards, I tell to him." And he fled.

Mary turned around, gave James a bleak look, and saw her children for what felt like the first time in a fortnight. Charlotte nuzzled her for attention, and Mary's arm encircled her. Emanuel, though, lay listless, causing her to remember him as he had been once before, when they had been washed out to sea in the cutter and she thought he was dying. She took him into her arms and rocked him gently. His weight was next to nothing.

When she looked up again there was an Englishman standing at the bars, one she had not seen before. Immediately several of the *Bounty* prisoners called out, "Doctor Hamilton! Thanking you, Sir, for being so kind. Show us some mercy, if you please, Sir. We swear to you we never were mutineers!" And other remarks along those lines.

"What's this about fever?" Hamilton snapped.

"See for yourself, Sir." James motioned to Matey, who was still moaning for water. "That man yonder is burning. If it's the fever he has, there will be no containing it down here in the hold."

Mary rose and said, "Better the guards lower our ration by bucket and not come below while the fever burns. Pray have me unshackled that I may carry water—of which we have none at the moment—to those too ill to move."

"You're safer at a distance," Hamilton noted dryly.

"'Tis of no interest to me whether I live or die."

"I should think you would have some fear of Hell, Madam."

Mary turned her gaze on him, that direct look so inappropriate for a woman of her class when speaking to a man of his, and asked, seriously, "Can there be more heat there, Doctor? Or more suffering?"

Hamilton turned away. To the guard he said, "Send for the armourer's mate."

Mary was unshackled and a short time later the hatchway was opened to permit the lowering of a bucket of water. Mary gave water to Emanuel and Charlotte, then went to Matey. She tried to lift the old man's head to give him a drink, but he snarled like a wounded animal and curled into a protective ball. Then, suddenly flinging himself upright, he pushed her aside with unnatural strength and shrieked at Will, "Filthy snitch! Murderer!"

With that he collapsed against Mary's legs and died.

Will may or may not have heard him, for he was sick as well, and moaning piteously. Mary ripped a bit of fabric from her tattered sarong, dipped it into the bucket, and began to do what she could to lower his raging fever.

"Ah Mary, why did I do it?"

"God only knows," she said dully.

"Is there a God?"

"Who knows?"

"He'll be so angry with me for what I done. But I did love you, Mary. Had my eye on you from the first. I'm crazy in love with that Cornwall girl, I told my mates, and someday she'll love me, too. But you never did, did you, Mary?" His voice faded to a whisper. "Never, never."

"Wild, foolish William," she whispered sadly. "You understand so little."

Mary was not required to nurse Will or any of the other men after that, for by nightfall all the sick ones were removed to hospital in Batavia in hopes of preventing the fever from spreading to the rest of the ship. Only Emanuel remained, because Mary concealed the fact that he was ill, and continued to cool and hydrate him as best she could.

It was remarked at least once a day that Edwards seemed intent on lying in the stinking port of Batavia until all had perished. What they did not know then, but later learned, was that he had had considerable difficulty in finding ships to transport them onward. During the delay, hardest hit were the mariners who had taken shore leave. Within days of Matey's death, seven of the *Pandora* crew took sick and died, and as many from the *Rembang* crew.

The tolling of bells could be heard from the town, and the sound of drunken sailors singing Christmas carols in English and Dutch, when Mary next saw Dr. Hamilton. He descended into the hold, accompanied by one of the English mariners. Mary, sitting on the filthy floor with Emanuel in her arms, did not bother to rise.

The doctor spoke to her through the bars. "I am sorry to bring such news on Christmas Eve, Mrs. Bryant, but your husband has passed away."

"Most surely he suffers less now than those he betrayed," she said bitterly.

Hamilton ignored her remark, and further informed her, "Captain Edwards ordered burial earlier this afternoon, with none from your party in attendance."

"What does it matter?" Then, struggling to her feet, Mary asked, "Tell me, Doctor, is the moon full?"

He gave her a startled look. "Why, I believe it is. Or nearly so."

"Pray allow me a moment on deck."

"Why, I could not grant such a request if I were inclined to—which I most certainly am not," he said bluntly.

"But you must," Mary stated. "You see, my son has died."

Involuntarily, Hamilton took a step back and glanced down in horror at what he had taken to be a sleeping child. "I . . . I will inform Captain Edwards. Perhaps he will consent to read a service tomorrow."

At that, the wall behind which Mary had concealed her feelings cracked, and she cried out, "This baby requires no prayer nor forgiveness for anything! If Captain Edwards is a praying man, let him pray for his own black soul!"

The English mariner accompanying Hamilton murmured, "Excuse me, Sir, but the men will complain if the captain makes them attend a funeral on Christmas Day. And if she puts it over the side herself, it'll save others from handling the corpse."

Hamilton pursed his lips and, speaking not to Mary but to the sailor, said, "It is unhealthful to keep a body aboard in this heat, and a danger to all if it died of the fever. Can we drop it overboard here in the harbour?"

"What with the filth already floating in this harbour, dead bodies not excepted, where's the harm, Sir? There's no more flesh on the mite's bones than a smallish fish."

"Then let it be disposed of tonight," Hamilton decided.

With that they left the hold. Mary reached down and ripped another strip off her once-beautiful sarong, and wrapped it around the naked baby in her arms.

Down the line of shackled men, Pip, trying to comfort Charlotte, was himself weeping. James began to recite the poem, *The Phoenix and The Turtle*, about the funeral of a turtle dove attended by other birds. Others joined in, all having learned it by heart from hearing James recite it many times over back in the dungeon. One by one their voices broke with emotion and they could not go on. When at last a jailer came and motioned Mary to follow him out, only the voices of James and Charlotte followed her in mournful chant:

"Beauty, Truth, and Rarity,
Grace in all simplicity,
Here enclosed in cinders lie

Death is now the phoenix' nest,
And the turtle's loyal breast
To eternity doth rest"

Up on the deck, in fresh air for the first time since leaving Kupang two months earlier, Mary held her dead baby over the railing and let go. The small body struck the water with an almost inaudible splash, and disappeared.

Then, under guard, Mary was returned to the hold. Charlotte immediately came to her and asked in a fearful whine, "Where's Emanuel?"

"He died, like the turtle dove," Mary told her.

"What did you do with him?"

"I put him in the water."

"Will you put me in the water when I die?"

Mary wrapped her arms around the child and said,

"I will never put you in the water, darling. You shall come with me all the way to England."

"When are we coming to England, Mummy?"

"Before this year is out, my love. Our next port will be Table Bay, on the southern tip of Africa. Then on to beautiful England."

The Indian Ocean

Batavia (Jakarta) to Capetown

Edwards was unable to secure passage from Java to South Africa for all his crew and prisoners on a single ship, so some of the *Bounty* men, including Bryn and Morrison, travelled on different vessels. Mary felt considerable sympathy for both—Bryn on account of his blindness and Morrison for having suffered unspeakable abuse at Edwards's hands for being a Methodist—but the one's whining and the other's incessant praying had frayed everyone's nerves.

The passage from Java to South Africa took three months. The conditions in which they were confined took a terrible toll on their bodies and a greater one on their spirits. Edwards kept them as wretched as possible, yet not quite starved to death, as he was determined to see the *Bounty* men hanged. Nor did he wish lighter sentences for those from Botany Bay. As the ship progressed toward the southern tip of Africa, few escaped some form of ill health. And always there was the hunger. One gloomy day, as they sat in irons watching the shadows of rats move back and forth around the edge of the hold, Scrapper remarked, "I reckon the only good thing about us gettin' so little to eat is we don't leave no scraps, so even the rats go on about their business looking elsewhere for grub."

Charlotte, never a robust child, was wasting away. Thomas Burkitt, one of the *Bounty*'s able seamen who had been in on the mutiny but chose not to go with Christian, was especially gentle with her. He never failed to offer the child bits of fish head with the bones picked out, or other solid food he found in his slop which might provide some small nourishment.

"I've got a native wife back in O'Tahiti," he told Mary one day. "Name of Mary, too. And ye won't believe it, but we had a little daughter about the same age as this one of yours, that we christened Charlotte."

"A native wife named Mary?" Mary asked doubtfully, imagining the aboriginal natives of Australia and their strange-sounding names.

"That wasn't her Tahitian name," Burkitt explained. "'Twas one I give her. We all done that with our wives, give 'em proper Christian names." He sighed. "Ah, what a fine woman my Mary was. And a beauty to boot."

That set the others to talking about the women they had loved and been forced to leave back in O'Tahiti. Cox, manacled at the opposite end of the line, blubbered like a baby about his poor sweet Florie, whom he believed he would never see again.

As the ship inched its way across the Indian Ocean, the captives chained in the hold heard rumours that more men from the *Pandora* crew had died, giving rise to certainty that they would perish as well. But in spite of the conditions in which Edwards held his prisoners, the captives all survived that leg of the journey—save one.

It came about during a terrible storm such as Mary herself had never known, unless it might have been that one the night they were landed in Botany Bay. But that night they *were* landed. Now they were on the high seas, deep in the bowels of a ship that rolled horribly, flinging them about and causing the fetters to cut into the flesh of their legs. Although she was not on deck to see the near-continuous lightning, thunder cracked so close at hand that it was often hard to believe the ship had not been struck. The Dutch mariners were in such a panic that they would not stay on deck but came tumbling down below.

The prisoners were unshackled and taken to man the pumps although, weak as they were from lack of exercise and near-starvation, Mary doubted they would be of any use. Water rose a foot or more in the hold, convincing her that death would come by drowning. Later she learned that Cox and Luke were not put to the pumps, but taken up to repair a broken yard. The storm, which had hit full force in the wee hours of the morning, raged all through the day. It was near dark before the sea calmed and all were back in their shackles. All but the one.

"Where's Cox?" Mary asked, seeing that his fetter lay empty.

Luke pushed away the mug of gruel Mary had just dipped up for him, and dropped his chin onto his chest without reply. Mary had never seen him so morose, and guessed at once that something terrible had happened.

"Luke!" she cried. "What's become of our Coxie?"

Luke's shoulders convulsed with sobs. It was some considerable time before he could speak. At last he got a grip on himself and told what he had seen.

"High on the mast Cox was, fixing a broken yard, on account of them Dutch sailors being too fearful of thunder and lightning to make the climb. I was a little below, hanging on for dear life. The ship was pitching every which way, sometimes keeling over till I thought the mast was going to slap the water."

"He fell?" Mary cried in horror.

"Nay, Mary, he didn't fall," Luke choked. "He jumped. I seen him clear. Drove the last nail into that yard, then climbed up on it and stood there clinging to the mast. Then he lifted the hammer high over his head and dove into the sea like he meant to bash it to death."

There was a shocked silence. Then Pip spoke hopefully. "Cox is strong as a bull, he is. Maybe he swum to land."

"I did see a lighthouse," Luke confirmed. "It wasn't far off."

"Sure he's on shore now and free as a bird," Scrapper predicted. "The lucky dog."

"Or he's in the water," Charlotte put in. "Like Emanuel."

James leaned along the line of shackled men to take Mary's hand in his, for he must have known what she was thinking.

"Don't you suppose he might've made it?" asked Pip, who was seated next to Mary. "Even with the sea so rough?"

"Cox couldn't swim," she said quietly. "Not even in calm waters."

The Final Voyage

Capetown to London

They reached the southern tip of Africa and anchored in Table Bay on March 18, 1792. James roused Mary from the stupor into which she had fallen, and repeated the rumour that they were to be transferred to an English ship, the *Gorgon*, commanded by a Captain Parker. "They say Parker is a humane man, and his wife sails with him. I should think this bodes well for the remainder of our journey," James offered encouragingly.

Mary glanced along the line of men whose clothes had long since rotted away, so that their nudity was nearly complete. Mary herself, weighing less than ninety pounds, wore only a scrap of the sarong she had been wearing when thrown in the Kupang dungeon six months earlier. Charlotte, mere skin over bones, was naked entirely.

"If he recognises us as human," she said dryly. "Let us hope that he does not share Edwards's view that we hardly need feeding, and iron fetters fit us better than clothing."

The longboat carrying the *Bounty* sailors was launched first, and came alongside the *Gorgon* while the boat carrying those from Botany Bay was still a little way out. From afar Mary could hear the prisoners being treated to insults from passengers hanging at the rail. The air was filled with such remarks as "Bloody pirates!" and "Sure and I'd know 'em for mutineers anywhere." "What a rough-looking bunch!" "Look at them tattoos!" "Can you believe they're English?"

As their boat approached the ship, Mary kept her eyes downcast. Being as unkempt as the *Bounty* men and nearly as naked, she expected the same sort of scorn from this audience of properly-dressed Englishmen.

Suddenly the air was filled with exclamations of an entirely different sort. "Bless me!" bawled a familiar voice. "If it ain't them that bolted with Mary Bryant!"

She looked up in amazement. At the railing were Sergeant Scott, Lieutenant Clark, Captain Tench, and other mariners whom she had last seen in Botany Bay, staring with astonishment as great as her own.

"Why, it's the girl herself if it ain't her ghost!" exclaimed Scott.

"Impossible!" Tench shaded his eyes to get a better

look. "By God, I believe it is! Hey there, Mary! Mary Bryant!" Clark called.

Mary did not respond. She was engaged in trying to get Charlotte to cling to her back so she could climb the ladder to the ship's deck, for she knew it would frighten the child to be taken up in the sling. Then, realising that Charlotte was not strong enough to hold on, Mary asked the oarsman to give her a bit of rope to bind the little girl to her body. Only when she began to climb did Mary realise how weak she was herself.

Behind her, waiting his turn, James touched her ankle and said, "Hold your head up, Mary. It is an amazing thing we have done, and they know it sure as we do."

Mary was too preoccupied with hanging on and raising herself hand over hand up the ladder to care about impressing others. Six months as Edwards's captive had robbed her of muscle, and left her spirit just as depleted.

When at last she reached the deck, hands stretched out from every direction to help her aboard. "Upon my word, but I never expected to see you alive again!" Scott exclaimed.

Near nude though she was and not caring at all, but perhaps because James did care, Mary stood as tall as her five-foot-four frame would allow, and tried to smile.

By then James was on the deck beside her, and Tench was saying, "Brown, you rogue! Whatever are you doing in the company of mutineers?"

"I say, Sir, it is as great a surprise to see you," James

said. "How is it that so many mariners from Botany Bay are aboard this vessel?"

"Our tour of duty is up. Replacements permitted some of us who came out on the *Charlotte* to go home. By God, but this is incredible! Where is that rascal Bryant?"

"Taken by fever in Batavia. Old Matey died there as well. Cox the carpenter we lost on this final leg of passage." James paused and added, "Mary's son Emanuel perished of the fever around the same time as his father."

Tench turned to Mary. "Mrs. Bryant! I am so sorry."

Others, including the wives and children of some of the officers, crowded around, full of curiosity about the journey which Mary and her companions had survived. Scrapper began to boast, but the others were satisfied to answer questions as asked.

As conversation swirled around them, Lieutenant Clark unfastened the rope which bound Charlotte to her mother and lifted the child off her back. "Hello there, Charlotte. Do you remember me? Dr. White is aboard. Won't he be surprised to see you!"

Mary moved a little away from the crowd, for she did not feel strong enough in body or mind to deal with so much excitement. Taking in her new surroundings, she noticed that three were watching from the bridge. One was obviously the ship's captain. Next to him was the First Mate, and a woman, probably the captain's wife of whom James had spoken.

Suddenly Mary had a sense of having spent the whole of her life looking up at people who were looking down on her. The English judge who had sentenced her first to hang and then to be transported instead. Governor Wanjon who had sent her to the dungeon. Captain Edwards who believed that being chained in the hold of a ship for half a year was appropriate punishment for being who she was and doing what she had done. All leading up to this moment—a moment in which she no longer cared about anything.

Or so she imagined. In reality, there was the promise she had made to Charlotte to take her to England. It was the one thing she could do, and wanted to do, before judging men put an end to her existence on earth.

Some of Edwards's mariners approached, carrying manacles to re-secure the prisoners. The First Mate hastened down from the bridge and called them aside for private words. The discussion grew heated, so that everyone on that part of the deck overheard.

"You might have considered the fact that there are officers' wives present before bringing naked men aboard," the First Mate informed them curtly. "I have been ordered to take charge of the prisoners. You may report that to your Captain Edwards. If he has objections, let him take up the matter with the captain of this ship." The First Mate then ordered his own men to take the captives below without manacles.

As Mary stood in line to go into the hold, she looked beyond the railing of the deck for what she could see of sea and sky, not knowing whether she would glimpse either again before reaching England. Then she followed the others into the hold.

It saddened her a little that the *Bounty* sailors, who had suffered alongside them for more than half a year, were placed in a separate cell. She had grown fond of the two youths, Heywood and Ellison, even though the latter admitted that he had participated in the mutiny. Burkitt said he had been involved, too, but how could she hold it against him when he had been so kind to Charlotte while pining his heart out for his own wife and daughter back in O'Tahiti?

Although she would miss those men, whom she had come to think of as friends, Mary was relieved to find herself and Charlotte sharing a cell with only James, Luke, Pip, and Scrapper. It was a cramped space and the hold of the ship was oven hot, but no longer were they shackled to floor boards and forced to lie in their own filth. Each prisoner had been provided with a hammock. In the past Charlotte would have slept in the curl of her mother's body, but the child had grown tender in the joints, and cried out when anyone touched or tried to move her. Mary asked for and got a separate hammock for Charlotte, which she hung touching her own. James hung his hammock on the other side of Mary's. With the hammocks of Pip, Luke, and Scrapper strung up alongside, there was no space whatsoever to walk around. But that hardly mattered. During their first weeks aboard the *Gorgon*, while the ship yet lay in the harbour, the heat of the hold, combined with weakness from starvation and lack of exercise, inclined them to inertia.

From the time they had first been shackled on the *Rembang* six months earlier, Mary had begun to draw in on herself. She rarely spoke, and roused only to meet the most basic necessities for Charlotte. Sometimes even those were not attended to unless James or one of the others reminded her. She was of course aware of James's presence and to some degree comforted by it. But in a state where it was almost beyond her ability to care for her child and herself, she really had nothing left over for him.

He must have been aware of the reason for her withdrawal, though, for when it became apparent that on this ship they would not be starved, he had, in an indirect way, spoken of it. Passing her a cup of stew (Mary no longer rose from the hammock to serve even herself, let alone others in her party, as she had done in times past), James said, "After a week or two of decent rations, I expect our minds will be less dull."

He said no more, nor did he need to. Mary knew that he longed for a resumption of the lively and tender conversations they had enjoyed during that one golden month in Kupang. She felt much the same, but whereas there remained some semblance of hope in James's eyes that this might yet come to pass, she was sure that such moments would never come again. Her feelings, insofar as she felt anything, consisted of wordless black rages.

The only times she felt truly alive were in dreams, when she imagined herself attacking a man. Often this took the form of her lunging at Edwards or Wanjon or Will with a blade—the knife having been pulled from the folds of her sarong, or having magically appeared in her hand. But, as dreams are wont to do, hers often turned to nightmares, and she would wake with a pain in her chest, convinced for a second or two that the villain had turned the knife on her and that she was the one about to die. It would take her a moment to realise that she was alone in her hammock, neither dead nor dying. Often in her hand would be the wooden comb Bados had carved for her back in Botany Bay which, through all her trials and tribulations, she had carried tucked inside what was left of her sarong.

About a week after boarding the *Gorgon*, the captives were given cast-off clothing collected from passengers and mariners. The sailor who brought the garments told them that Edwards had been opposed to this charity, but Captain Parker had decided that they were to be allowed on deck as soon as the ship sailed. He would not have the wives of officers on board further insulted by the sight of nude prisoners.

The day after they received clothing to cover their nakedness, the hatch opened, but no one immediately descended. Instead, a discussion commenced on deck, in voices loud enough for those below to hear most of what was being said. The loudest voice was that of Edwards, which the prisoners knew well and had come to dread. He was saying, in a petulant tone, "I have no choice but to abide by your decision, Captain Parker, but I strongly protest these criminals being allowed out of irons."

"It would seem that you make no distinction between men charged and those proven guilty," Parker observed.

And Edwards's unimaginative response, "I don't know what you mean, Captain."

"As the *Bounty* sailors have not been tried, one cannot say with certainty that all are mutineers," Parker explained patiently.

"As for the others, surely you would not keep a woman in irons!" exclaimed the high-pitched voice of a woman whom Mary guessed to be Mrs. Parker.

"I certainly would," Edwards asserted. "And have done these six months past. There is absolutely nothing of the gentle sex in Mary Bryant. They say she showed not a sign of grief when her husband died, and put her infant son over the side with neither tear nor prayer."

"You are quite mistaken!" protested Tench. "The child Mrs. Bryant has with her now was born on our voyage out. I observed them daily, and I assure you, no high-born lady could have been more tender. The Bryants were model prisoners on that voyage, and in the colony as well, except for Bryant's delving into the black market. I wager it was for the children's sake that they made their bid for freedom."

"But how did they get to Timor? And with all alive?" wondered Captain Parker.

"What an intriguing woman," mused his wife.

"Pray do not misplace your admiration, Mrs. Parker," scolded Edwards. "The woman is in no way remarkable."

That brought a snort of derisive laughter from Dr.

White. "Except that with a babe in each arm, she sailed a boat all the way to Kupang. And am I not correct in saying that *their* vessel did not founder on a reef?"

"They are less than the vermin that feeds upon them," Edwards muttered.

"A great many humans do not rise above the level of vermin," came Dr. White's dour comment. "Nevertheless, it is a remarkable thing they have done."

"Indeed it is," Tench said eagerly. "With your permission, Captain Parker, Dr. White and I will proceed to interview them."

"If you wish," Captain Parker said easily. "But I daresay you won't stay long. Given the kangaroos and other wildlife we are transporting, the stench in the hold is overpowering. You would do better to wait until we sail, and the prisoners can be brought on deck."

At this point Edwards launched into a protestation against the notion that the prisoners should be allowed to take exercise, but Mary had ceased to listen, for even listening took energy she did not have. She lay sweltering in the heat and the mindless rage that now so often consumed her; she was hardly cognisant of her surroundings until James's voice broke through.

"Mary! Get up. Captain Tench and Dr. White are here."

"Dr. White?" Mary struggled to her feet and tried to collect her thoughts. "You ought not to be here, Sir. 'Tis not a fit place for the living."

"You and the rest of this lot seem alive enough," he said, in his usual cranky way. Then he squinted past her to Charlotte, who lay naked and unmoving in her hammock. "Good God! Tench said she was thin, but the child is a perfect skeleton!"

"After being starved for six full months, what would you expect?" Mary spat.

Tench cleared his throat and said, speaking to Mary but in a voice meant for all to hear, "Mrs. Parker would have you and your child put in a separate cell, Mrs. Bryant, to prevent molesting by the men. But the ship has only the two, and the other is taken up by prisoners from the *Bounty*. She did ask me to enquire as to whether you are being abused. If so, her husband, the captain, will see that the man is properly punished."

For a moment Mary stared blankly, her thoughts coming slower than in the past. Then with that sudden vehemence which, since their recapture, sometimes came exploding out of her without premeditation, she cried, "Abuse? What does she know of abuse? Who among these men—" she flung out her arm to include the four men who shared her cell, "—could imagine doing to a woman what that vile Edwards has done to us all? If Captain Parker would mete out punishment, let him not start with these men, my brothers all, but by hanging—"

"Mary, Mary!" James grasped her arm and tried to pull her from the bars which she was gripping with unnatural force. "Be quiet!"

"—Captain Edwards!" Mary shouted. "Hang him, I say! Hang him! Hang him!"

"Stop it!" White snapped, adding his authority to James's pleadings. And to Tench, "Captain Parker fairly warned us—the stench down here is unbearable. Let us continue the interview later, when we are out of the harbour and the prisoners can be brought on deck."

The two visitors exchanged a meaningful glance and quickly left the hold.

"Oh, Miss Mary!" Pip whispered in a frightened voice. "Ye ought not to've said such a thing. I'm sure they was meaning us well."

For a moment longer Mary stood gripping the bars as if her hands were welded there. Only when she turned around and saw how the men were staring at her did she realise what she had done; how, just as she let her rage take possession of her back in Kupang, and had offended Governor Wanjon to the point that he gave no consideration to her supplications, so might she have done again with the officers from Botany Bay.

"Reckon we ain't got all that many friends," Luke said. He turned his back on her, muttering, "Seems like we might be showing respect to them that is."

From further along in the hold, Ellison called out, "That your little Captain Mary down there trying to stir up a mutiny?" Amidst raucous laughter, he added, "Don't count us in on this one. We done had ours, and it ain't done any of us a bit of good!"

"Them *Bounty* boys got a point," Scrapper said laconically. "Don't know 'bout a woman, but a man could get a flogging for saying how one of His Majesty's officers oughta be hanged."

Mary looked from one to another, last at James, whose worried eyes said all those things and more. "Oh James," she moaned. "Have I lost my mind?"

"Not your mind, Mary," he said gently, putting his arm around her and urging her back to her hammock. "There was nothing illogical in what you said. It's more a matter of self-control, upon which you once prided yourself, and which served you well as a means of getting things done. Flying into a rage was necessary in Batavia, as the fever going about might have killed us all, and there was no other way to bring attention to our situation. But in our present circumstances . . ." His voice trailed off, as if he could not bring himself to criticise her as the others had.

"I don't know what comes over me that I behave thus," she said.

He looked at her thoughtfully for a moment, then replied, "It has been clear to me for some time that when a body is as wasted as ours are, the mind is likewise weakened. I suppose the same applies to self-control. But I believe, truly I do, that as we recover our physical strength, those other parts of our personality will regain their vigour as well."

"Those are comforting words," Mary said, and closed her eyes and went to sleep.

Dr. White did not take his own advice about waiting till the prisoners were brought on deck to see them. The next day he returned to the hold, this time alone. Again, James had to rouse Mary from her hammock, for it was to her the doctor wished to speak. "I came to see Charlotte," he said abruptly. "Bring her to the bars."

Mary hesitated. "She cries when I try to lift her. It pains her."

"I did not ask what she wanted," White snapped. "Do as you're bid, woman."

Charlotte did cry when Mary picked her up, and continued to do so as her mother held her near the bars for Dr. White's inspection.

He looked at the suppurating sores on the child's bone-thin thighs, but all he said was, "You have been aboard for more than a week. Has she put on no flesh at all?"

"She will not eat," Mary admitted. "I believe it is scurvy, for her teeth have loosened and fallen out but for one."

"Hold her close and open her mouth so I can examine it," the doctor instructed, and muttered to himself, "As if I could see a damned thing down here in the dark."

Mary, cajoling the child to open, got the mouth opened wide enough for the doctor to run a finger around inside. "As might be expected," he snapped. "Full of cankers. Once scurvy reaches this stage it's damn near fatal. What she needs are citrus fruits."

"Are they to be had?" Mary asked anxiously.

"I will have some sent down," White said, "But the acidic nature of such foods makes eating them agony once the mouth is so raw."

True to his word, Dr. White saw to it that a lime each day was send down for Charlotte. But as he had predicted, the child screamed in agony when the juice was squeezed into her mouth, and she gagged, and absorbed but a few drops of what was given to her.

They set sail soon thereafter. To the prisoners' relief, they were allowed to spend the morning hours on deck where the temperatures, although still stifling hot, were not as high as in the hold.

One day, as Mary sat with Charlotte, trying to keep her cool with a wet rag and the fanning of her palms, Captain Tench wandered by. "Mrs. Bryant," he said pleasantly. "The heat is quite unbearable, is it not?"

"Bearable," she said shortly. "And awful."

"It must have been hot in that open boat, too, when you were sailing the Coral Sea," he continued, no doubt hoping to lure her into a conversation about the adventures of their escape. When Mary did not respond, he continued, "Of course, one had to mind the reefs there. How was it that you steered clear of them?"

"'Twas easy enough," Mary said impatiently. "When I felt coral teeth rising up to bite a hole in the boat, we turned aside."

Tench stared down at her uneasily for a moment, then said in a dubious voice, "I see. Well, uh, good day to you, Ma'am."

Dr. White, who had observed the exchange, said, "I see your interviews are not going very well, Mr. Tench."

Tench grimaced. "Oh, the others are inclined to

talk. And except for young Scrapper, not inclined to boast. But her—." He motioned toward Mary.

"The criminal mind is not given to reason," pronounced Edwards, who, although uninvited, had wandered over to join the conversation.

"I confess I find her strange," Tench admitted.

"She has suffered a great deal," White said shortly. "I suspect that she now stands just this side of madness."

Edwards's small lips curved into a mirthless smile. "Perhaps it will ease her hanging."

The heat was horrible on deck, and even worse for the prisoners during the hours they were confined to the hold. Mary stripped off the dress Mrs. Parker had acquired for her, and went back to wearing what remained of the sarong, a mere strip of fabric knotted about the waist. Yet there was nothing sensuous in that nudity, for neither her bare breasts nor her legs retained enough flesh to give them womanly curves.

Charlotte's agony was so great when touched that her mother's arms were no longer a comfort. When Mary realised this, she offered the only thing available that might provide a little solace. She told stories, and called on the others to do the same during all the hours the child was awake. For Mary, nothing existed except her daughter, whom she might have seen—could she have borne the knowledge—was dying.

In fact, children were dying all over the ship. Within a month of their sailing, Clark wrote in his journal that seven of the mariners' children had died, most of these being around Charlotte's age or younger. Only a miracle might have ensured that Charlotte, disease-ridden and starved beyond recovery, would survive. On this voyage there would be no miracles.

In the late afternoon of May 5, the air was rent with screams. A sailor came tumbling down the ladder to find Mary at the bars, holding Charlotte in her arms. Around her crowded the four men, terrified by their own helplessness.

"The bosun says shut the bleedin' bitch up if I have to pitch her oversides," the tar barked.

"Please fetch Dr. White!" James begged, as he tried to comply by covering Mary's mouth with his hand.

"Come, fellow, you can see she's plumb off her head. You want her quiet, bring the doctor," Luke urged the sailor. "He's the only one can settle her down."

"What if he won't come?" the sailor asked dubiously.

"He'll come, Sir, I know he will," Pip put in. "He's fair fond of the little one."

"Make haste, Sir!" Scrapper panted, as he tried to assist the others in getting Mary into her hammock. "This ain't—!"

Just then Mary got one of her arms free and bashed Scrapper across the face, bloodying his nose. The sailor shook his head and disappeared.

It was not long before the hatchway opened and Dr. White descended, along with the turnkey.

"It's Charlotte," James said, and mouthed the word, "Dead."

"Mary!" White commanded. "Bring Charlotte to me."

"No!" Mary shrieked, clutching the limp body to her breast. "She is going with me. To see England."

White wiped perspiration from his brow, and muttered, "Perhaps she sees it now."

"To walk the fields of Cornwall, and pick wildflowers along the lane!" Mary insisted.

The doctor shook his head slowly from side to side. "You are bound for prison, Mary. That is no place for a child."

"In all the world," she said dully, "no place for my child."

White motioned for the turnkey to open the door. When the door was open, he said, "Come, then. Bring her up into the sunshine."

Mary followed the doctor obediently, whispering to the little body as if it were alive.

"Doctor?" the turnkey called after him.

Dr. White looked back. The turnkey motioned toward Mary's companions, asking if they were to be allowed to accompany her. White nodded. The turnkey held the cell door open, and the men filed silently out.

Up on deck, only a few of the ship's company gathered for the funeral service. It might have been the heat, because the sun was just touching the horizon, and as yet there was no relief from the day's sweltering temperatures. Or maybe they stayed away because it was only a convict's child. Or because in recent days they had seen too many children die already.

Captain Parker came to the railing with a Bible in his hand. Mary gave him a suspicious look. He cleared his throat and began to read, "The Lord is my shepherd, I shall not want."

Mary interrupted loudly. "She is cold, Dr. White. Feel her hands. Is she not cold?"

White took the dead child from her. "We are very near the place where Charlotte came to life, Mary. God wants to take her back and you must let her go. Do you wish to kiss her once more?"

Obediently, Mary kissed the lifeless cheek.

Captain Parker continued reading. "He maketh me to lie down in green pastures. He leadeth me beside still waters."

Dr. White held the little body over the railing and let go. Mary watched it fall. Then, without warning, she flung herself at the doctor like a wild animal. Screaming incoherently, she tore at him with teeth and nails. White was so taken by surprise that he sustained several bites and bloody scratches before Tench and Gardner, who stood closest, leapt forward and pinioned her.

Almost immediately, Mary ceased to flail and went limp. Although her eyes remained wide open, she was obviously not seeing anything around her, nor did she respond to their entreaties. For a moment the onlookers were silent, aghast. Then Mrs. Parker said quietly, "Perhaps we were praying for the wrong soul."

From that day in early May until the ship sailed up the Thames in mid-June, Mary spoke not a word. Her mates tended her like the invalid she was, cajoling her to eat and to take sips of water, for without urging she would do neither. She left her hammock only when they pulled her from it and moved her up on deck with considerable effort, two pulling her from above, and two below boosting her from behind.

While on deck, James never left her side. If it was hot, they took turns fanning her, and if it was rainy, they huddled with her and held a bit of canvas over her head. She paid them no mind, other than to occasionally jerk against their grip. The wooden comb Bados had made stayed tucked into the waistband of the half-sarong she still wore, but her hair remained uncombed and her body unwashed.

She was in those days something of a curiosity, with passengers and crew wandering by from time to time to observe and comment on her condition. As she appeared oblivious to their presence, they thought nothing of making remarks in her presence. Whereas at the start of the voyage she was called "the girl from Botany Bay," they later began to refer to her as "the mad woman."

Dr. White checked on her daily, sometimes giving James a curt command as to a detail of her care. One morning, as Mrs. Parker was accompanying White on a stroll around the deck, she stopped in front of Mary, and asked, "Does she ever speak?"

"Not as far as I know," White replied, and looked at James, who shook his head.

Mrs. Parker held a handkerchief to her nose to ward off the smell of Mary's unwashed body. "Despite her class, I had hoped to see something of consequence in the poor creature's character."

"It is difficult to judge character in one drained by grief," White snapped.

The captain's wife, perhaps offended by White's abrupt manner, lifted her chin. "Many of our seamen's wives have lost children on this voyage, and do grieve, I assure you, Doctor. But never have I seen one sink so low. What excuse can there be for such behaviour?"

White stood for a moment glowering down at Mary, as if infuriated by the sight of her. But the doctor was only considering the question. At last he said, "It seems to me that women bear suffering like beasts of burden. Some take load after load until they are broken. Others are like the Spanish ass. When the weight is more than they can carry, they simply lie down, and nothing on earth can induce them to move until the load is lightened."

"Indeed!" Mrs. Parker seemed intrigued by the comparison. "And which manner of woman is this?"

"Madam, I do not know." With that White turned and limped away on feet that always pained him.

Mrs. Parker, still staring at Mary, murmured, "What a shame she does not pray."

She started to follow Dr. White, then turned back and asked James, "Is there a particular reason why, after being supplied with a perfectly decent gown, she persists in going naked but for that rag knotted about her waist?"

James stood slowly and with a correct and courteous bow, replied, "I understand how Mrs. Bryant's manner of dress must offend you, Madam, and all the ladies on the ship. She did wear the gown for a time, but removed it in the heat of the hold when her child was dying and grief overcame her sense of propriety. We men who are confined with her have too much respect to lay hands on her in the intimate way that would be required to dress or bathe her."

He hesitated and added, "We do pray daily, as you yourself suggested, that she might soon recover enough to do for herself."

Mrs. Parker's eyes opened wide, no doubt surprised that a man she had taken to be a rough criminal should be so well-spoken. "Then I shall pray for her as well," she said, and moved away to rejoin Dr. White.

Soon after this conversation, the *Gorgon* reached England, and anchored at Portsmouth.

"Five years we have been gone," James whispered to Mary as they lay in their separate hammocks that night. "We have sailed clear to the other side of the world and back again."

Mary did not respond. She was not merely in a separate hammock, she was in a separate world—a world in which there existed nothing but a blackness of rage. When James came to feed her of a morning, sometimes he found her clutching the wooden comb in her hand, but did not understand why this would be so, for she had not combed her hair since Charlotte's death. He had, several times, tried to take the comb from her to do the combing and braiding himself, but she had clutched it tightly, and would not give it up. At length it would find its way back into the waistband of her sarong.

Not until they learned from Mr. Tench that on the morrow they would be taken from the ship to stand before a magistrate did James enlist the other men to help him do what he had told Mrs. Parker they would not do. They forcibly washed Mary as well as they could and dressed her in the gown given her by Mrs. Parker. Although it was far from fresh, it was not as filthy as her remaining scrap of sarong. Nor would it have her attracting stares on the streets of London as if she were a witch.

Difficult though it was to wash and dress her, it was more difficult still to persuade her to give up the comb. Finally she drew in on herself so completely that she did not seem to notice when James took it, and did not struggle during the hours it took to untangle her long hair and re-weave it into a braid down her back.

When James had finished that task, he put the comb back in her hand, closed her fingers around it, and slipped hand and comb into a pocket of the gown. It was all Mary had in the world to call her own, and he wanted to make sure she knew where it was. If indeed she knew anything at all.

It was in this condition that Mary, along with the other prisoners, was taken from the ship. As they were about to be placed in a police van for conveyance to court to appear before a magistrate, Mary suddenly lifted her head. Looking about at the gathered crowd, she spoke her first word since Charlotte's funeral. "England."

"Yes, Mary," James said, joy leaping in his eyes. "England."

He must have believed, just then, that she was to recover her senses as quickly as she had lost them. But this was not to be.

England

When the five from Botany Bay appeared before the magistrate, Mary stood with lowered head, refusing to communicate with the court or with those around her by so much as a glance. Her behaviour might have been deemed a form of insanity, and perhaps it was. But James, recalling Dr. White's words about how some women were like those beasts of burden that simply laid down and refused to move when their burden grew too great, clung to the notion that this was what had driven Mary to close her senses to what was going on around her, and that once that burden lightened, she would return to normal.

Standing before the magistrate, he pleaded Mary's cause, which she was neither willing nor able to do for herself. "She is not insane," James assured the judge, "but lost in grief, by reason of both her children dying in the past six months, the last barely five weeks ago."

"Such love as she had for her babies you can't imagine," Pip put in. "Sure and it was for their sake that she made a bid for freedom, for she oft said they was innocent and didn't deserve to grow up away from their native land."

"She fussed over them regular-like," Scrapper put in. "Don't I wish my mum had set such store by me."

"Her original offence had no violence in it," Luke offered. "A gentle lass she is, by her very nature."

Mary remained slumped and silent, in a posture which might have suggested shame or bereavement. In truth, it was fury. For a full year she had struggled to keep it in check, but with the death of Charlotte it had come to dominate her soul. Although she had been willing to hope as long as there was hope, now that there was none, why should she not draw strength from her rage and use it for a final act of defiance? Thus the determination to never again look up to men who were looking down on her. Judge her they would; that she could not prevent. But her participation was hers to decide, and her absolute intent was that there would be none.

The magistrate was favourably impressed by the fact that Mary's companions, rather than pleading their own cause, had spoken up on her behalf. Having no notion that the bowed head was intended as an act of defiance, he felt enormous sympathy for the starvation-thin woman standing before him. After sending the lot of them to Newgate to await trial, he told the press, "Never have I experienced so disagreeable a task as being obliged to commit this poor soul to prison."

One week later, the five of them were brought to stand trial at the Old Bailey. By this time the men were aware of the publicity surrounding their case. In addition to press accounts, there were pickets in support of them in the street outside the courtroom. They learned that, even before their arrival back in England, the tabloids had made of Mary a celebrity, first as "The Girl from Botany Bay Who Got Away," and later as, "The Girl from Botany Bay Who Almost Got Away". Now, in part because she was silent, everyone felt at liberty to project onto her whatever they liked. Most saw the great sailing adventure as a heroic act undertaken for her children's sake, one which demonstrated the courage and character of a true Englishwoman. Despite flourishes added to the story by newspapers that did not feel wholly bound by the facts, this was not far from the truth.

The Crown Prosecutor may have felt some sympathy as well, or else he was influenced by the press's expressions of sympathy, for he did not call for the bolters to be hanged. Outright leniency, though, was out of the question. As he explained, if the Government went so far as to "do a kind thing," that would give encouragement to other prisoners to try to escape. With these considerations in mind, the penalty imposed was for all five to, "remain on their former sentences until they should be discharged by due course of law."

Given conditions inside Newgate Prison, such an

indeterminate sentence certainly met the Crown's criteria of not being a kind thing. Survival depended entirely upon the treatment received in lockup—and on whether one succumbed, as most did, to gaol fever.

As they left the courtroom, Mary to be taken to a ward in Newgate apart from James, Luke, Pip, and Scrapper, only the men said goodbye. Mary did not speak, nor lift her head, nor even move unless someone took her by the arm and drew her along. Was she sad? Was she sorry? Was she sane? As long as she showed no awareness of what was going on around her, and neither her face nor her eyes revealed what was going on in her head, how could anyone know?

A decade later, one Elizabeth Fry would bring about prison reforms which would include sleeping pads, so that inmates were not forced to lie upon the cold stone floor. Rules of decorum would be instituted to prevent the kind of chaos that reigned in the women's wards during Mary's incarceration. Although dogs had recently been banned from the prison, inmates were still allowed to bring children, poultry, and pigs. All contributed to the noise and filth, and all went unnoticed by Mary. If she recognised this as the place where she had met Florie, Cass, and Colleen six years earlier, she gave no sign of it.

Mary's notoriety had preceded her into the ward. Where other vulnerable women might have been abused by fellow inmates, most of the prisoners stood back, a little awed by the tales that had circulated regarding where she had been, what she had done, and what she had endured. The few inclined to molest her, as she curled herself into a ball against one wall, were quickly blocked by others who set themselves up as her defenders. It was an unusual situation, one the jailers admitted to visitors that they themselves had not seen before.

There were visitors. Some were merely curiosity-seekers come to gawk at the adventuress from Botany Bay, but at least one had a serious interest in seeing justice done. This was the writer James Boswell, a Scottish lawyer, member of London's literary elite, and old college friend of Henry Dundas, the Secretary of State for Home Affairs. Boswell had a reputation for taking on causes for humanitarian reasons, and in particular, ones involving "unfortunate" young women. None of his friends were surprised when he showed a keen interest in the affairs of "the girl from Botany Bay."

At least, his interest in her was keen as long as he was merely reading about her in the press. When he actually visited her in Newgate, he was nearly shocked into abandoning her cause. Although she was young—only twenty-six to Boswell's fifty-two—she was not beautiful. Nor was she, in his opinion, even sane.

"I'd not go in there if I was ye," warned the turnkey when Boswell insisted on being permitted to enter the narrow exercise yard where upwards of forty women were engaged in all manner of activities from washing clothes to quarrelling to using chamber pots. "These 'uns is rough, and could do a man harm." The turnkey pointed to what appeared to be a heap of rags against a far wall. "Not that one, a'course, yer Mary Bryant. She ain't moved yet of her own accord."

"That's her?" Boswell started at the body indicated. "Rouse her and bring her to the bars. Tell her a friend wants to speak to her."

"Ain't no rousing her," the turnkey explained. "I can bring her, forcible-like, because I done it before. But she won't look at ye nor speak a word, and quick as she's let, she'll flat turn away."

"Then I will go in," Boswell decided, for he could not believe that anyone who had done what Mary was reputed to have done could be entirely unreachable.

The turnkey instructed the prisoner designated as wardswoman to accompany Boswell across the court-yard to where Mary lay. The stench of the area was enough to induce gagging, for, in addition to the filth one might expect in such an overcrowded space, there were, in nearby chambers, the corpses of prisoners whose families had not yet come to claim them. Upon reaching Mary's side, Boswell spoke her name. She did not move.

The wardswoman grabbed Mary's forelock, jerked her head up, and cackled, "You got a gentleman 'ere to see you, dearie."

Although Mary's blue-grey eyes were open, they stared vacantly, in such a way as to give Boswell the creeps. They were, he recounted later, as empty as those of a dead person.

But he was not a man easily put off an idea, and so he seated himself uncomfortably on the stone floor next to her and proceeded to talk. Other women collected in a circle around them, some making lewd remarks or calling out answers to questions he put to Mary. Boswell soon concluded that conversation was doomed in such an atmosphere, even if Mary were inclined to respond, which clearly she was not. Deeply disappointed, he said, "I will try to visit again, Mary, but I do not know if I can, for you see, I myself have been sentenced to death."

Mary's body jerked, and she turned her head just slightly to see him out of the corner of one eye, which was bluer than Boswell had first thought. This indication that she was in fact listening, and even comprehending, was there for only an instant, and then was gone.

Encouraged, he said, "The doctors give me no more than two years to live. Perhaps not even that long. But long enough, I hope, for us to become friends and share our histories. Would you like that?"

Something like a curtain drew over her eyes, causing them to revert to their original cloudy appearance, more grey than blue. When it became apparent that there would be no connection, verbal or otherwise, Boswell struggled awkwardly to his feet and left the ward.

Although Mary was not inclined to bestir herself, she had not been unaware of Boswell's presence nor uncomprehending of his words. She operated more on feeling than thought these days, and her feeling about the man, whose name meant nothing to her, was that he was both kind and lecherous. His comment about being under sentence of death she did not believe. But then, she believed little of what was said to her by anyone, which was why she paid more attention to the squealing of rats scrabbling around the edges of the ward than she did to any words. Still, it was a startling thing for the man to say, which she had not expected.

Some would say later that it was Boswell's interest that revived Mary, and perhaps that was a factor. He did leave money with the warden to pay the garnish which would ensure that she received a reasonable ration of food, and had soap and other items for which all prisoners paid or went without. He did the same for Pip, Scrapper, James, and Luke, housed in a men's ward on the other side of the prison. It was in his mind even then that if he could not get a story from Mary, he might learn details of the trip from them.

A more likely reason for Mary's return to something like normal was the simple passage of time. Several weeks after Boswell's visit, Mary's fingers touched the comb in her pocket, and she drew it forth. She examined the smooth wood and delicate workmanship, drawing pleasant sensations from the feel of it. It recalled to her Bados's large hands, not as he was delicately carving this very item, but how they trembled when he held the compass. Another day she examined the teeth of the comb closely, to see if a few strands of Charlotte's golden hair might yet be caught between them. One morning she remembered the feel of the comb as James had pulled it through her own hair on the last day they had been able to touch one another, as he tried to make her presentable for appearing before the magistrate. She brought her waist-long braid around into her lap and tentatively fumbled the comb through the loose end, below where it was tied.

This is what she was doing—this and remembering things that had been shut out of her mind for many months—when a ruckus broke out near the ward entrance. Mary did not look up or pay any attention whatever, but here is what was going on:

A well-dressed woman, and a well-known one, for she had been the madam of a bawdy house until her arrest following the suspicious death of one of her gentleman clients, had just been admitted. Her expensive clothing was awry and her elegantly-styled hair had come undone. Immediately upon entering she began to put herself right, buttoning this, straightening that, patting something else back into place. Seeing Mary fiddling with the comb, she made straight for her.

"My dear," she carolled, "allow me to borrow your comb."

Mary responded as she always did, which is to say, she did not respond at all. The newcomer, used to having her way with men and women alike, reached down and snatched the comb from Mary's hands. She held it up to the light to examine it for lice before putting it to her own head. Mary slowly stood up, with her back to the wall, and reached for the comb.

"A moment if you please, dear," the woman said sharply, holding it out of Mary's reach. "I shan't be long."

The words were hardly out of her mouth before Mary had grabbed her by the hair and flung her to the floor. The comb went flying. Mary turned from the woman at once and picked it up. She had no more than dropped it back in her pocket when the woman grasped her by the arm, and plunged her hand into Mary's pocket in pursuit of the comb. Without a sound or change of expression, Mary backhanded her in the face, knuckle hard, exactly as Will had hit her on more than one occasion. The stranger screamed and fell back, suddenly occupied with trying to staunch the flow of blood from her nose.

Women came running from all over the ward as those closest to the altercation began shrieking that the girl from Botany Bay had come alive and was on the verge of murdering a fellow inmate. The wardswoman pushed her way through the crowd just in time to see the new inmate spattered in blood and Mary—

Mary had dropped to the floor and curled into a ball. The wardswoman grabbed her arm, intending to jerk her to her feet. Then she let out a piercing scream as Mary sunk her teeth into the woman's hand. That brought the turnkey, who ordered Mary to get up and gave her a kick in the kidneys to make his point. Still Mary did not rise, so the turnkey lifted her bodily and flung her over his shoulder like a bag of potatoes, which in limpness she much resembled.

Out of the ward he marched, and to one of the refractory cells used for incorrigible prisoners; the one chosen had been vacated only hours before by a woman taken out to be hanged for having murdered her husband. Mary was flung down so roughly that her head struck the stone floor hard, a blow that left her unconscious.

When she came to and felt inclined to lift her throbbing head, she saw that she was in a room about six feet wide and eight feet long. At one end was the heavy wooden door through which she had been carried. At the other end, a high iron-barred window let in a little light. A chamber pot, a candle stand without a candle, and a stone bed with neither pad nor coverlet made up the contents of the room. Mary dragged herself onto the bed, which was more in the nature of a bench and no less hard than the floor. She reached into her pocket, felt the comb still there, and smiled.

From that moment on, Mary spent hours each day combing her hair, keeping it clean of lice and tangles. In the whole of her life, it was the first time she had ever been absolutely alone for an extended period. Such solitude was not a situation she would have requested, or even thought possible this side of the grave. Yet quite by accident, the small cell gave her precisely what she had been trying to create through emotional and mental withdrawal: a space which shut out almost everything, to the point that she could cease to participate in a world which had become intolerably unjust. There was no escaping the prison stench or the clamour that went on out in the exercise yard, but with stone walls and iron grates separating her from all that, she no longer had need of a mental barrier. She relaxed, and within a few days her mind had begun to form the occasional coherent thought.

Very likely she would not have remained in a refractory cell long, for there were surely more violent inmates than she, had it not been for another incident. Although she had begun to recover, she was not far enough along to deal with the unexpected appearance of a person whom at first she did not recognise, and when he recalled himself to her, she could make no sense of the purpose of his visit, and therefore responded in a way deemed most inappropriate.

Normally visitors and inmates exchanged words only in the visitors' box, wherein they were separated by about three feet. This separation, along with the watchful eye of a warden, ensured that no contraband items were passed from one to the other. But with the payment of a fee anything was possible at Newgate. Mary's visitor, as curious as all the rest of England about the girl from Botany Bay, did not wish it known that he had paid her a visit. Thus he paid a tidy sum to be admitted to her cell. As she had been quite calm during the two weeks she had been confined there, the warden who accepted the payment foresaw no problems.

The slender young man in clerical garb followed the turnkey along the corridor to the cell, holding a white silk handkerchief to his nose in a futile attempt to block out the smell of humans, animals and corpses grown putrid in the summer heat. The heavy wooden door was opened to reveal Mary sitting on the stone bench which served as a bed. Immediately she got up, moved to the far wall, and stood with her back to the man who had just been let in.

When she failed to acknowledge his presence, he said, in a high-pitched voice which revealed his nervousness, "Mary?" When still she did not respond, he tried again. "Mary Broad?"

The use of her maiden name so startled her that Mary turned and looked at the man, but still said nothing.

"Do you not remember me, Mary? I am Adam. The same whose father was the parson at the church you attended before . . . before . . ." He swallowed, and after a moment, tried again. "I last saw you in the lane, as I was departing for college. Do you not recall?"

He took a few steps toward her. As his features came clear to her in the dimly-lit room, Mary at last spoke. "I remember how long your lashes were, Adam, and how they lay against your cheek when your head was bowed in prayer."

Adam's intake of breath was audible, so startled was he by her recollection of such an intimate detail.

"You have hardly changed at all," Mary continued, meaning that his face still matched the one she had dredged up from her memory.

"I shouldn't think so." He laughed nervously. "After all, it has only been six years. You look . . . different. But I'm certain your heart is the same," he added.

"My heart?" Had Mary been in a humorous frame of mind she would have laughed, but as it was, only her tone of voice reflected how ridiculous she thought it was that he imagined he could be certain of what was in her heart.

Flustered, Adam answered quickly, "I mean, in your love for God. Your trust in Him."

"Ah yes," Mary said vaguely, and, with a fingertip, began to trace a pattern of light and shadow cast by the bars of the window upon the wall.

Emboldened by her passivity and full of a sense of mission, Adam moved closer. "He will redeem you, Mary. I know He will. You know the story of the prodigal son; we learned it together in Sunday School. Believe me, God loves a prodigal daughter no less."

"How fortunate," she said ironically.

Warming to his subject, Adam continued, "We all have sinned—"

"And been sinned against," Mary interrupted bitterly.

"His mercy is infinite! It shows itself—"

Mary whirled on him, her face contorted with rage. "In fits and starts, and sometimes not at all! Where was God's mercy when I called out to Him for my children's sake? Better to believe He doesn't exist than to imagine He deliberately allows such innocents to suffer!"

The outburst shocked Adam to the core. "We are all born in sin!" he exclaimed.

"Sin? Sin?" she hissed into his face. "Until you've seen the cruelty I've seen, you have no idea! You want a sinner? Seek out Captain Edwards, who killed so many on that final voyage, and brought back innocents to hang!"

"You cannot claim innocence!" Adam protested,

trying to reclaim the upper hand in a dialogue on God's mercy, a subject he surely knew better than she.

Mary's voice rose to a shrieking crescendo. "I claim innocence for my children because they *were* innocent. If they're not in Paradise I want no part of it, nor of the God who betrayed them!"

The jailer, who had remained just outside the door— ostensibly in case of trouble but in fact because he had found it profitable, in the past, to observe the goings-on in private cell tête-à-têtes about which he was later paid to keep silent—opened the door with a chuckle. "Had enough of 'er, yer Reverence?"

Adam inched toward the door. "I shall return next week. I can see this will take time."

Mary slumped onto the bench. "It has taken time, Adam. All the time I've been away. More time than you can imagine. One does not come back from that kind of journey."

Reassured by her seeming return to reason, Adam said softly, "You are back, Mary. And I will return."

"No," Mary said flatly. "You are you and I am a woman you have never met, nor would want to know, nor could ever understand."

"Ah, but God understands."

In a flash, Mary was on her feet again, screaming. "Out! Out! I'll not be understood by a God who murdered His own son and mine as well!"

Adam vanished through the doorway. The turnkey, still chuckling, listened to the young parson's footsteps as he fled down the corridor. Then he shook his head in pity at the sound of Mary's sobs coming from inside the cell.

It was this incident, when related to the warden by a shaken young clergyman and confirmed by the turn-key, that kept Mary in a refractory cell. The warden also felt called upon to warn James Boswell, when the writer requested another interview, that the girl from Botany Bay had turned violent.

Boswell's long delay in paying Mary another visit was partly due to the fact that he had been very ill, for he suffered not only from malaria and gonorrhoea, but also from bouts of depression. When he was sufficiently recovered to again be up and about, he did go to Newgate, but not to see Mary, as his first visit had convinced him it would be a waste of time. Instead, he visited her companions in the men's ward. They gratified him with a good deal of information about their journey from Botany Bay, but asked repeatedly for word of Mary. Finally he promised he would visit her again and report back to them. That was when they informed him of her confinement in solitary, something not known by the general public but circulated by word of mouth throughout the prison.

At first Boswell was inclined to disbelieve the rumour. He found it incredible that the pathetic rag of a woman he had tried to interview a month earlier had even regained the power of speech, let alone the energy to attack people in the violent ways described. Such incidents, if they had occurred at all, would have been greatly exaggerated in the telling. Still, Boswell was curious enough to want to see for himself. Despite the warden's warnings, the writer paid the bribe required to enter the cell of the prison's most exotic inmate.

"A Mr. Boswell here to see ye," the turnkey told Mary gruffly. "Better behave yerself this time. Anymore outbursts like before and we'll have ye in shackles."

"Mrs. Bryant!" Boswell greeted her with the cheerful optimism that was his style. "I bring greetings from those who travelled with you from Botany Bay. They are most anxious about your health. I promised that I would report back to them as to how you are faring."

Boswell saw the spark of interest that flared in Mary's eyes, but was dismayed to see it immediately extinguished. Although she had not moved from the stone bench upon which she was seated, he felt her withdrawal.

He had no clue as to the confusion that existed in Mary's mind about the others, and most especially about James. She remembered in great detail their escape from Botany Bay, and also their time together in Kupang. But she had no memory of what transpired during their last months together; she only knew that during that final voyage Charlotte had somehow been lost. And she remembered James combing her hair. Why he had done that she had no idea, for she did not recall their appearance before the magistrate, nor being in the dock at the Old Bailey. Had the men been brought to Newgate like herself? Returned to Botany Bay? Or hanged? Even if James was still alive, was it not probable that his love for her had died? After all, it was the workings of her mind he had loved. She did not need to be told that for the past many months her mind had scarcely functioned at all.

Thus, when Boswell indicated that he had news of her friends, Mary longed for that news as she had once longed for a sip of water on a deserted isle. Simultaneously she feared it, for what could be more painful than learning that James was alive but had ceased to love her? Unless it was that he loved her yet as she loved him, but with no hope of ever consummating that love, as they had promised each other, in freedom or not at all.

As Mary sat in silent confusion, Boswell lowered his corpulent body onto the stone bench next to her and proceeded to tell her of his visit to the men's ward. "The visitors' box kept them about a yard away, so we had to shout to make ourselves heard above the din. I asked them what I might have sent in to ease their confinement, expecting the usual requests for tobacco and the like. But all they clamoured for was news of you. Your Mr. Brown, now, he also asked for books, if you can believe that. I asked him what sort, and he gratified me by indicating that he had read my interview with the Corsican revolutionary Pasquale Paoli. When I told him I had recently had published a biography of Dr. Johnson, he immediately solicited a copy! By Jove, but I was surprised!"

Boswell smiled in a self-satisfied way, and rattled on. "I thought he was putting me on, not expecting someone of his class, and from the Colonies at that, to be so well-read. But when he added that anything by the Bard would be equally welcome, and spontane-ously, the three standing with him began to recite *The Phoenix and The Turtle*, well, can you imagine the in-congruity of four men shouting out those verses over the din of the ward?"

He glanced at Mary, and was startled to see si-lent tears trickling down her cheeks. Mention of that poem brought to mind how all the prisoners in the hold, including those from the *Bounty*, had re-cited it by way of eulogy for little Emanuel.

"Why, Mrs. Bryant!" Boswell was astonished. "Have I upset you? I am so sorry!"

Mary dried the tears with the back of her hand, and said only, "Broad."

"I beg your pardon?"

"My name is Mary Broad."

"Yes, of course!" Boswell brightened. "That was your maiden name, was it not? In one of the newspaper ac-counts I recall reading that. Actually, I have been won-dering about those stories, Mrs.—uh, Mary Broad. Just how much of what has been reported might be true?"

There was a silence; the sort which at first Boswell would take for slow-wittedness, but which he would later come to understand was something else. At times it was a lack of interest in answering the question, but at other times, thoughtfulness. In this case it would seem to be the latter, for she eventually replied, "How much of anything is true?"

Boswell raised an eyebrow. "I suppose that depends on what one believes."

"Belief has little to do with truth," Mary said flatly,

in a tone which suggested that she had dismissed him as some kind of fool.

Boswell was more excited than offended to hear such pithy remarks coming from the mouth of this infamous yet largely unknown woman. Drawing out a pad and pencil, he asked, "Do you mind if I take notes on our conversation?"

"Will they be used against me?"

"Oh no," Boswell assured her. "On the contrary. They might be used to help you."

"Help me be hanged, or returned to Botany Bay?"

Boswell frowned, for it seemed to him that she had misunderstood the judgement already rendered, which was that she was to remain in prison for an indeterminate period of time. There was every likelihood that she would perish of typhus, or "gaol fever" as it was called, for this was the fate of most confined here for very long.

"Have you a preference?" he asked curiously.

This time it was even longer before she replied, "If I were put on a ship, I could cast myself into the sea. I like the sea. 'Twas where my father ended his days. And my children."

"What if you are compelled to live?" he asked gently, his innately sympathetic nature coming to the fore.

"I do not live now," she said simply.

"I grant you this is hard, Mary, but surely it is life!"

With words still coming slowly, but definitely moved along by thought, she replied, "Life has light, and colour. There is no colour here."

It was then, finally, that she looked at him, and he back at her, until he replied, "Your eyes are very blue."

She continued staring at him a little longer, then dropped her gaze and asked, "What is it you want of me, Sir?"

"To understand something of your nature, dear girl. But perhaps I already do."

"Perhaps you never shall," she contradicted.

"You think not? Pray, tell me why."

"England is very far."

"England? Far?" His brows puckered with incomprehension.

"Far from Botany Bay."

Mary grew moody after that, disinclined to provide even cryptic responses to Boswell's questions. After a few more questions, met with silence, he took his leave.

Boswell followed the turnkey back down the corridor with a jaunty step. The girl from Botany Bay was proving ever so much more interesting than he had imagined. She would provide stories with which he could entertain his friends for weeks!

A month passed before Boswell visited again, and again the delay was by reason of ill health. When at last he felt inclined to revisit the bolters from Botany Bay, he was received with the utmost courtesy by the men. The same could not be said of Mary. His September visit unfortunately coincided with a hanging. Boswell himself would not have thought this worth mentioning, but the jailer, as he was searching through his keys for the one to her cell, asked, "Did ye see the execution of the mutineers, Governor?"

"No," Boswell answer shortly.

"Hanged by the neck, they was, the three of 'em. And left to dangle two full hours to make sure they was no coming back to life."

At last the turnkey got the door open and Boswell entered quickly, not wanting to hear more morbid details. But already too many had reached Mary's ears. As soon as the cell door closed, she turned on him and demanded, "Who?"

"Three of the *Bounty* mutineers," Boswell said, taken aback by her intensity. "If I recall the names correctly from the morning paper, it would be Burkitt, Ellison and Millward."

"What foul deeds pass for justice in this country!" Mary hissed.

"You think they were not deserving?" Boswell personally believed that if anyone deserved to hang, it would be mutineers.

"They were abused beyond endurance before the mutiny, for which they were scarcely to blame! And afterwards, tortured more than those who celebrate their deaths can possibly imagine! And that I know for a fact, for was I not with them?"

"You were—oh, my dear! Were you and they returned on the same ship?"

"So we were! Separate cells we had in the dungeon of Kupang and later on the *Gorgon*, but for the five months from Kupang to Capetown, shackled side by side we were in conditions as foul as a privy. Yet in all that time, even the two who admitted to being party to the mutiny never lost their humanity."

"Which two would those have been?" Boswell asked alertly. At last he was beginning to get the kinds of stories he sought from Mary, related to her travels, and he was mightily intrigued.

"Ellison claimed to have participated, but he was only a boy, not above sixteen when the mutiny occurred. Burkitt said he knew of it in advance, so I suppose he was in on it, too. But neither chose to go with Christian, wanting only to escape the brutality of Captain Bligh."

Pacing like a tiger, Mary went on, "Burkitt had in O'Tahiti a native wife he'd given the name of Mary, and they had a daughter the age of mine, whom they called Charlotte, too. Of all the *Bounty* prisoners, none was kinder to my little girl. Why, he gave her food from his own portion!"

She stopped before him and stared angrily into his face. "You cannot know, Sir, until you have been as hungry as we were, how starvation is one torture, but to take a bit of food your whole body is craving and put it in the mouth of another and watch them swallow it down brings on a suffering just as intense. This poor pock-marked Burkitt did for my child when Captain Edwards was starving us all to death!"

"There was another youth, Peter Heywood," Boswell began tentatively. "And a man by name of Morrison, both recommended to His Majesty's mercy. I expect they will be pardoned. Also a cook's assistant—"

"Willy Muspratt," Mary supplied. "Flogged by Bligh

more than once, they said, and yet all agreed he had had no part in the mutiny. Did they hang him, too?"

"Muspratt was sentenced to die," Boswell told her. "But he wasn't hung with the others this morning. Perhaps there has been some reconsideration, and he will be pardoned as well."

"Pardoned!" Mary spat the word bitterly. "How is it that some are pardoned for crimes they never committed, while others are never called to account for the crimes they did? Mark my word, Mr. Boswell, Captain Edwards, murderer of children and the parents of children, will walk the good earth into old age."

Boswell stayed a while longer, but Mary lapsed into a moody silence, and he could get no more out of her. At last he took his leave, tipping the turnkey on his way out, and leaving extra money with the warden to ensure that Mary had decent food and other necessities.

Mary suffered a period of depression after that visit, but by the time Boswell came again she had come out of it and, if not cheerful, was at least receptive to his company. Little by little she came to trust the roly-poly man for, despite the lecherousness she sensed in him, he never presumed to touch her. Physically unattractive though he was in most respects, his eyes were genuinely kind, and he had a serious interest both in her adventures and in her unconventional ideas.

Only once did she seriously offend him, and that was on a visit when he undertook to read to her one of his lengthy poems, entitled, *No Abolition of Slavery or the Universal Empire of Love.* As he perched his bulky body on the stone bench and read aloud, she sat on the floor at his feet as, long ago, she had sat at the feet of her father as he spun tales.

Boswell read with such cheerfulness and droll expressions that she enjoyed his recitation even though she barely understood what the poem was about, only dimly perceiving that it had something to do with goings-on in the House of Commons. Not till many pages along did she grasp that it was a rant against those who would abolish slavery.

At that she rose and walked to the end of the room and stood under the barred window with her back to him, as she was wont to do when she did not wish to be engaged. Her silence and the set of her shoulders caused Boswell to stop reading.

"Are you not understanding, Mary dear? Would you have me break the rhyme and provide explanations for the difficult parts?" he inquired solicitously.

"I doubt you can explain to me what you do not understand yourself," she snapped.

"I beg your pardon?" he asked, scarcely believing she could have said such a thing. "What in this verse, which I myself have written, do you imagine I do not understand?"

"I wager you have never known a black man, or have any idea how they're treated."

"What? You consider me insensitive on the subject? Did you miss the line where I remarked that the conditions in which slaves are transported should be improved?"

Mary turned around and glared at him. "Ah yes, so, as you would have it, they can sing, sing, sing while they toil as time flies by on downy wing. Filled with joy they are because in sickness they are never neglected, and their wives and children always protected!" she recited in a tone of dripping sarcasm, somewhat scrambling the words but with meaning intact. "Ah, Sir, I have met some fools in my time, indeed I have. Given your kindness to me and my companions, it pains me to discover that you are one of them."

Boswell rose, red-faced and sputtering. "You speak as if you know something of slaves yourself, which hardly seems credible!"

"Indeed not!" Mary gave him a look of contempt "What could I know of a black man with whom I spent many months, who made for me this very comb—." Here she reached into her pocket and flashed the carved comb in Boswell's face. "And whose hands I last saw holding the compass I used for our escape from Botany Bay—a compass which enabled him to make his escape, along with a most beautiful woman who threw in her lot with him."

This outburst, one of the longest Boswell had heard from Mary, left him both infuriated and intrigued, for up to now he had heard nothing about a black man who sailed with them, or how he had evaded capture.

As he gathered up the pages of his doggerel and called to the turnkey to come let him out, Mary saw she had hurt his feelings, and later she was sorely ashamed. Once again she had let her temper flare, and probably had damaged a relationship which had resulted in benefits not only to herself but to James, Luke, Scrapper and Pip, who had more need of kindness than she. What she needed was—well, truth be told, she had no idea. What does a person who has already lost everything and has no future to look forward to, really need?

Certainly she did not need memory, for that only intensified her sense of loss. Nor did she crave kindness, for it was a reminder of decent people among whom she was not considered fit to mingle. Not that all people who were kind could be thought decent, nor did everyone who imagined themselves decent practice kindness. These thoughts she brushed away, for they were among the many things she did not need.

Ah, James, she thought, *as for this mind of mine which will not be done with thinking, whose way of proceeding you most admired, that is the thing I now need least of all.*

Mary might have imagined that she no longer needed her mind, but once the grief which had muddied it began to abate, she did use it. First and foremost, she undertook to be civil to Boswell when he next appeared, as she could not avoid the fact that his interest in their story had generated some benefits for Pip, Scrapper, Luke, and James. Boswell had hinted that he wanted to help her, too, but she sensed his lecherous intent and remained prickly in his presence. Why indulge him when, unlike Captain Smit, Boswell had nothing she wanted? All she had ever cared about was now gone or, like freedom itself, was beyond her reach. And, she supposed, beyond the reach of Mr. Boswell.

It was a good long while before Boswell came again. When at last he did, she made a point of behaving toward him in a courteous manner. Instead of turning away or ignoring him until he spoke, she put out her hands in greeting. "Mr. Boswell, how nice to see you," she said, and discovered that she actually meant it.

He beamed his delight at the warm reception and replied, gallantly, "You look very handsome, Mary. If your presence were not required here, I would take you to meet my friends."

She snatched her hands back from him as if he meant to drag her out to meet strangers that very moment. "I should not like that, Mr. Boswell!"

He laughed. "And why not, may I ask?"

"Ah, you would not understand, Sir."

"Do give me the opportunity," he implored, lowering his bulk onto the bench and patting a place beside him. "Come, my dear. Explain yourself."

She hesitated, then sat, not quite where he indicated, but close enough to not cause offence to him or unease to herself. As for explaining, she hardly knew where to begin. Could she describe how the mere mention of "meeting friends" caused her heart to contract with aching for friends she would never see again? Or that knowing such a simple thing was forever impossible was like knowing one's life was ended already? Although those things were in Mary's heart, she did not have the means to put them into words. Instead, she spoke of her behaviour, feeling that this, at least, Boswell would understand.

"When I left England," she began tentatively. "its customs were strong in me. But now I often fail to think of pleasing others. Yet for your kindness these past months, it would sadden me to conduct myself in such a way as to cause you shame. As I most likely would if I were brought into the presence of your fine friends."

"Dear Mary!" he exclaimed. "Have I not proven myself to you by now?"

"Proven yourself?" Mary frowned, not understanding what proof he might suppose was needed for anything. "In what way?"

"Have I not demonstrated that in my presence you may conduct yourself exactly as you please?"

"Ah, I see. 'Tis true, you have never censured me for my behaviour." She added, more to herself than to him, "With so little time, and all of it to be spent within these walls, it can't really matter now, can it?"

Boswell smiled broadly, "Perhaps you are wrong in your suppositions as to what the future holds. The Home Secretary was a school chum of mine. I have communicated with him on countless occasions regarding your case. Believe me, dear girl, when I say there is hope!"

If he had anticipated that Mary would throw herself on him in a spasm of gratitude, it was only because he did not understand the workings of her mind and so was unaware of her ability to look into the future and see how one thing would likely lead to another.

She rose from the bench and moodily began to pace the cell from door to window and back again.

"Tell me, Sir, what hope is there for an Englishwoman who does not bow to her betters? One who shows anger when felt and will not pretend to beliefs she does not hold?"

"But my dear!" Boswell exclaimed excitedly. "Those are the very habits of one who harbours an independence of both mind and spirit."

Mary considered this notion, which had never occurred to her before, then dismissed it. "In a man, perhaps. But in a woman, those are deemed the habits of one not fit to be a wife or mistress or servant. Perhaps not even a decent trollop."

Boswell burst into such a fit of laughter that his whole robust body jiggled. Then he sobered and said, "I daresay you speak the truth. Remarkable that you should discern it."

Mary shrugged. "If the whole world can discern it, how is it so remarkable that I can?"

Then she turned the subject away from herself, for she had long since discovered that thoughts of her personal situation were among the most depressing. "What of you, Mr. Boswell? Is there any power that will pardon you, that you might live long and happily?"

At that he sagged a little, and replied, "Long, I fear not. But if I live to see you free, Mary, that will give me more happiness than I have known since . . . ." He paused, and smiled slyly, "Since my wilder moments as a young man."

Mary sat down next to him then, and, for the first

time, voluntarily put her hand in his. For a long while neither spoke, but sat in companionable silence. In Mary's mind, which was never as quiet as her person, the only question was which of them would be first into the grave. She felt sorrier for Boswell than for herself, because she had nothing more to lose.

On each of Boswell's subsequent visits, Mary endeavoured to give him what he seemed to want most from her: tales of her travels in far places. She even told him about the deaths of her children, and was gratified when he wept as if their loss had been his own.

"You must miss them terribly," Boswell said sympathetically.

"No."

He looked as shocked as if she had said she had strangled them. "No?"

"By day I can barely remember their faces. It's as if they were tots I only heard tell of and never really knew." She paused and added, "Nights I often dream of them, and they are as real as in the flesh. I do not miss them then, for it seems that they are with me."

Boswell continued to bring books, pamphlets, and poems to read to her. Mary enjoyed these more than conversations about herself. Perhaps because of her reaction to the pro-slavery poem, he did not again read anything he had written. He brought some things by Dr. Johnson, who he said had been his boon companion until that great man's death eight years before.

"Once," Boswell grinned, "Dr. Johnson criticised me

for eating oats for breakfast. He said that in England a man would not think of eating oats; that they are fed only to horses. I replied that this must be why in England you have better horses, and in Scotland you have better men."

They laughed together. Then Boswell grew teary as he recalled the death of his best friend. This time Mary wept with him for his loss, as he had wept for hers.

Having no calendar or means for determining the date, Mary did not know when she woke up on the morning of May 1, 1793, that it was her twenty-seventh birthday. Nor did she know, when Boswell came to visit, so ill that he required the assistance of his manservant to walk the distance down the corridor to her cell, that he carried news which would turn the life that she no longer deemed worth living upside down. Which is to say, it was about to be put right side up again.

When the turnkey opened the door and she saw the pained paleness of Boswell's normally ruddy face, she rushed forward to help him to a seat on the stone bench. But he waved her off, and said, "Dear Mary, this is the last time I shall visit you."

"Please tell me that is not so!" she cried, for she had grown truly fond of the jolly man whose illness made him seem so much older than his fifty-three years.

"Perhaps our next visit will be in my quarters." He attempted a smile which came out more as a grimace. "These days, my doctors get very cross with me when I go out, and my body protests even louder."

Anxious on account of his condition and thinking

his invitation for her to visit him a humourless joke, Mary urged, "Do come and sit, Sir, for I can see it pains you to stand."

"Nay," said Boswell. "My carriage waits without. I came only to give you the news, which will be given to the warden by the Sheriff of Middlesex on the morrow."

"What news might that be?" Mary asked anxiously, for all she could think was that any news pertaining to her situation could not be good.

"As I told you before, I have been lobbying for your release for many months. And not only I, but a great many other people. At last a pardon has been granted. Within a day or two, you shall be free to go."

"I . . . alone?" Mary was so stunned she could scarcely breathe. "My . . . friends?"

"We are still working on that," Boswell replied. "I can only assure you that they have not been forgotten."

She fell against Boswell's ample chest and began to weep, for it was all too much to take in. "But I have nothing to give you in return," she blubbered.

"I have done much good in my life," Boswell said immodestly, "and have got much good in return. But sometimes it benefits a man to do good for the sake of goodness alone."

✧

How much Boswell had done for Mary she did not know till the following day. This was when she was released, having served the seven years to which she had originally been sentenced, plus six additional weeks.

Mary did not walk out of the prison alone, for Mr. Boswell had sent his solicitor to explain to her that she was to receive an annuity of ten pounds for the rest of her life.

"He also instructed me to give you this purse, which contains a sum of money for your immediate expenses. Can you think of anything you need right away?"

Mary stood on the paving outside Newgate Prison and looked up at the grey sky. Were she in Cornwall the sky would be blue, and the sun would be spreading its warmth across the land. But here in London the sky was overcast, and a cold spring wind bit through the ragged gown that she had worn night and day during the eleven months of her imprisonment at Newgate.

"Yes," Mary said. "A cloak."

Epilogue

Mary stayed in London for a month, feeling that she owed it to Boswell to visit him on those rare days when he was well enough to receive guests. She also went regularly to visit the men in prison and paid the warden to ensure that they received basic necessities. But, tormented by guilt for the fact of being free when they were yet locked up, and seeing with her own eyes that Boswell was dying, she grew increasingly depressed. At length she herself grew ill, and the five men conspired to persuade her to leave the city.

Where was there to go but to the cottage where Mary had once lived? It was derelict, of course, its meagre contents long gone. She supposed her mother's treasured Bible had been taken for compensation by whoever came to remove the body. The few utilitarian items left behind had probably been scrounged by neighbouring families as poor as her own had been.

Mary went into the village to purchase candles, a few cooking utensils, garden tools, and bedding. Villagers stared with mouths agape but none approached her. Even clerks in the shops, who chattered gaily with everyone else, handled their transactions with her in silence and looked past Mary to the next customer in a way that said they could scarcely wait for her to leave so they could begin to speculate about her.

Her quiet manner did nothing to give offence, which made it easy for people to project upon her their notions as to the kind of woman she was. Opinions varied widely, but most would have agreed that the single word *strange* summed her up. Had Mary known this it would not have troubled her, as she had not regained the capacity to care what others said. The skill of ignoring what seemed irrelevant—if that could be called a skill—caused her to barely notice.

In any case, her contact with local people was slight. Her visits to the village were infrequent, and the road she took to get there was some distance from the cottage, on the other side of a field. No one chose to visit her. That was just as well, for the hut remained in a derelict condition, its roof fallen in. Mary placed her bedding in a corner of the room and fashioned a lean-to over it to keep off the rain. There she slept, sometimes in deepest peace and sometimes in heavy sorrow, aching for friends and family lost.

Once each fortnight she went into the village and, with the aid of a solicitor, composed a letter to Boswell. In early September he replied with news of her friends, which she very much craved. He said that all four had been pardoned and released from prison. Whereupon young Pip had astonished everyone by enlisting in the marines and getting himself assigned to a ship bound for the South Seas.

Mary looked up from the letter for a moment and smiled, imagining Pip in a mariner's uniform. He had done this thing, she knew, in hopes of getting back to Kupang, where he might see Mira again. And if he did? Mary did not have to be told that if babu was the Dutch word for slave, and Pip could buy her freedom, he would do that, and either bring her home with him or remain there to be near her.

Boswell's letter went on to say that he had spoken to Luke in the courtroom just after the pardon was read. The country man said he was going home to find out if his wife was still waiting. He allowed that he would not hold it against her if she had given up hope and wed another, since more than once he too had thought himself as good as dead. Wife or no, he still had his children to look forward to, as it was unlikely that all had perished in his absence.

Scrapper, Boswell noted, had in that same court-room been approached by a journalist who offered to buy him a pint in exchange for tales of his travels with "the girl from Botany Bay." Boswell said he encountered the scribbler a week later and asked if he had got the story. The man said he had, at a cost of not one but a whole night's worth of pints. Worse yet, when he got home he discovered that his purse was missing; where and how it had been lifted he could not be sure.

Boswell's missive ended with a wish for Mary's happiness, followed by a postscript: "I was struck down by the ague that day in the courtroom, and was forced to hasten away before I had a chance to speak to your fourth companion, the Canadian. He came by the following day, but unfortunately I was still indisposed, and unable to receive him. He left a book I had lent him, along with a letter of thanks, but it made no mention of his plans."

Mary laid aside the letter, read many times over in the two days since its arrival, and went out to work in the garden. Chopping weeds and turning up the soil in a plot seven years fallow had been exhausting to start. But a summer of hard work had transformed both Mary and the garden. Her muscles had regained their firmness, and summer sunshine had changed her prison pallor to a healthy tan. Her hair, which had darkened during confinement at Newgate, again showed streaks of blonde.

It was that hour in late afternoon when greenery takes on a golden hue, and the sun, having lost its intensity, enfolds the body like a warm embrace. Mary crouched in the midst of the garden and stuck a finger into the dirt alongside a carrot, to judge its readiness for harvest. She decided the carrot was fat enough, and had just grasped the feathery top to give it a yank when she looked up to see James standing a dozen yards away.

She did not rise at once, nor did she speak; she simply pushed back a lock of hair that had fallen across her eyes, in order to see more clearly. His image seemed solid enough, yet so did many others that had appeared to her since returning home. How many times had she dropped her hoe and run across the field because a red-haired woman passing on the road looked like Colleen? And what of that time in the village when all heads turned—and hers as well—to gape at a black man carrying a dark-skinned child, and for one heart-stopping instant she believed the man was Bados?

Often—much too often—Charlotte and Emanuel had appeared out of nowhere, only to disappear in the same mysterious way. The most terrifying moment was but a week ago, when she imagined she saw them standing together at the edge of the cliff. Heart in her throat, she had gone flying down the path to prevent them from falling over. Even after she reached the place where she imagined they had been, and chided herself for not grasping that it was only a hallucination, still she had clambered down to the beach and searched the rocks to be certain that no small bodies had tumbled there.

True, none of those apparitions had ever come as close as this one, which was standing at the corner of the cottage, only a dozen yards away. Slowly, she rose and waited to see if he would speak, because that was something which, as far as she knew, only the living could do.

The thing that might be James reached up and touched a bit of thatch that brushed his dark brown hair. "Your cottage roof is in need of repair," it said.

"Indeed it is." Mary spoke softly, because if it was an apparition she did not want it to go away. "Back in Botany Bay my friend Colleen said that when there's a garden to be made and a roof to be mended, best do the garden first, for a little rain is not likely to kill a person, whereas hunger can."

She paused and added, "Besides, 'tis a job I cannot do alone, and I have no friends hereabouts."

"Here is one," he said, twisting round and round the hat he held in his hand, "who would wed the mistress of the house, before or after fixing her roof."

This made Mary smile, for while she did not know if apparitions spoke, she was fairly certain they were never so nervous as to crumple a perfectly good hat.

"The mistress of the house has an annuity, so is dependent on no one, nor inclined to wed. Would this friend be willing to share her bed outside the bonds of marriage, but in freedom, as once he promised?"

"Only if that freedom inclined her to stay with him all their days."

"In body I can make such a promise, but in mind . . ." Mary's voice faded and she looked away. "I do wander."

He came close to her then, laid a hand on her cheek, and turned her face to look at his. "And where do you wander to, Mary?"

"Mostly into the past, to be with my children. Although sometimes they come here."

"And would I be with you there?"

Mary considered. "Perhaps. But most of the time, I think I must go alone."

She looked up at him, into those brown eyes flecked with bits of gold that held the light of intelligence within. "All I could promise is that, if that friend were waiting for me here, his love for me, and mine for him, would always bring me back."

Acknowledgements

"Boswell and the Girl from Botany Bay," Frederick A. Pottle's 1932 Presidential Address for the Elizabethan Club of Yale University, provided valuable source material, although without my friend Andrew Gibson, who found it in his university library and obtained a precious copy, I never would have seen it. Thanks also to Les Cole, who found primary-source newspaper accounts from 1792 in the British Museum. John Varley helped me track down details about the six-oar cutter, and my daughter Jona's insightful comments on the manuscript were especially helpful. Above all, thanks to Derek, my partner in love, writing, and everything else.

Rosa Jordan is an internationalist who explores the world physically and intellectually, always probing for the point at which political and social realities intersect with personal courage and compassion. After a decade of freelance reportage, she authored the autobiographical *Dangerous Places: Travels on the Edge*.

Then she embarked on a series of children's books set in Florida: *Lost Goat Lane, The Goatnappers,* and *The Last Wild Place. Lost Goat Lane* was nominated for the 2006-07 Chocolate Lily Award, a finalist for the 2005 Silver Birch Award, and shortlisted for the 2005 Red Maple Award.

Next she set out to cycle Cuba's 4000-km coastline, which resulted in *Cycling Cuba*.

For Jordan, writing is the link between the edgy places she is drawn to and what she considers a truly idyllic home life in the Monashee Mountains of British Columbia. For the past decade, she has been social justice program director for Earthways Foundation, which has supported her in developing a jungle cat reserve in Ecuador's Choco rainforest and a food security program in a war-ravaged Mayan village in the highlands of Guatemala.